CEMETERY
ROAD

ALSO BY TOM LOWE

A False Dawn
The 24th Letter
The Butterfly Forest
The Black Bullet
Blood of Cain
Black River
Destiny
Cemetery Road

CEMETERY
ROAD

A Sean O'Brien Mystery / Thriller

TOM LOWE

K

Kingsbridge Entertainment

Registered with the Library of Congress, and U.S. Copyright Office. First cataloged December, 2015, Author - Lowe, Tom, 1952 –

　　1. CEMETERY ROAD—fiction. 2. The Preacher—fiction. 3. Florida Panhandle—fiction. 4. Ghosts of the river—fiction. 5. Shorty's—fiction. Title—Cemetery Road

CEMETERY ROAD – is distributed in ebook, print and audiobook editions. Audiobook published by Audible. Printed books are available from Amazon Inc, bookstores and libraries.

Cover design by Damonza. Formatting print and digital conversion by CreateSpace.

ISBN-13 9781518718281
ISBN-10 1518718280

First edition: December 2015. Published in the USA by Kingsbridge Entertainme

Although CEMETERY ROAD is a work of fiction, it is inspired from the history of the former Florida School for Boys near Marianna, Florida. The reform school was opened in 1900. It operated for 111 years before closing. At one time it was the largest reform school in America. Some children were sent there for "truancy" and "incorrigibility." Others were wards of the state and sent to the school because they had nowhere else to go. In 2011, the state of Florida reported that the school was closing for budgetary reasons. In the few years before closing, some of the men who were confined within the school as children, reported that they and others incarcerated there were victims of severe physical and sexual abuse. And they allege that there were children who never left the reform school alive, buried in hidden graves. Prosecutors have said that there wasn't sufficient evidence to prove or disprove the allegations.

After the school closed, a forensics anthropology team from the University of South Florida secured permission to use grand-penetrating radar and other forensics tools to locate fifty-five graves, and fifty-one bodies. Some of the children, investigators believe, died from a fire and disease. For others, the causes of death were apparently not recorded at the time and difficult to establish decades later. The forensics team used mitochondrial DNA and was successful in identifying a few of the dead children by matching DNA with living family members. At the time of the publication of this novel, the investigation was continuing.

ACKNOWLEDGMENTS

Often I'm asked which one of my books is my favorite. I don't have a favorite, but I do have my favorite part of each book. It's right here where I have the opportunity to thank and recognize those who've helped me launch another novel.

For CEMETERY ROAD, a special thanks goes to Helen Christensen and Darcy Yarosh for their attention to detail and proofreading my books. To the hard working production team at Amazon CreateSpace: Maria Martin, Jamie Lee, Carina Gilbert, Kandis Miller and Brianne Twilley. You're the best. And finally to my wife, Keri, for her skills as an editor, her patience, perseverance, and her laugh. She makes the often-cloistered life of a writer a little easier.

I tip my hat to you, the reader. If this is your first time reading a Sean O'Brien novel, welcome. If you're returning, thank you for your loyalty and continuing the journey. I hope you enjoy CEMETERY ROAD.

For Melissa Lowe,
and for…
All the children who entered the doors of the Florida School for boys, and especially to those who never left.

"Some people regard it as their right to return evil for evil and, if they cannot, feel they have lost their liberty."

- Aristotle

PROLOGUE

Jackson County, Florida - 1964

His sister was the only one he'd miss. He didn't want to leave her, but at age thirteen there wasn't much he could do. He would return one day to get her—to rescue her. Andy Cope sat in a hard, wooden chair across the counter from the principal's secretary, a heavy woman with listless eyes and turquoise-framed glasses worn halfway down her nose. Her bottle-blonde hair was pulled back into a tight bun that looked to Andy like a hornet's nest. She picked up the phone, stuck her thick finger into the rotary dial and made a call that would forever change Andy's life.

He glanced at the clock on the wall behind the woman. 11:15. Andy knew the freight train would rumble by the school at 11:30 sharp, always slowing to a crawl at the crossing, sometimes coming to a brief stop in Marianna. Andy hoped today the train would be making that stop. He could run all the way to Marianna if need be. He was athletic. Strong for his age. Handsome angular face, his brown hair cut short. Green eyes, often guarded, suspicious. A small, white crisscross scar above one of his dark eyebrows. He watched the sweep second-hand on the clock as the secretary spoke into the phone.

"We have one boy today. His mother and Mr. Gillespie signed the papers. Warden Beck is expecting him by three. Are you coming in a bus or is the truancy officer picking him up?" She paused, listening—looking over her glasses at the boy, her eyes superior. Andy held her stare, unblinking. She said, "That'll be fine. Thank you. Darlene, how's Harold? Betty told me he's fixin' to get out of the turpentine business."

The principal, a tall balding man in a cotton seersucker suit, came out of his office, his wingtip shoes hard against the pinewood floor, the smell of cigarette smoke on his clothes. He looked down at Andy. "Maybe schoolin' isn't for you, son. You lack motivation and discipline. They'll teach it to you at the Florida Home for Boys. You'll grow up quick down there. It's for your own good. When you come back here, you'll be changed."

"I'm never comin' back here."

The principal rocked slightly on his brown, polished shoes. "I suspect you're right about that. Boys like you are born bad. Wicked seeds are planted amongst the moral seeds in the garden of good and evil." The principal's mouth turned down. He adjusted papers atop a clipboard, two fingers on his right hand yellowed from cigarettes. He tucked the clipboard under his arm and walked out into the hallway, the school bell ringing as the door closed.

Andy looked at the clock, felt his stomach churning. 11:25.

He heard the train whistle in the distance. Soon the train would roll by the old high school, shaking the bedrock of the building. Andy knew he had to be by the tracks when the train slowed. Had to hop a freight to escape. He wouldn't be sent to reform school. *Hell no.* He'd heard rumors of the place. Horrible rumors. Some boys went in and never came out. Those that did were forever spooked. Distrustful. Fidgety. *Actin' like they'd been in some kind of war. Maybe they had been.*

The door to the office flew open. A large-breasted teenage girl with shoulder-length red hair stepped into the room, her face shiny and flushed. "Miss Belle...I need to go home."

The secretary looked up from her paperwork, her head rising just above the reception counter. "You sick again, Linda Sue?"

The girl glanced over to Andy Cope. She swallowed dryly, licked her lips and approached the counter. She lowered her voice, clearing her throat. The secretary stood, waddling to the desk. The girl looked back over her shoulder for a second at Andy and then whispered something to the woman.

Andy saw blood trickle down the inside of the girl's left leg, the back of her dress red and stained. He looked away.

11:28. The train whistle blowing. Coming closer.

The secretary exhaled an exasperated sigh. "Let's get you to the bathroom." She opened a hinged, wooden half-door in the center of the counter desk, the girl stepping through, two spots of blood the size of pennies where she had stood. The secretary looked over to Andy, pointed her short index finger at him. "Andy Cope, you sit still. I'll be back in a minute. Mr. Gillespie is out in hall. Stay put, you hear?" She turned, the girl following her to a faculty bathroom.

Andy stood, peering through the glass window, the principal in the corridor talking with a teacher. Andy knew the hall beyond the principal's door led to a series of backrooms and an exit on the west side of the building, the side facing the railroad tracks. As he started to turn—to run, his sister Caroline appeared in the foyer. She looked at the principal speaking with a teacher and then she looked over to Andy. He raised his hand, slowly, watching his only sister for a moment. She bit her lower lip, holding library books against her chest, lifting her head, a slight nod.

He smiled and then turned, running. He ran hard down the hall, three offices vacant during the lunch hour, the rumble of the train engine muffled through the building. At the end of the hall was the exit door. The door to freedom. Andy jostled the handle. Locked. His heart sank. There was a noise. Metal and wood. Something scraping on the floor. A black man in his sixties, salt and pepper hair, came out of the janitor's closet, a mop in one hand, bucket in the other, perspiration beaded on his forehead. He looked at Andy, the man's prudent eyes assessing a scared kid. He knew the boy. Always a polite kid—a boy with a soul older than his time on God's earth.

Andy stood straight. His jawline hard. "Can you let me out?"

"Andy Cope, what's your hurry, son? This school's got a big ol' front door, too."

"James, they're trying to send me to reform school. I done nothin' wrong. Just been late to school a few times. It's on account..." Andy held back his words, his eyes watering.

The old man shook his head. "I 'spect I know why." He reached for the key ring on his belt, opening the door, the sunlight pouring inside.

Andy nodded. "Thank you."

"Don't get caught. If you do, they cain't know it was me who hepped you. Understand?"

"Yes. Much obliged." Andy ran down the sloping schoolyard, jumping a drainage ditch filled with dark water, running toward the tracks. The freight train was slowing, the engine closer to the crossing, the caboose trailing around the bend. Andy looked for a boxcar with side doors open. He ran adjacent to the rolling train, his mouth dry, heart pounding—sunlight flickering through the open spaces between boxcars.

The janitor stood in the shadows of the school door. He whispered. "Come on, Andy. Run! Faster!"

The train whistle blew a long blast, the boxcars picking up a notch of speed. Andy ran hard as he could, his leather shoes hitting gravel and wooden crossties, the smell of diesel in the air. He jumped, reaching for the iron ladder. He caught it, his body swinging like a flag in the wind for a few seconds.

A man in a pickup truck idling at the crossing watched the boy clinging to the ladder, watched him fighting to get a footing on the moving train. The man spit a stream of tobacco out the truck's open window. He thought he recognized the boy. He'd know for sure when the train came closer, if the kid didn't fall to his death.

Andy pulled hard, lifting his body higher from the ground. He tried to sling his legs up to the boxcar platform. His right leg slipped, the train picking up speed. He tried again, reaching deep inside for more strength. He pulled his body further up, grabbing the side of the door and crawling into the cavernous mouth of the open car.

The janitor nodded, watching the train gain speed. "Good luck, Andy Cope. You're gonna be needin' it." He stood there for a few more seconds, the sound of steel on iron fading, the caboose growing small in the western horizon. He blew out a long breath and closed the door.

The man in the pickup truck stopped at the crossing, watching the train roll down the tracks. He saw the boy crawl into the shadows of the boxcar. The man stared into the open boxcar when it passed in front of his truck. A shaft of sunlight broke through the side door, the flash illuminating the scared face of Andy Cope.

The man spit the finished wad of tobacco out of his mouth. When the caboose rolled by and the crossing lights stopped flashing, the man put his truck in gear and mumbled, "Andy Cope. Bet your daddy would like to know where you're at, boy. You just jumped a freight train bound for nowhere."

Andy sat in the shadows, watching the countryside roll by, the warm summer wind drying the sweat on his face, the song of the rail playing through his free soul.

ONE

Florida - Ponce Inlet - Present Day

The letter came to a place where letters were never delivered, at least not to me. I was paying my boat-slip rent at Ponce Marina when the dock master, a wiry man sporting a salt and pepper stubble and wearing a sweat-stained Hatteras ball cap said, "Oh, Sean, I almost forgot."

"Forgot what?"

"The letter."

"Letter?"

"Yeah. Arrived last week. I walked down to your boat. *Jupiter* was buttoned up tight. Nick Cronus said he hadn't seen you in a few days. Said you were probably at your river cabin. I don't have a forwarding address. So, I figured you'd stop by sooner or later. I'll get it." He shuffled across the small office, a large corkboard on one wall filled with fliers advertising boats for sale. Half a pot of burnt black coffee smoldered on a burner.

The dock master hummed the song, *99 Bottles of Beer*, while leafing through a wire-mesh basket filled with mail. "Found it. Some damn neat handwriting. Maybe it's an old girlfriend. Maybe not. I hear that's what Facebook's for. That's why you sure as hell won't find my face on Facebook."

He handed the letter to me. "Thanks, Al. Come on Max." I left the office, Max my ten-pound dachshund romping a few feet ahead of me as we opened the gate to L dock. She paused, watching a brown pelican perched on a creosote-stained piling, the bird shifting its weight from one webbed foot to the other, its head tilted, a big yellow eye watching Max. "Come on,

1

Kiddo, leave the neighbors alone." Max snorted and we continued our hike down to my old boat docked at the very end of L dock.

A gentle wind from the east, toward the Atlantic Ocean, blew across the marina, the scent of blackened grouper and garlic crab coming from the Tiki Bar, a rustic wharf bar that could imitate restaurant status. A day-charter fishing boat chugged from Ponce Inlet and the Halifax River into the marina and around the long piers moored with dozens of yachts and sailboats. The fishing boat, *Lucky Strike*, was filled with tourists and the day's catch. Screeching sea gulls followed the boat's wake across the water.

I looked at the envelope. Letter-perfect penmanship. It was addressed to Mr. Sean O'Brien, care of Ponce Marina. On the top, left side of the envelope was the return address. Just an address. No name of the sender. The return address was in Jacksonville. I didn't know anyone there. If it was something ominous, and if the sender licked the envelope before sealing it, he or she might have sealed DNA with the glue and paper.

I needed a knife. "Come on, Max. I bet Nick has a fillet knife on his boat. If Nick's not out fishing, we'll pay him a visit." Max walked faster, almost prancing, head held high, parading down the dock. She knew Nick's boat, *St. Michael*, but more importantly, she knew Nick was an excellent and generous cook.

A trail of white smoke puffed from under the hood on a small barbecue grill near the center of *St. Michaels'* cockpit. The double doors to the salon were wide open, Greek music coming from inside the fishing trawler, a boat with the lines and lineage from those that sailed the Mediterranean for centuries.

"Hot dog!" bellowed Nick Cronus, stepping from the salon to the cockpit, a Corona in one hand, a spatula in the other. Max sprinted across the auxiliary dock that ran parallel to *St. Michael*, bounding down the three wooden steps leading to the transom. Nick set his beer on a small table and picked up Max. "Where you been, hot dog? Sean kept you away from your marina family for too long." Max licked Nick's chin. He held her to his wide chest, picked up his bottle of Corona and danced in a circle to the music, Max almost smiling.

"Nick, do you have a fillet knife?"

"Do the fishes swim in the deep blue sea? Of course I have a fillet knife, I have three of 'em. I used one a half hour ago to fillet some grouper and reds I caught. I put some on the coals for you and hot dog." Nick set Max down, sipped from the bottle and opened the grill to turn over a large piece of fish. He sang something in Greek, closing one eye to avoid the smoke. Years of working as a fisherman gave him a body thick with muscle. His bushy dark hair was a mop of wavy locks, skin the shade of light tea. A full moustache covered his upper lip. His eyes were bright, playful, matching his steady grin. He was loyal, fearless, and after I pulled two bikers off him a few years ago, he said we were brothers for life.

I stepped down onto the cockpit, Nick reaching under the grill for a fillet knife. He handed it to me and I sliced the bottom portion of the envelope. He said, "I just rip open my mail. You do it the fancy way."

I handed the knife back to Nick, unfolded the letter inside and read. It was written in hand. Probably from an expensive fountain pen.

Dear Mr. O'Brien,

By the time you get this letter I will be dead. I'm told the cancer will take me in six months, but I refuse to burden my family with that.

One of the true highlights of my life was the day I chartered your boat for a fishing trip. It had been a very long time since I felt that good about life and my place in this life. I remembered you telling me that you had been a Miami homicide detective. Something in my gut tells me you were good at it, too. I can understand how the death of your wife could make you seek a career change.

I was forever changed many years ago by the horrible abuse inflicted upon me and other children at the Florida School for Boys in Marianna, Florida. Grown men beat us so brutally our underwear was imbedded in our buttocks. In 1965, a boy named Andy Cope was murdered. He tried to run away one rainy night and they just shot him in the back. The men threatened me, men who were evil and filled with hate. And I kept silent. I now know that, for years, I suffered from post-traumatic-stress-disorder. I'm not making excuses. I've lived with that guilt all my life.

The local police say it's a cold case with no evidence or a body. And now, on the eve of my death, I want to try to right a horrible wrong. I believe at least one of the men who did this is still alive. In this envelope, you'll find the key to a post office box. On a separate paper, I've included the location and box number.

I'm hoping you might take a look at this case because Andy wasn't the only one to die. It was like a death camp for boys. They buried Andy one rainy night down there. I sent a photocopy of this letter to Andy's only sister. There may be a statute of limitations for rape and abuse – but not for murder. Should you decide to take this case, I've enclosed compensation in the package at the postal box as well as something tied to the murder, only if the right investigator could find the other parts. You can simply tear this letter up and walk away, but in my heart, I don't think you will.
- Curtis Garwood

I reached in the envelope and lifted out a single brass key and a note: **P.O. Box 129, Daytona Beach.** I held the key in the palm of my hand for a few seconds, thinking about what I'd just read. Nick sipped his beer and asked, "Sean, what the hell's in that letter. Looks like you saw a ghost."

"Do you remember a charter customer we had a few months ago—his name was Curtis Garwood?"

"Since you, or we, only had a few, I remember them all. Wasn't Curtis Garwood the tall guy who wore the Florida Seminoles cap?"

"Yes."

"Nice fella. What about him?"

"He's apparently dead."

"Dead? Damn, man. I'm sorry to hear that." Nick made the sign of the cross. "How'd it happen?"

"I've read a few suicide notes…but I've never read one addressed to me."

"Oh shit."

"And this key is to a post office box that might have something in it that will shed some light on a murder of a child."

"Murder…a kid?"

"And it may have happened more than fifty years ago."

TWO

Jesse Taylor sipped his morning coffee at his kitchen table, checking to see who'd died. Since turning sixty-five, he read the obituary listings in the Jacksonville Times Union before he read the sports section. At least once a month, he'd found an obit—a death notice—about someone he'd known. Mostly it'd been men. Fellas who had shared the same hardscrabble lifestyle Jesse lived all his life—lived still. Paycheck-to-paycheck. Hand-to-mouth too often. Hard to hold a steady job when you held steady anger. Cheap wine and weed would take the edge off, but Jesse hated the hangovers, hated himself for relapsing.

His thick, white hair was thinning, a pink scar now visible an inch above his left temple. He shook open the newspaper, his sea-blue eyes narrowing through weak glasses, drugstore readers he'd bought almost two years ago. He glanced out of the kitchen window and watched a twenty-year-old pickup truck rattling through the trailer park, which was dotted with sagging and faded mobile homes. The sun was clearing the top of a cottonwood tree. A skinny, mixed-breed dog sniffed through garbage that lay spilled from a trashcan tipped on its side.

Three wives had left him through the years. The longest marriage lasted than a decade. He tried counseling. Tried religion. Nothing worked for long. The demons circled in the shadows just beyond the edge of his peripheral vision, the frail spokes on a rickety wagon pulled by a stubborn mule hitched to his subconscious. He hated the failures, but more importantly he hated how he'd failed as a father. He'd sworn never to beat his sons like he'd been beaten. But maybe back then, when he was locked away for truancy from school, the men had left more than scars across his butt and legs.

Maybe fifty-two years ago they'd beaten his soul out of his body.

They'd wielded a wide leather strap, similar to the straps barbers used to keep an edge on their razors. The boys were told to lie face down on a cot, grip the crossbar at the head of the cot, bite into a soiled pillow that reeked of dried vomit, blood and salty tears. And then the first crack of leather across buttocks. *Ka-pow.* It was the first lash that hurt the worst, Jesse remembered. It usually drew blood. After the twentieth stroke, you were almost numb to the pain, pieces of underwear embedded in the bloody wounds. By the fortieth lash, your soul had crawled away to hide. Your spirit, broken and severely wounded, seemed to leave your body behind in a hot, smelly room with dried blood splatter on the walls and ceiling in an isolated building the men called the White House.

"You scream, boy, and we start over again," Jesse remembered the man in the black fedora say the first time. *"Bite into that pillow. It's for your own good. You hear me, boy?"*

Jesse blinked hard, glancing down at the newspaper, his wide hands smoothing out the fold, his eyes moist. He studied the obituary. *Lots of deaths this week. Mostly older folks. People in their eighties.* A combat World War II veteran. A former Detroit Tigers pitcher who retired to Florida twenty-five years ago. A seventeen-year-old girl who died when her car was struck by a drunk driver.

And then there was a name he knew.

It was the last name on the list. Curtis Garwood, originally from Tallahassee, a resident of Jacksonville since 1999. Graduated from Florida State University. The survivors include his wife, two grown children, and one grandchild. The cause of death wasn't listed. Curtis Garwood dead at age sixty-four. The obit described him as a loving husband and devoted father. *Then God bless you*, thought Jesse. *You managed to somehow bury it when so many of us who were held there never did. Never could.* He exhaled deeply, the sound of an acorn popping off the aluminum roof, the last drip of coffee falling into the carafe, the coffee maker exhaling a *whoosh* sound. The obit read that in lieu of flowers, the family requests donations to be made to St. Michael's Hospital. Jesse glanced up from the paper for a moment. He recognized the name of the hospital. It was for psychiatric patients.

He pushed his glasses up on the bridge of his nose, reading the name of the funeral home. He reached behind, removing a stack of newspapers, picking up a phone book and rifling through the pages. He found the number and punched the keys on his phone.

"Anderson Brothers Memorial Services, this is Shelly. May I help you?"

Jesse cleared his throat. "Yes...a friend of mine passed."

"I'm sorry for your loss. How may I help you?"

"His name is Curtis Garwood. It looks like your funeral home is doing the arrangements. When's the viewing?"

"I'm sorry, the family requested a closed casket service. It's tomorrow between one and five."

"I'm coming from out of town. Did Curtis pass away in a car accident?"

"Not that I'm aware of. It appears the cause of death was suicide. I'm sorry. I understand that Mr. Garwood was about to enter hospice care for a terminal condition."

"Thank you, ma'am." Jesse disconnected. He flipped through a small Rolodex, finding a card under index marker G. He lifted out the card, stained and worn thin over time. He studied the name for a moment, then dialed the number. "Hank, it's Jesse. Did you hear that Curtis Garwood died?"

"No. How'd it happen?"

"Suicide."

After a few seconds of silence, the man said, "Damn, Jesse...I'm sure as hell sorry to hear that. I haven't seen Curtis in years. Like all of us, though, I know his burden was heavy."

"Yep. Maybe some of 'em are still alive. They need to pay for what they did to so many boys. You want to go with me...back to Jackson County?"

"You fall off the wagon again? Jesse, you been drinkin'?"

"No. I haven't touched whisky in sixteen months. Curtis might have had cancer in his body, but his soul was eaten up way before his body took sick. I'm goin' back there. I think Harold Reeves still lives in Marianna. "

"What could you and Harold do? Don't be dumb. We've talked about this before. It's been too long. Too damn many years. That storm is way behind us. The statute of limitations has long passed. Nobody gave a damn then. Nothin's changed. Give it up, Jesse. It's not worth it. Not now. Not anymore."

"If anything happens to me. I want you to know that Winchester 71 you always liked is yours. Gotta go, Hank." Jesse disconnected, stood from the table and walked to a locked gun case in the corner of a small living room. He unlocked the case, removing a pump 12-gauge shotgun and a Colt .45 pistol. He set the firearms on the kitchen table, lit a cigarette, and inhaled deeply, blowing smoke out of his nostrils. He picked up the newspaper, staring at the obituary notice and said, "Maybe after I'm finished you can rest in peace, brother."

Jesse stared out the kitchen window, the skinny dog leaving the spilled garbage and loping through the trailer park, ground muddy from last night's hard rain, the call of a large crow coming from the top of the cottonwood tree.

THREE

I saw Max's radar go off. She stood on her hind legs in *St. Michaels'* cockpit, front paws bracing against a deck chair, her ears raised as high as dachshund ears can be lifted. She growled, the fur down her long spine bristling. I looked in the direction she stared, her posture like an African meerkat watching a lion approach.

Ol' Joe, a hefty tawny cat with more orange than black fur, strolled down the middle of L dock as if he owned the marina. He'd been here as long as most of the boat owners could remember. He was a cat that belonged to no one in particular, but most everyone in the live-aboard community would leave food for Ol' Joe. Nick was his favorite host.

Nick held a bottle of beer in one hand, using a spatula in the other hand to turn the fish on the hot grill. Popeye like, he closed one eye, the smoke from the coals swirling around him. He glanced over to Max. "I see what's got your panties in a wad, hot dog. Don't mess with Ol' Joe. That cat's got scars older than you." Nick reached in the cooler and lifted a grouper from the chipped ice. In a blur, he filleted the fish, tossing the fillets on the grill and throwing the fish head up to the dock where the cat approached.

A large brown pelican swooped down, landing on the dock less than six feet from the fish head. And now Ol' Joe was on one side, the pelican on the other, the fish head in the middle. It was more than Max could handle. She paced and barked. The pelican charged for the food, the cat leaping in and sinking its teeth into the fish, old scars across the cat's face resembling seared battle wounds. The pelican backed away, wings half extended. Ol' Joe casually picked up his prize, lifted his head, turned around, and sauntered back down the dock.

He swaggered right by Dave Collins, who was heading our way with a Styrofoam coffee cup, newspaper and a tablet. Dave, mid-sixties, broad-shoulders, neatly trimmed gray beard, white hair, wore a tropical print shirt, shorts and flip-flops. Coming closer to *St. Michaels* he said, "Foul verses fur and fang. No contest. My money's on Joe every time. But I'm not sure he has much fang left, but he's never lost his chutzpa." Dave grinned and sipped his coffee.

Nick wiped his hands on a paper towel. "Ever notice how the gulls go away when Ol' Joe's on deck? When Joe was younger, I'd give him a fish. Next mornin' he'd bring me a rat. Tit for tat or rat, I figured. I'm making super grouper subs. Come aboard."

"Twist my arm." Dave walked down the short secondary dock next to *St. Michael* and stepped over and onto the cockpit, taking a seat in a canvas deck chair. Max followed him, wagging her tail. "How's my favorite doxie?" Dave lifted her to his lap.

After retiring from a life-long career as an intelligence officer, and a twenty-five year marriage that crumbled, Dave spent most of his time living aboard *Gibraltar*, a 42-foot trawler moored across the dock from Nick's boat. Dave's analytical mind was always churning through the domino effect of current political events and their human and economic consequences. He was a fierce chess player, blogger, and he averaged reading three books a week, mostly non-fiction. I never knew him to forego a cocktail when the sun began to set in the harbor and Halifax River west of Ponce Marina.

Nick opened a Heineken and set it on a small metal table in front of Dave. "Ah, such service, Nicky. And I didn't even have to ask."

"Thought I'd give you somethin' to sip on 'cause I know my man, Sean, is gonna tell you about the letter he got in the mail from a dead man."

Dave inhaled deeply, sipped his beer and said, "You know, I was just assuming Sean was here because it's the first of the month. He's probably paying his slip rent, and just maybe he and little Maxine would spend some time aboard *Jupiter*. Sean, you've become Thoreau, and that cabin on the river is your Walden Pond."

I smiled and took a seat across the table from Dave, setting the letter on the tabletop. "I just rescreened the back porch. And now that I'm here at the marina, I was going to replace some of the isinglass on *Jupiter*."

"Was? What's preventing it?"

"Nothing, at least not yet." I motioned toward the letter on the table. "A few months ago, a guy by the name of Curtis Garwood chartered my boat. Nick and I took him out in the reefs for a day. He caught fish. But he did something at the time that none of my other customers ever did?"

"What's that?"

"Catch and release. Didn't matter what he caught, we'd get the fish to the boat, and he asked Nick to release them."

Nick nodded. "Yeah, that about drove me nuts. Snapper, wahoo, trout… he'd send 'em all back to Poseidon. For me, a Greek fisherman, it was almost sacrilegious." Nick touched the small gold cross hanging from his neck.

Dave watched the condensation sweat from his bottle and asked, "So, I gather the letter on the table is from this guy who paid big bucks to catch fish, but not boat them. And, based on Nick's introduction, I deduce this guy's dead. Now, I'm damn curious. What's in the letter?"

"A job offer."

"A dead man offered you employment?"

"Not on-going work. If I take it, this would be for one thing."

"And what's that?"

"To solve a cold case—a murder."

"How cold?"

"More than fifty years."

Dave glanced over to a 40-foot Sea Ray moving slowly across the marina waters. "Why'd he pick you?"

"He gives his reasons in the letter."

Nick fixed three po-boy sandwiches filled with hot grouper, feta cheese, red onion, olive oil and peppers—all served on paper plates. He joined us at the table, a fresh beer in his hand. "Let's eat."

I gave the letter to Dave. He put on his bifocals and read silently. The sound of chuckling gulls passing over the marina and the gurgle of a diesel cranking from a Hatteras leaving M dock were the only noises filling the air.

Dave pushed back from the table, looked over his bifocals to me. "Curtis writes that he believes one of them is still alive, but he didn't leave you with his name."

"That information might be in the separate package he sent to the post office box."

Dave took a large bite from his sandwich. He chewed slowly, his face pensive. He opened his tablet and said, "I went through Marianna, Florida, three or four years ago. Didn't see the reform school Curtis mentions, but I did see a way of life that hasn't changed much in decades." He hit a few keys on the table, reading in silence and then clearing his throat. "Jackson County is about as Dixie as you can get. It's the only county in Florida that borders both Alabama and Georgia. The last black man publically lynched in America was hung by a rope from an oak next to the Jackson County Courthouse, and they hung him after they'd beaten him to death."

Nick sipped from his beer. "What the hell did he do to deserve that?"

"Allegedly raped and killed a woman."

"Allegedly?" Nick used a toothpick to stab a piece of feta cheese on his plate.

"He never lived long enough to be tried for the crime. That happened in 1934. The Florida School for Boys was in business thirty-three years before the last public hanging in America. Sounds like the local demographics probably made for a rather shallow employee pool. That reform school operated one hundred and eleven years. The state closed it in 2011, ostensibly for budgetary reasons. This came after reports of child abuse through the years and a lawsuit filed by some men held there as children. A judge tossed it out because the accusations were far beyond the statute of limitations. And the state attorney said there wasn't enough evidence to prove or disprove the allegations of child abuse." Dave shook his head. "And more recently, Curtis writes that the police weren't too interested in a cold case, this one the murder of a child."

I nodded. "But it's not a case until someone in law enforcement makes an effort to investigate and hunt for a body. And what if Curtis Garwood was right, what if there are more bodies of kids—boys buried in hidden graves somewhere on the property?"

Dave pursed his lips and exhaled. "Then, perhaps, it could be a lot of cases…maybe America's killing fields—victims who were runaways, maybe considered by some as throwaways. Too bad Curtis waited so long, and now, at this late state, if he was a witness to Andy Cope's murder, Curtis is dead, too. Not a lot you could do, Sean."

Nick shook his head. "Yeah man, sounds like others have tried to do something. A judge tossed out one case. And the DA said he's got nothing, one way or the other."

I thought about Curtis's letter. "Nick, do you remember when Curtis Garwood caught the fish…he stood on the transom just long enough to look that last fish, a wahoo in the eye, before releasing it?"

"Yeah, he seemed to stare at 'em, kinda like he felt sorry for the fish."

"When he was bringing the fish in, when he stood next to the transom on *Jupiter*, I noticed severe scarring on the back of his legs above the knees."

"Now that you mention it, I remember it, too. It was hard not to notice. Man, I just figured he was burned bad in a fire."

"A fire doesn't leave deep crisscrossed scars like that. That type layering, most likely, was caused from repeated beatings."

I pulled the brass key from my shirt pocket and set it on the table. "This key opens the post office box Curtis mentioned in his letter, and in that box is probably the last thing on earth Curtis Garwood ever mailed."

Nick blew out a long breath. "Yeah, but do you really want to know what's there?"

Dave leaned forward. "Sean, Curtis Garwood was a customer on your boat for one day. He's dead. You're under no obligation to accept a job he offered you before his death."

"I know that. But he left a fee in that package, probably cash. I need to return it to his family."

Nick grunted and stood. "What if there's something in there that convinces you to hunt down a fifty-year-old ghost? I'd just write return to sender. I don't care if the sender is dead."

I lifted the key off the table, the sun over my shoulder reflecting from the brass surface, the hole drilled in the center like a dark unblinking Cyclops' eye in the hot Florida sun.

FOUR

J esse Taylor hadn't been back in decades, but yet he felt the urge to vomit. The sheer visuals he saw made him nauseous. He drove slowly down the road on the perimeter of the old reform school, renamed the Dozier School for Boys, the late afternoon sun popping through the tall pines. The razor-wire fence seemed to border the property for miles, the brick buildings behind the fence giving the deceptive look of a boarding school tucked away in an idyllic pastoral setting.

Jesse drove with his windows down, the smell of pinesap and honeysuckles in the warm Florida breeze. Yet, he could remember only the smell of other things here, the acrid odor of urine-soaked cots because the boys were too badly beaten to walk to the bathrooms, and the stench of sweat, blood and dried tears on the filthy pillow in the small building called the White House. Instinctively, Jesse reached for his pistol in the center console. He shook his head and mumbled, "They're all gone…the bastards have left the building."

He drove past the entrance to the property, intent on driving State Road 276 toward Marianna a few miles away. But then Jesse looked to his right, down the long entrance drive. A lone pickup truck was parked near a guardhouse, the gate behind it pulled across the driveway. Jesse slowed, breaking as he passed the entrance. He made a U-turn in the road and drove back to the main entrance, and then turned into the drive. He felt his stomach tightening the closer he came to the fence. His heart beat faster, palms moist, his mind racing back to the day he was brought here in the backseat of a deputy sheriff's car. It was a Ford, no air conditioning, the spongy seat cushion material sticking through parts of the seat, the smell of the deputy's aftershave in the car.

He blew air out of his cheeks and slowed to a stop as a tall man in his early sixties, clipboard in one hand, phone in the other, stepped from the guardhouse. He walked with a slight limp over to Jesse's car. "Private property here. What's your business?"

Jesse half smiled. "I'm not much of a businessman. Just headin' into town, thought I'd stop to see this place. I know it's closed. Didn't know whether it might be open for inspection."

"Why do you ask?"

"I heard the place was for sale."

"Thought you said you weren't a businessman. I need some ID."

"On second thought, I really don't want to go in there." Jesse looked at the man's nametag: *J. Hines*. He remembered the name from a Hines family in Jackson County. "Are you Johnny Hines? Little Johnny Hines?"

"Who are you?"

"You're all grown up. I'm the guy who used to give your older brother, Frank, a noogie on his towhead. I'm Jesse Taylor."

Johnny Hines' eyes opened wide, a vein pulsed in his neck. "I remember you. You were locked up here one time."

"So were a lot of kids."

"We heard you were messed up in Vietnam. Didn't you spend some time in a hospital? We heard it was a psych ward."

"In those days, nobody knew a whole helluva lot about the ghosts of war."

The guard wasn't sure what to say. He put the clipboard beneath his armpit and touched the tip of his nose with a finger, the fingernail chewed down. "Why you back in town?"

"That's one fine chamber of commerce greeting. What ever happened to your brother, Frank?"

"He retired from United Trucking. Lives outside of Panama City."

Jesse nodded. "And I'm bettin' you worked here at the old school at one point."

"Did sixteen years before they shut it down. How'd you know?"

Jesse stared at him for a moment. He grinned. "Lucky guess, I guess. Was Hack Johnson still around when you worked here?"

"No, he'd already gone."

"I imagine he's probably dead by now, old age and whatnot."

The guard said nothing for a few seconds. "He's long since retired."

"Which means the old bastard is still alive, right?"

"Why'd you come back, Jesse? After all these years, you here for a funeral or something?"

"Something like that. What if I came back to say hello to old acquaintances like you?" Jesse lit a cigarette, blowing smoke out his open window, the guard straightening. "See you around, Johnny. If you run in to Frank, tell him the first round of pool is on me." Jesse started forward, making a U-turn in the wide driveway and heading back to the road. He looked in his review mirror and watched as Johnny Hines wrote down his tag number and then punched the keys on his phone.

— —

A man with a deep, southern accent answered after two rings. "What's up?"

"Amos, it's Johnny at the gate to the school. Is Hack there?"

"Yeah, but he don't come to the phone. You know that."

"Give him a message. A guy just stopped here at the gate."

"What guy?"

"Name's Jesse Taylor. Born and raised in Jackson County. He joined the Army to leave this place. Came from a trailer trash mama who died with a needle in her arm. He spent time in Dozier before the name was changed. He asked me if Hack was still alive."

"So, what's he got, an old grudge?"

"I don't know. I do know he was a Green Beret at one time. Got captured in Vietnam. We'd heard he'd somehow strangled one of his guards, took his weapon away and shot his way outta those bamboo cells and managed to find his way through the jungle back to the American forces. They say he wound up in a Army psych ward for a year or so."

"Why you tellin' me this shit, Johnny. You think this sicko is gonna hurt my grandpa?"

"Because your grandpa pays me to tell him."

FIVE

I thought about what I tried not to think about. I stood on a ladder propped up against my ramshackle cabin on the St. Johns River, forty miles west of Ponce Inlet, replacing some of the corrugated tin over my screened back porch, which faced the river. I wanted to bury myself in physical work—to sweat, to keep busy doing what I often did to restore a 65-five-year-old home that I'd bought in foreclosure after the death of my wife, Sherri. I'd replaced rotten wood, fixed plumbing, painted, remodeled the living room, kitchen and generally given the old place a new look without diminishing its rustic charm.

I glanced down at Max who sniffed the grass and pine straw near the base of the ladder. "Step back, Max. I need to drop some of this roofing." She looked up at me, tilting her head, as a lizard bolted from a cabbage palm next to the house, running to a cord of wood that I'd recently chopped. Max gave chase, and I dropped a piece of old tin from the section I'd just replaced.

We'd moved here from Miami after Sherri died from ovarian cancer. Max was Sherri's last gift to me. And so now it was the two of us—me at 6.2 and 205 pounds. Max standing on short dachshund legs and weighing in at ten pounds. We were the odd couple—together by fortuitous design. My wife had been a wise woman.

I climbed down from the ladder. In the back of my thoughts, the murky image of Curtis Garwood's package stuffed in a dark post office box hung like an mysterious piñata just on the edge of my sight. It had been three days since I read his letter, plenty of time to reflect on the day he had chartered my boat, *Jupiter*. I'd been trying to recall and restore bits of conversation that might give me better insight into what Curtis had gone through as a boy—how he'd persevered.

"Come on, Max. Let's take a break." I sipped from a bottle of water, sweat dripping off my face, shirtless, wearing a pair of faded shorts. Humidity thick. Temperature in the upper nineties. "Let's go down to the water, see if we can catch a breeze." She snorted, running ahead of me toward our dock.

The old house sat in the center of almost three acres, on a bluff, over-looking the river. The highest section of the property was an ancient shell mound built centuries ago by the native people, the Timucua. It was con-structed from tons of oyster and clamshells on the highest section of the property. Some of these old mounds were simply trash dumps. Others were sacred burial grounds. A Seminole Indian friend of mine says the mound, one hundred feet from my cabin, was used for ceremonial purposes.

Three large live oaks, thick limbs cloaked in beards of Spanish moss, stood sentry in my backyard. We walked under the boughs, a mourning dove chanting in the adjacent woods. My dock, most of the old boards I'd replaced, jutted eighty-feet into the river. To my left, the St. Johns formed an oxbow, the slow-moving black water nudging off a cypress-covered jetty. The river was 310 miles long. My cabin was near the halfway point between the headwaters and the Atlantic Ocean east of Jacksonville. It was the only major river in America that flowed north.

Across the river was the Ocala National Forest, more than 800 square miles of thick woods, swamps, and luminescent springs bubbling up from the earth. The spring water came from a hallowed source, percolating for years through vast underground limestone caverns, aquifers restoring rain-water into nature's untouched holy water.

I stood at the edge of my dock, looked at the wind across the dark water, looked for signs of knobby eyes breaking the surface. My Indian friend, Joe Billie, had given me a lesson on swimming with alligators. Don't swim in a lake or river if the wind's causing the water to be the slightest bit choppy. Today, the water was flat calm. No wind. No gators in sight. I turned to Max, who stood right beside me. "What do you think? You spot a gator anywhere?" She looked up at me from scanning the river, her head making a short dachshund nod.

"Okay, I'll do a fifteen second swim to cool off." I set my phone on the wooden bench I'd built, turned and went headfirst off my dock, slicing through the river with little sound, the water cooler the deeper I swam. It was twenty feet deep at the end of my dock. I touched the sandy belly of the river with one hand, turned and swam to the surface. I kept noise to an absolute minimum, treading water quietly, the cries of an osprey overhead, the smell of blooming heather in the air.

I floated on my back for a moment, Florida in the summertime down by the river. And then Max started barking. Nothing calls a gator to dinner faster than a barking dog, especially a small barking dog. I was about twenty-five feet off the end of the dock. I looked around, and there it was. Maybe at seventy-five feet away. Next to a bald cypress tree. I looked at the unblinking eyes imbedded in knotty hide—just above the surface.

Judging from the space between the eyes, I figured the gator was a big one, maybe ten feet. I had twenty-five feet to the dock ladder. The gator had seventy-five feet to me. And he or she had a large tail. I swam, clearing the distance in seconds. I grabbed the rungs to the ladder and pulled up to the dock, standing next to Max, water dripping from my body, the gator nowhere in sight.

I turned to Max. "Thanks for ringing the dinner bell with your bark. On second thought, maybe you were sounding the alarm for me." She wagged her tail and looked toward the area where the gator had been. I picked Max up and sat down on the bench, scratching her behind the ears.

I checked my phone. One missed call, and it was from Dave. I played his message: "Sean, if you get this, call me as soon as you can. You have a visitor, and it's related to the letter Curtis Garwood sent you. He sent it to someone else, too, and she's here at the marina asking for you."

SIX

Jesse Taylor hoped he'd be there, but he wouldn't bet the farm on it. Jesse could detect from the phone call that Harold Reeves was only meeting him because of their history together as kids. Both had been robbed from a natural transition, a coming of age, from boy to man. Maybe Harold would show up at the Waffle House. If not, that would speak volumes in a small town of less than ten thousand people. And it would mean that Jesse was going to start from scratch to find old men long overdue to be prosecuted, or the graves of those who died in their care.

Jesse locked the door to his room at the Heartland Motel, a chalky-white, single story, ragged structure that had a lot of tread wear since it was built in the 1950s. He left behind the chemical bleach smell in his room and walked across the parking lot, which was peppered with cracks and water-filled potholes. He stopped to light a cigarette, looking down at his reflection from the black water inside one pothole, mosquito larvae wriggling at the surface. He had forty-five minutes before his meeting with Harold at the restaurant, a few blocks from the motel.

He walked to the corner on Lafayette Street and headed right, stopping at a crossing, waiting for the light to turn green. A Marianna Police Department cruiser eased up to the intersection, stopping, the officer's eyes hidden behind dark glasses, but Jesse knew the patrolman was watching him. Jesse lit a cigarette and crossed the road, his eyes trained on the sidewalk in front of him. The patrol car drove by slowly, the officer turning left.

The Jackson County Courthouse was to his right. Old live oaks stood on the grounds, the limbs casting dark shadows over concrete shrines to the Civil War. Jesse knew the exact tree that the mob had hung Claude Neal from in 1934. A year before Jesse's father had beaten his mother senseless, the old bastard had proudly pointed it out to him, like the tree was a monument. *No wonder I never amounted to much. Maybe I can still right a wrong or two.*

Jesse sat on a bench, watching people coming and going from the building, attorneys carrying briefcases bulging with files. People carrying human baggage, often stuffed with shame or hurt. Looking for some way out of a bad situation. But it was here where Jesse's situation went from bad to horrible. He stared at the exterior of the building, remembering the day he was sentenced here. The outside of the courthouse had been updated, but it was the inside where Jesse's life was forever changed.

He remembered the elderly, white-haired judge who wore a black robe and a reputation of stubbornness. *In God We Trust* was highlighted on the dark wood wall behind the judge's bench. He never looked at Jesse as he sentenced him to ninety days in the Florida School for Boys. It might as well have been ninety years, because if Jesse lived ninety years, he felt his soul would never be cleansed of those ninety days. He blew a long breath out of his cheeks, his chest hurting. He glanced at his watch and walked toward the Waffle House.

Approaching the restaurant door, Jesse could see his reflection in the glass, and he could see the patrol car making another round down the street, the same officer in dark glasses looking toward the Waffle House as Jesse went inside.

Half of the booths were filled with diners. Four people sat at the counter, two paramedics, radios on their belts, and an earpiece in one ear. Jesse walked by the counter, looking for Harold Reese. *What the hell would he look like today?* Jesse spotted one man, sitting alone in a back booth, the furthest one from the front door. It was Harold.

Jesse walked up to him and said, "Been a long time. I think the last time I saw you was at Daytona, the time Dale died."

"Yep. He was the best. Junior's junior. What can I say? How you been, Jesse?"

"Somehow I find a way to climb outta the fox holes of life, barely."

"I know what you mean." Harold wore faded jeans and a NASCAR T-shirt. His whiskered face was deeply lined from age and the Florida sun. He had the look of a man who'd made his living outdoors, a farmer or fisherman.

Jesse took a seat opposite Harold. "I sure appreciate you meeting me."

"No problem. We sort of grew up together." Harold sipped black coffee.

"Man, what keeps you here. After the shit you experienced at the school, how could you have walked the same streets as those butchers through all these years?"

Harold looked out the window to the steeple of a church in the distance. He turned his pale blue eyes to Jesse. "Where could I have gone? I got deep roots in Jackson County. My granddaddy fought the yanks in the battle of Marianna. I have forty acres, a small house that's long been paid off. I hired on with the post office and somehow managed to stay as a letter carrier for thirty years, and then I retired. I was lucky, after a lot of failures, to find a good woman who could put up with me, my quirks. And today we have two grandchildren."

Jesse smiled. "I'm happy for you. You're a better man than me."

"On the phone you told me about Curtis Garwood's death. Reading his obituary made you want to come back here, why?"

"Because it reminded me of how our lives got derailed off the tracks by some mean sons-a-bitches that never paid for what they did. I've been thinking about this for years."

"You picked a helluva time to start your crusade. Most of those men are dead. The state attorney looked at it a few years back. Said nothing was prosecutable, statute of limitations and whatnot."

"Murder's prosecutable. Curtis's death—by the way, he took his own life, brought back memories of Andy Cope. They were good friends. You remember Andy?"

"Yeah. His sister has tried more than once to get an investigation going. But man, you're talking about a kid who vanished a long time ago."

"I know they killed Andy in there one night. It was the night Andy told me and Curtis he was gonna run away. He wanted me to go with him, but

I was too damn scared. I heard the shots, between booms of thunder. I'd just taken the garbage out. I didn't see 'em killing Andy, but we never saw him after that night. He never ran away. They shot him. Curtis was never the same. He never talked about it either. There's no mistaking the sound of a 12-gauge shotgun firing double-aught buckshot. I've fired enough rounds through the years."

Harold looked around the restaurant. "Jesse, lower your voice. This town's got bigger ears than you understand. You need to go talk with Andy's sister, Caroline Harper. See what she's been up against. I'll give you her address."

"Caroline Cope…I remember her. So she's been trying all these years to find Andy?"

"I believe she gave up on finding him. She'd hoped to find what happened and who did it. Now, I think she just wants to find Andy. To find his grave, I guess."

Jesse looked across the restaurant for a second. "I remember Andy and Caroline walking home from school. Always together. He tried to take care of her, and he was just a kid, too."

"Yeah. Her husband died a few years ago, heart attack. She has one daughter who lives in California. When the state attorney was looking at claims of child abuse in 2010, right before they shut the place down, Caroline was doing all she could to get investigators to look into what happened to Andy. She didn't get very far. Nobody in this town wants to go there. It's like they just want to distance themselves from a sleeping evil right on the edge of Marianna. I'll give you directions to her place. Another thing, the state's got that place up for sale. They may have an offer on it. I heard a developer wants to build houses and golf courses—a damn country club."

"Somebody's got to stop that. Nobody should be playing golf over the bones of kids. I got to do something quick—"

"Ya'll ready to order?" A waitress approached the table. She was in her early forties, green eye shadow, a fingernail-sized birthmark on her neck, and graying hair in a ponytail.

Harold said, "Just more coffee, Lisa"

Jesse leaned back in the booth. "That's fine for me too."

She nodded and left. Jesse lowered his voice. "I believe there are a lot more bodies buried around that school. There has to be. We both knew kids like Andy who simply disappeared, never to be seen or heard from again. They didn't run away, Harold. For God sakes, you know that. Nobody has a right to build over them."

Harold stirred sugar into his coffee. "Jesse, you ought to leave it alone. Just go on back to Jacksonville and forget it, okay?"

"No, I can't. Not any more. I stopped at the school on the way here. It's all locked up. Spoke with a security guard, Johnny Hines. Remember him?

Harold nodded. "What'd you tell him?"

"I asked him if Hack Johnson was still above ground."

"What'd he say?"

"Let's put it this way, he didn't say Johnson was dead."

Harold released a deep breath. "You asked the wrong guy. Hines is tight with the Johnson family. Might as well be on their payroll. Now they know you're in town."

"You were a letter carrier. What's their address?"

"He lives way the hell back in the swamps. He's got a hundred acres, fenced. His family lives back there in trailers, doublewides. They pretty much sum up the definition of survivalists. I heard the grandsons cook meth and sell it. One of those boys, his name's Cooter Johnson, drives around town in a late fifties model Ford truck, painted canary yellow. He shoots pool a lot at a place called Shorty's. But if I were you, I sure as hell wouldn't go in there alone."

"I got no beef against a grandson. I'd like to pay the old man a visit, though."

"You don't know if it was him who killed Andy. Johnson was one of the meanest. He liked to see blood fly on the first lick of the strap. You could never get to him today. And if you decide to head back in those swamps, then you'll be doing what Curtis did. You'll be committing suicide."

SEVEN

Curtis Garwood left a clue, but he didn't leave a name. Before I returned Dave's call, I remembered in Curtis's letter he wrote that he'd sent a copy to Andy Cope's sister. I stood on my dock and called Dave. He answered after a half dozen rings. "Sean, I was just leaving the Tiki Bar, heading back to *Gibraltar* for an espresso. Where are you?"

"Standing in wet swim trunks."

"Poolside, no doubt, with a lovely lady, perhaps?"

"Max is the lady. The river will do as a pool in ninety-nine degree Florida heat. Who's my visitor?"

"Name's Caroline Harper. She drove down here from the panhandle, Jackson County to be exact."

"Let me guess—Andy Cope, the boy Curtis mentioned in his letter, was her brother."

"*Was* seems to be the operative term. I spoke with her briefly. Met her in the marina office paying my slip rent. She was asking where she might find you. I told her that you and I were friends and that I could get a message to you if it was important. After some gentle prodding, she shared that she'd received a copy of Curtis's letter and then wanted to meet Sean O'Brien, someone who might help find her deceased brother's grave. Sounds like a tall order to me."

I said nothing. The sound of a bumblebee darting in and out of the lavender trumpet flowers that were growing across an embankment and down my seawall invaded the momentary silence. The flowers were thick, and in the breeze they resembled cascading water spilling over a sluice into the river.

"Are you there, Sean?"

"Yeah, I'm just thinking."

"Did you, perchance, pick up the second letter or package Curtis mailed to the postal box?"

"No."

"Understood. Whatever it contains, I surmise, will be in someway linked, even by proxy, to Miss Harper or most probably to her brother, Andy."

"I think the reason Curtis sent a second package is because he knew, if I opened it, if I take it, I would deal with whatever's in the envelope and accept his offer."

"It's not as much an offer, Sean, as it is a challenge, a proverbial Oedipus riddle. And speaking of the Greeks, Pandora's box was not a box. It was a simple looking jar—until it was opened."

"And it was a myth, but don't tell Nick."

"What shall I tell Miss Harper? I left her at a corner table in the Tiki Bar overlooking the marina. She ordered hot tea and said she'd wait there until I told her whether or not I reached you. Time hasn't been too kind to her, Sean. She has the thousand-yard stare, the look of someone who's been denied of the one thing that propels all human growth."

"What's that?"

"Hope."

I watched Max chase a field mouse as we walked toward the cabin. Dave exhaled in the phone. "I can tell her you're not accessible, send her back to the Florida Panhandle. You're under no obligation to meet someone who sort of materialized here at the marina, connected to you only because she was copied on a letter addressed to you. This is not a chain letter, however, it has that ominous feel. What would you like for me to convey to Miss Harper?"

"Tell her to order another cup of tea. I'll be there soon."

EIGHT

Caroline Harper seemed out of step in a dockside bar filled with people who walked to the beat of a different drummer. The Tiki Bar was about half filled with shrimpers, deck hands, boat captains, weekend bikers, and tourists on all-day happy hours. It wasn't hard for me to spot her. She sat alone, reading a book at a corner table in the bar. The rustic bar was a restaurant stripped of any pretense. It sat above the marina water on stilts. Its thatched roof of dried palm fronds was somewhat covered in pelican poop, the wooden sides of the bar faded from time and salt water. Plastic windows were rolled up, and a breeze carrying the scent of garlic crabs and broiled fish drifted across the Ponce Marina.

Dave had described her well—early sixties, platinum gray hair pinned up, the pensive face of a woman who'd endured a hardscrabble life probably more difficult than most. She'd set her paperback book on the table, one of a dozen large wooden spools previously used by utility companies to store power-lines. The tables were shellacked, turned on one end and bolted to the knotty pine floor, which was stained from spilled beer, grease, and sometimes a splatter of blood.

Max followed me through the restaurant, her tail wagging when Roberto, the cook with a full beard and belly to match, came from the kitchen near the bar and said, "Hey, little Max. You wanna fry?"

She snorted and Roberto used one of his large hands to lift a French fry from a bamboo basket lined with newspaper. "Sean, last time I saw Max,

Nick Cronus brought her in here and let her sit on a barstool for a little while."

"She likes German beer. It's the dachshund in her." I grinned. "Come on, Max. One's enough." She followed me across the restaurant to Caroline Harper's table, diners in tank tops and shorts pointing at Max and smiling. Caroline Harper looked up, not sure whether to smile or ask me a question. I said, "Are you Miss Harper?"

"Yes. Please call me Caroline."

"I'm Sean O'Brien. Sean works fine for me." I smiled.

"Thank you for willing to meet with me. Please, sit." Her pale blue eyes tried to mask worry, maybe fear. She glanced down as Max approached, sniffing the base of the table and sitting next to my feet. "Your dog is so precious. My neighbor had one for years. How long have you had him or her?"

"Definitely her. Long enough to know each others quirks." I smiled, letting her take the time she needed, hoping my comment would put her at ease.

"It looks like she knows her way around this restaurant. How'd you choose a dachshund?"

"I didn't. My wife Sherri did a few months before her death. And so now it's Max and me.

"I'm sorry for your loss. Your friend, Dave, said sometimes you live on your boat here at the marina."

"I have an old cabin about fifty miles inland. My boat's an ongoing work in progress."

"Is that the boat Curtis Garwood chartered?"

"Yes."

Her chest rose, she swallowed dryly. Caroline reached in her purse and withdrew a photo, placing the picture on the table toward me. It was the image of a boy, maybe twelve or thirteen. Handsome. Staring directly into the camera lens. "That's a picture of my brother, Andy. Curtis mentioned him in his letter to you."

I said nothing, picking up the photo and looking closer at it. I could see a dusting of freckles across the boy's forehead. I set it down. "And I'm sorry for your loss, too. He looks like a fine boy."

She smiled. "He was…he was the best older brother a girl could hope for. We did a lot together growing up. Andy had to grow into…he became more of a protector for me than our stepfather. I'd always suspected they'd killed Andy while he was being held in the Florida School for Boys. My family received a letter and a brief call from the warden telling us Andy had run away. But where would he go? He was only thirteen. I'd heard talk that there might be hidden graves of boys killed and buried on that reform school property. I've tried to get the police to open a file, to start a case. They still call him a runaway, a missing child. And after all these years, they won't do anything, especially in Marianna."

"And then you received a copy of Curtis Garwood's letter."

"Yes! It was like a new door had opened where one had been nailed shut for years. I was so sorry to read Curtis took his own life. I remembered him as a kid who had lots of those little Matchbox Cars. When the other boys didn't spend time with Curtis, Andy did. Curtis was always trying to get money to buy more of those little cars." She bit her lower lip, looking at her brother's picture. Then she raised her eyes up to me. I could see a vein pulsating on the right side of her neck. She took a deep breath. "Sean, would you…could you maybe look into Andy's disappearance? He didn't deserve that fate. He was just a boy—a child. He was sent there because he skipped school twice. The principal wanted to make an example out of Andy. My brother was so bored in that country school. He had a quick mind, and he could make a hundred percent on tests without having to study. He liked the library and read voraciously, something our stepfather ridiculed him for doing. He simply didn't like Andy, and our mother was too scared, a self-inflicted learned weakness, to do anything about it. Our stepfather accused Andy of stealing money from his wallet. He even called the police to our house to scare Andy. A few weeks later, Andy told me in confidence that he suspected one of his friends, a boy who'd been at our house that day, had stolen the money. But Andy never accused him of it. You know who that boy was, Sean?"

"Curtis Garwood."

She lifted her eyebrows. "That's impressive. How'd you know?"

"Lucky guess."

"Andy said two days after the money went missing, Curtis had a dozen new Matchbox Cars." She leaned back in her chair, watching a family enter the restaurant and take seats around two of the spool tables. She stared at a boy who was about the age of her brother in the picture. She said, "That family just seated by the waitress is a happy family. You can tell by their smiles, by their joking with each other. The oldest boy reminds me of Andy. The boy handed his mother the menu first. He's quiet. He's considerate. You can tell. He's going to have a chance to come of age, to live his life. Andy never got that. It was as if he was born in the wrong time to the wrong family." She looked at me and said, "Will you help me?"

"I'm not sure what, if anything, I could do. If your brother was killed, his killer or killers are probably dead by now. There may be no one left to bring to justice."

"Sean, my brother, and other boys like him, were considered by the state as nobodies. Throwaways. No one was ever held accountable because no one cared. Even if you can't find any of the men responsible for my brother's death, maybe you can somehow find my brother's grave. A few years after Andy never returned home, my mother divorced our stepfather. She married a decent man. They're both dead, buried in a plot next to my grandparents. I want to find my brother's hidden grave and bring him home to the family plot. Will you help me?"

I nodded. "I'll look into it. Do what I can. At this point, I don't want to promise you something I can't deliver."

"Oh, but you're wrong, Sean. You've already delivered it to me. You've given me something I haven't felt in almost a lifetime."

"What's that?"

"Hope."

She reached in her purse and removed a second, identical photo of her brother. "Please, take this. If you need a reminder of what I'm hoping for, it can be as close as your shirt pocket. Where will you start?"

"By looking in a post office box."

NINE

There's something odd about opening a post office box that's not yours. It's almost like opening a letter that's not addressed to you. I thought about that, stepping inside a post office I'd never been to, opening a box I've never seen. I walked up to box 129 and inserted the brass key. And there it was, a manila envelope fitting neatly into the large box. I glanced over my shoulder. Three people, less than twenty feet from me, stood in line at the counter to claim packages or buy stamps. The clerk, late fifties, bloodhound eyes, glasses perched at the tip of his nose, looked over at me with a detached glance.

I pulled the package from the box and read the address. The same neat handwriting, the same fountain pen. Curtis Garwood had written my name in the address, but at this point, it didn't make it much easier. I started to open the large padded envelope on a table used for preparing packages. I glanced at one of the three cameras I'd spotted entering the building and thought otherwise. If it was some kind of physical evidence in the killing of Andy Cope, the evidence chain had been broken a long time ago. But there was no need to empty the contents on government cameras.

I walked across the parking lot to my Jeep, the hot sun on the back of my neck. I sat behind the wheel, lowering the windows and using a knife I carried in my console to carefully open the package. There were two stacks of one hundred dollar bills, a hand-written letter, and something at the bottom of the package. I looked inside and saw a shotgun shell. I found a pencil in my console, inserted it into the open casing and lifted out the shell. It was a spent shell—the casing, and it was one of the older varieties, a paper casing with small images of pheasants on the exterior. I lifted the shell to my nose. I could smell the faint odor of burnt powder from a 12-gauge shell that was probably fired a half-century ago. I set the shell on the top of the console and read the letter—most likely the last thing Curtis Garwood wrote in his life.

Dear Sean –

If you're reading this, I can assume you've decided to take the job, and for that I'm eternally grateful. I've enclosed fifteen thousand dollars for your expenses and time. That's the best I could do. The shotgun shell I've included in here was used to kill Andy Cope. I say that because I was hiding when I saw three men chasing Andy one night. I'd taken the trash out and decided to spend a few minutes smoking a cigarette behind a brick tool shed. A thunderstorm came from nowhere. That's when I heard them chasing somebody. It was three men. Although their backs were turned to me, as they chased him, I heard one of them yell, "Stop! Don't make us cut you down, Andy."

The man who yelled was the one we called the Preacher, because he liked to quote old testament Bible verses before he beat us. He had a tattoo of the Southern Cross on his right forearm. He called his tattoo the Southern Cross of Justice. They shot the first round in the air. Andy stopped and turned around. Then there was a crack of lightning and Andy ran. The man in the center, I believe it was the Preacher, shot him in the back as Andy ran toward the only oak tree in the field. That's where he fell, at the base of the tree.

The men picked up the first shell casing. But they couldn't find the second. In that burst of lightning, I saw the casing fall behind a log. The next morning I found it, and I've kept it all these years. I hid that night while they picked up Andy, his head hanging down and his body limp. I knew they'd killed him, and I knew they'd do the same to me if I told anyone. I have few regrets in life, but that's one I'm taking to my grave. Wherever they buried Andy, I believe other boys were buried there, too. They had no right to do that to kids, and that's all we were — scared kids. I hope you will find courage and success where I could not. And I pray for your soul, Sean, because if you go there, you will meet some people who sold theirs a long time ago.

    Sincerely,
    Curtis Garwood

I sat there for a few seconds, thinking about what Curtis had written, thinking about what Caroline Harper had said, the mournful loss of her brother. I picked up the spent shotgun shell again, looked at the indentation strike mark on the primer, lifting the casing to my nose for a moment. Somewhere in the mixture of scents, the tarnished brass head, the scorched powder, was the scent of death. Not tangible in the physical sense, but perceptual in the sense of the unconscionable, gunning down and shooting a child in the back.

I reached in my shirt pocket and took out the photo of Andy Cope, the smattering of freckles just visible on his forehead, the bright look of optimism and courage in his eyes. I knew there was something about Andy that stayed with Curtis Garwood throughout his life. Maybe it began as a debt of boyhood gratitude for keeping Curtis's theft a secret. Maybe it was because Curtis knew Andy was going to escape the night he was killed and he was forced to witness Andy's execution. For Curtis, it was the one-two punch of guilt and grief that he fought all his life because of the good he didn't do, until now, and he blamed himself because no one else could.

On my way back to the marina I would call Caroline Harper and tell her what I found. Then I'd plan a trip to Jackson County, and there I had no idea what I'd find.

TEN

The last time Jesse Taylor entered the Jackson County Courthouse he left in a deputy sheriff's car. And, today, he was here to see the sheriff. He'd called to make an appointment, but was told the sheriff was tied up in budget meetings. Asked what it was in reference to, the receptionist said Jesse could speak with an investigator within the cold case division.

The investigator was forty-five minutes late. Jesse sat on a hard plastic chair inside the receiving lobby of the sheriff's department. Three chairs down was an African-America woman, leafing through a tattered copy of People Magazine, one of the pages falling to the floor. She picked it up, glancing over to Jesse. He could see that her face was slightly swollen on the left side, her left eye dark with bruises. She quickly turned her head.

Jesse looked at the clock on the wall close to the reception desk. *More than fifty minutes late.* He got up and walked over to the woman behind the counter. She stopped pecking at the keyboard in front of her, looking up at Jesse. "Yes sir." Her tone was flat. Hair bobbed around her ears, round face, multiple piercing spots on her earlobes. No earrings.

"I was wondering if you heard from Detective Larry Lee. He's almost an hour late."

"He's still in the field. Last communications he said he was heading back to the station. Detective Lee knows you're here, sir. It's been a busy day. Active cases are a priority."

"You mean over cold cases."

"I didn't say that. Please, just have a seat."

35

Jesse turned to walk back across the lobby just as two men came in from the entry hall. They were laughing at something. One wore an open brown sports coat, white shirt and khaki pants, badge barely visible on his brown belt. He had a neatly trimmed salt and pepper beard on an angular face, toothpick in one corner of his mouth. The other man was tall, wide-shoulders, his dark hair cut military style. He picked up two messages on the desk, waited for the receptionist to press a button under her counter to allow him access to a locked door near the desk. He turned to his partner, "Catch you in a few. We'll go over the Barfield case."

The man in the sports coat nodded and turned toward Jesse. "Are you Mr. Taylor?"

"Yes sir."

"I'm Detective Lee. How can I help you?"

Jesse looked around for a second. "Do you have somewhere we can talk, maybe an office?"

"This'll be fine." He pulled out a small notebook. "I can jot down what you have to say and take it from there. As I understand it, you wanted to meet about an incident at the Dozier School, correct?"

"They called it the Florida School for Boys when I was there. What I want to talk to you about isn't no incident. It's murder."

The detective tilted his head, lower jaw tightening. "Murder? What murder, and when did it allegedly happen?"

"It was in 1965. The victim's name was Andy Cope."

"How do you know this?"

"I heard the shooting."

"So you were in juvie. What were you in there for?"

"I took a car for a joyride."

"You stole a car, right?"

"No, it was my old man's car. Rather than punish me like a father, he liked to have the county do it. He could spend more time drinking. Detective Lee, the night that Andy was killed I knew he was going to make a run for it. He wasn't at breakfast the next morning. His family never saw him again, and they were told Andy ran off, maybe hitchhiked outta there. But it never happened."

"You heard a shooting, which meant you never saw it, correct?"

"Yes, but—"

"Ever see a dead body?"

"No. Didn't have to. Andy wasn't the only one not to make it outta there alive. A kid told me he saw a black boy's severed hand in the hog slop one day." Jesse glanced at the woman sitting in one of the plastic chairs. She closed her eyes for a moment. "Detective, you got a lot of cold cases on that property. And there are people here in this county that never were investigated for them."

"Mr. Taylor, a case, at least to me, gets cold if I don't have somebody in cuffs after forty-eight hours, not fifty years. And this county has investigated allegations such as yours. The state attorney says there has never been sufficient evidence to prove or disprove abuse or even a killing in the old school. Some fellas like you filed a class action suit, think it was in 2010, and the judge threw it out because it vastly exceeded any statute of limitations."

"That doesn't apply to murder."

"There's no dead body, no crime scene…nothing."

"Look…if they build condos and golf courses over that land, the devil will do a dance over graves 'cause he was at the school when I was held there. I could see it in the eyes of the men who beat me. See the hate and the downright evil. They were the criminals, not the kids. Maybe you can take a team out there and start doing some digging. I'm bettin' you'll find graves of kids never reported dead in any official records."

"Mr. Taylor, I want to thank you for coming by today. However, I'm not going to get a court order to start excavating hundreds of acres of property based on hearsay. Now, I've got other pressing cases I have to get to." He closed his small notebook, turning to leave.

"Detective Lee, you know an old timer here by the name of Hack Johnson?"

The detective looked at his pen, clicking the top and placing it in his shirt pocket. "Can't say I do. Why?"

"Because he could lead you to where they're buried."

The detective stared at Jesse for a few seconds in silence, the soft buzzing of a phone call coming from behind the reception desk. He walked away, his hard soles loud against the tile floor, exiting left through the same door that his partner had used.

Jesse shook his head, turned and started for the entrance door when the black woman set the People Magazine down and said, "Sir." She stood and walked his way.

Jesse stopped. "Yes?" He tried not to stare at her eye, partially swollen shut—the white of the eye strawberry red.

She glanced around, lowering her voice. "I didn't mean to overhear your conversation with the policeman, but I heard you talking about a killin' at that reform school."

"Do you know something about that?"

"Way 'fore I was born, they sent two of my grandma's boys there. One time I heard her tell my mama that my Uncle Jeremiah, when he was a boy in there, he saw 'em shoot a white boy."

Jesse looked over her shoulder at the receptionist. "Let's step out in the hall."

"I cain't be gone long. My boyfriend violated his 'straining order. Now he's gonna go straight to jail."

Jesse looked at her eye. "He hit you?"

She nodded, sniffling.

"Come on." He led her to the hallway. "Let me ask you something, did your Uncle Jeremiah ever go by the name Jerry?"

"Some folks called him that. When he was little they did mostly, I'm told."

"Where's he now?"

"He stays in an old school bus parked in a pecan grove somewhere. My mama, his sister, said after he got outta that reform school he was never the same boy. He don't talk much. He's a picker. Apples. Grapes. Watermelons. Stuff like that."

"You mentioned two boys. Did Jeremiah have a brother in there?"

"His name was Elijah. I never met him. Grandma says those men tol' her Elijah up and run away from that reform school. Grandma and my mama said they never saw him again. Nobody did. Grandma believes they kil't him in there. Buried his lil' body somewhere. All she wants to do now is put flowers on his grave. But there ain't no grave to go to."

"How do I find your grandma?"

"I'll write down her address. There's a picture of a redbird on her mailbox. If you go to her house, go in the daytime."

"I understand. Thank you. What's your name?"

"Sonia Acker. All my life I heard stories about my lost Uncle Elijah. My grandma has one picture of him. He was about nine, dressed for church on an Easter Sunday. He had the biggest smile. She keeps that picture on her mantle next to a picture of Jesus. Write down your number. If I see my Uncle Jeremiah, I'll give him your number."

Jesse wrote his number on the paper napkin she gave him. "Take care of yourself, Sonia."

"I don't know where they put Elijah. But if you find boys buried at that school, look in two places. Look for a graveyard for white boys and one for black boys. They won't be buried together." Her eyes filled with water, a single tear falling from her swollen eye onto the marble floor in the hall of justice.

ELEVEN

I walked down L dock toward my boat with payment-in-full from a dead man. The money was still in the envelope. I didn't count it. No reason to. There was no return address on the package. And for me, there was no turning back. I'd made the commitment to Caroline Harper. By opening the sealed package, I'd closed the deal with Curtis Garwood too. And now I had a narrative of Andy Cope's last day on earth, a description of a tattoo, the name of a man Curtis called the Preacher, and a 12-gauge shotgun shell.

And fifty years from the point of origin—from the day the shell was fired.

A squadron of gulls flew over the marina just above masts of the sailboats, the gulls laughing, darting toward Ponce Lighthouse. I walked down the dock, playing over in my head the two conversations I'd had with Caroline, the one at the Tiki Hut and the other on the phone when I called her after I'd read Curtis's letter. She didn't know anyone called the Preacher in Jackson County. Had never heard her mother mention a person by that name. The description of the Southern Cross tattoo meant nothing to her. But she was intrigued with the possibilities of what the shell casing might bring. *"At least that's real evidence,"* she'd said.

But what were the real odds of ever finding the shotgun? Betting men simply wouldn't wager. Caroline said I'd given her something—hope. But I was doing so on speculation, the probabilities so low that that no one could calculate those odds. I'd have to figure a way to improve them, to shorten the distance, condense the years between a crime or crimes and the perpetrators.

I walked toward a 42-foot Sea Ray, open cockpit, exterior painted deep blue. I heard a woman laugh, smelled a whiff of cigar smoke. They were in the cockpit—an older man and a younger woman, the music up. The man was in his early sixties, mostly bald, wearing an unbuttoned, green tropical shirt, belly hanging over the swim trunks, a thick gold chain buried in his chest hair. A stogie was in one corner of his mouth. He sipped scotch from a heavy cocktail glass before setting the drink on a table. "I'm getting more ice," he yelled, turning to enter the salon.

The woman was in her late-twenties, sitting in a lounge chair, black hair swept up, dark tortoise shell glasses on a striking face. She wore a bikini top, exposing ample cleavage, white shorts not much larger than bikini bottoms. She was deeply tanned, a rum punch in one hand, fingernails fiery red. Norah Jones was on the wireless speakers singing *Turn Me On*. The woman lowered her sunglasses and smiled at me, uncrossing and crossing her feet at the ankles, slightly shifting her body in the lounge chair. I returned her smile and kept walking.

I walked toward *Jupiter*, my 38-foot Bayliner I'd bought for ten cents on the dollar in a DEA sale. It was at the very end of L dock. I knew Max was either on Dave's boat, *Gibraltar* or Nick's boat, *St. Michaels*. She had the best of both marina worlds—the relaxed and quiet crossword-puzzle-solving atmosphere around Dave's boat, with a Gershwin tune or jazz usually played softly. She might choose to be on Nick's boat, *St. Michaels*, following Nick in a Zorba-the-Greek dance. It all depended upon whether she wanted a nap or if she was hungry.

It was Nick's boat at the moment. I spotted her sitting in a canvas chair, opposite Nick. He sat with a reel he'd removed from one of his many rods. Nick was using a light oil to clean the reel, a web of fishing line piled next to his bare feet. He was animated, gesturing and chatting with Max. She seemed to listen patiently, and then she turned her head my way, jumping from her chair, tail wagging. Nick looked up. "Sean, you walkin' like an Indian or what? Didn't hear you, and I don't even have my music on. How long have you been standing there?" He glanced down at the package in my hand.

"Just got here. How's Max?"

"Hot dog's the best. She's a watchdog. Gulls stay off *St. Michaels* when she sits out here. Max is better than a wooden owl. Gulls are on to that decoy crap anyway. Kinda like a crow sits on a scarecrow's stuffed shoulders." He grinned, pleased with his analogy. "So, what the hell did you find in that post office box. Looks like you brought it to your marina home, and that probably isn't cool. I can tell 'cause Max looks worried."

Max looked at me and then at Nick. I lifted up the package. "I couldn't return it because there is no one to return it to."

"So, what's in this one?"

"Where's Dave?"

"When you answer my question like that, man I know the shit's rising in the bilge. Dave's on *Gibraltar*. Probably watchin' C-Span or sleepin' after he got tired of cussing whatever the hell's on C-Span."

"Politicians, mostly. Let's go find him, and I can show you both what I received from Curtis Garwood."

We crossed the pier and walked down the ancillary boarding dock that ran the length of the trawler, all the way to the transom. Dave sat at a small table on the cockpit, laptop open, his bifocals balanced near the tip of his nose. He had sliced cheese and crackers on a large plastic platter, a bottle of cabernet and a half-filled glass in front of him.

"Perfect timing, Sean. I was just doing a little research on the Dozier School for Boys, formerly the Florida School for Boys. You can change the name, but you can't exorcise the demons from the hundred and eleven year history of that place. Come aboard little lady and gentlemen." Dave stood, getting two more glasses from a small wet bar on deck.

We took seats around the table, Max sniffing the corners of the cockpit, satisfied, she sat near Nick, hoping for a handout. She was never disappointed. Dave poured wine in my glass and Nick said, "I'll get a brew." He stepped to the wet bar, opened the mini-fridge, taking a bottle of Guinness and popping the top.

Dave leaned forward. "I assume the large envelope you came with brings new revelations."

"More puzzles than revelations."

"Unless Curtis Garwood left you with hard and tangible physical evidence, he, even though deceased, and Caroline Harper, very much alive, won't have a legal chance in hell considering the circumstances. Statute of limitations overrides any civil or criminal charges of abuse at this point. Only the crime of murder, excuse the pun—still lives, should you find evidence that may connect some very faded and distant dots."

I reached inside the package and set the shotgun shell in the center of the table. "The dots just got a little closer."

TWELVE

Jesse Taylor wondered if she'd remember him. He remembered her. Little Caroline Cope, holding Andy's hand, walking around mud puddles on the way home from school. He recalled her wearing a Tweety Bird yellow raincoat with a ripped hood, her nose running in a cool April rain. *Funny*, he thought. *Can't remember my debit card pin number, but I can remember bits and pieces of childhood and slow-motion images of survival in Nam.*

He pulled into the driveway, the house a1950's ranch style. Maybe a half-acre yard mixed with Bermuda and St. Augustine grasses, a few weeds in the dry patches. He crushed the remains of a cigarette in the car's ashtray, stopping next to the brick home. He got out and walked down the slate rock path leading to the front door. At this moment he wished that Harold had given him Caroline's phone number as well as her address. Maybe he should have called first. And now he's showing up after fifty years. Why hadn't he come earlier? Why did it take reading Curtis Garwood's obituary to motivate him? *Because the abuse of a child leaves scars that never fuckin' heal. That's why.*

He knocked on the wooden door, paint fading, the scent of blooming azaleas next to the house, a butterfly darting over the pink blossoms. The door slightly opened the length of a brass chain. Jesse nodded, looking into the same pale blue eyes he remembered so long ago. She'd aged well. "Caroline, I don't know if you remember me. Harold Reeves gave me your address. I'm Jesse Taylor. I went to school with you and Andy. Andy was in my grade. And he and I wound up in reform school together."

She stared at him a few seconds, the chant of a mourning dove coming from the adjacent wooded lot. "Jesse Taylor...yes, yes, I do remember you."

"Can I come in? It's about Andy."

"Yes, of course." She slid the chain off the lock and opened the door. "Please, come in. Can I get you something to drink? Coffee or maybe some water?"

"No, I'm fine."

"Let's go out on the porch to visit."

He followed her through the home filled with antiques, family photos, and furniture that was worn but comfortable. She led him to a fully screened back porch filled with lime green and yellow overstuffed pillows on wicker furniture. Ferns grew from large copper vases in three of the four corners. She sat in a rattan rocking chair. Jesse took a seat on a couch opposite from her. "You have a real nice house, Caroline."

"Thank you. It still has a lot of Jim's touch. Can't bring myself to change much. We were married thirty years before his heart attack. I still have some of his clothes in the closet."

"I understand."

She crossed her legs, just moving the rocking chair, waiting for him to speak. He cleared his throat, "Caroline, I had coffee with Harold Reeves. He told me you'd been trying for years to get somebody to investigate your brother's disappearance."

"That's right. It's been the same excuses: no body no crime, especially in Jackson County."

"I was there the night they shot Andy."

She stopped rocking, leaning forward. "Did you see who killed Andy?"

"No. It was rainy and foggy that night. I was taking out food waste to the hog pen. I heard two shots, and I knew Andy was gonna try to make a getaway that night. Maybe there's something I can do to help you."

She smiled, her eyes narrowing some, probing. "That's kind of you, Jesse. What made you think of Andy after all these years?"

He looked through the screen toward the back yard, a soft breeze blowing around the tall pines and creating a jingle from wind chimes hanging in one corner of the porch. "I hadn't really stopped thinking about Andy. I thought about him when I was in Vietnam gettin' my ass shot off. I thought of him when I saw kids his age in the park or the playground. And I thought of the hell those men put kids like Andy and me through. The beatings were so bad we bled through our underwear for days. And then I saw a death notice in the paper. It was Curtis Garwood's obituary. I remembered he was Andy's best friend, and after I learned Curtis committed suicide, I knew the bastards that beat us had taken another life. Curtis just suffered for fifty more years beyond Andy."

"Right before he took his life, Curtis copied me on a letter he'd sent to a man Curtis had hired as a charter fishing guide. The man's name is Sean O'Brien. He has a charter boat near Ponce Inlet. In the letter to Sean, Curtis had talked about Andy. I have an extra copy. You can take it."

"Why would he send that to a fishing guide?"

"Because, before he was a fishing guide, Sean O'Brien was a homicide detective down in Miami. He'd apparently impressed Curtis enough to hire Sean."

"Hire him?"

"Yes, he wanted Sean to investigate Andy's death, to investigate the abuse you were talking about. After I received my copy of Curtis's letter, I drove down to the Ponce Marina to speak with Sean. At that point, he hadn't decided whether he'd look into the case. I pleaded with him to please try. He finally agreed. After that, he went to a postal box to pick up a package Curtis had mailed, probably sent the same day the letter was mailed. Sean told me that in the package Curtis said that three men were chasing Andy that night. And although Curtis didn't get a clear look at the men's faces, he did recognize the voice of one of the men. He said it came from a man the boys called the Preacher."

Jesse leaned back on the couch, touching his whiskered chin with a finger, his jaw-line rigid. Caroline studied him for a moment. "Who's the Preacher, Jesse? Do you know?"

"We didn't know most of their names. It was Mr. this or Mr. that. We knew them by the nicknames we gave the men. That's how we could whisper stuff without it gettin' back to the bastards."

"In the package, Curtis included a shotgun shell casing that he'd picked up that night. In the fog and rain, the men apparently couldn't find it. It was from the shooter's gun. This is the first physical evidence we have."

"The question is where the hell's the gun? You need something more, Caroline."

"We don't have anything more."

"What if you had an eyewitness, a grown man who was there as a boy and saw them shoot Andy that night."

"As far as I know there isn't a eyewitness."

"Maybe I can find one for you. And if we're real lucky, maybe he won't be afraid to tell us who pulled the trigger that night."

"What do you know, Jesse? Do you *know* someone who was there… someone who saw it clearly and who can identify the killer? Even if the killer is dead, we'd have a name. We'd have a case, and we'd have cause to go in there and find my brother's grave before they start building golf courses and condos."

Jesse said nothing, looking down at the scars across the tops of his weathered hands. "I don't personally know anyone who saw it. I might have a way to find somebody. He's a local recluse, keeps to himself. Maybe he'll talk to me."

"Be careful, Jesse. There's a reason he hasn't talked. One man was going to, maybe twenty-five years ago. Before the grand jury was convened, they found his body floating in the Chattahoochee River. His tongue had been cut out. Let me give you something."

Jesse looked at his hands, silent.

Caroline stood, walking over to a bookcase, removing a pen and post-it notes. She wrote something, giving the paper to Jesse. "Take this. It's Sean O'Brien's number. Please share with him anything you have, okay? He's done this before, Jesse. He'll know how to use it in the legal sense. Write your number down here, too." She watched Jesse struggle to write, his right hand not able to fully enclose around the pen. "Take your time, Jesse."

"What they did to Andy, to Curtis, to me and hundreds of other boys wasn't legal. Maybe in this county, they'll just look the other way. Kinda like slapping an old Nazi on the wrist for death camp crimes 'cause he's an old man. Bull shit." He stood, handing the piece of paper to Caroline. He smiled, glanced toward the woods and then looked at Caroline. "I remember you and Andy walking home from school after a hard rain. He was holding your hand and guiding you around mud puddles. At the very last one, you just jumped in and stomped up and down, laughing your head off. You made your brother laugh, too. You were wearing a yellow Tweety Bird raincoat, and it had a rip in the hood. You didn't care. I always liked your spirit, Caroline."

She smiled, rising from the rocking chair, reaching out for the paper. She noticed the scars on the tops of his hand. Caroline gently held his right hand, lifting her eyes up to him. "What happened to you?"

"I got those scars because I tried to cover my butt one time from the beatings. Preacher was infuriated. He screamed at me and forced me to hold my hands against a concrete cinderblock in the White House, and he brought the strap down hard, three times. The third time broke bones in my right hand. The bones never healed properly. Even after all these years, it's hard to hold a pencil to write."

She looked at him, his eyes watering, embarrassed. He glanced away, to the edge of the pinewoods. She continued holding his hand, the wind chimes tinkling, a tear rolling down her face. "Jesse, I am so very sorry."

THIRTEEN

After I finished reading Curtis Garwood's last letter, Dave Collins stared at the shotgun shell in the center of his table. Nick sipped from his Guinness, feeding Max a shard of Havarti. Dave reached for a small, clean cheese fork and inserted it into the open end of the shell casing. He lifted the shell and inspected it. "I haven't seen one of these since I was a lad. It's made of durable paper. Today's shotgun shells are plastic, of course. And look at the images of pheasants in flight on the casing."

Nick blew air out of his puffed cheeks. "Why the hell did Curtis keep that thing all these years? He sees his friend shot dead, and he picks up the shell casing the next morning. I don't guess he could have given it to the cops, considering the shit he was dealing with at the time."

Dave's brow furrowed, studying the shell. "The letter doesn't say who shot the kid. So maybe he kept it because one day he thought it could be linked back to the shooter. Or maybe it was to remind him never to forget."

Nick shook his head. "In the meantime, fifty years pass, and my man Sean's got the baton handed to him. But what the hell can you do with an old shotgun shell. You can't trace those loads. And you don't have a body to see if the rounds match. You can't lift prints off a fired shell, especially after so many years. So all you have, Sean, is a creepy souvenir from a murder."

"Maybe not. In lifting fingerprints the conventional way, you're right. But if a print is on a brass shell, when that shell fires there can be a chemical reaction between the salt from the print and heated brass. It can create a corrosive imprint, almost like a branding iron burning a mark into something."

Dave set the shell down. "Indeed. You can't see the print like you might on a window. And the perp can't wipe it away. To find if there's a latent print, forensic techs shoot a high voltage charge through the brass, that couples with the application of a special powder that adheres to the print's ridge points."

Nick looked at the shell in front of him. "So if the shooter used his thumb to push that shell into the shotgun, the print might be there...even after half a century."

I nodded. "And that means, if a print is there, it came from one person—the man who shot Andy Cope in the back."

Dave laced his fingers over his stomach, looking at a white pelican waddling across the dock railing. "So we know that Curtis describes the perp, or one of the three men, as someone called the Preacher. This guy has or had, assuming he's dead, a tattoo of the Southern Cross on his arm. If he's not dead, he's probably close to it. What does Caroline Harper want you to do?"

"To prove that her brother was murdered. There may be no one left to prosecute, but it'll help bring closure to her. And in the end, if she has one wish left on earth, it's to find her brother's grave and bury him in a family plot away from where he was shot and killed."

Dave shrugged his wide shoulders. "You know, Sean, you are under no obligation to chase ghosts for Caroline Harper or for Curtis Garwood."

"I told her I would look into it."

"But you never simply look into something. You go full bore until there's nothing left of the onion to peel away. You go to the core. And, in this case, particularly, that might prove to be one hell of a dangerous place to be. You agreed to nothing with Curtis. If you can't find his heirs, then find his favorite charity. Give the money to them. Walk away with a clear conscience. All you ever did was to take Curtis Garwood on a fishing trip. The rest, even his sending a copy of the letter to Caroline Harper, was his choice. It wasn't something you solicited."

"But I do feel an obligation, and here's one reason." I reached into my shirt pocket and pulled out the photo, propping it up against the shotgun shell. Dave and Nick leaned in to look at it, Nick folding his arms across his chest. "I feel an obligation to a kid—a victim. His name is Andy Cope, and he was killed by those responsible for his welfare while in custody of the state. He and other kids like him were the throwaway boys. The nobodies, the ones to be made examples of…And, too often, they've become captive prey in the hands of sexual predators on the department of corrections payroll—to become the whipping post to men whose hatred and psychosis were further unleashed with each cut of the leather strap."

Nick adjusted his weight in the deck chair and blew a low whistle through pursed lips. "Every time I see that look on your face, man, I know you've made your decision."

My phone buzzed. I recognized the incoming call. It was the number Caroline Harper had given me. I answered and she said, "Sean, it's Caroline. I wanted to let you know I had a man knock on my door, someone I hadn't seen since I was a little girl. His name's Jesse Taylor. He was a friend of Curtis Garwood and Andy's. Jesse's been gone from this area for many years. He returned because he read the obituary for Curtis. Something about how Curtis died…the suicide, well it really hit Jesse hard. He wants to do something. His heart is in the right place, but he's not trained to investigate. I'm worried. As a kid, Jesse was always funny. And now he has some of the saddest eyes I've ever seen. I asked Jesse to call you. If he doesn't, would you mind speaking with him, just to let him know you're looking into things, and he doesn't have to?"

"Do you have his number?"

"Yes, I can text it to you. There's something else. Jesse said he's trying to find somebody he says was an eyewitness to my brother's killing. He wouldn't tell me who, though. Whoever this person is, he was probably incarcerated in that awful place when this happened…just another boy. And he's probably someone who's also been afraid for years to speak up. Maybe you can find him before Jesse does."

FOURTEEN

He looked for the gray mailbox with the small redbird painted on it. Jesse Taylor drove his car slowly down a backwoods hard-packed dirt road, braking when he approached a gray mailbox. Most of the mailboxes, he thought, were some form of gray. But none of them had a redbird painted on the side. The houses in the neighborhood reminded Jesse of where he grew up. Tired, old cinderblock homes, cobbled together in the fifties and sixties. Scraggly yards with "the wash" hanging from clotheslines. Drainage ditches that never drained. Mosquitos that never left.

Jesse lit a cigarette, exhaling smoke through his nostrils, his left arm propped on the open window of his truck. He drove a little farther, the country road winding through piney woods, laced with hammocks of cabbage palms. He stopped at a slate gray mailbox, a large dent in the center, the front hanging by its hinges, just moving in the breeze as if the mailbox was yawning. A wasp's nest grew from under the box, resembling a fist-sized barnacle. "Imagine you don't get much mail," Jesse mumbled.

He looked up toward the house partially hidden behind sickly pines, the blockhouse painted olive green, a blue minivan on jacks, smoke curling from garbage burning in a rusted fifty-gallon drum near the dirt drive. A skinny black man in dungarees and a white, loose-fitting tank top split firewood with a double-blade ax, stopping to watch Jesse pull away from the dented mailbox at the foot of the man's gravel driveway.

Jesse drove fifty yards farther without seeing another house. Just as he was about to look for a spot to turn around, he saw one last mailbox. Slate gray. And, from the distance, he could see something red, not much bigger than a large strawberry. Driving closer, the strawberry became defined, portraying a cardinal perched on a small a branch. Green ivy snaked up the wooden post supporting the box. Jesse grinned. "You've arrived at your destination." He crushed his cigarette in the ashtray and turned into the driveway.

The house was wood frame, brown veneer siding, small front porch, and rose bushes blooming below the windows. The yard had patches of Bermuda grass scattered between the areas of sandy ground. No cars in the driveway. Jesse could see someone sitting on the porch in a foldout metal chair. He parked and walked up to the porch, the sound of a barking dog coming from somewhere in the neighborhood. "Excuse me, ma'am...are you Mrs. Franklin?"

A black woman in her mid-eighties sat in the chair, a paper bag at her feet, a Folgers coffee can for a spittoon. She was snapping green beans and putting them in the bag, her fingers and knuckles twisted from arthritis. She wore a red scarf on her head, purple summer dress with white polka dots, face deeply wrinkled, eyes puffy from allergies—suspicious from familiarity. She reached into a plastic bucket, lifting out a handful of beans, cutting her eyes up at Jesse. "What you won't?"

"Ma'am, your granddaughter, Sonia, sent me."

"Why she do that?"

"My name's Jesse Taylor. I grew up not far from here. I wound up in the Florida School for Boys for nothin' really. Sonia told me about two of your sons that were there. I remember Eli."

She stopped breaking the green beans, turning her head toward Jesse. She said nothing. He nodded. "Sonia was tellin' me about how Elijah never returned home. Said the warden told you Elijah broke out and ran away... but you don't believe that, right?"

"You knew my boy, Elijah?"

"Yes ma'am. He was quiet. I didn't know him really well."

"You know who kil't him?"

"I have a good idea...the same bunch who killed Andy Cope."

She angled her head studying him. "Why you here now...after all this time?"

"Because a fella I knew just killed himself. He was in that school about the same time your boys were there. The stuff we went through, the beatings—the…it's something that never leaves you. It changes you for the rest of your life. A boy we knew, Andy Cope, was killed in there, too. Miss Franklin, the state's gonna sell that place and some developer will build tennis courts, golf courses and houses all over there—over the boys buried somewhere on that land."

She stopped snapping the beans, shifting her weight in the chair. "Ol' death come in my house last year and took my husband. He was sufferin' with the cancer. Death had no right to take my baby, Elijah, away from me. Time don't heal a mama when her child be kil't on account of a mean person. They tol' us Elijah run off, but we know'd better. We had nobody to hep us, exceptin' God. Is my prayer finally bein' answered? Did God send you?"

Jesse grinned and shook his head. "No ma'am. I'd probably be the last guy on earth God would send to do anything."

"Why?"

"Just the way I turned out, I suppose. Maybe I can do somethin' good with the time I got left. I believe Eli, Andy Cope and no tellin' how many others, are buried on the reform school property."

"I want to bring my boy home. My husband's in his grave behind Shiloh Baptist off Leaning Tree Road. You know where that's at?"

"Yes ma'am."

"Rest of my family's there, too. I pray I can find lil' Elijah's body and take him home to be with the family. 'Spect I'll be there 'fore too long."

"Maybe we can find Eli and Andy Cope. Sonia said your other son, Jeremiah, might know somethin' about who killed Andy. Do you know who that could be?"

She snapped a green bean, her nostrils widening. "He tol' me about it when he got outta there. It was after Jeremiah had night sweats so bad I couldn't keep a dry T-shirt on my boy. He cried and I'd rock my son back to sleep. Them men's hurt him…they hurt him real bad. He ain't never been the same. Police never cared."

"What'd he tell you about them killing Andy Cope?"

"He said, mama, they kil't a white boy in there. Shot him down like a dog with rabies. He seen the man…the one who done it. But he wouldn't tell me his name."

"Where's Jeremiah?"

"He brung me these here beans. He's a picker. Sometimes I don't see him for months on account of the harvest here and there."

"If he's here, Mrs. Franklin, whereabouts might that be?"

She lifted the open coffee can to her mouth, spitting a dark stream, the hint of snuff tobacco in the air. "He stays in a bus."

"A bus?"

"An old school bus. It's what he likes. Mr. Haines took a liken' to Jeremiah. Sold him some land and an old bus forever parked on that land. It's a pecan grove off Stevenson Road. The old bus is down by a creek on the back of the property. It don't run. Best tell him his mama tol' you to visit."

Jesse nodded. "Much obliged."

She looked up at him, sunlight popping through the limbs of a cottonwood tree, brushing her face in soft light. Jesse could see her eyes glisten. "After all these years, I don't pull the covers over me at night without thinkin' 'bout my boy, Elijah. Hep me find lil' Elijah, wherever they put him. I want to bring my boy home 'fore the Lord takes me home. Can you hep an old woman?"

"I'm gonna try."

FIFTEEN

I t was a rare night, even for night skies around the Atlantic Ocean. No wind. No clouds. Stars hanging like holiday ornaments. The atmospheric conditions were optimum for those with telescopes and curiosity. The midnight hour was approaching, and Max was taking me for a walk around sea oats and sand dunes near the marina. I'd spent the last hour doing research on the former Florida School for Boys, and the late night walk was a welcome relief.

We headed back down L dock, Max scurrying, stopping, sniffing. We walked by dozens of boats, most dark and quiet. But this is a marina and for some, a license to host non-stop parties. We strolled by a houseboat with multi-colored Japanese lanterns hanging from all corners and most of the ropes. I heard people laughing, and then a woman's high-pitched laugh, the smell of burning marijuana twisting from the open salon doors and windows, the revelers trying to sing *Wild Horses* along with the Rolling Stones.

We walked by the 42-foot Sea Ray, the boat that I'd seen the older man entertaining the twenty-something brunette, him drinking scotch, her sipping rum punches. The windows and salon doors were open. No sign of the woman. Through the open hatch, I heard the staccato clatter of heavy snoring, Max pausing and raising her ears, then trotting down the wide dock.

We walked by Nick's boat, the sounds of Greek music and a woman's laughter coming from *St. Michael*. Dave's boat was fairly dark, bluish wavering light from his television flashing through two porthole windows.

We boarded *Jupiter,* all 38 feet snug in her slip, the rubber bumpers, groaning as the hull drifted close to the docks. "What do you say we go topside, Max? I don't feel like buttoning *Jupiter* down and turning on the canned air. "

She snorted. I lifted her under one arm and climbed the steps to the fly bridge. Earlier, I'd unsnapped and rolled up all of the isinglass. I set her on the sofa, and I eased into the captain's chair, a mild breeze from the ocean escorting the briny scent of salt in the air.

I looked over the marina, lights from boats reflecting off the dark water, a sailboat halyard tinkling against the tall mast, tie-down ropes groaning in a rising tide. I couldn't remember a recent time the sky was as bright. The last time was deep in the Caribbean. Tonight was the kind of starry night that inspired artists like Vincent Van Gogh to interpret and paint the universe.

I thought about what Curtis Garwood had written describing the man he called the Preacher. I thought about the Southern Cross tattoo Curtis had mentioned. *The Southern Cross of Justice.* Max jumped up into my lap and curled into a dachshund ball. I scratched her behind the ears. I looked at the large compass in front of me, locking on the S for south. Then I followed the sightline due south.

And there it was.

A small cross in the night sky. Compact but an impressive constellation. Four bright stars, just above the southern horizon on a hot summer night in Florida. It looked like a cross slightly tilted to the left, a faint fifth star in the lower right side. I remembered something I'd read studying Dante's *Inferno* years ago. In *Purgatorio,* Dante called the Southern Cross the *Crux.* He'd attributed four human virtues to each star: *justice, temperance, prudence* and *fortitude.*

I wondered about the faint fifth star. What did it represent, if anything? Was it a virtue or a darker component of the human psychological profile? Maybe it meant free will. Was it really there, a pure free will? Or was it more like the off and on dim light of the dim fifth star? A free will, something we believe is part of our psyche, yet find there are forces that bend that will to suit their agenda. Maybe it's not free. Maybe it's learned or borrowed. What kind of will, human desire, compels grown men to inflict crippling beatings on children? What kind of free will voluntarily strips human flesh from live Death Camp prisoners in Germany and fashions that skin into lampshades?

I looked at the ancient light from the cross falling to earth, traveling through space and time from a small constellation so far away. And I thought of an ink tattoo on an old man's forearm, the ink probably faded, but the original influence still there, right below his skin, right behind his hard eyes.

The last time I remembered seeing the Southern Cross was when my wife Sherri and I took our final trip together. She wanted to sail before she became too ill to sail. We chartered a 40-foot Beneteau out of Grenada enjoying seven splendid days and nights at sea exploring the islands. It was a night not unlike tonight that we were sailing south on a fair wind from Carriacou to St. George.

The Southern Cross was our prime navigation tool, hanging over the bow-sprint at the edge of the horizon, a nightlight from the heavens. We followed the light of the cross, the wind to our backs, the deep purple night sky a backdrop to an interstellar show. I remembered Sherri laughing, the wind in her hair, a glass of chardonnay in one hand. She danced on deck and began singing. Her voice was still strong, and she sang with flirtatious and unfiltered passion. She smiled at me, singing the lines from a Crosby, Stills and Nash song called Southern Cross. *When you see the Southern Cross for the first time, you understand now why you came this way. 'Cause the truth you might be runnin' from is so small…but it's as big as the promise, the promise of a new day.'*

She'd walked back to the helm, smiling, the moonlight seemed trapped in her brown hair. The boat slipped through the clear water, creating a slight green phosphorus trail in the warm sea. It was a night I'll never forget. She took my hand from the helm and touched her face with the tips of my fingers. We kissed and then we made love under the stars, the light from the Southern Cross guiding us on our journey.

I rubbed Max's head as she slept in my lap. I propped my feet up on the console, and watched the night sky. A meteor soared across the sky in a fiery rooster-tail streak, the marina bobbing in tethered slumber. I wanted to reach out and knock on heaven's door. Instead, I stared due south at the smallest constellation with perhaps the most symbolism. The twinkling four stars were mesmerizing with bright light as if a heavenly cross was sowed at the foot of the visible universe. The dim fifth star was there, too, in the shadow of the Southern Cross.

I wondered how Vincent Van Gogh might paint that.

SIXTEEN

Jesse Taylor felt for his gun under the truck's seat. He'd pulled off Stevenson Road after passing a rusted sign that read: **Shelled Pecans ½ Mile Ahead**. A barbed-wire fence ran along the boundary of the land, pecan trees growing as far as the eye could see. Jesse parked under an oak tree on the opposite side of the road. He pulled up his right pant leg and slid the .25 caliber pistol into the ankle holster.

He locked his truck and walked across the road, the steamy air pirouetting just above black asphalt baking in the sun, the drone of grasshoppers flying over the property. Jesse approached a locked cattle gate, a single sign in the center with hand-written words that spelled: **No Trespassing**. He looked around and then climbed the gate, jumping onto the sandy soil. He followed the dirt road, not much wider than a trail, the road twisting through the grove, pecan shells cracking under his boots.

After a quarter mile, Jesse spotted an old school bus parked under the pecan trees along a creek at the base of the property. Much of the yellow paint on the bus had faded. Vines grew up the sides. Brown rust spots were under the windows and along the back emergency door, below the words: **Stop When Red Lights Flash**. He stood behind a large pecan tree, lifting his pistol out of the holster and slipping it into his back pocket.

Jesse took a deep breath and walked up to the front of the bus, the door wide open, the whirr of a bee circling around the right front tire, the rubber faded and cracked but the tire was still inflated. He knocked on the open door. "Jeremiah, your mama told me where to find you. She was snappin' beans you brought her, right there on her front porch. She reminds me of my grandma, the way she took a liken' to snuff."

Silence. The bee returned, flying near Jesse's face. He swatted it, turning his head and sidestepping. "Damn bee!"

"Why you got a gun in your pocket if'n you talked to my mama?"

Jesse whirled around to face a tall black man. Jeremiah Franklin stood ten feet away. He wore bib overalls, a white T-shirt with holes in the center, his bare arms muscular, large hands, steady coal black eyes, a bit of gray in his hair. He held a three-prong pitchfork in one hand, staring at Jesse. "I'm hopin' you don't reach for that pistol in your pocket."

Jesse raised his hands, shook his head and smiled. "No…hell no. I'm not reachin' for my gun. A man never knows if he'll walk up on a rattler in this country."

"What you want wit' me?"

"Jeremiah, do you remember me? I'm Jesse Taylor. First time I saw you it was below the Bellamy Bridge on the Chipola River. You and some old man were fishin' and ya'll were hookin' blue gill like nobody's business. I was fishin' just down river from you and never got a bite. The old guy you were with sort of took pity on me and showed me the right way to thread a worm on a hook."

"That was my grandfather."

"He was good with a cane pole. It wasn't long after that I was sent to the Florida School. My stepfather told the law I stole his car. I was barely fifteen. How is a few minute joyride and comin' back home stealin' a car? Anyway, you came into the school not long after your brother, Eli, was sent there. I think ya'll were about a year apart in age. I guess kids like you and me were lucky. We walked outta there. Your bother and others like Andy Cope didn't."

Jeremiah said nothing. He held the pitchfork, his dark black skin glistening under the Florida sun. He stuck the pitchfork in the soil. "I remember you. Why you here now?"

"Because another one of us died, a fella named Curtis Garwood…you might recall him, too. Anyway, he killed himself, and in the suicide letter he wrote a lot of it had to do with his suffering through the years because of what happened to him at that school. Curtis said he heard them shoot Andy that night. It was pourin' rain, but he heard it. Said the man's voice sounded like the bastard we called the Preacher. What'd you see that night?"

He folded his large arms. "What makes you think I seen anything?"

"Because your mama told me what you told her when you got out. Look, man, I served in Nam, and nothin', not a damn thing I saw and experienced, and I saw the worst, none of it affected me like what they did to me in that school. They had no right, Jeremiah. We were just kids. The shit they did to the white kids wasn't nearly as bad as what they did to the black kids. I remember you told me you saw the hand of a little black boy in the hog trough. Did you see 'em shoot Andy? Who pulled the trigger?"

"Ain't nothin' you can do. Them days are gone, buried, man. Nobody cared then and nobody sure as hell don't care now. Look at all the hate in this country. Ain't nothin' changed."

"I've changed, or maybe I'm changing. Took me all my life, but I finally figured if I'm not contributing to good then I'm part of the bad. After I read Curtis's obituary, I read a letter he wrote to an investigator who's working for Curtis's sister. Curtis said he heard Preacher's voice that night before they shot Andy. This thing could get some momentum and maybe a grand jury will do something. If nothin' else, we might get court orders to hunt for bodies on that land before it's a fuckin' golf course. You want a smoke?"

"Don't smoke."

"Mind if I do?"

"Long as your lighter ain't in your back pocket?"

Jesse grinned. "I don't blame you." He lifted a cigarette pack from his shirt pocket, shook one out, pulled the lighter out of his front jeans pocket and lit the cigarette, exhaling smoke through his nostrils. "Man, I wouldn't blame you if you ran that pitchfork right through me. Like I say, the black kids got it worse than the rest of us." He smiled. "But at least you can use your hands to pick an apple off a tree. Preacher got pissed 'cause I tried to use my hands to cover my ass when he was beatin' me, blood flying on the walls of the White House. So he had another man hold my wrists, putting my hands on a block to teach me a lesson."

Jesse held the cigarette in his right hand, slowing turning the back of the scarred hand around. He smiled. "Remember when you told me to call you Jerry? You said you didn't know any black kids named Jerry, but a few had the name Jeremiah. You brought me a peanut butter sandwich one night when they kept food from me because I spit in the grass."

Jeremiah stared at Jesse's hand, then looked into his eyes. "Yeah, I remember. I was in a tree the night they shot Andy."

"A tree?"

"The lone oak a little ways past the hog pen. I'd just taken the last of the kitchen scraps to the hogs, and for some reason I just kept walkin'. Then I heard 'em chasin' somebody. There was a low-hanging branch on that old tree. Made for easy climbing. I used to jump up, grab it and climb into the tree. It was the only place I could get away without running away. Somehow, man, I felt closer to the stars just bein' twenty feet off the ground. Andy was running across the field. They were chasin' him, laughin', callin' him names like sissy and faggot. When Andy ran toward the tree...they shot him dead right below me. I was so scared they'd hear me up there. I could smell the whiskey all over them when they lifted up Andy. After they left, I stood on a limb, shaking, hugging the tree and cryin' like a child."

Jesse nodded. "You were a child. Who killed him?"

"One of the reasons I'm still alive, still here in Jackson County, is 'cause I never said anything. They would have kil't me like they did my brother, Andy and others. If word got out I was gonna testify today, they'd probably hang me."

"You can get witness protection. Stay out of sight 'til the trial."

"How 'bout after the trial? Who's gonna keep 'em away then?"

"Answer me this then...is he still alive?"

Jeremiah said nothing.

"Your mama wants to bring Eli's body home to a proper resting place. What you say could make that happen."

"She's the only reason I stay here."

"Man, if you follow the picking seasons, once this is over you can keep goin', never come back."

"Isn't that running away? This old bus ain't much, but I got two deeded acres on this creek bank. One day I plan to build a little house here. It's funny in a weird way—I follow the pickin' seasons, workin' with crops, and all I ever really wanted was to put down roots. Maybe find a wife. But I never stopped lookin' at shadows on the wall." He watched a dragonfly hover near the top of the school bus. "Lemme think 'bout it. I'll talk to mama, and I'll let you know."

"I'll write down my number. I need to ask you this…is he still alive?"

"He's above ground."

SEVENTEEN

When I closed my laptop, I opened a possible door into the Florida School for Boys. Since I walked Max at sunrise, I'd been sitting in *Jupiter's* salon researching the former reform school, which closed in 2011 under the name Dozier School for Boys. I knew its history, the names of superintendents through the decades, the complaints of abuse filed against the school, and had a possible glimpse into its future. The Department of Corrections was taking bids from development companies interested in purchasing the land and buildings. There were a few days left before the sales window expired.

I was about to become an interested party.

"Max, hold the fort down while I shower and pack." She was lying on the salon couch, eyes half closed. She lifted her head and yawned. I shut down my computer and hit the head for a shower. I hadn't been under the water thirty seconds before I heard my phone ring. I finished, towel dried, put on fresh jeans and a sports shirt. Fine attire, I figured, for inspecting property.

I picked my phone off the bar in the salon. A voice-message was waiting for me. "Hey, I'm trying to reach Sean O'Brien. This is Jesse Taylor—a friend of Caroline Harper. She wanted me to give you a shout. She said you're good at this investigation stuff. There's a lot of shit goin' on up here in Marianna that you need to know about. It goes back to when I was locked up at the school from hell. Maybe I can help you…maybe we can turn over a few rocks and watch the spiders run…right a few wrongs that are long overdue. You got my number. I'll tell you what I have so far."

I hit the redial button. After three rings a voice-mail message begin: "This is Jesse. You know what to do at that damn beep."

"Jesse, looks like I just missed you. This is Sean O'Brien. Caroline and I both appreciate you looking under rocks. You might want to take it easy until I can get up there. I'd like to hear what you've found, maybe what you suspect. But it's probably a good thing to keep a low profile. I'll call you when I get to Marianna." I disconnected and scrolled down my contact list until I found the name and private number of an FBI friend of mine in Tampa.

Carly Brown answered on the second ring. "Sean O'Brien. What do I owe the honor of this call? Maybe it's personal and you have a magnum of champagne and a sailboat for a long weekend."

"It's good to hear your voice. How've you been, Carly?"

"No complaints. I have twelve years with the bureau now. If they ever reassign me to a field office in North Dakota, that's when I'll turn in my badge. Hey, I hear you're doing some PI work."

"Off and on. More off than on."

"It's always on here. What's up? Are you in Tampa or are you coming to town. Just want to know what I'll need to tell my current flame—a flame that's more like a candle flame." She laughed and I couldn't help but smile.

"Carly, I wish I were in Tampa. I'm about to head to the opposite end of the state, a town called Marianna."

"Sound's like a town named after some guy's wife. What's there?"

"Maybe a lot of bodies—bodies of kids." I told her most of what I knew and then asked, "How long would it take to do an electrostatic recovery analysis on the shell, the brass head?"

"It depends. So you think there's a latent and micro-etching that might produce a find?"

"Maybe. Only one way to find out. Can I overnight the casing to you?"

"Sure. If this does turn into a killing field for kids, the bureau will be there anyway."

"Thanks, Carly. I owe you one."

"You owe me nothing but three days and nights on blue water. Bye, Sean."

I dropped the shotgun casing into a Ziploc bag, placed it in a small shipping box and labeled it. I'd stop by the post office and send it next-day delivery to the FBI office in Tampa. I packed a bag, extra rounds for my Glock, locked *Jupiter*, and hit the dock with Max trotting a few steps ahead of me.

Nick sat in *St. Michael's* cockpit taking a large fishing reel apart, a web of fishing line next to his bare feet. He was mumbling, cursing, his monologue cutting from English to Greek and back again. He looked up at us and grinned. "How long you and hot dog been standin' there lookin' at me like I was a bear?"

"A grizzly wouldn't need a rod, reel and two-hundred yards of line to catch a fish dinner."

Nick lifted a large ceramic mug of coffee, steam spiraling from the top. "And good mornin' to you, Sean O'Brien. You and Maxie just roll outta the sack, huh? You get into some ouzo last night and didn't invite me?"

"Actually, when Max and I walked by *St. Michael* a couple of hours ago, she almost barked when she heard the snoring coming from your salon. Thought it was a hibernating bear."

"Come here, hot dog. We gotta talk." Max looked at Nick, snorted, and then headed towards Dave's boat, a trace of Canadian bacon in the air. Nick shook his head. "You're a ten-pound traitor."

"She smells bacon from Dave's galley. Come on, Nick. Give your thumbs a rest."

The three of us walked down the narrow boarding dock that led from *Gibraltar's* bow to stern, the smell of bacon, Irish cheese and dark coffee greeted us. Dave stood in the galley making breakfast. He looked over his bifocals and shouted, "Come aboard! Thank God I have people and a pooch to help me eat this feast. I was about to send an invitation, but you beat me."

We entered through the open sliding glass doors, Dave coming up two steps from the galley with a platter of omelets, potatoes and onions, and at least three pounds of Canadian bacon stacked like hotcakes. Max almost did a backflip. We took seats around a square table that substituted as a large chessboard on occasion. I glanced over the bar to the wahoo mounted and hanging on the wall. I thought of Curtis Garwood, thought of the scars on the back of his legs.

Dave said, "I have paper plates that look like bone china. Pile it on gents. Maxine, we'll give you some bacon and eggs." Dave fixed Max a small plate and set it on the floor of the trawler, Max finished the scoop in seconds. The rest of us took our time.

I said, "Speaking of Max, if you guys can keep an eye on her for a few days, I'd appreciate it. Her leash is on the nail in *Jupiter's* galley next to her dog food."

Nick shook his head, lifting Max to his lap. "Hot dog won't be eating that stuff. Between Dave and me, she'll eat like the dachshund duchess of the docks."

Dave sipped black coffee for a second and then said, "From what I've been able to discover, just doing a little research, is the state—at least the Department of Corrections, has no real interest or anything to gain by investigating decades of alleged impropriety, abuse and maybe even murder. When they closed that institution in 2011, they pretty much dusted off their hands of any culpable liability. And now they want to sell it and let some developer sweep a century of dirt under the rug. You will be the camel sticking his nose under a closed tent."

Nick swallowed a mouthful of omelet. "Where can you even start, Sean? It'll be like stepping into Mayberry—a place where nobody even jaywalks. Hear no evil and all that shit."

Dave nodded. "Nick's got a point. The philosophy behind the archetypal three wise monkeys, from the Buddist viewpoint, is to stay away from trouble by not listening to it or not repeating it. In the western world, it's more about turning a blind eye. In Marianna, the old reform school was probably one of the largest employers. Generations worked there. If someone were ever brought to trial, a change of venue may be the first move a prosecutor would request. You'd have to find irrefutable evidence." He glanced at the small box. "Is it there?"

"It's the shotgun shell casing. I'm sending it to a friend of mine, and FBI agent. She's going to see if an electrostatic charge can reveal a print."

Nick used a paper towel to wipe coffee from his bushy moustache. "Shit, after fifty years, the genie might stick his redneck head outta the bottle, or in this case, the shotgun shell."

I removed a folded sheet of paper from my pocket and handed it to Dave. "Here are some names and numbers. I found the name of the listing real estate broker the state is using to show the property. He's a broker with a good batting average. There's strong interest from a corporation called Vista Properties. Maybe you can find who's the decision maker, and who're his or her allies in Jackson County. Call the listing agent and tell him you're interested in the property, ask him if the local airport can accommodate a Gulfstream G650 jet—but before you fly in for an inspection, you will have your representative go by for the pre-inspection."

Dave smiled. "And you, Sean, no doubt, are my representative."

"Yes. I pulled satellite images of the property and buildings. I have a good feel for the logistics. But the place is locked and guarded. Admittance is by invitation only. Thanks for the breakfast. I need to be hitting the road."

Dave poured more coffee into his cup, looking up at me through the steam. "Be damn careful, Sean. This one has layers of bureaucratic complicity all over it, very dangerous because of where the dotted lines may lead. Maybe that little box in your hand will open the Pandora's box. If not, after so many years, you're looking for a needle under a hill of hay."

"But if you set fire to the hay, the rats will run. After the hay has burned, the needle will be there. It might be charred and blackened, but in some form, it'll be there. I just have to use a magnet to draw it out—to find it." I petted Max on her head, turned to leave, looked at the glass eye of the wahoo on the wall and remembered the expression in Curtis Garwood's eyes when he released his wahoo back to the sea.

EIGHTEEN

He'd seen her name in the local newspaper, and now he needed to find her. Jesse Taylor used a red pen to circle her name in the *Jackson County Patriot*. The story was about how she'd managed to get convictions in difficult cases up and down the Second Judicial Circuit in the state of Florida, a district encompassing six counties from the Gulf Coast to the Alabama/Georgia state lines. She'd been in her current job less than two years. Previous to that, assistant state attorney, Lana Halley, worked as a prosecutor in the Ninth District, the Orlando area. Not only did Jesse circle her name, he underlined the reporter's name, Cory Wilson.

Jesse sat in the lobby of the state attorney's office in the courthouse, the folded newspaper in one hand, feeling a touch of familiarity, *been there and sort of done it*, he thought when he'd met with Detective Larry Lee. The lobby floor was old marble, highly polished, an afghan rug near the reception desk. A large painting of former president Andrew Jackson sitting in a saddle on a white horse, hung on the wall above two walnut doors leading into the offices. Jesse shifted the newspaper to his other hand, staring up at the painting; Jackson's eyes seemed to look through him—a nonverbal invitation to leave the county that bore his name.

The double doors opened wide and a woman walked out into the lobby, dark blue suit, high heels that sounded like taps on the marble floor. Jesse recognized her from the black and white picture in the paper that accompanied the article. She almost took his breath away, black hair to her shoulders, emerald green eyes, and dark eyebrows against radiant skin. She had a winning smile, one that could probably open the minds of any jury. Jesse suddenly wished he were thirty-five years younger. She walked across the lobby, extending her hand. "Hi, I'm Lana Halley. You must be Mr. Taylor. How are you?"

"Fine, thanks. I appreciate you taking the time to see me on short notice."

"You told my assistant it was urgent, time sensitive and could have implications to multiple, unnatural deaths. You hit all my buttons."

Jesse reflexively licked his dry lips. He lifted the folded paper. "I'd done my homework. Read the story about you, how you're a victim's rights kind of lawyer. The article said how you'd come from nothin', a broken home to put yourself through law school and try to turn things around for others. I think that's a noble thing to do, Miss Halley."

She smiled. "Please, call me Lana. You can't believe everything you read in the news. That reporter included more than he really had to. I understand this has to do with the old reform school. Let's go to my office. I only have a few minutes, but I'm an excellent listener."

"That's always a good start."

He followed her across the lobby, before walking through the open doors. Jesse glanced up at Jackson on the horse, the president's eyes narrow, following him into the halls of justice. They walked through a maze of corridors, paralegals in cubicles tapping on keyboards, sorting through files and staring into computer screens and case histories. She led him into a small office, took her seat behind a desk that was free from clutter, one file folder in the center, an American flag on a wooden pole behind her, a picture of her in a graduate's cap and gown, an older woman resembling Lana, standing next to her. No father.

"Please, have a seat." She gestured to one of two vacant chairs in front of her desk. Jesse sat in the chair next to the window, overlooking the courthouse square. He held the newspaper on his lap, his hands sweaty. She glanced at his scarred hands and then looked up at him. "What's this about multiple unnatural deaths, you mean murder?"

"Yes. I don't know how many. What do you know about the Florida Home for Boys?"

"Not a lot. I came here after it was closed."

"I spent almost a year in there for taking my pop's old car on a ride for half an hour one night when I snuck outta the house to meet a girl I was sweet on."

"Sounds like your father went to an extreme."

"That's putting it mildly. I'll be brief. The men in charge of us were as brutal as Nazi guards, maybe worse 'cause they got to administer punishment. By this I mean boys, some young as nine, forced to lie on their stomachs in a small building. The men would take turns beating us. A kid would get at least thirty hits from a long leather strap with a small shard of metal in it. Blood would fly like a damn slaughterhouse." She listened, swallowing dryly, jotting an occasional note on a clean legal pad. He told her about Andy Cope, the letter from Curtis Garwood. Then he added, "I have an eyewitness to Andy's murder."

"Who is that?"

"He's name's Jeremiah Franklin. His brother, Elijah, never made it out of there alive."

"Do we know if the perpetrator is still alive?"

"Jeremiah says he is."

"What's this man's name and what role did he play at the school?"

"Jeremiah wouldn't give me his real name."

"Why?"

"He's afraid. He's a black man living in the country in Jackson County. When we were kids, many of us were locked up due to petty stuff like truancy, maybe stealing a candy bar from a five 'n dime. We called the meanest of the staff, the Preacher. He'd try to justify his bloody punishment from Old Testament Bible verses. He always talked about the wrath of God and Sodom and Gomorrah."

"If the man who allegedly did these things is alive, would Mr. Franklin testify?"

"He's considering it."

"But he hasn't said anything in fifty years. And from what you tell me, there's no physical evidence that can, beyond a reasonable doubt, firmly put this man at the scene the night Andy Cope was killed, correct?"

"I don't know. Caroline Harper mentioned a shotgun shell casing… maybe…"

"Maybe we'd find the gun after half a century. I'll need a lot more if I'm to present this to a grand jury." She glanced at the watch on her left wrist. "I have to go. Thank you for coming."

Jesse looked out the window to the courthouse square, the lofty oaks barely moving in the warm breeze. He watched an elderly black man in overalls slowly walking down the sidewalk, shuffling by in front of polished stone monuments to war. He eased down to sit on a park bench, tossing a peanut to a squirrel hopping close to him.

"All I want, and all Caroline Harper wants, is for somebody to look around the school property for hidden graves."

"And that takes probable cause and a court order." She lifted up the file in front of her. "A class action suit, claiming abuse from former residents of the school was tossed out in 2010 because the judge said the statute of limitations had long expired. The Florida Department of Law Enforcement did an extensive review, and those findings were presented to this office. The state attorney, my boss, said that based on the information, he couldn't prove allegations of abuse. In other words, Mr. Taylor, the assertions aren't prosecutable."

"What if I can get somebody to help me? Somebody to look around with me, a fella with a background in law enforcement."

"That's the job of either the Jackson County Sheriff's office or the police, depending on the scene of the crime. I'd give them a call."

"Already done it. Met with Detective Larry Lee in the sheriff's department. He gave me every reason why this is not even a cold case 'cause he says it isn't even a case 'til there's a body."

She stood. "I'm sorry for what happened to you as a boy and how that was allowed. Corporal punishment in the state ended in 1968."

"There's a big difference between a spankin' and a beatin'. And I'd say shootin' a kid in the back is the ultimate corporal punishment. Thank you for your time." He turned to leave, lifting his phone, scrolling as he walked to the door, putting on his glasses, mumbling. "O'Brien…got his number somewhere."

Lana said, "May I ask who you're referring to?"

"Fella's name is Sean O'Brien. He's helping Caroline Harper look into what happened to Andy. Why? Do you know this guy?"

She clutched the file to her breasts and walked Jesse to the door. "Yes, I do know him. I prosecuted a case in Orlando. Mr. O'Brien had been trying to find someone who killed a college girl and her boyfriend in the Ocala National Forest. It involved a drug cartel. He and a Seminole Indian friend entered the forest on behalf of the girl's mother. And in the end, the state had only one of the accused to stand trial."

"Why'd you only have one guy to put on trial?"

"Because you can't prosecute dead men. Four of them never made it out of the forest alive." She paused and exhaled a deep breath. "Mr. Taylor, I want to make this clear to you…do not begin some kind of a vendetta hunt or blood feud in Jackson County. It won't be tolerated."

NINETEEN

Dave Collins was in his element of plausible denial. Somehow, I thought, you can take fieldwork from the retired intelligence operative, but you can't screen out the covert gene that makes deception work well. I mailed the package to FBI agent Carly Brown in Tampa, and had just returned to the road in my Jeep when Dave called. "You'll be meeting with real estate agent Ben Douglas at the gates to the former Dozier School for Boys. Benjamin and I had a nice chat. The local airport can indeed accommodate private jets. I told him that my representative, Sean O'Brien, is my senior advisor, and a man whose judgment in commercial property I trust implicitly."

"Did he ask you what you might have in mind for the property?"

"Indeed. I told him that, as a private equity firm, if I decided to add it to the portfolio of one of our companies, then it's all about location, price, and the cost of conversion. He was quick to let me know the local zoning board had already given the green light for single and multi-family development, including golf course construction. And he was also quick to point out that there are other bids in and the window of opportunity is closing. Can you be there by four o' clock?"

"Shouldn't pose a problem."

"Oh, and one other thing…the Florida Department of Law Enforcement will have a rep there, too. Her name is Lisa Kurz. She's a public relations person for the state. Maybe she's there to sell you on the future and gloss over the histories of a dark past."

"We'll see. How's Max?"

"In the hands of Nick at the moment. I'm not sure who's walking whom, but last I saw Max was leading Nick down the dock."

— ■ —

Jesse Taylor paced the floor of his small motel room, windows open, a warm breeze coming through the blinds. He wore a white tank top. Jeans. No shoes. He looked through his wallet, retrieving a folded piece of paper. He dialed the number. After four rings, there was a long beep, indicating it went to voice-mail. He said, "Hey Sonia…it's Jesse Taylor. We met in the sheriff's office lobby. I need to talk with your Uncle Jeremiah. It's urgent. I need his number or he needs to call me. You got my number. Call me, okay?"

He disconnected, lit a cigarette, stepping outside to smoke it. Jesse leaned back against the white veneer wall, traffic stopping and starting at the intersection near the old motel, the smell of diesel exhaust coming from across the road. He thought about Curtis Garwood's letter, thought about Caroline Harper. Remembering what the old black woman, Jeremiah's mama, had said on her porch while snapping green beans. *'After all these years, I don't pull the covers over me a night without thinkin' 'bout my boy, Elijah. Hep me find lil' Elijah, wherever they put him.'*

Jesse looked across the street, the neon glow of the word *Cocktails*, coming from a sign high above a bar. At that moment, the neon resembled a lighthouse beckoning Jesse across a troubled sea to a safe harbor, if only for a short stop. He crushed the remains of his cigarette against a steel post, flipping the butt into a pothole in the parking lot. He returned to his room, got dressed and drove three hundred yards to the fleeting promise of confidence.

— ■ —

The interior of the bar was dark, small wattage lights flickering from overhead fixtures, a Carrie Underwood song on the jukebox, the smell of spilled beer on the mats behind the bar. A middle-aged woman with dark hair pinned up, wiped shot glasses with a white towel, smiling at Jesse when he took a seat at the bar. He looked around—only three customers in the middle of the day. A man sat with a woman in a burgundy booth, stuffing coming from the cracked plastic seat cover. One man sat at the far end of the bar nursing a thin beer in a glass mug.

"What can I get for you?" asked the woman, setting the white towel down on the bar.

"Shot of Crown. Can of Bud."

"Comin' up." She hummed to the song on the jukebox, cracked open a cold can of Budweiser, and poured a shot of Crown Royal, setting them both in front of Jesse. "You wanna run a tab?"

"That'd work."

She smiled and went to the other end of the bar to refill the customer's mug.

Jesse knocked back the shot of Crown and took two long pulls from the can of beer, the alcohol giving him a light burn in his throat, quickly hitting his empty stomach. He finished his beer and sat on the stool, reaching in his front pocket, getting out the card with Detective Larry Lee's name and number on it. A woman said, "Sheriff's office, Glenda speaking."

"Detective Lee, please."

"Hold please."

Jesse gripped his phone, the alcohol entering his bloodstream, a Tim McGraw song, *Like You Were Dying*, coming from the jukebox. "Detective Lee."

"Detective, this is Jesse Taylor."

"Talk to me, Jesse. You got anything more to go on?"

"How 'bout an eyewitness, that good enough for you?"

"Depends. Who's your witness?"

"Promise me one thing."

"What's that?"

"You'll get him in a witness protection program if he agrees to testify."

"We'll do what we can. We're not in the business of endangering witnesses. What'd he see?"

"Andy Cope's murder, that's what he saw. And he's been scared to tell anyone because he has no trust in the justice system. I'm hopin' you can prove him wrong, Detective. His name's Jeremiah Franklin. Lives in the sticks off Stevenson Road, beyond a pecan grove."

"Who does he say did it? The perp still alive?"

"He's still alive. To get the story and name from Jeremiah, you'll have to convince him that he'll be safe. Then, Detective Lee, you can solve what I'd imagine is the coldest case in Jackson County history, at least in the last fifty years."

"Does this Franklin have a number?"

"Don't you guys ride out and speak to folks face-to-face anymore?"

"Not after a half-century. He can come in here and talk with us. I'll call him and extend the invitation."

"That's bullshit. You want me to do your job?"

"That might be the last job you ever do. You been drinking, Jesse? You're slurring your words a tad. A few years ago that would have been a violation of your parole."

"So you spend time checking me out and no damn time investigating the murder of a child. That's such crap."

"Don't let the booze talk for you, pal. Be careful driving. You never know who'll be following you back to your motel. You really don't want a DUI in my county."

TWENTY

Some places with a dark history have a strong sense of presence, often palpable. It's something I felt years ago visiting Arlington National Cemetery and Andersonville, the site of a Confederate Civil War prison camp. I sensed this today driving slowly by the closed reform school near Marianna. The steel gray of a razor wire fence juxtaposed in front of a cobalt blue sky with white clouds drifting serenely far above the tree line on the property.

Prison fences don't surround most cemeteries, but most cemeteries aren't the place where the living has died. Here it was different. The brick cottages and other buildings scattered among the live oaks and the pines looked pastoral, resembling a boarding school for children of prosperous families. The institution could have doubled as an elite military prep school, one where trust-fund graduates were groomed and destined for West Point, the Navel Academy or Ivy League colleges.

It wasn't.

If looks can be deceptive, this place, based on Curtis's letter and what I'd read, could have been a façade for a Hollywood horror movie. The fence went for hundreds of yards. I slowed to a stop well before coming to the main entrance and the gate. I played back the satellite images in my mind. Now at street-level, I had a very good idea of what I was seeing. A large black crow landed at the top of a roof on the closest cottage and called out, cicadas hummed in the pines.

I looked for the building known as the White House. I knew the basic area where it was, but I couldn't see it from where I stopped my Jeep. I could see the cottages, rolling landscape, a ball field, maybe an abandoned swimming pool in the distance. It had the trappings of a Hansel and Gretel world—candy cane houses of terror, a place where witches and warlocks ruled and abandoned kids would have to find ways to survive, to outwit the ogres or suffer the consequences. But it wasn't a Grimm's fairy tale, it was real—a deserted reform school with more than a century of charade. From the outside looking in, most people would see tranquility, never recognizing deception.

I reached in my pocket and pulled out the photo of Andy Cope and whispered, "Are you somewhere in here? Maybe with your help I can help your sister." The big crow called out again and flew away, to the north, toward another field. I looked beyond the fence and spotted a tree line in the distance. I started my Jeep, put it in gear, and headed for the entrance to the Dozier School for Boys.

After a few minutes, I turned right into a long drive that led to a locked gate across the entranceway. There was a guardhouse, lots of shade from live oaks, dappled sunlight coming through the branches. A pickup truck was parked to the left of the guardhouse. There were two other vehicles, a blue Toyota and a white Chevy Malibu parked in the shade.

I stopped in front of the guardhouse, could barely make out the man behind the dark glass windows, variegated sunlight reflecting from the glass. I parked beneath one of the oaks along the driveway and got out. A mockingbird danced on a limb above me, its call sounding like a car alarm going off.

There was movement from both cars. A man in the Toyota finished a phone call and came toward me. A woman in a business suit followed him. The man wore designer jeans, button down white shirt and a dark blue sports coat. His blond hair was gelled, short. The woman wore her brown hair up. I could see a strand of pearls at the base of her neck as she approached. Both were in their late thirties.

The man extended his hand well before he got to me. "Are you Mr. O'Brien?"

"That'd be me." I shook his hand.

"Delighted to meet you. I'm Ben Douglas. Your employer, Mr. Farnsworth, sings your praises."

"He's too kind."

The woman extended her hand and looked up at me. Wide smile. Freshly applied lipstick. High heels. It would be challenging to walk around the property, lots of grass, in heels. That might be a good thing—an early exit. She said, "I'm Lisa Kurz. It's good to meet you, Mr. O'Brien."

"Please, Sean works even better."

She smiled. "Your timing is excellent, assuming there's a strong interest from your company. The state's had the property on the market for eight months. If you see potential, there's still time for a bid. Ben will give you the particulars. I can help you with the history of the property and what the state may be willing to mitigate for serious offers."

I could tell Ben Douglas was waiting for her to pause so he could begin his pitch. He jumped in and said, "Let's show you around. I think the property will speak volumes for itself. Mr. Farnsworth mentioned his interest in converting the land into an old Florida-themed development, something that reflects a turn-of-the-century feel, upscale houses, all with front porches—homes that invite neighbors to be neighbors, not strangers. Large backyards. Lots of green space and natural park-like settings. Florida at its finest, like the grand seaside cottages and homes of yesteryear with all modern conveniences."

I smiled. "Turn-of-the-century...going back to when this place was envisioned and built."

Lisa Kurz didn't pause a beat. She said, "It was a splendid time in Florida, the winter destination for much of the Northeast and Midwest. But as the state grew with permanent residents, a need for a juvenile facility like this was apparent. The state didn't want to build something that looked like a prison—after all, these were boys. So they created a rural campus-like setting that had a lot of the attributions of a working farm. It would keep the kids busy, out of trouble, and give them a skill in agriculture."

I nodded. "I suppose it's all about planting seeds. The harvest will tell how well that was done."

She smiled, but kept her lips together. Ben Douglas was about to say something when the guard approached. He walked with a light limp to his right leg, carrying a clipboard, mid-sixties, tall, military haircut, black shoes reflecting the sunlight. "How you doin'?" His accent was Deep South, gruff. He wore a silver ring on his right hand with a U.S. Marines insignia in the center. His nametag read: J. Hines

"I'm fine, thanks."

He nodded. "I know you're with these folks. I just need to see an ID before you walk the grounds."

"No problem." I opened my wallet and displayed my driver's license, keeping my left thumb over the last few digits. He looked at my picture and then looked at me. As he started to write the number, I closed my wallet, putting it back in my pocket. "If you need a number, you have my license tag. My meeting today with Mr. Douglas and Miss Kurz is confidential, per the wishes of my client."

He started to say something, but Lisa interjected. "It's okay, Johnny. Mr. O'Brien is with us."

He stared at me. I could tell he was trying hard to make the connection. The mockingbird flew to a tree above the guardhouse, blurting out car alarm shrieks. Then the guard said, "O'Brien...Sean O'Brien. You have a good visit, you hear."

I didn't know how long my tour of the facility would be. But I did know I'd just been made.

Johnny the guard knew my name.

TWENTY-ONE

It was an impromptu stop. Something unplanned. But, as Jesse Taylor knew, not a whole helluva lot had been planned since reading Curtis Garwood's obituary. Jesse thought more about death now than ever. Or maybe he was thinking more about life—living life. Maybe if he could find some kind of closure for Andy's sister, Caroline Harper, he'd find it for himself.

Jesse spotted the small sign on the one-story building and hit the brakes, looking for a place to turn around. He cut through a parking lot in downtown Marianna and drove back to the building. The sign on the side of the brick read: *Jackson County Patriot – On Guard Since 1879*. He parked in the lot, picked up the newspaper on the seat next to him and whispered the reporter's name, "Cory Wilson…let's see if you're here."

Jesse entered the building, walking down a short hallway decorated with awards and accolades the newspaper and its reporters had won through the years. The reception area was really a long counter, a small stack of newspapers on one end, business cards near a ceramic bowl filled with peppermint candies. People worked at desks in an open office setting, most seemed attached to computer screens. One larger man, with flushed skin, puffy face, strands of comb-over hair feathered across his scalp, ate a hamburger and fries at his desk.

A middle-aged woman in jeans and a yellow blouse stitched in butterfly images, stood from her desk near the counter and met Jesse. Her dirty blond hair was pulled tight in a ponytail, round face with a narrow smile, capped teeth. "Can I help you? You lookin' to place an ad? We have a special this month that applies to print and online too."

"No ma'am, I'm not here to buy an ad, but I do like your newspaper. Been reading it every day since I got back in Marianna."

Her smiled dropped a notch. She tilted her head, folding her arms, trying to place his face somewhere in her memory. "How may I help you, sir?"

"Is Cory Wilson here today?"

She glanced over her shoulder. "He's here. Do you have an appointment?"

"No, I have something even better."

"And what might that be?"

"A story. I have a damn good story for him."

Another woman, mid-twenties sat at her desk near the counter. She looked up from her keyboard, overhearing the conversation. She picked up her phone, buzzed a man sitting next to the man eating the hamburger, and said something into the phone.

Cory Wilson stood from his desk and walked across the newsroom to the counter. He wore his plaid shirt outside his jeans, brown hair combed back, angular face, a week's worth of stubble growing, rimmed glasses. He picked up a mint from the bowl, glanced at the man and nodded. "Hey, are you my three o' clock appointment?" Cory smiled.

The receptionist said, "He didn't make an appointment."

Cory broke the mint between his back teeth and said, "Probably my mistake. I have time to chat. Thanks, Deloris."

She shrugged and lumbered back to her desk, leafing through ad copy. Jesse cleared his throat. "Are you Mr. Wilson?"

"Cory's fine. We're not formal here. Can I help you?"

"You cover the police beat, right"

"Cops and crime."

Jesse glanced around the large room. "You got somewhere we can talk. Be frank with you, I'm getting tired of speaking with people in their lobbies."

"Sure, come to my desk." He unlatched a swing-through door built into the counter, Jesse following Cory back to his desk. "Have a seat."

Jesse sat in a chair on the opposite side of the desk, glancing around the room, the man eating the burger was wiping mayonnaise from the corner of his mouth.

Cory leaned back in his chair. "What do you have?"

"How familiar are you with the Dozier School for Boys?"

"Not much. I've only worked here for a year or so. I know the state closed it. Apparently, budgetary reasons, why?"

"I was in there before they changed the name, back in the mid-sixties. Here are just some of the permanent souvenirs they gave me." Jesse placed his palms on the desk, the scarred back of his hands visible to the reporter.

"Jesus…what happened to you?"

"They beat me to a pulp, the men who worked there. I wasn't alone. Dozens and dozens of us, through the years. I believe there are a lot of hidden graves there." Jesse told him about the brutal whippings, Curtis Garwood, the letter and about Andy Cope. "Maybe you could interview Andy's sister, Caroline. She's got a lot to say and don't mind sayin' it to who-ever will listen. But that's one of the glitches. Nobody listens. State wants to sell that place and sweep all the shit under the rug."

"Let me look at some of the files." Cory tapped his keyboard and began reading the screen. "Between tossed out class action suits to a lack of tan-gible evidence, looks like there was nothing police or prosecutors could take to trial. What's different now?"

He lifted is hands. "Is this enough tangible evidence?"

"To do forensic work, maybe bring in ground-penetrating radar to hunt for bodies, there'd have to be something way beyond those scars. And, please, I mean no disrespect. Based on what you told me, what they did to you and others is unconscionable. But the prosecutor is probably right. To go to the jury, to send a man to life in prison or lethal injection, there has to be evidence that will push the reasonable doubt from the minds of a jury." Cory exhaled and looked toward the man who'd just finished eating at his desk. "Wallace, can you come here for a minute?"

He brushed breadcrumbs from his lap and waddled over to Andy's desk. "What's up?"

"Wallace Holland this is Jesse Taylor. Wallace covers a lot of areas, including the courts. Jesse lived in Jackson County years ago. He spent a few months in the Dozier School. He believes there could be bodies—bodies of kids killed while in there, buried in hidden spots on the property. I know you've covered a lot of the events related to the old school. You ever hear of unsolved murders in there?"

Wallace smiled, a piece of lettuce between his teeth, mayonnaise spot on his white shirt "Oh sure, as a reporter I've heard all the rumors. Fact is there are no facts, at least provable facts related to child deaths. The last investigation a few years ago had a lot of innuendo but no prosecutable evidence." He chuckled. "I doubt if there would be many people left to prosecute. Hey, I gotta hit the head." Wallace nodded and walked away, the smell of French fries and hamburger still lingering.

Cory said, "I'm sorry. I'm sorry for the suffering you and other boys had to endure while in that place. But like Wallace said, there's no evidence to take to a grand jury. As a reporter, I've got to have facts. I wish you luck."

"Why don't you look into who wants to buy that property? Why is the state on a fast-track to sell it? If there are bodies hidden in there, murder victims—that would hold up a sale for years. That could be one helluva story. You might win a Pulitzer Prize."

"I'm interested in accuracy."

"What if you had someone who witnessed Andy's killing?"

"An eyewitness? Who?"

"He's scared, and for a lot of damn good reasons. He's black and lives out in the sticks. He was in there when I was, and they killed his brother, too."

"What's his name?"

"I can't tell you that, at least not now. Maybe soon. He's gonna meet with me again. I believe he'll finally talk 'cause his aging mama wants to find her son's body and bring him home, to get him the hell outta the place where he was murdered."

"Jesse, look at the reality of the situation. If this man was an eyewitness, from what you told me, it was a rainy night. It's been decades. The witnesses' credibility will be questioned. If the shooter is still alive, it'll simply be his word against the witness unless there's physical evidence to connect the man to the murder."

"Are you a golfer?"

"I enjoy the game."

"Could you imagine teeing off and knowing that a few feet below your ball was the body of a boy? Not just dead...but murdered. Thanks for your time."

TWENTY-TWO

The guard gate was about to open when it happened. The temperature dropped quickly, the sun became absorbed by dark clouds rolling in from the northeast, and a cool breeze set in, blowing across the reform school property, tree limbs swaying. I glanced up and saw the mockingbird fly from one of the oaks at the entrance and head into the surrounding woods. Lisa Kurz flashed a tense smile. Ben Douglas looked at his watch.

Johnny Hines stood in the guard shack, the gate's electric motor straining, gears grinding, as if a chainsaw were getting pinched by a partially cut limb and the pull of gravity. Finally the gate swung open, the three of us walking onto the property. Ben said, "I have lots of photos, including aerials, easement locations, utilities, schematics—everything you'd need to take back to Mr. Farnsworth." He grinned. "But I know the most important thing is for you to inspect as much of the property as time will permit to get a gut feeling for its vast potential." He handed me a three-ring binder, tabbed with more than two-dozen categories.

I followed him, Lisa following me, making our way across the property, Ben stopping to point out various buildings, speaking briefly about their former use and at greater length about their potential. We walked by a dozen timeworn brick cottages, a three-story dormitory, offices, out buildings, and a long-abandoned swimming pool. Stagnant water remained, pooled from rains at the deeper end, frogs leaping into the black water, tadpoles thick as maggots. I could smell a putrid odor similar to fish rotting in the hot sun.

Lisa said, "I'd mentioned mitigating potential. The state is willing to remove this old pool, pay for any well water samples, and clean up a long abandoned muck pit where hog waste was stored. That is a tiny fraction of the vast amount of pristine acreage here. The topography would be perfect for a world-class golf course. You could even build thirty-six holes, a full clubhouse and have plenty of land for single and multiple family units."

Lightning streaked through the northeast sky. The temperature dropped another few degrees and the wind picked up. Lisa clutched her purse strap hanging from her right shoulder. "Looks like a storm's blowing our way. It might be a good idea to head back."

Ben considered the sky. "It might go around us. That's odd—the weather forecast said it was supposed to be hot and dry. Let me show you a couple more things." He led the way around small buildings that had been standing on the property for more than a century. Up close, the architecture was an austere brick and mortar, designed to keep people from leaving.

No visible bars, but an invisible caging hung over the landscape like a morning dew.

I pointed beyond an outpost building to small crosses in a lone field. The crosses were made from sawed PVC pipe, all the same size, some falling down. "What's that?"

Lisa looked in the direction I pointed. "It's been here forever. There was a fire more than a hundred years ago. Unfortunately some of the boys lost their lives."

"Did all of them die in the fire?"

"From what I understand, most. There was disease, such as typhoid, that hit the area. With little or no drugs in those days and factoring on the remote and rural area, the state lost some of the juveniles—or rather the residents. It was tragic."

Some of the juveniles. I glanced around. "Are those the only graves?"

I saw her cut her eyes to Ben. He cleared his throat. "Absolutely, at least to our knowledge."

"The reason I ask is because of the special treatment that goes into construction around a known cemetery."

Lisa nodded. "Of course, the pipe crosses would have to be replaced with more decorative headstones."

"Would you have names to go on those headstones?"

She clutched her purse tighter, knuckles growing white. "All of that can and will be addressed to match or exceed zoning covenants when we get close to a contingency offer." She looked at her watch. "I must be getting back. I happened to be in Marianna when Ben called. I work out of Tallahassee. Can I answer any other questions?"

"No. Not at this time." I smiled.

She almost clicked her high heels as she turned to leave. "Ben, you might want to wrap it soon. The weather looks like it's taking a turn for the worse." A gust of wind blew her hair. "It was nice meeting you, Sean. We hope to hear from you or your representative soon." She walked quickly down a path, her heels pounding the chipped and broken concrete.

Ben flashed a wide smile. "Anything specific you'd like to see? Our daylight's fading fast."

"I'd like to see a bathroom. Too much coffee on the drive here."

"I'm sorry, but everything's locked. I got here as quickly as I could after I spoke with Mr. Farnsworth. I wasn't near the office to pick up a ring of keys. We can open the buildings tomorrow, if you like. We have to keep this place locked up. If not, even with security, vandals will get in here and create a mess."

"I understand. Maybe tomorrow…when Lisa mentioned the animal pens, specifically the former hog pens, I'm sure I could take a leak there. Where are the pens?" I smiled.

Ben grinned. "It wouldn't hurt if you did, that's for sure." He pointed to the north, and stepped away from the building we were standing next to, walking toward something that resembled a tool shed. "I'll show you."

I followed him for about seventy-five feet, stopping when he did close to the shed. He pointed toward a field. It was larger and longer than a football field. The grass looked to have been recently cut by a tractor pulling a large mower. He gestured to the north. "See that lone oak way out there to the right?"

"Yes."

"It's back in that vicinity. Not much left. A barn-like building, maybe a few pens. There's a shallow and dry area where waste was disposed. You don't want to walk that far to pee."

We could hear the rain coming before we saw it, a torrent moving through the woods. Ben said, "I can run to the car and get some umbrellas. I got two from a golf tourney I was in last year. They can almost pass as beach umbrellas."

"I'll be fine. You go on. I'll wait for the rain to slack and find a tree to pee under."

He stared at the woods in the distance, the sound of rain like a waterfall. "Maybe I should stay with you."

I smiled. "Sometimes it's best to let the buyer take the wheel. I won't be long."

He opened his mouth to say something when lightning struck the roof of the old high-rise dormitory, less than fifty yards from us. "We need to get out of here. When I was a kid I saw lightning strike a small herd of cattle north of Tampa. It was on our neighbor's farm. The bolt killed seven of eight cows."

"You head back. I'll take shelter under the awing on that shed. If I try to run, I might spring a leak. I have a weak bladder from a tour in the Mideast. I'll speak with Mr. Farnsworth tonight. Tell the guard I'll be out shortly. Just had to find a place to pee, okay?"

He nodded, inhaled a deep breath as rain slapped the tree leaves, fat drops smacking the concrete pathways. He looked toward the sky, the reflection of lightning in his eyes. "I look forward to talking with you or Mr. Farnsworth. Be safe!" He turned and ran, a wall of rain chasing him.

My next stop would be to a lone oak—the place where Andy Cope may have died.

TWENTY-THREE

I stood beneath the awning, rain pelting the tool shed, wondering how long I had before the guard would brave a thunderstorm to find me. Maybe Ben Douglas told him to let me take my time. Maybe not. I removed Andy Cope's picture from my shirt pocket, looked at his face for a moment, before transferring the photo to my wallet—the driest place for it.

Lightning struck a tall pine near the tool shed, a severed limb crashing through the boughs hitting the ground, bouncing once, thunder echoing from the old buildings. I felt the atmosphere change. The charged ions part of the air I breathed, green spots floating in front of me, my eyes trying to adjust, ears ringing. The hair on my arms stood, almost bristling like an animal. Maybe some part of the lightning had traveled through me, leaving me unhurt. Something was different, as if the powerful bolt had split atoms, the landscape momentarily altered in a bluish wash slowing down the pendulum of time and the perception of dimension.

I looked out in the field, through the marsh in the distance, and I saw what resembled the silhouettes of three men. They were upright effigies out of sync in the balance of sky and earth—almost standing on the edge of the world. They moved stealthily, in no hurry—their prey losing ground. The men wore fedora hats. Dark clothes. One appeared to be holding a shotgun. White lightning veined through the sky in front of them, and for a heartbeat, outlining the dark images in a rim of white.

I stepped from the awning, walking across the muddy field in the rain, instinctively reaching for my Glock, which I'd left in the Jeep. I walked more than a hundred yards, following the men—my mind racing back to Afghanistan, back to the time I tracked three members of the Taliban. *Move on.* Today, I could hear the mud sucking at my shoes.

I wiped the rain from my face, picking up my pace, the three men reaching a vanishing point, crumbling into the purple vista. They were gone. Disappeared. But the lone oak was there, standing tall in a remote corner of the immense field. I approached it, the rain tapping against the leaves. It was one of the largest oaks I'd ever seen, huge knotty girth—outstretched limbs larger than most trees.

I knew the oak was very old, probably been here since the Seminole wars, maybe Indians or soldiers had hidden behind it. And now I was betting that a boy was shot and killed in front of it. I imagined what the oak might have looked like when Andy Cope was a boy. How many feet had it grown since that time? If he had been taller than five feet when he was hit with buckshot…where would the killer have aimed? And where might that spot or pattern of buckshot be today, if even only one of the steel balls was imbedded in the tree?

I looked at the tree trunk, my eyes slowly moving upward. All the gnarled bark appeared the same, growing with continuity, the same ridges and small crevices in a natural pattern. The tree's exterior, the way the bark grew with lines and shapes, was it's own fingerprint. I looked for the scar— the artificial blemish.

And there it was—the one flaw.

It wasn't from rot, disease, or some organic reason. It was as if the oak had been injured, the bark growing around a puncture wound in a circle that resembled a dark inverted doughnut. I placed my right palm against the tree, moving up the trunk, feeling for the irregularity. The rain fell through the leaves and limbs, falling on my face. At my height, a little over six-two, I could just reach the indentation.

I used the small light on my phone to examine it. The hole went less than an inch into the bark. I opened a blade on my pocketknife to dig in and around the perimeter of the pit. In less than thirty seconds, I felt metal against metal, the dull tap that comes from manmade material.

I pried a small steel ball out of the tiny crater, holding the buckshot in the palm of my hand, the rain falling on it, washing off small specks of bark and tree sap like the erosion of dried blood dripping between my fingers. I had the shotgun shell. I had buckshot. But I didn't have the man who pulled the trigger. I glanced around the landscape.

Are you buried out here somewhere, Andy? I found the buckshot, and I knew if I could find Andy's body, an autopsy might find matching buckshot. But where was the man who pulled the trigger?

The beam of a flashlight interrupted my thoughts. I kept my back to the light, quickly dropping the buckshot into my shirt pocket. I turned around slowly, the light bobbing up and down with the walking pace of the person who held it. I didn't move, keeping my hands visible. I knew who it was, and I knew he carried a gun. What I didn't know was whether his gun was in the hand that didn't carry the flashlight.

"What the hell you think you're doin' way out here?" Johnny Hine's southern accent was clipped, laced in fiery anger. He said, "No sudden moves and keep your hands where I can see them. You got a problem with that, Sean O'Brien? I know who you are. And now I want to know what you're doing standing out here in the rain? Don't give me a reason to drop you under that tree."

TWENTY-FOUR

J esse Taylor drove slowly through downtown Marianna thinking about the justice system, thinking about a shot of Crown chased by a cold Bud. He pulled into the parking lot of the *Heartland Motel*, parking near his room, 29, the pulse of blue and yellow light from the neon sign falling against his face. The "l" in the sign was burned out, spelling *Heart_and Motel*

He lit a cigarette and thought about the human heart, whatever the hell that meant. What it really meant was greed—the gap in justice between the wealthy, their high-paid attorneys, and the rest of us. The injustice in true due process of laws written for 'we the people.' He could see the indifference and the bias in the eyes of the detective. He saw the look of anxiety in the eyes of the assistant prosecutor who'd have to open a case that her boss said wasn't provable. Maybe the reporter would investigate who's behind the sale of the property. Greed.

He blew smoke out the open window. He could go in his room, listen to the rattle of the box air-conditioner. Watch a cable news program. His blood pressure was high enough. He picked up his phone and dialed Caroline Harper's number. "Hi, Jesse."

"How'd you know it was me?"

"Because you wrote your number down. I programmed it into my phone."

He nodded, exhaling cigarette smoke out the window. "Look, I've been trying to run down some of this stuff about Andy, trying to close loose ends. It's gonna take a little longer than I thought."

"I understand. Have you spoken with Sean O'Brien?"

"Left him a message. He left me a message. We'll connect. In the meantime, I was seeing if I could find some stuff to help him…you know, maybe get some of the legwork outta the way so he could come in and drill down further."

"Where have you been?"

"Met with the cops—a detective. He was nothing but excuses as to why he can't open a case. I got so pissed I met with an assistant state attorney. She gave me about seven minutes. I even spoke with a reporter, the guy who covers cops and crime. Everybody wants me to do their jobs…to go out and bring evidence to them."

"Jesse, please let Sean make those inquiries, okay?"

"I sort of stumbled onto something that could change everything."

"What?"

"When I was talkin' with a sheriff's detective who couldn't give a rat's ass about what I was tellin' him, a black girl overheard my conversation. When the cop left, she approached, saying she'd always heard one of her uncles was killed in there, too. She had two uncles in the school about the same time. One left. One never did. The one who got outta there may be the only eyewitness to the killing of Andy."

"Oh dear God…where is this man?"

"He lives in an old rundown school bus way the hell out in a remote part of the county. He's still scared after all these years. I spoke with him. He told me he was hiding up in an oak tree when the men were chasing Andy and shot him near the base of the damn tree. They never saw him, but he saw the shooter."

"Who did it?"

"He wouldn't tell me. Which does tell me the killer is still alive. Old, but alive. The man I'm talkin' about is afraid if he testifies, somebody…maybe the old man's family, maybe some crazy racist, will kill him. I told him about how the state's in a hurry to turn the property over to developers. There was a spark of fire in his eye. He said he'd speak with his elderly mother. She wants to find and bring home the body of her other son…but you gotta know that old woman sure as hell doesn't want to lose another one in the process."

"What can you do?"

"Nothing. Maybe the cops can give him some kind of witness protection. It'd be hard to park a squad car out front of his house because he lives behind a pecan grove in the backcountry. A reporter I spoke with said unless there's physical evidence to put the old man on the scene when Andy was murdered, it could boil down to the eyewitnesses' word against the shooter, and that ain't enough for lady justice to look at this with both eyes open."

"Call Sean, okay."

"Yeah, I'll get to it. What are you doing tonight?"

"Fixing some dinner."

"I guess it's that time of night. Figure I'll grab a burger somewhere, get an early start in the morning."

"Jesse, would you like to come over and join me for a bite?"

He looked in his rearview mirror, watching the traffic beyond the parking lot. Something caught his eye—a yellow truck. Stopped at a traffic light. Not just any late-model truck, but rather a 1950's model. It reminded him of his stepfather's truck years ago. And he remembered something else, something Harold Reeves had said in the Waffle house, *"One of those boys, his name's Cooter Johnson, drives around town in a late fifties model Ford truck, painted canary yellow. He shoots pool a lot at a place called Shorty's. But if I were you, I sure as hell wouldn't go in there alone."*

Jesse crushed his cigarette in the ashtray. "Hey, Caroline, I think I'll take a rain check on dinner tonight. I got somewhere I need to be. Goodnight."

"Goodnight, Jesse. Be very careful."

He disconnected, started his car and turned right out of the motel parking lot. Went back toward town, hoping he'd find the yellow truck. Looking for a place called Shorty's.

TWENTY-FIVE

Johnny Hines, the lone security guard, came closer—a flashlight in his left hand. His right hand on the pistol grip, the pistol still in his holster. He stopped about ten feet from me and said, "Like I say, I know who you are. What I don't know is why you're here. Why's that, Mr. O'Brien?"

"The people I represent are interested in this property, this facility. That's all you need to know. I was invited here, and now I'm going."

"Wait a damn second! I say when you leave. Why are you way the hell out in this field, and in the middle of a thunderstorm? What are you looking for?"

"There's very little time to assess this property. The option for bids is rapidly closing. I'm trying to maximize the time I have. The storm blew in quickly, and it didn't stay long. The others chose to leave. I wanted to wait it out. And now I'm going to take a hot shower and get into dry clothes." I started to walk past him. He followed, the mud sucking at his black rubber boots, his raincoat making a swishing sound as he walked. I felt my phone buzz in my pocket.

He said nothing until we got within thirty yards of the gate, his breathing labored, his right hand still on the pistol grip. He stopped under the lights from the gate and said, "What's a sharpshooter doing out here looking at this place?"

"Pardon me?"

"I read about you. It was in one of my gun and ammo magazines. The story was how a sniper—you—took out a plane trying to leave a small South

Carolina airport to drop a dirty bomb over Atlanta. They said you took the shot from an old weather tower at the airport. Said you shot clean through the window of a moving plane on the runway, managing to miss a hostage and still take out the terrorist pilot. The article said it was the shot heard around the world because it set some kind of distance and accuracy record. I found your picture online. Must have been taken a while ago, but it's you."

"Do you have a problem with a radical terrorist, en route to bomb an American city, being killed?"

"I got no problem with that. The story didn't have much about your background. Said you served tours in the Middle East. My problem is why would somebody like you be snooping around this old reform school in a thunderstorm?"

"What if the company I represent wanted to build a paramilitary training facility on this land? Something better than Blackwater in North Carolina. Imagine that."

"An antiterrorism training camp in Jackson County?"

"That's confidential."

"I understand."

"If word gets out, it could jeopardize millions of dollars, have a detrimental impact on the Jackson County economy, and be a blow to Homeland Security and our antiterrorism initiative. Do you follow me?"

"I gotcha. There's a manual button by this breaker box. I'll open the gate for you." He stepped over to a gray box on a steel post, pressed a button at the base of the box. The small motor whined and the gate began retreating across the drive.

I walked through, nodded to him in passing—wondering how long before most of Marianna, Florida, heard that a paramilitary operation was considering establishing a presence here. I unlocked my Jeep, checked for the Glock under my seat. Everything in order. Then I checked my phone. Two voice messages. "Sean, it's Caroline Harper. I spoke with Jesse Taylor tonight. He's supposed to get in touch with you. I'm worried. His intentions are honorable, but he's sort of a loose cannon. He said there's a witness. Someone who saw Andy shot...a boy, at the time, who was in the reform school the same time Andy and Jesse were there. Jesse will only say the man is black, afraid to testify. Maybe you can find him. Thank you."

I looked in my side mirror and saw Johnny Hines in the guard shack, pacing like a hungry rat in a cage, phone to his ear. Maybe he was speaking with real estate agent Ben Douglas, or maybe PR rep Lisa Kurz. I didn't really care. I'd found what I wanted. I lifted the piece of buckshot from my front pocket. I knew if I could find Andy Cope's body, there'd be a good chance forensics would discover a steel ball just like this in his remains.

After fifty years, I wasn't worried about breaking a chain of evidence. That chain had long since rusted due to time and disregard, or indifference. I was concerned with connecting the dots to create enough heat to spark a confession or a grand jury investigation.

I had a piece of buckshot.

I had the shell casing.

If lucky, I'd get a print off the brass. And if I could find the man who fired the shotgun shell, it would be a match. Not one made in Heaven, but more like what Dante referred to in *Purgatorio*—Italian for purgatory. After climbing from the depths of Hell in *Inferno*, Dante wrote about scaling Mount Purgatory in the Southern Hemisphere—a mountain built in strata's from the seven deadly sins. I thought about the Southern Cross I'd seen ascending in the night sky from the Southern Hemisphere and wondered, for what possible human virtue, could the man dubbed by the boys as Preacher, have chose for himself when tattooing the cross on his arm. The four attributes—justice, temperance, prudence and fortitude—didn't fit a monster.

Maybe the small steel ball in the palm of my hand somehow represented a physical linking to justice. But would I have to climb an elusive mountain to find it? Florida has no mountains. It has lots of swamps and people who know how to survive in them. I knew what Dave would say. *When I was up to my ass in alligators, it might be hard to remember my original goal was to drain the swamps.*

I dropped the buckshot in a plastic bag, started my Jeep and headed toward Marianna.

TWENTY-SIX

It was another place. Another time. But *Shorty's* was the kind of joint that Jesse Taylor used to score rent money. Half a lifetime ago, he had a custom-made cue stick and a reputation that got him banned in more than a dozen pool halls from Jacksonville to Daytona Beach. Those days, the hustling, the cons, the fights—were history. But history had taught him lessons about human nature, especially when it came to sports betting—putting folded money on the line and watching a man's eyes change when the gambling hook was set by a challenge.

He thought about that as he slowed in front of a one-story cinderblock building washed in red and white neon. The sign read: *Shorty's Billiards*. It hung from chains fastened to a rusted pole that was bolted to a concrete block near the roof. But it was the parking lot that Jesse scanned as he pulled off the street. And there, to the far left, was the custom yellow pickup truck. Jesse counted eleven cars in the lot and two more pickups. Three motorcycles were in a handicapped space near the front entrance.

Jesse parked, lighting a cigarette and blowing smoke out his open window. He glanced over to the yellow truck, where a diffusion of red neon gave the truck a slight rosy-pink look. Moths circled the sign, the raucous beat of a driving bass guitar coming from inside the building. Jesse reached in his console and lifted out a .25 caliber pistol. He pulled his right pant leg up to his calf muscle, shoving the pistol into an ankle-strap holster, pulling his pant leg down.

He locked his car and walked across the lot, stepping on flattened beer cans, the smell of burning marijuana in the night air, an electrical buzzing sound coming from the neon sign. He looked up at two bikers leaning against a wrought iron railing on what would pass as a porch entrance. Both bikers wore shabby, thick beards. Lot's of black leather. Fur on arms and chests. Ink tats covering most of their arms. One wore an American flag as a pirate's bandana.

Jesse walked straight toward the front entrance. As he passed the bikers, the man in the bandana said, "Wanna meet Miss Chrystal? She's cooked up all nice and fine. Guaranteed to take you places you'll never go in that old car of yours."

Jesse stop walking for a second, inhaling a last drag, blowing smoke from his nostrils, looking the biker in the eye. "When you bury a military veteran and you salute the American flag draped across his coffin, you won't wear our flag on your head." Jesse flicked his spent cigarette into the lot, sparks popping. He turned back and walked toward the door.

"Pops, you're fuckin' crazy. It ain't my flag." The biker drained the beer from a Miller can, dropping it to the lot, crushing the can under the heel of his black boot.

When Jesse opened the door to *Shorty's*, he was met with the smells of sour beer, sweat-laced testosterone and weed. A woman shrieked and laughed at the bar. From the vintage Wurlitzer jukebox, Charlie Daniels belted out *The Devil Went Down to Georgia*. Jesse stepped inside, eyes adjusting to the semi-darkness. He counted seven pool tables. Single lampshades hanging from the ceiling bathed each table in soft cones of light, shadows and silhouettes of players moving in and out of the light.

Jesse approached the bar. Every stool except one was taken. A huge sign on the wall behind the bar read: *Jack Daniels Spoken Here*. Jesse sat on the stool, resting his arms against the timeworn wooden bar, the old knotty pine long since stained from spilled whiskey and branded by smoldering cigarettes. A twenty-something blonde bartender in short cut-off blue jeans, tank top exposing ample cleavage, pulled a draft beer, looked at Jesse and said, "Be with you in a sec."

"No hurry." Jesse pushed back in the stool, his eyes fully adjusted to the low light. The man sitting next to him had the look of a gym rat. Black T-shirt stretched over chest and arms thick with sculpted and steroid-enhanced muscle. He wore his hair in a military cut. Face ruddy. He stared ahead at a large-screen TV, sound muted, a NASCAR race on the screen.

"What can I get for you, hon?" The bartender blew a strand of dirty blonde hair from her shiny face and smiled. She wiped her hands on a white towel, the song on the jukebox *Bad to the Bone*.

Jesse said, "I'd like a shot of Crown and Bud in the can."

"You got it." She dug for the can in a metal tub partially covered in cracked ice, popped the top on the beer, poured a shot of Crown Royal and placed both in front of Jesse. Taking the twenty-dollar bill he held between his fingers, she said, "Be back in a minute with change."

"Sure, I ain't going nowhere."

She moved down the bar, filling another drink order, working her way to the cash register. Jesse took a deep breath, feeling the beat of his heart pulsating under the holster strap near his ankle. He reached for the shot of Crown, downing it, then taking a long pull from the beer. The man looked at Jesse's hand and then slowly raised his eyes back to the TV screen.

Jesse glanced around the room. The crowd appeared to be mostly working-class folks—people who earned a living with their hands and skills handed down from fathers and grandfathers. Bricklayers. Plumbers. Construction workers. Somewhere in the bunch of leather and denim was a fella who may have learned an awful vocation from his grandfather—the call of the devil. Handed down in the bloodline. Taught by example. Somewhere in here was Cooter Johnson.

The man sitting next to Jesse reached for a sweating bottle of beer. When he did, Jesse could see a tattoo on the man's upper arm. It was the insignia of the Army Rangers. Jesse sipped his beer for a second. He looked at the man and asked, "Were you in the Army?"

The man slowly turned his head toward Jesse, his face impassive. Jesse said, "Spotted your tat. You may have trained the same place I did."

"Where's that?"

"Fort Benning."

The man nodded. "Don't see a lot of guys your age having gone through the program."

Jesse grinned. "We're a rare breed, I suppose. Not too many of us left. I was in the 75th. Sent to Nam. It wasn't long after Hamburger Hill. The enemy had a hell of an ax to grind after that shit. I stayed through something called the Easter Offensive, and I can tell you it was offensive, on a lot of levels."

The man studied Jesse a few seconds. His face softer. He extended his hand. "Name's Ace Anders."

"Jesse Taylor. Pleased to meet you, Ace. What are the odds of a couple of Rangers sitting together in this dive bar? Is Ace your real name?"

"Yeah, my old man named me that."

Jesse smiled. "He must have been a card."

Ace grinned, lifting his beer in a toast. "To us...Rangers lead the way."

"I'll drink to that." They toasted, Jesse draining a final swallow from his can. "That was good. Think I'll have another."

"You ain't payin'. When you guys came back from Vietnam you got shit on. Too many Fonda types gave you a lotta crap. Brother, I want you to know I salute you. And ya'll should have gotten the recognition you deserved surviving that jungle warfare." He got the bartender's attention. "Lucille, another round for my new friend, Jesse." He slapped Jesse on the back.

The bartender brought the drinks and set them in front of Jesse. She took another order and Jesse turned toward Ace. "Much obliged." He drained the Crown, his face flushing, the pulse beat under the ankle holster slow and steady. "Ace, how long you lived here?"

"All my life. That's why I joined. I was glad to go to Iraq just to get the hell outta here."

"I hear you, brother. I couldn't help but notice the custom '57 model truck in the lot. You know if that bad boy might be for sale?"

"Don't know. Guy that owns it is shootin' pool at the last table before the johns. Name's Cooter Johnson. He's the tallest one at the table. Wears that damn Mohawk haircut. Dresses like a Viking. Got a bunch of piercings in his face, God knows where else."

"Is he a bettin' man?"

"He can work a table, why?"

"Because I wanna see how good he can work a table." Jesse stepped off the stool, and made his way though the crowd.

Two women, both in tight jeans and T-shirts, danced with each other near one table, the jukebox playing the Door's *Midnight Special.* Jesse approached the pool table and watched the final shots. Cooter Johnson, hair spiked in a five-inch Mohawk, open leather vest, large hands, long arms, gestured to a right corner pocket before lining up the cue ball and tapping the eight-ball into the pocket. He stood and grinned. Long, narrow face. Reddish whiskers like weeds. Silver piercings in his lips. Gold ring through one nostril.

A lumpy man in ragged shorts and a white T-shirt shook his head. "Damn, Cooter. You might as well be playin' by yourself."

Jesse stepped under the wash of light, looked at Cooter Johnson and then set down a hundred-dollar bill on the side of the pool table. Jesse said, "No reason to play by yourself. Now you got my ol' pal Ben Franklin and me. Maybe he can become your BFF. Maybe not."

Cooter Johnson stared hard at Jesse and said, "Rack 'em."

TWENTY-SEVEN

Cooter Johnson spotted the cue ball off-center on the lower portion of the pool table. He leaned over with a customized, engraved cue stick in his hands, lining up the shot. Jesse looked at the big man's left hand, the letters *e-v-i-l* tattooed on the tops of four fingers, just below walnut-sized knuckles. A dozen people sat in chairs, leaned against the bar, or stood in a buffer around the perimeter of the table, sipping beers, watching the opening break. The smell of sweat mixed with perfume, a tinge of smoke drifting through the light over the table.

Jesse overheard one man in the shadows say to another, "I bet Coot takes him down fast. I'll wager the old man will leave at least five on the felt."

"You're on, Lofton. I'm bettin' the graybeard will do better."

Johnson glanced up at Jesse before breaking the rack; the *whack* sounding as if a firecracker popped, balls zipping around the table. The striped thirteen-ball recoiled from the far railing and rolled slowly back toward Johnson, falling into the right-side pocket. Johnson cut his eyes up to Jesse. "Thirteen's my lucky number. One down seven to go." He lined up another shot, calling it with the point of the cue stick, quickly taking it, the nine-ball dropping.

Jesse could hear laughter, low conversations, the crackle of money. Johnson had an opening, easily sinking the four-ball. Someone in the crowd made a catcall. A shapely brunette in hip-hugging short shorts, a tight T-shirt that read, *Shorty's Good Eats*, brought a shot glass filled with Jack Daniels.

Johnson paused, took the drink and knocked it back, Creedence Clearwater Revival on the jukebox singing *Bad Moon Rising*.

Johnson motioned toward the twelve-ball and a corner pocket. He leaned down, lining it up, looking at shot probabilities after dropping the ball. He tapped the cue ball. It hit the twelve too hard, causing the ball to drift to the center of the table. Jesse looked at the layout, figuring angles and where the next shot might lead. He chalked his cue stick, walking around the table, doing the geometry in his head.

Johnson snorted. "C'mon, man. You got nothin.' Left you nothin'. So go on and take your nothin' shot, and I'll close this down. You'll feel the pain in your wallet."

Jesse found the angle. He said, "Six in left corner."

Johnson grinned. "No fuckin' way. Take that shot and game's over for you old man."

Jesse lowered himself against the table railing, his body loose, his eyes cutting from the cue ball to the six. He tapped it, the cue ball kissing the right side of the six and sending it into the left corner pocket."

A woman applauded from a table. Someone hooted. *Bad Moon Rising* sounded louder from the jukebox. Cooter Johnson seemed amused, stroking his copper beard, shifting his weight from foot to foot. Jesse met his eyes, stepped around the table, motioning to the side pocket next to him. "Let's send number three home." He bent down, sighted the shot looking at the tip of the stick, striking the cue ball. It recoiled from the opposite railing, the three dropping into the pocket.

"WooHoo!" shouted a woman standing by the biker wearing the American flag bandana.

Jesse stepped to the end of the table, tapped the left pocket with his hand. "Let's bring four back to here." He lined up the shot, taking it quickly, the four ball traveling almost the entire length of the table and falling in the pocket. He cut his eyes up to Johnson. A vein pulsed on Johnson's forehead, close to his temple, as if a larva was wriggling, trying to escape through a pore. Johnson used the back of his left hand to wipe sweat from his brow.

Jesse aligned another shot. "Seven in the side." He struck the left side of the cue ball, putting spin on it, the ball recoiling from the rail and tapping the seven into the pocket. Jesse looked up at Johnson. "Four solids in the hole. Four to go."

Ace Anders watched the game from the bar. More than that, he watched the people watching the game. The bartender looked at him and said, "Looks like your new pal is kicking Cooter's ass. It's about time somebody did."

"I don't know what Cooter hates most, losing or the embarrassment of losing."

Jesse could feel Johnson's anger growing. *It's how you play the game*, he thought. "Five in the right corner." He tapped the cue ball, banking off the railing to sink the shot.

"I'm smellin' blood," said a potbellied man, grinning, wearing a Tampa Bay Rays hat, holding a can of beer and eating a piece of beef jerky.

Jesse pointed toward a side pocket. "Number two is gonna be retired." He popped the cue ball, sinking the shot in a blur of moving colors.

Johnson licked his dry lips, pacing half way around the table. He gripped his cue stick, knuckles white. He said, "You miss the next one, I'll clear the fuckin' table. I like comin' in strong from behind. The world loves a winner." He looked at an attractive woman sitting at a table with two other women. "Ain't that right, Sarah?"

"That's right, Cooter."

Jesse said nothing. He stepped to the end of the table, near Johnson and said, "You're blocking my shot."

"Don't see a shot from down here."

"Move and I'll show you."

Johnson reached in front of Jesse, putting his open armpit near his face, chalking his cue stick, and then slowly stepping aside.

Jesse tapped a left corner pocket. "Number one's going here." He struck the cue ball, sending it off two railings and rolling into the one ball, dropping it in the pocket. Johnson's eyes bulged, the vein in his forehead twisting in an S rotation.

Without hesitation, Jesse said, "Eight in far right corner." He hit the cue ball hard, the eight ball vanishing in a streak of dark color. Jesse reached for the hundred-dollar bill. "Looks like you aren't taking Ben home tonight."

"Double or nothing, pops."

"You owe me a hundred dollars. Pay up."

"You can take your Ben Franklin and shove it up your ass."

Jesse smiled, still holding his cue stick. "Where'd a young fella like you learn to talk so nasty? You lost. Tonight, you're a loser. And now it's time to pay your dues."

"I don't pay shit to a hustler. You got no manners comin' into my house with your shit. You got a choice…you can leave or I'll escort you to the county line. And when I'm doing it, I'll teach you what your old man shoulda taught you."

"He didn't have a chance because your grandpa was beating the blood out of me. I was just a kid at the Florida School. He was one of the staff, except he was a little different. He loved boys…loved 'em in a peculiar way. If they didn't share the love, or if they cussed, like you're doing, he'd take his wide leather strap and beat 'em until the whip was splashin' blood on the walls. Kinda like painting with human blood."

A murmur came over the crowd. The *whumping* rotation of a paddle fan could be heard between the changing of music on the jukebox.

The bartender signaled a new waitress and said, "You better find Ernie."

"The bouncer?"

"He's the only Ernie we have. He's probably outside smoking. Get him. Now!"

TWENTY-EIGHT

After leaving the shuttered school, I drove through a misty rain toward Marianna, thinking about the voice-message Caroline Harper left me—how a witness, a boy at the time, had seen Andy Cope shot. *"He was in the reform school the same time Andy and Jesse were there. Jesse will only say the man is black, afraid to testify. Maybe you can find him."*

To find him, I'd have to find Jesse Taylor. I could see that my next voice-message was from Jesse's number. I played it, the Jeep's wipers pushing the droplets off the windshield. "Hey, Sean…Jesse gettin' back with you. Man, I don't play this telephone tag thing so well. Maybe we can meet up. I'm stayin' at the Heartland Motel, room 29. Come on by, and we'll go for a coffee or a bite. In the meantime, I'm droppin' by a pool hall called Shorty's. Maybe take in a game or two. If you come by, I'm wearin' a black T-shirt and a LA Dodgers ball cap."

I checked my watch against the time of his call, found the address online, and then set my GPS address for Shorty's Billiards. With the description he left, Jesse Taylor would be easy to find. What I didn't know was why he'd picked this particular bar to visit on a rainy night in Marianna, Florida.

— ◾ ▬

Cooter Johnson grinned, a reddish eyebrow rising, eyes flat. Johnson set his personal cue stick on the table, reaching for one propped against a post.

He broke it in two pieces, dropping the smaller end and keeping the thicker section with jagged shards. He moved around the table.

Jesse stood his ground, holding the cue stick like a baseball bat. He swung hard. Johnson used his three-foot piece to block the swing. Jesse's cue stick shattered, one piece flying above the crowd. Johnson shoved the serrated wood under Jesse's chin, turning it into his flesh. Blood rolled down the stick. Jesse was pinned against the pool table. He used his right hand to feel for a side pocket, to find a billiard ball. He gripped a ball, smashing it hard against Johnson's forehead. The blow tore away a flap of skin, blood pouring down Johnson's face, mixing in his red beard.

"Get him, Coot!" shouted a stocky man wearing a Tampa Bay Bucks T-shirt.

Johnson slammed his right forearm into Jesse's mouth, loosening teeth, blood streaming. Jesse brought his knee up hard into Johnson's groin, the big man reeling backwards, shaking his head like a dog coming from water, blood spraying across the pool table. Johnson charged. He pushed Jesse against a wooden support beam that went from floor to ceiling, his head crashing against the hard wood. The blow stunned Jesse, causing him to slip down the post onto the floor, his head and back propped up against the pillar.

The biker wearing the American flag bandana smirked and said, "Hey, Cooter. Hold his hand up against the post. We'll pin his paw to the pole. Teach the fucker a lesson."

Johnson grabbed Jesse's left wrist, lifting his arm and holding Jesse's hand above his head, against the post. Johnson glanced at the scars. "Your hand looks like a possum's ass. Stick him, Danny."

The biker grinned, pulling a knife from his belt, and stepping closer to the post. He drew back with the serrated-blade knife, targeting the back of Jesse's hand.

Ace Anders jumped from his barstool, pushing through the crowd, shoving a raucous man out of the way. Ace ran up behind the biker, wrenching his arm, knocking the knife to the floor. He hit the biker in the jaw, the blow causing the bandana to fly from the man's head.

In an instant, Cooter Johnson swept the knife off the floor, charging for Ace.

Jesse shook his head, vision returning. He pulled up his pants leg, drawing the pistol from the holster. He fired a round into the ceiling. Dust and a piece of black tile fell. The crowd was silent, people backing away, the warm air smelling of beer and blood. Jesse stood on wobbly legs, pointing the pistol at Johnson. "Drop the knife!"

Johnson tilted his head, glaring. "You gonna shoot me in front of all these witnesses?"

"That's your choice. But if you don't lose the knife, I'll decide for you."

Johnson released the knife, dropping it to the floor. Jesse said, "I'm giving you a message to take to your grandpa. Tell the old pervert that Jesse Taylor's back in town, and he's comin' to see him. He may not remember me, but he hasn't forgotten what he did to me at the school for boys. He liked it too much to forget." Jesse cut his eyes over to Ace. "Let's go."

Ace nodded, shoving the biker out of the way. Jesse kept his pistol pointed at Johnson. He ran toward the doors with Ace in the lead, the music changing, CCR belting out *Run Through The Jungle*.

They opened the door to the cool night air and the blinding spotlights from a half dozen squad cars. A deep southern voice on a bullhorn said, "Police! Drop your weapons! Now! Lie face down on the parking lot. Arms out! You got three seconds!"

TWENTY-NINE

I'd been in the Shorty's Billiards parking lot, sitting in my Jeep and speaking on the phone with Dave Collins, when it happened. The pool hall must have been just over the city/county line, because I watched a half dozen Jackson County Sheriff's squad cars pour into the parking lot followed by two Marianna police cruisers. Deputies and officers drew weapons, advancing toward the building. Spotlights trained on the door when two men stepped into the light. I recognized one of them immediately—only because Jesse Taylor had left a description of himself. *'If you come by, I'm wearin' a black T-shirt and a LA Dodgers ball cap.'*

And there he was. Standing in the harsh wash of intense light from the SWAT team. He wore a Dodger's cap and black T-shirt that read: *Harry's Beach Bar – St Pete, FL.* He had blood on the front of his neck. Some had soaked into his T-shirt. He dropped a small pistol and stood next to another man—a large man. Military haircut. Both men held their hands up, blinking in the bright light, trying to see beyond the moving silhouettes with weapons drawn. A deputy shouted, "Lie down! Arms and legs spread!"

"What's happening, Sean?" Dave asked.

"I think I just found Jesse Taylor."

"Where?"

"Lying face down in the parking lot of a pool hall. He's with another guy. It's a SWAT assault. Police are surrounding them both. An arrest is definitely going down. Looks like my meeting with Taylor will be postponed."

A deputy wearing a bulletproof vest shouted to the men, "You're under arrest! Don't move! Bag his gun, Derek."

Dave said, "I could hear that. Stay low. Sit tight, Sean. Whatever Jesse Taylor has just stepped into has the trappings of a small town setup. What has he done to justify a SWAT assault? He told you he was dropping by the bar to shoot a game or two of billiards. The question is…who'd he play against? What was at stake? What happened in there?"

"Don't know. I do know that Jesse Taylor was carrying a pistol in his right hand. He followed orders from the deputies and tossed the weapon. Talk with you later." I disconnected, lowered the diver's side window on my Jeep and watched them take down Jesse Taylor and the other man. They brought the men to their feet, handcuffed and dirty from lying facedown in a parking lot. The officers holstered their guns, the crackle of police radios echoing off the small building now splashed in a shower of blue, red, and white emergency lights.

I watched the proceedings from the shadows in my Jeep, close enough to hear, yet not to be in the way. A woman, maybe she was the bartender, and a fortyish man I figured was the manager—perhaps Shorty—poked their heads out of the door. An officer waved them outside and questioned them. Two more officers entered the bar. Jesse Taylor looked up at the moon and blew a sharp breath from his cheeks.

A tall man dressed in a sports coat, tie loosened, walked from an unmarked car around the officers. I saw him pull one aside, speaking in hushed tones. Then he approached the officer next to the manager and bartender, speaking briefly, questioning the manager. The tall man, a detective no doubt, nodded, not taking his eyes off the men in handcuffs. I could tell from his body language he was familiar with at least one of the two men. I assumed it was probably the guy with the gym body and military haircut.

The manger and bartender returned inside the bar. The detective approached the handcuffed men, two deputies standing next to them. The detective smiled, shaking his head. "Mr. Taylor…we meet again. Now it's under much different circumstances. There have been some laws passed since you lived here and spent time in the old reform school. You can't pull a pistol on a man and shoot it."

Jesse stared at him. "I fired at the ceiling."

"But you, according to eyewitnesses, pointed a handgun at a man and threatened his life. Maybe the bullet in the ceiling was really meant for Clarence Cooter Johnson, but in the scuffle—the fight—it discharged into the ceiling. That would be attempted murder."

"If I'd attempted it, you'd be carrying him outta here in a body bag. It was self-defense."

"Did he have a gun?"

"He had a knife, and he was about to stick it into the back of the man standing next to me."

Ace nodded. "That's right. This man saved my life. You ask anybody in there, people who aren't Cooter's friends, and you'll hear the real story."

The detective ran his tongue along the inside of his left cheek. He stepped closer to Jesse and looked at him as if he was inspecting an animal for parasites. "You smell of some serious drinking. Booze and guns make a deadly mix. When you spoke with me, I told you there was no tangible evidence to substantiate your accusations. And now you start creating problems. Hunting down relatives of people you think did you a wrong turn or two. So would this have been some sick sort of revenge killing? You start trying to wipe out the old man's seeds off the face of the earth? Is that what this stuff tonight amounts to?"

"Cooter Johnson and that biker with the American flag bandana on his head, they tried to stick a knife through my hand and pin it to a post. I was shootin' pool with Johnson. He lost. That's when his temper, his demons, came out. He had the same look in his eye tonight as the old man did when the bastard was beating and abusing me as a kid."

The detective crossed his arms and stood on the balls of his wingtip shoes for a second. "This isn't the Old West, Mr. Taylor, where you can go about vigilante hunting of people." The DA's going to set an example with this one." He glanced over to an officer. "Give them both a breathalyzer. Book 'em. I'll be back later for questioning."

"What a damn minute!" Jesse said, his chest swelling, words slightly slurred from alcohol. "What about the fella who was an eyewitness to Andy Cope's killing at the school? Did you interview him?"

"We rode out there. It looked like whoever lived in that old bus is gone. Maybe your witness is picking grapes in California. Migrant's don't have a whole lot of credibility." He looked over to a deputy. "Book these two. They're under arrest."

The officer nodded. In one hand he held a sealed and marked plastic bag with Jesse's pistol inside it. He signaled for two officers to escort Jesse and the other man to two separate squad cards. I got out of my Jeep and walked toward the entrance to Shorty's.

THIRTY

They put Jesse in the back of a squad car as I approached. A deputy looked up at me and said, "Crime scene, sir. Stay back!"

I smiled. "Sorry, didn't see any of that yellow tape you guys put up. Was the crime here in the lot or inside? Because if it's not inside, I'd like to enter."

Before the deputy could answer, the detective looked in my direction and said, "Hold on! You got a hearing problem?" He finished jotting something in a small notepad, closed it, placing the notepad in his inside coat pocket. "This entire place is a crime scene. Beat it."

"It can't be much of a crime since you just arrested those two guys and you didn't read them their Miranda rights."

He looked at me as if I'd just landed my spaceship in the lot. "Sure we did."

"I've been here the whole time. Didn't see it."

A deputy, late twenties, concerned face said, "Detective Lee, sir. I think he's correct. No rights were read to the—"

"Shut up, Parker! When and if you become a detective your opinion matters." The detective turned toward me. "Who the hell are you, Sherlock?"

"Name's O'Brien...Sean O'Brien." I could see Jesse stare at me, his mouth opening slightly.

The detective said, "If, in the remote chance, they weren't read their rights, they will be read before interrogation. Are you a lawyer? You represent one of them?"

"No, but it's pretty common knowledge that without a Miranda warning, the suspect's rights can be violated, meaning the answers they gave you here in the parking lot would be inadmissible, should this go to trial." I lifted my phone from my pocket. "Got it here in high-def video."

"Give me that!"

"Not without a warrant. By then it could be all over the Internet. And there's no delete button."

The detective's eyes burned. He looked above the flashing blue and red lights, slowly turning his head back to me. "Where you from? What do you want?"

"Worked homicide with Miami-Dade. I'm in real estate now. I've never seen either of those two men before tonight. What do I want? For those two gents, all I want is a fair evidentiary hearing. From what I heard, looks like no one was hurt inside. No real property damage except a bullet hole in the ceiling. That probably adds to the appeal of the place."

"These men will be questioned further, booked into the county jail and have a bond hearing before a judge. You wanna be there with your little video, fine. See you in court asshole." He turned, walking toward the swarm of officers and lights, signaling for two deputies to drive off with the men arrested.

I watched them drive away, Jesse Taylor looking at me out the side window. He nodded in a gesture of thanks or maybe acknowledgment. I walked toward my Jeep just as more than two-dozen people spilled from inside Shorty's Billiards. Some lit cigarettes, inhaling deeply, trying to calm the small part of the brain that was demanding a nipple of nicotine. They hung back in small packs—the leaders easy to identify. Lots of enhanced hand and body movement in pockets of black leather and denim. Adrenaline mixed with booze and egos.

Two officers followed behind a tall man wearing a spiked Mohawk haircut. Tats covered his muscular arms. The man held a blood-soaked cloth to this forehead. He spoke with the officers—one scratching notes, the other on his radio mic. I watched the detective approach the man with a familiarity I've seen in the body language of undercover cops communicating with street informers. Loose. Casual. Both parties glancing around the perimeter, eyes always moving, trying to make the awkward look routine. The better the actor, the better the act.

The detective wasn't a very good actor. Mohawk man was most likely the one that tangled with Jesse and the guy with the military haircut. And from the loud interrogation I overheard, the tall guy with the Viking complex was probably Cooter Johnson. I thought about what the detective had said to Jesse: *'You start trying to wipe out the old man's seeds off the face of the earth.'* So who was the 'old man' and what was his relationship to Mohawk? Maybe a grandfather? Uncle?

I got back in my Jeep, bar patrons drifting to their cars, trucks, or motorcycles, engines cranking, the metallic clattering noise of tires driving over flattened beer cans. I watched Mohawk and a woman in tight jeans, tank top, and boots get into a late fifties model yellow Ford pickup. I jotted down the tag number. They pulled out of the lot and turned right. I followed, keeping a reasonable distance, thinking about more of the conversation between Jesse and the detective.

I trailed the yellow pickup for a few miles south on Highway 71, past a barbecue joint, a truck stop and finally into the lot of a $49 dollar a night motel at the I-10 interchange. I'd hoped he might lead me to his home, or maybe a home he shared with others in his clan. Not tonight. Tonight his female companion would tend to his wounds. I had a feeling Jesse Taylor, angry and inebriated, may have done more damage to Mohawk's ego than the cut on his forehead.

I turned around in the parking lot of a Dollar Tree store and headed back to town. I thought about Jesse Taylor, his struggles leading to an arrest and at least one night in jail until a bond hearing. And I thought about parts of the interrogation and Jesse's response in the Shorty's lot.

The most disturbing was the reference of an eyewitness to Andy Cope's murder. It sounded to me as if Jesse had given the police the witness's identity. Which, in the vast majority of cases, would be the best thing to do. But after I watched the grilling and arrest, I had my doubts. *'It looked like whoever lived in that bus is gone. Maybe your witness is picking grapes in California. Migrant's don't have a whole lot of credibility.'*

Why wasn't the detective, and maybe his peers, putting any time and real effort into Jesse Taylor's allegations? Maybe it was because of the same roadblocks Caroline Harper had faced. In the minds of investigators, through the years, Andy Cope was simply a missing juvenile. Probably a runaway. Maybe kidnapped off the road. Like hundreds of others, it was something that could never be solved. Too much time gone. Too little evidence. No witnesses. That *was* the case. Not now. Who was the man in the bus? Where was it? And most importantly, where was he?

I needed to talk to Jesse Taylor. And I needed to do it quickly.

THIRTY-ONE

Police don't use a squad car to subtly tail a suspect. They use a marked car to make a statement. *You're under surveillance*, even if it's only until you reach the city limits. After I'd left Shorty's Billiards, I looked in my rear-view mirror and saw a sheriff's cruiser follow me for a few blocks before pulling away, making a U-turn in a 7-11 parking lot and heading toward town. I drove up to the drive-through window, bought a fish sandwich and a cup of black coffee.

The motel vacancy sign was flickering when I parked my Jeep in front of the office. It was a single-story 1960's vintage motel on the fringe of Marianna. I paid cash, the balding clerk smelling of gin and tobacco. There were mostly pickup trucks in the lot, a three-quarter moon rising over the top of cabbage palm trees, the scent of camellias in the warm night air.

I returned to my Jeep, parking a few spaces away from my room, thinking about the phone messages I'd exchanged with Jesse Taylor—the look on his face in the back of the cruiser as they took him away. I called Caroline Harper, got her voice-mail and said, "Caroline, it's Sean…I was on my way to meet Jesse Taylor here in Marianna. I saw him arrested in the parking lot of a bar. From what I can gather, he got into a fight with a family member of someone who worked at the reform school when Jesse and Andy were held there. Looks like Jesse had been drinking. There will probably be a first appearance court hearing in the next day or two. I plan to be there. Just wanted you to know."

I disconnected, slipped my Glock under my belt, picked up the bag I'd packed, locked the Jeep and walked toward my room—number seven out of fourteen, cicadas shrieking from the palms and pines beyond the parking lot.

The room smelled musty—cigarettes, bug spray and bleach. Carpet thin and worn. I tossed my bag on a blemished dresser, a small TV on top of the table. I checked the bathroom and small shower. Both clean. Above the single bed a black ant crawled down the frame of a print depicting an eagle flying over the tops of pine trees.

My phone buzzed. Incoming call from Dave Collins. "Sean, I've been doing a little digging on the politics between Jackson County and Tallahassee."

"Tallahassee?"

"As in the governor's office. Although the state is ostensibly accepting open offers for the old reform school property from anyone with a deep checkbook, seems likely that the final nod will go to a Miami corporation called Horizons Inc."

"Who are they?"

"A multinational corporation. Real estate. Telecommunications, cable, Internet, cellular, restaurants, manufacturing and venture cap investments. The company's board is a who's who of Silicon Valley and New York conglomerate and investment companies."

"Let me guess…Governor Burnett's got presidential aspirations, and he begins to build buddies and raise millions. All his new friends, of course, will eventually expect some kind of a return."

"Elections and presidents, unfortunately, are bought and sold like global commodities. There's no secret that Burnett has his eyes on the White House. The CEO of Horizons, James Winston, just hosted an exclusive, five-thousand-dollar-a-plate dinner party at his house in Palm Beach for the governor. Of course, Burnett's handlers are only conducting an exploratory campaign to determine the viability of a presidential run. In the meantime, they don't have to abide by contribution guidelines, meaning they can raise millions until there is an official announcement."

"How does all of that tie in to the sale of the old school?"

"Representatives from Vista Properties, a division of Horizons, made a presentation to the Jackson County Planning Commission last week. The people from Vista rolled out extremely detailed plans for a huge and very exclusive country club community, something they're calling Chattahoochee Estates. When it all sails through the county commission, and it will, you can bet the proverbial farm that the governor and CEO James Winston will be in gleaming hardhats, holding polished shovels for the official photo-op groundbreaking ceremonies."

"Send me a picture of James Winston and his contact info. Maybe all bets will be off if I can get excavations going before they bring their shiny shovels and news media."

"The media will be key to you prying the long-closed door off this thing. But that won't be easy to do unless and until you have definitive evidence and someone with the chutzpah to obtain a court order and, considering the circumstances, it may have to be signed by a federal judge."

I told Dave about Jesse Taylor and said, "I have to get to him before he continues to be a one man tornado, creating an environment of heavy local suspicion, meaning possible old evidence might be tossed, lips sealed, and even an eyewitness neutralized. And that's assuming Jesse doesn't get himself shot and dumped somewhere in the swamps."

"Considering the new revelations you're dealing with now...the possible family and political ties to an old murder and child abuse, that, compiled with the new interest in a massive property with huge development potential, along with the neat scenario of literally paving over a long festering sore in the state's past—you better move quickly while you can."

"How's Max?"

"Sean, your ability to catalog or change subjects at the blink of an eye always amazes me. Max is fine. She's sleeping on my couch. The little lady spent most of the day with Nick. I think they both wore each other out. When I went to get Max, I have the evening shift now, Nick was sawing logs on his couch, while Max slept on his bean bag chair in *St. Michaels'* salon."

"I'll be back as soon as I can."

"The law of averages isn't stacked in your favor on this one. I really hope Caroline Harper appreciates your efforts. Your other client isn't around to know the difference."

"You never know, Dave. Maybe, somehow, he'll know the difference. Goodnight." I stared at the photo of James Winston that Dave just sent. Winston was close to sixty. Gray hair. Intense eyes. I glanced up at the moonlight streaming through the window and thought about how the moon has no light of its own, a dark mass moving in a circle. The moonlight is only a reflection of sunlight. But tonight it looked brilliant over the palms. No one shines alone. We all need a hand, a guiding light sometimes.

And so it was for Caroline Harper, maybe even Jesse Taylor. The question was—would I have time to really help either one? Similar to the orbit—the perfect ring the moon travels, this case had no real beginning or stopping point. Maybe the point of entry started 111 years ago when the first kids were confined in the reform school. But the ending, the finish line was not marked, at least not yet. The old buildings would eventually be leveled. The debris hauled away. The misery carted off like cracked rubble. The boys, the survivors now all in their sixties and seventies, would soon be gone. Expensive meals, wines and liquors would pour from posh members-only lounges in the new country club.

Maybe. Maybe not.

I slid my gun from my belt, placing the Glock on a nightstand. I removed my shirt, felt the small photo of Andy Cope in the pocket. I set it next to my pistol, the moonlight falling against Andy's face. His time had been so short. But I knew time was always borrowed. Always on loan, rented. Never owned. I glanced down at Andy's picture, hoping for his sister that I could borrow a little more time to carve justice on a headstone that wasn't erected. Because the murder of a child—a crime buried without justice, should never be forgotten.

I lay down on the hard mattress, listening to the distant and lonely refrain of a train whistle. I stared at the irregular ceiling tiles, looking for a point of entry into the past, hoping I wouldn't find myself backed into the corner of a sleepless night.

THIRTY-TWO

Jesse Taylor didn't consider himself a deeply religious man, but tonight he was. He whispered a silent prayer before making the only phone call he'd get before being booked into the Jackson County Jail. He made the call from the sheriff's department after an hour of further interrogations with Detective Larry Lee. Jesse had demanded to speak with a lawyer. But there was one big problem. He didn't have a lawyer. He looked across at the bare interrogation room, mostly white, dark scuffmarks on the floor near the table. One-way glass with oily handprint smudges on the glass.

A black phone hung on the wall. With a trembling hand, he called Caroline Harper.

"Hello." Her voice had a tenor of suspicion.

"Caroline, this is Jesse. I'm so sorry to bother you, but I really don't know a lot of people here with the exception of Harold Reese."

"What's happened, Jesse? Sean O'Brien said you were in some kind of trouble. Where are you?"

"I never formally met this guy, O'Brien, but I sure as shit saw him in action tonight. He's a big guy who's not afraid to stand up to a bully detective. He stood up for me as this detective was pissin' on my leg. I got hauled off and never got a chance to thank O'Brien. But now I'm about to be locked up in the county jail on trumped up charges"

"What charges?"

"I didn't do anything, really. Mostly it was self-defense. I was at this bar, maybe I did have one more drink than I shoulda, but that's 'cause I don't drink anymore. No tolerance. Caroline, I confronted a fella by the name of Cooter Johnson. That's probably not his real first name, but his last name's dead on."

"What do you mean? What happened?"

"This guy's one of the grandsons of Hack Johnson. Johnson was one of the meanest S-O-B's at the school. He'd beat boys within an inch of their life. I don't know if it was him who shot Andy that night, but chances are that Johnson was one of the three men chasin' Andy into the marsh."

"What did you do to his grandson?"

"We tangled. Both of us got in licks. His posse, some bikers, was closing in when I pulled out a pistol and fired a shot."

"Dear God…"

"Not at anyone. I shot into the ceiling to stop 'em from coming. They'd have crippled me for life, or worse. They all ran like rats on a sinking boat. Another fella helped me get outta there. They locked him up too. His name's Ace Anders." Jesse blew out an extended breath. "Look, I don't have a lawyer here. Don't know a soul. I'm low on cash. I got to go before a judge tomorrow for a hearing. Maybe you could recommend a lawyer, somebody who'll take payments. I have a sorry heart, and I'm damn remorseful to have to ask, but I—"

"It's okay. I'm glad you called. I want to help you. It's the least I can do for what you are trying to accomplish. I have a dear friend, we went to Florida State together, and he's a good attorney. His name's Daniel Grady. I'll call him. He'll be there for you, Jesse."

"I can't thank you enough. I made a mistake in one way by drawing out Cooter Johnson, but I confirmed something else, too."

"What?"

"He's got the same cold, flat eyes as his grandpa. If there's a soul behind those eyes, it's already been repossessed by Satan. I'm certain of that."

━ ━

When I got to the courtroom, Caroline Harper was already there. She sat to the far left of the room, Jesse Taylor and a half dozen other defendants were seated near a vacant jury box close to a table reserved for attorneys. One man in a suit sat at the table, his briefcase open, going through a file.

I took a seat next to Caroline. She smiled and said, "Thank you for coming. I feel bad for Jesse. He let his temper, fueled by alcohol, get the best of him."

"Who's the man at the table?"

"Daniel Grady. He's been my family lawyer since we graduated from college. He does a lot of wills, trust, a few divorces, and more than his share of DUI cases."

I looked to my right as the state prosecutor entered the courtroom. Watching her walk by, I knew Jesse Taylor might not be going back to his motel room soon. She was all business. And I recognized her.

I glanced over to Caroline and asked, "How much serious criminal defense work has your friend done?"

"I'm not sure, why?"

"Because Jesse's about to have his butt handed to him. I recognize the state attorney. I don't think she's ever lost a case. I do know that she takes no prisoners. Before this dog and pony show starts, get the attention of your attorney and tell him that Jesse Taylor was questioned in the parking lot, arrested but never had his Miranda rights read to him. Tell him you have a witness. And you'd better do it now, before the prosecutor gets started."

THIRTY-THREE

She was fearless. That's what I remembered most about Lana Halley. Facing possible retaliation—death threats, for her relentless prosecution of a Mexican drug lord captured in Florida, she persevered. As an assistant state attorney, her bold approach garnered headlines for her and a life sentence for the accused. Lana Halley always did her homework. She had a steel-trap mind for details and the big picture, the tentacles of the crime and the criminals. And she had the confidence to cut the legs off any weak defense. Her liability...*they're all guilty*.

A first-appearance bond hearing doesn't usually give a prosecutor much time to prep. Not her. Lana's attention to detail would prove uncanny. I remembered it when she prosecuted the head of a drug cartel caught doing business in the Ocala National Forest. She'd been resolute in the courtroom. And now, here she was, working in the Second Judicial District, geographically closer to the state capital, Tallahassee and the power base.

She walked by the dozen or so spectators, her posture straight, confident. The courtroom audience was seated, most of them probably family members of the people about to go through a bond hearing. I spotted Mohawk man. He had a large bandage across his forehead. Arm in a sling. He sat with almost a dozen people in one row near the front. Men, women, teenage boys and girls. Jeans and T-shirts. The oldest man around fifty, wore a T-shirt with a Confederate flag on the front. No grandfather figure, all family members bearing a slight resemblance to the man I heard the detectives refer to as Clarence Cooter Johnson, AKA Mohawk. They were fair-skinned, probably linked to Scandinavian ancestry.

I looked around the room. One man sat by himself near the front row, close enough to hear everything. With his wrinkled khaki pants, denim shirt, sleeves rolled to his elbows, he was one of the best dressed in court. He scribbled in a small notebook, taking notes, using his phone to shoot video. Definitely a reporter. This wasn't a trial. Nothing high profile. So why was he here? And why was he scrutinizing only one of the people facing the judge? Why was he looking at Jesse Taylor? I watched him as he observed the proceedings.

Lana Halley wore a beige suit, black hair up, strand of pearls beneath a white blouse unbuttoned below her neck. I saw her glance at the row of people, six, who were facing the judge, most here because the state required their first appearance hearing to be held within twenty-four hours of arrest.

She held her eyes on Jesse for a few seconds longer than I would have expected. He looked at her, a hopeful expression on his whiskered face, his physical manner transparent. It was then that I could tell that somehow he knew her. And she knew him. Had he been in trouble before? Had she prosecuted him in a previous case? It didn't appear likely. There was no indication of contempt from her or from him as often the case when the system cycles habitual offenders in and out of jail like a roll of the dice in a game of Monopoly. Too often the inmates are 'just visiting,' serving no hard time.

I recognized one of the other men held for a first appearance. He was the stocky man with the military haircut I'd seen with Jesse when they were both arrested. A sixty-something man in a suit, silver hair, rimless glasses, briefcase opened at the table, sat next to Jesse, studying papers. He looked up as the judge entered the courtroom.

"All rise!" barked a stout bailiff.

The judge, face thin, shaggy white eyebrows, motioned for the spectators to sit. He placed bifocals on his nose and shuffled through case files stacked at the side of his desk. After less than twenty seconds, he cleared his throat. "State of Florida verses defendant Jesse Ryan Taylor. Is Mr. Taylor present?"

The man in the suit, briefcase open, nodded. "Yes, your Honor. Mr. Taylor's represented by counsel."

The judge cut his eyes toward Jesse. "Mr. Taylor, you're charged with aggravated assault, public intoxication, and last but not least—discharging a firearm in a public facility, endangering the lives of the public. Do you understand the charges, Mr. Taylor?"

Jesse nodded. "Yes sir. But—"

The attorney stood. "Your Honor, I'm requesting a bond hearing today as well. My client poses no threat. He was born in Jackson County. Has ties to the community and should be released on his own recognizance."

Lana Halley rose from her chair. "Your Honor, the state disagrees. The defendant, Mr. Taylor, may have been born here, but he hasn't returned to the area for decades. Some of his youth was spent in the Florida School for Boys. He's lived in the Jacksonville area most of his adult life. So why is Mr. Taylor here, back in the county after decades? His actions in Shorty's Billiards define his intentions."

The judge leaned forward, bushy eyebrows rising, peering over his bifocals. "We don't prosecute intentions, Miss Halley. Only actions that break the laws of the land."

"I understand, your Honor. However, for the purpose of establishing an appropriate bond, the state will show at this hearing how, in Mr. Taylor's case, his actions in the bar are commensurate and inseparable with intent. It's not unlike the gunpowder behind a bullet. Separate, both are harmless. Together, with a hair trigger connected to a personal vendetta fueled by alcohol…it's a lethal mixture."

Caroline Harper looked over to me and whispered. "I'm praying for Jesse. She makes him sound like a terrorist."

I looked at the reflection on the judge's glasses, a glint of light coming from the back of the courtroom. The doors had opened and closed. I turned slowly and saw the detective who arrested Jesse entering, standing for a second before taking a seat in the back row. This wasn't a criminal trial. But in the last few minutes it was taking the appearance of one.

And I might become its first witness.

THIRTY-FOUR

Lana Halley never made direct eye contact with the detective, but I knew she was aware he'd arrived. Her delivery was a little sharper, going for a closing in a hearing that wasn't even an arraignment. Maybe it would never make it to the arraignment stage if Jesse's attorney could get it tossed out for a Miranda rights violation.

Lana stepped in front of her table, arms and body relaxed. "Mr. Taylor came to the state attorney's office a few days ago. He did so, voluntarily, because he wanted the office to convene a grand jury to look into alleged improprieties at the Florida School for Boys during the time he was incarcerated there. Mr. Taylor, after all these years, still carries a resentful grudge, a potential dangerous revenge against anyone who worked at the school during the time he was confined there."

I watched her rapid presentation, pausing for the right effect, looking from the judge back to Jesse and his attorney. Now I knew why I was picking up on the awkward familiarity that I first noticed when Jesse watched her walk into the room. He'd met with her earlier. Not good.

Lana said, "Your Honor, police reports citing eyewitnesses, indicate that Mr. Taylor singled out one man, Clarence Johnson, who was playing billiards, simply because Mr. Johnson's grandfather worked at the former reform school. Mr. Taylor, according to the reports, started the altercation, resulting in gunfire and oral threats to both Mr. Johnson and his grandfather, who wasn't present at the time."

"Your Honor," the attorney lifted both hands, palms out, glaring at Lana Halley. He shook his head. "The prosecutor is basing her allegations purely on hearsay, accounts that police got from witnesses who are friends or colleagues of Clarence Johnson. My client did not start the fight. He was defending himself. He had no choice but to stand his ground, and he has a witness as well. He's seated in this courtroom, and he's a decorated former member of the U.S. Army Rangers. Ace Anders is charged with aggravated battery for helping Mr. Taylor exit the building before a mob descended on Mr. Taylor for winning a game of billiards, and defeating Mr. Johnson in front of his friends. Mr. Taylor also was an Army Ranger who served in Vietnam. The state sites the information on the arrest report as her source. We have a witness who says Mr. Taylor wasn't read his Miranda rights before, during, or after his arrest. So we contend this first appearance should be a last appearance and my client released immediately."

The judge leaned forward, tilting his head as if he wanted the attorney to repeat the statement. "Is your witness in the court?"

The attorney looked back toward Caroline and me. I stood and said, "Yes, your Honor, I'm here." I could feel Lana Halley's eyes boring into me.

"Your Honor," she said in an annoyed tone. "This is not a criminal trial. It's purely a first appearance where the defendant is apprised of his charges."

The judge grunted. "I'm aware of how a first appearance hearing works."

Lana smiled. "The arresting detective, who's in this courtroom, told me that most of the questioning was done, or attempted to be done at the sheriff's office. But Mr. Taylor demanded his lawyer, and so we're here today with his attorney and the fact that when someone comes into this town, he doesn't get a pass to attack people and fire a pistol in a crowded bar. The defense is correct, Mr. Taylor served in Vietnam, and according to Mr. Taylor, he still suffers from PTSD today."

Jesse started to come out of his seat. His attorney motioned for him to sit.

Lana seized the moment. "The state contends that he's not stable, and he's a man who has proven he will fire a live round in a crowded indoor area.

Maybe the next place will be a crowded theater. We argue bond, if offered, should be set at the maximum under Florida law."

Jesse shouted, "My PTSD didn't come from Nam! It came from the hands of men beating and abusing me at the school. They were supposed to help us. And the state of Florida let the bastard's do it! That's my fucking PTSD!"

The judge pounded his gavel. "Order! No more outbursts in my court! Bond is set at twenty-thousand dollars. Bailiff, escort Mr. Taylor out. Next case." Two bailiff's moved toward Jesse.

Lana was impassive, lifting another case folder.

Caroline held one hand to her mouth for a second, "That's not fair. Jesse is a victim here, too."

As a husky bailiff escorted Jesse from the table to an exit door, he turned, looking our way, his face hurt, filled with anger. He stared at Lana Halley for a moment, her concentration already shifting to the next case as they led Jesse around the judicial Monopoly board of power and politics, going directly to jail.

THIRTY-FIVE

Cooter Johnson led the parade across the marble floor of the old courthouse. His family, laughing and swapping stories, snaked out of the building. They stopped on the top steps, some of the adults lighting cigarettes, celebrating their win over Jesse Taylor. One man, his salt and pepper beard full, grinned, slapping Johnson on his shoulder. I watched their interactions, their unabashed revelry. I assumed Jesse was probably locked away, inside the county jail, wondering how he'd make bond.

Caroline Harper came out from the restroom waiting for her attorney to appear in the hallway. As she walked in my direction, I watched the reporter interview Lana Halley near a far side of the foyer. They stood next to a large painting of seventeenth century Spanish explorers coming ashore on a Florida Gulf coast.

I wondered what questions the reporter was asking. And what was Lana telling him? Why would a reporter cover a first appearance hearing in a case that wasn't a capital offence? No murder. No massive embezzlement schemes. Maybe it was a slow news day in Marianna. When Caroline approached, I asked, "Did you know that Jesse had gone to the state attorney's office before the meltdown in the bar?"

"He mentioned three places he'd gone, and this was after I asked him to wait for you. He met with a sheriff's detective, someone in the state attorney's office and a reporter. He told them about Curtis' letter. I'm not sure who in all he met with, though."

"I am. The detective was in the courtroom. He sat in the last row. Just listening. He was the same guy that arrested Jesse in the Shorty's parking lot. And now I'm sure that the person in the SA's office is Lana Halley, and the reporter interviewing her now was probably the guy Jesse went to see. Do you know what Jesse told the state attorney?"

"He said he told her about Andy's death…about Curtis Garwood's letter. What can we do?"

"I can do some form of damage control, where necessary."

"I'll bail Jesse out of jail. I feel it's the least I can do. His heart is in the right place. Too bad it can't control his anger. But I can't fault him for that either. Not after the life he's lived."

"Don't bail Jesse out immediately. I want to look around, and I'd prefer it if he wasn't in the near vicinity. Give me a day."

Caroline's attorney approached. She said, "Daniel, I want you to meet Sean O'Brien. I mentioned a little about Sean to you earlier. He's helping me look into the disappearance and death of Andy. Sean, this is Daniel Grady."

Daniel extended his hand. I shook it, and he said, "Looks like you already got a good start. Your observation of the violation of the Miranda rights will go a long way if this ever goes to trial."

"Maybe the alleged victim will come to reality and drop charges."

Daniel scanned out the front door, some members of the Johnson family were still smoking cigarettes on the outside steps. He said, "Somehow I don't think they'd do that." He cut his eyes to Caroline. "Jesse's bond is fairly low. It could have been higher. Judge Rollins likes to make an example out of a defendant who has an outburst in his courtroom. I maintain Jesse was standing his ground in what was about to become a mob mindset. Unfortunately, he didn't have a permit to carry the pistol. I'll speak with Jesse to see if we can offer a plea bargain with the state. No jail time. But he'd possibly wind up with doing some community service; maybe pay for the repair to the ceiling in the bar."

I looked across the hallway, Lana Halley was finishing her interview with the reporter and said, "Somehow I don't think she'll do that."

Daniel nodded. "You could be correct. She's fairly new to the Second District. However, her reputation precedes her. I hear she's a ballbuster. Sorry, Caroline."

Caroline smiled. "Daniel we've know each other far too long to make apologies for gutter talk. Sometimes it's the best way to make a point. I just want to help Jesse. As a little kid, I remember how he played with Andy. When I see Jesse, somehow I see the innocence he shared with Andy…and now I see the pain. Finding Andy's body, I think, is as important for Jesse as it is for me."

Daniel dipped his head slightly, lips tight. "I'd try to get a court order to excavate if I had something tangible to leverage in front of a judge."

"Maybe, now that Sean is here, we'll find something tangible. Let's get coffee. Daniel, I need to know the procedure for bailing Jesse out of jail. Sean, can you join us?"

My phone buzzed in my pocket. I looked at the incoming call, remembered it was the number of the real estate agent. "I need to take this. I'll catch up with you."

THIRTY-SIX

When I looked up and saw Lana Halley walking in my direction, I didn't want to take the call. I'd make it quick. I answered. "Hey, Sean, it's Ben Douglas. Hope things are going well. I wanted to catch up with you. One of the security guards at Dozier is saying some crazy stuff about you. We need to talk."

Lana Halley was less than twenty-five feet away. Unsmiling.

"Are you there, Sean? Look, Mr. Farnsworth's not returning my calls."

"I'll call you." I disconnected as Lana Halley broke into a wide smile, briefcase in one hand, purse in the other. "Hello, Lana."

"Sean O'Brien. It's been awhile. I'm trying to remember if I ever thanked you for testifying in the Pablo Gonzalez murder trial."

"No thanks needed. You did your job. In the end, that's what counts."

"And you did your thing too. In the end, the body count saved the tax-payers a lot of money—the OK Corral in the Ocala National Forest. That alone took the argument of self-defense to a whole new perspective."

I said nothing.

She smiled, gazed out the door for a moment, and then looked up at me. "What brings you to our little hamlet? Marianna doesn't seem like the kind of place a former Miami homicide investigator would find very fun."

I smiled. "Sometimes the most fun is found where you least expect it. Often in quiet places. Occasionally the quiet is indicative of the mystery and secrets some people want buried."

She studied me for a few seconds, the daylight coming through the large windows lustrous in her deep blue eyes. "You think there are hidden secrets in Marianna?"

"Every town has them. Some more than others."

"So let me understand this…were you there when Detective Lee or his arresting officer allegedly failed to read rights to Taylor?"

"Yep. No alleged. It happened. "

"Why are you here, Sean? Why stick your nose into what amounts to a bar fight? I'm here because it's my job. You…I'm not really sure who you are. Maybe a wayward knight with a rusty Achilles heel and some personal mission to fix it by fixing others."

"Is that what you think?"

"I'm not sure what to think, at least not yet. But if you stay, I will know soon enough."

"If I stay, you will because I'll let you know."

She held her eyes on mine, smiled and tilted her head, the light gleaming off one pearl earring. "Not that it's not nice to see a handsome face like yours, but I'd really like to know what mysteries and secrets you think are in Marianna, Jackson County or the whole Second District. Maybe I could be of help."

"You can help by cutting Jesse Taylor some slack."

"Why would I do that?"

"Because he went to you. He confided in you, telling you about the murder of a boy, Andy Cope, killed when Jesse was in the school for boys. And you're asking for maximum bail in what you just said was a bar fight?"

"What are you insinuating?"

"How much does the sale of that property have to do with keeping Jesse Taylor quiet?"

Her eyes narrowed. "After prosecuting Gonzales, you should know me better than that."

"Then why don't you level with me? Jesse told you about the letter Curtis Garwood sent to me. So you know exactly why I'm here. You didn't have to ask. The question you could have asked is how you, as a prosecutor, can bring closure to people like Caroline Harper, Jesse Taylor and other families—people who've seen and lived with a lifetime of the psychological effects of child abuse. Those scars don't disappear. What else did Jesse tell you?"

"Any information I receive from a—"

"Victim? Because that's what he was."

"Sean, we worked together once. I overlooked your vigilante methods then. But I won't do it again. If you take the law into your own hands, if you violate someone's rights, I'll vigorously prosecute you. Are we clear?" Her eyes bored into mine, nostrils just flaring. Then she turned to walk away when a man approached. He wore a thousand dollar, slate charcoal gray suit, almost my height. His platinum hair was perfectly combed. Lean face tanned.

He nodded at me, smiled at Lana and said, "Good job on the prelims. I've had to move Robert to the Jefferson case. I'm trying to avoid a bottleneck. Judge Reynolds seems to be more about a defendants right to a speedy trial than ever before." He looked back at me and extended his hand. "I'm Jeff Carson. I don't think we've met."

I shook his hand. "No we haven't. I'm Sean O'Brien."

Lana said, "Sean's a former Miami-Dade homicide detective. He helped bring down Mexican drug lord Pablo Gonzales when he was caught in the states."

Carson crossed his arms. "I remember that one. Impressive. What brings you to Marianna?"

"A friend wrote to me, suggested I come visit."

Carson smiled. Perfect teeth. "Who's your friend? We might have a mutual acquaintance."

"He's dead."

Carson stared at me. "His name was Curtis Garwood." I didn't blink and said, "He was a survivor of the Florida School for Boys. Now it's referred to as the Dozier School. You can change the name but you can't change the history of abuse."

He looked directly at me for three seconds, his pupils closing a touch. "Indeed," he nodded, lifting his right hand near the cleft in his chin. "All that was way before my time. Even my predecessor in this office, Charles Perry, said there wasn't enough evidence to prove or disprove any allegations of wrongdoing. Unfortunately, the statute of limitations of long ago expired."

"Not for murder."

He angled his head, glanced toward the main entrance to the courthouse, and then looked at me. "Is that why you, a former homicide detective, is here...to investigate a murder?"

"Probably murders, plural. Caroline Harper has tried to speak with your office. She believes her brother, Andy Cope, was murdered and buried on that property."

He smiled. "We always encourage the sheriff's staff to investigate cold cases. It's up to them to prioritize and bring their findings to this office."

"You can call for a grand jury investigation. And you can get a court order to dig around the property to see if there's evidence of bodies."

"Mr. O'Brien, you just heard me speak to Lana about a district judge's mandate for quicker turnaround times from arrest to trial. We don't have the time nor manpower to begin archeological digs on state property. Perhaps you can ask the Florida Department of Law Enforcement, to poke around. Nice meeting you." He turned on his Brooks Brothers lace-up shoes, gestured for Lana to follow him and walked down the hall, turning around a corner.

I saw a man standing to the far right of the corridor—the reporter. He lowered his camera and left the building.

I called Dave Collins, got his voice mail and said, "Dave, give me a call. There are some shadows on the wall here in Marianna. Maybe you can shine a light into some dark places for me."

THIRTY-SEVEN

I t's the unscheduled stops that sometime lead to a destination. But you often don't know it until you go back and remember where you were at the milepost of an investigation. I was about to leave the courthouse when I smelled fresh roasted coffee. I walked around an alcove, the scent of brewed coffee leading me.

People moved in small herds up and down the halls in search of courtrooms and, for some, justice. Two baristas worked behind the counter in the coffee shop, grinding beans and pouring coffee. There were at least a dozen small tables and chairs scattered in the nooks of the shop. I ordered a large black coffee to go.

As I waited for the barista to fill the order, I glanced around the shop. People, most dressed in professional attire, sat at a few of the tables engrossed in hushed conversations. At a table tucked in the far reaches of the shop, I spotted the detective sitting with state attorney Jeff Carson. They were drinking coffee from paper cups, talking quietly. Carson doing more talking than listening.

I paid for my coffee and left. The fresh air and sunlight was a welcome change from the courthouse. Two members of the Johnson family lingered near the building, still talking, probably about Jesse Taylor. One man, the guy with the full streaked beard, laughed at something, and then the two men walked away, going separate directions. I came down the courthouse steps and followed the bearded man, keeping my distance.

He kept to the sidewalk, walking under the deep shade of the live oaks. He stepped up to a late model pickup truck. Someone was sitting on the passenger side of the truck, cigarette smoke curling out the open window. The passenger appeared to be an old man. I moved faster. My Jeep was parked less than three spaces from the truck.

The older man wore a Stetson hat, white T-shirt. The bearded man got into the driver's side. He didn't start the engine immediately, instead the two men sat there talking. I walked behind the truck, memorizing the license tag number, moving near the passenger side of the truck. I pulled out my phone, pretending to send a text standing beside a locked mid-eighties model Ford Taurus. I tried to get a glimpse of the man wearing the Stetson, but the hat was too far down on his forehead. He held the cigarette in his right hand. Claw-like. Hand knotted from arthritis, nicotine stains between two fingers.

The motor started. I feigned taking a call, turning back toward the passenger side, the sound of a George Jones song coming from inside the truck. A gust of wind blew through the trees, the branches moving, dappled light falling against one side of the truck. The old man knocked the ash off the cigarette, light from the sun illuminating a tattoo on his forearm. Although the ink was faded, and his skin flaccid, I could tell the tattoo was the same image Curtis Garwood had seen as a boy.

There was no mistaking a tattoo of the Southern Cross.

I stood there as they drove away, a blue jay shrieking in the branches of the live oak, the wind dying and the deep shade returning. I walked to my Jeep, thinking about Curtis's letter, thinking about the scene I'd just witnessed in a court of law. As I unlocked the Jeep, my phone buzzed. Caroline Harper said, "Sean, Jesse called me. He's officially been booked and fingerprinted, and he's angry. I told him I was going to make bond as soon as I could. He wants to speak with you."

"I'm sure you didn't tell him I asked you to delay making his bond. He could speak with me when he's out. Did he say why he wants to talk?"

"He said it has to do with that eyewitness he mentioned…the man, who as a boy, witnessed Andy's murder. Jesse's afraid, now that he's in jail, someone will harm the man."

"And that could only mean that Jesse's told someone the witness's name."

"Maybe Jesse told the police, or the state attorney. After what happened in court, he could have a good reason to be frightened. Somebody doesn't want the truth out. What can we do?"

"I'll speak with Jesse in the county jail. In the meantime you can begin the bonding out procedure."

"So you don't want a day delay now, correct?"

"In view of what's happening, Jesse might be much safer out of the county jail. That can be a place where fatal accidents or restraints happen."

"I'll go to my bank for the bond money. Please hurry, Sean."

I started to open the door to my Jeep when I saw a moving reflection on the side window. It was that of a man, and he was quickly approaching me. I opened the door, knowing my Glock was within reach. I turned to face him. He was the same reporter I'd seen in the courthouse hallway, but not the reporter I'd spotted in the courtroom. Big guy. Scruffy. Loose tie. Short sleeve pale yellow shirt outside his pants, the wind lifting his comb-over hair.

He said, "Excuse me. Are you Sean O'Brien?"

"Who wants to know?"

His smile dissolved, his chest rising and falling. Nervous. His breath smelling like burnt beef brisket and onion rings. "I'm Wallace Holland with the *Jackson County Patriot*. Can we talk?"

"I'd really enjoy a nice chat here on the shady square, but I'm in a hurry."

"Are you representing someone looking to buy the old Dozier School for Boys?"

"If, and this is only if, I were…any information pertinent to a purchase or even an inspection is confidential due to the nature of competitive bidding. Now, I must be going."

"So you're saying no comment, correct?"

"No, I did comment and I told you why there is no further comment. In the what, where, how and why part of journalism I gave you the why, probably the most important part of a story, I'd imagine, right?" I smiled.

He didn't. His eyes widened, suspicion behind his glasses. I noticed a mustard stain the size of a bird dropping on his red tie. "I know that you're the same Sean O'Brien who fired the shot that took out a terrorist plane on the runway. So why would you be interested in the state property? Is this about building some sort of paramilitary facility there?"

I said nothing.

"Who are your backers? You do realize that all particulars to the sale of taxpayer-owned properties will be open for scrutiny?"

"If the taxpayers had really owned that reform school, maybe there'd have been better scrutiny and less exploitation of kids. By the way, a plane can't be a terrorist, only the pilot or a passenger. No more than a bullet is a terrorist until a coward aims and fires it into someone's back. When you spell my name, it's O'Brien with an *e* not *a*. I know accuracy is everything to you guys. Just a suggestion." I smiled.

His mouth contorted, trying to form a question, his lips looking as if he'd bitten into a lemon. I got in my Jeep, started the engine and drove toward the county jail. In my rearview mirror, the reporter stood vertical like an unmade bed, his fingers punching the keys to his phone.

THIRTY-EIGHT

The feeling was always the same—a type of mental castration. A prison setting does more than confine and segregate humans from the outside. It's the inside, the human mind, that's really trapped in a mental sterility by virtue of being locked in a six-by-eight foot cage. Even as a visitor, you can sense the edge of vulnerability. I felt it often working homicide in Miami, dealing with jails, inmates, prisons, and jailers. You, the prisoner—even someone being held on charges and yet to be tried for those charges, became insignificant the moment you put on the orange jumpsuit.

I thought about that as I cleared metal detectors in the Jackson County Jail, signed the visitor's paperwork, and waited for the jailers to bring Jesse to the visitation room. It was more of a large cubical than a room. Thick glass separating the visitor and the inmate, the ubiquitous black phone attached to the wall adjacent to the glass. I knew how jail begins to torment the human psyche. It doesn't take long. A rational man or woman may break a law, sin against society, and while locked in a pen, come to realize through that personal depravity, his or her own self worth. Sometimes.

A lanky guard in his mid-twenties, acne, round shoulders, led Jesse Taylor into the room. The guard moved over to a metal table and chair in a corner of the room.

Jesse picked up the phone. I did the same. He blew out a breath and said, "I guess you and Caroline saw all that shit that went down in court."

"Yeah, we saw it." I noticed the scars on the hand that held the phone. I looked at his other hand. Same thing.

"That damn detective is gunning for me."

"There are a lot of people who don't want the scabs knocked off the history of the old reform school."

"That's for damned sure."

"And right now you're a threat, coming from nowhere rattling cages just as the state is trying to make millions in a sale of the property."

"What those bastards did to us as kids is beyond criminal. It's like they wanted to experiment to see how much physical and mental abuse we could take before we died inside." He looked away, eyes blinking rapidly for a moment. Then he cut his head toward me. "You know, in a few years all of us in our sixties and seventies will be dead and gone. And the reform school will be a fancy neighborhood with winding streets where children can play safely. Nobody will know about kids like Andy Cope and the others. We were the throwaways. They didn't care then, and they don't care today."

"I care."

He looked at me, his eyes searching my face. "Why, man? You got no skin in the game."

"Because there's something about a brutal injustice that bothers me. And it really bothers me when it happens to a child."

"Even though you aren't family of the victims?"

"We're all related. That's the best answer I can give you."

He grinned and shook his head. "I always wondered why the family of man is so dysfunctional. Although I've done some bad things, I'm not a bad person. I'm just sort of despondent because of this nature verses nurture thing. I certainly didn't have any of the latter. I'm not a philosopher, but I have pondered whether we're born with a blank slate and life experiences become the writing on our wall. Or is some of that writing on the wall already there—a kind of invisible ink? Does it become more legible the more we find out who we are in life?"

"Maybe it's a combination of both, born with some inherited sense of survival—of mutual dependence, but too helpless to recognize or under-stand it if we could."

He nodded. "I got to believe that inherited thing can be handed down good or evil, too, like black or white seeds scattered by an unseen hand. Then the roots take hold. But will the person be rooted in good or evil soil? Guys like you, O'Brien, are a rare breed, I do believe. If you hadn't got Curtis's letter, if he hadn't gone fishing with you...what then? Nobody has been able to do anything—to prove anything. The whole damn town seems scared. And why's that? Who're they afraid of...a few old men today who coulda been guards in a World War II death camp? Maybe. Maybe there's more."

"Why did you want to see me before your bond is made? It shouldn't take too long to make bond."

"You never know, and because I'm afraid. Not for me, although they might bust me up in here. I figured after fifty years there'd be new generations of good people in this county...in law enforcement. That's why I gave the cops the name of an eyewitness, someone who saw 'em shoot Andy. Thought they might interview him and begin a real investigation. Now I believe I made a bad mistake."

"Did you tell anyone else?"

"I told a news reporter with the local paper, but I didn't tell him his name."

I thought about the reporter in the courthouse hallway who'd snapped my picture standing next to Lana Halley. "Was his name Wallace Holland?"

"No, it was Cory Wilson. Holland is another guy who works there. He seems like he couldn't give a shit if a hundred kids were buried on the property. The other guy, Cory, he's different. After I'd left, he called me, talked in sort of a whisper, like he didn't want anybody to hear him. Said he really wanted to write a story, but didn't have enough to go on, so he wanted me to let him know if I found something else. I think he's a good guy, just not a ball buster kind of reporter. Maybe I'm wrong."

"Did you tell anybody else?"

His eyes opened a little wider, looked over his phone and whispered. "Yeah, I gave his name to the assistant state attorney, the one givin' me shit in the courtroom, Lana Halley."

I said nothing.

Jesse continued. "The eyewitness was just a kid hiding in a tree on the reform school property the night they killed Andy. If I give you his name and address, would you ride out there and tell him to lay low. Maybe stay at his mama's place 'till we can get this sorted out? Maybe he can get into a witness protection deal."

"Write down the information, fold the piece of paper and ask the guard to give it to me. Tell him I represent you."

Jesse stared at me for a moment. I could hear his breathing in the receiver. He nodded. "Got it." There was a small note pad next to Jesse. He picked up a pencil with tooth marks on much of the yellow paint. He wrote down a few lines, folded the paper three times and looked toward the guard. "Sir, would you give this to Mr. O'Brien. He's one of 'em who represents me."

The guard stopped reading a Sports Illustrated magazine, slowly got up and walked across the room to take the piece of paper. He looked at Jesse. "Let's call this a favor, bud."

"Much obliged."

The guard went to the far right of the room, unlocked a door, locking it as he exited into the visitor's area. He handed the paper to me, said nothing, and returned to Jesse where he said, "Time's up, bud."

Jesse looked at me through the glass. "See you when I get outta here." He stood and the acne-faced guard led him away. I placed the folded piece of paper in my pocket and left.

I walked across the parking lot, the Florida sun shimmering off the exteriors of cars parked in the county jail lot, the asphalt searing. I'd left my Jeep under the shade of an oak tree in a far spot of the fenced-in lot. I unlocked the door, opened it, the warm air billowing out. I unfolded the paper Jesse gave me and read his note. **Jeremiah Franklin lives in back of a big pecan grove off Stevenson Road. Right past a sign about pecans for sale. Follow the trail beyond a cattle guard marked no trespassing. His house is an old school bus. Tell him you know me and his old grandpa taught me to fish on the Chipola River. He'll know you talked with me.**

THIRTY- NINE

I'd been on the road less than ten minutes when Dave Collins called. "Sean, the newspaper in Jackson County may not have a large local circulation, but their Internet presence is, of course, with no boundaries. I'd say they got a fairly good angle of you. The lady next to you looks very photogenic."

"Her name's Lana Halley. Assistant SA. She was the prosecutor during the Pablo Gonzales murder trial."

"Ah, yes. I recall her courtroom tenacity." Dave chuckled.

"What'd the reporter write?"

"Enough to fuel rumor mills from the state capital to Marianna and, no doubt, rush the sale of the property into the waiting arms of Vista Properties. The reporter is quoting a security guard at the property as one source. A man who says you told him your representative may be in the market to build a military training facility larger than the old Blackwater operation in North Carolina. Keep in mind, the word facility is derived from the French intonation, meaning toilet. The reporter went on to quote people within the department of law enforcement—the current custodians of the property, who have no official comment about you or their alleged negotiations with you. A real estate agent, Ben Douglas, is quoted as saying you appeared 'sincere' in your interest, but he's not received an offer from you or the person you represent. Perhaps I should call him with a comment or a financial bid based, of course, on contingencies."

"Maybe you can think of a way to stall the public announcement of a Vista Properties sale while I scramble for evidence."

"How's it going?"

I told Dave and then I gave him the tag number I saw on the back of the pickup truck. "The passenger in that truck was the old man with the Southern Cross tattoo. See if you can find an address."

"I can do that. Where are you headed now?"

"I'm en route to Jeremiah Frankin's place. It's an old school bus in a pecan grove. Maybe he'll tell me what he saw. I'm hoping he'll give me the ID of the guy who shot Andy Cope in the back."

"After that, the challenge will be to keep him safe while the wheels of justice turn ever so slowly in the county. You think Lana Halley's leaning on Jesse because someone's leaning on her?"

"She's not the type to succumb to pressure. But all that depends on who's applying it and the circumstances around it."

"With the Internet, these days things like career-killing compromising photos or other such humiliating materials can be pictures with a thousand words leading to two words…you're fired."

"I'd suspect she's more careful than that. Maybe it's something else."

"Maybe it's just the way she does her job, but the issue, based on what you told me, is this: why is she pursuing Jesse so aggressively after he first came to her looking for an open door to a grand jury?"

"Dave, see what you can find on her boss, state attorney Jeff Carson. I briefly met him. He's continuing a strategy, apparently set by the previous state attorney, of ignoring assertions because all this happened in the dark ages and none of it matters today. This is coming after a state investigation into purported abuse, and even after a class action suit was filed by a small group of men who were held there as kids."

"Give me a little time and I'll give you a dossier on his life."

"I'm sure you can. Since I'm driving, a short version will work for now." I could hear Dave's fingers moving across the keyboard in his boat.

After a few seconds, Dave grunted and said, "He's got the old Hollywood definition of movie star looks. Reminds me of the actor John Forsythe. Of course, I'm dating myself. So that's the guy Lana Halley reports to. Looks like Carson graduated from Florida State University with a law degree.

Clerked for Justice Bergman. Carson's worked in three judicial districts in the state, the Second District, his home, is where he became state attorney."

"What other districts did he work?"

"The first, which includes Tallahassee, and the eleventh, Miami-Dade."

"When in Miami-Dade?"

"He was there for three years…looks like he left five years ago. Why?"

"Because, when Lana introduced me to him, she told him that I'd worked homicide in Miami-Dade. You'd think a former prosecutor who worked cases there would have mentioned that coincidence. I never heard of him, and I was there at that time."

"I don't have to tell you it's a big district. Lots of crime. Lots of prosecutors. Maybe your ships never came into the same port. I'll see what I can dig up."

"Dave, I saw him again, a few minutes later in the courthouse. He was sitting in the back of a coffee shop talking with the detective that arrested Jesse Taylor."

"It's not out of the norm that a detective would meet with a state attorney."

"No, but this comes right after Jesse's first appearance. The SA was nowhere to be seen in the courtroom. So why isn't the detective talking with Lana Halley instead of her boss? And why meet in a coffee shop rather than the SA's office?"

"I can't answer that, but I can tell you who that truck is registered to. I just pulled it up. Someone named Loretta Johnson owns the truck. Her physical address is 1352 South Bayou Road…Jackson County."

I thought about Mohawk man getting in the 1950's model yellow Ford pickup truck. I reached in the Jeep's console, lifting out the paper I'd used to jot down the truck's tag number in the parking lot of Shorty's Billiards. I read the number to Dave. "Run this one too. I have a hunch it might be registered to the same person."

I heard Dave tapping the keyboard. "Why's that?"

"They appear to be a tight clan. The patriarch probably had them put their assets, cars, homes, in the name of a trusted family member in the event of trouble."

"Name as in one person?"

"Most likely the matriarch. Probably someone who's survived through the years by a learned helpless dependence."

"Ah...yes...that tag number reveals the following: the truck, a 1957 model Ford pickup is registered in the name of Loretta Johnson...the same address. Bingo. Give me a second, Sean." Dave worked the keyboard, whistling softly. He said, "I've pulled the satellite images of the location. Looks like some kind of compound back in the swamps. Lots of fencing. Some wetland. In the dry area, I'm counting five trailers...something that resembles an old farmhouse, a couple of barn-like structures. I see six pickup trucks and six cars. No neighbors within almost a mile. If you're thinking about going in there to question some of the clan, as you call the lineage, you'd better find some backup."

"I don't have an immediate reason to go in there. But that might change after I speak with the man who, according to Jesse, witnessed Andy Cope's murder."

FORTY

The brake lights were the first thing that caught my eye. The pickup truck, moving slowly forty yards in front of my Jeep, tipped me off to the sign. It was a black truck, gun in the center of a rack visible through the back window. The driver tapped his brakes, red lights on for a few seconds, off and on again. I could see the driver looking toward a locked cattle gate. A man in the passenger side stared through the back window, scrutinizing the entrance to the property and the massive grove of pecan trees. The pickup gained speed, moving on down the country road.

I passed a faded weather-beaten board from an old barn, the sign hanging from the fence by a rusted coat-hanger wire. Hand-written letters in white paint signaled that pecans were for sale a half mile ahead. It was the same sign Jesse had made reference to in the note he'd written. And on the cattle gate was another sign: *No Trespassing*. Who were the guys in the truck and why are they doing a drive-by, checking out the entrance to the property? I decided to pass the gate and turn around in a half-mile or so.

I placed a call to Lana Halley. Her assistant put me on hold long enough to ask Lana if she wanted to take my call. I made a U-turn. The recorded voice on the line was that of state attorney, Jeff Carson, his baritone voice reading the script, telling callers how the crime rate has been reduced in the district since he took office.

Lana picked up. "What's new, Sean? You still holding on to the Miranda card?"

"There's no need to use it. You know that. Jesse was surrounded by a pack of wolves in that bar. If he hadn't pulled a pistol, he'd have wound up in intensive care, assuming he lived."

"You make our little town sound like Dodge City."

I looked in my rearview mirror and saw the pickup truck cresting the horizon. "When Jesse came to you—when he told you about the death of Andy Cope in the mid-sixties, he told you about an eyewitness, a man named Jeremiah Franklin. Did you share that information with anyone?"

"That's really none of your business."

"Lana, right now it's very much my business. I have a couple of good ol' boys coming in my direction. It may be in reference to Jeremiah Franklin. If you shared the information with anyone, I need to know before the next thirty seconds expire."

I heard her exhale into the phone. "What do you mean?"

"What you tell me will help direct my next few moves." The truck came closer, moving through a pulsating shimmer of heat reflecting from the hot pavement.

"I warned you about any vigilante approaches in this county."

"Lana, did you share the eyewitness's name with anyone?" The truck was less than two hundred feet behind me, slowing.

"I'm only talking with you about this because of our symbiotic history together, but not much of what I'd call a professional working relationship."

"Did you share the name with the state attorney?"

"That's confidential." She hung up

Decision time.

I pulled off the road right before the cattle gate, rolled my window down and waited. I reached into the Jeep's console and set my Glock next to my right leg. The driver pulled up parallel with my Jeep, the passenger window down. The man on the passenger side wore a white stained tank top, arm filled with ink, a black onyx earring in the earlobe, his heavy face filled with scraggly reddish whiskers. The guy behind the wheel was a big boy, probably going close to 280 on what appeared to be a large frame. Fur and ink on his forearms. His shaved head almost touched the truck's headliner.

I recognized them from the courtroom, maybe part of the extended family or friends with the Johnsons. The man nearest to me nodded. No smile. His mouth turned down. He glanced toward the pecan grove and then leveled his eyes at me. "You need help, bud? You lost?"

I smiled. "I appreciate you fellas stopping. I'm fine. Just pulled over to return some text messages. You know how unsafe it is to drive and text."

He shook his head. "Nah, I don't. Ain't never text. If I got somethin' to say to a feller, I just find him and say it."

The driver removed what appeared to be a hand-rolled cigarette behind his ear. He lit it with a Zippo lighter, inhaling a lungful of marijuana smoke. He squinted, staring at me, trying to recall where he'd seen me, blowing smoke from his nostrils. He held the joint between two stubby fingers, pointing at me. "You're the dude who stood up in court and said that shit about Miranda crap. Bad move. Real bad move. We know how to handle crap."

I smiled, my hand wrapping around the pistol grip. "Just trying to be a good citizen."

The driver turned a little behind the wheel. He wedged the joint in the corner of his mouth, left hand on the steering wheel, his right hand propped on his seat near the headrest—closer to the shotgun. "First, we see your ass in court and now out here. Why you out here?"

"Last time I checked a passport wasn't required."

His hand moved a little closer to the shotgun. The passenger grinned and said, "You got a mouth on you. I could tell it from the courthouse, and I damn sure see it now. We can see from your tag that you're far from home. Volusia County is at least a five-hour drive from here. Now would be a real good time for you to go on back to whatever shit hole you crawled out from."

"I hear there's a lot of history in Jackson County, back to the Civil War and even the Spanish Conquistadors. I'm very interested in local history. So I think I'll stick around to learn more about the past. I'm sure you fellas can appreciate that."

The driver's right hand was on the stock of the shotgun. He tossed the joint out the window, bouncing off the side of my Jeep. The man on the passenger's side said, "Nah, we don't have much interest in history 'cause it's all in the past. Cain't change nothin' about it. We believe in changin' the future."

I nodded, looking past the passenger and toward the driver. "You tossed a hot marijuana cigarette out. That's the way to start fires. Most folks are a little more careful."

He grinned. Chuckled. "Earl, go smother the smoke."

"Sure, brother."

He opened the door, stepping out. I knew what was about to happen. As soon as the passenger had cleared the trajectory, the driver was going to lift the shotgun. Maybe it would be a warning. Maybe he'd pull the trigger. I wasn't going to find out. I moved the Glock to my left hand, holding it out of their line of sight.

The passenger closed the truck door, looking at me a second before searching the ground. He picked up the smoldering joint, taking a hit off of it. He stepped closer to my open window, turning to his friend. "No use wastin' good shit, big brother."

He turned back to me, tossing the joint in my face. The hot ash hit me above my left eye. I didn't give him time to pull his hand back. I grabbed his arm, keeping him in the line of sight. Blocking a potential shot from the driver. I slammed his elbow on the edge of the door, crashing my upper body weight into his wrist. The sound was as if an egg was dropped on a tile floor. The bone snapped completely through at the wrist. The man's hand flopping like a fish out of water.

He screamed, turning around. "Shoot the motherfucker!"

The driver tried to aim the shotgun. I grabbed the man with the broken wrist, my left hand gripping his thick neck. I held the Glock next to his round head, pointing the pistol at the driver's chest. "Drop the shotgun! Now!"

He stared down his barrel at me, his brother's head directly in the line of fire. I could see the guy in my grip turning pale. His head jerked back then forward, vomiting down his chest.

I stared at the driver and said, "He's going into shock. It'd be a good idea to get him to a hospital. Once shock sets in, he just got a little closer to his date in hell. Put the shotgun down!" The opening at the bore was wide—a 12-gauge. Double barrel.

He set the gun back in the rack, sliding across the seat. He came out the door and helped his brother into the passenger side of the truck. Then he slammed the door and ran around to the driver's side, climbing back inside the truck. He looked over his brother to me, the brother's head propped up against the headrest, his face bone white. The driver shouted, "Asshole, you broke my brother's arm! You're a fuckin' dead man!"

"And you're on video." I lifted my phone. "Got everything you said and did right here. The 4G quality of video in these phones is amazing. So if you try to file charges, it won't fly."

He lifted the middle finger on his right hand and started the truck. The sunlight shining through the front windshield cast the gun in the back window into a silhouette. Two triggers. He pulled away, peeling rubber, the truck fishtailing and gaining speed. When someone pulls a gun on me, especially a 12-gauge shotgun, time slows into slices of still life because violent death is imminent. The brain processes surroundings so fast they're seen in images of still life. I imagine for a suicide jumper, it's the freeze-frame views between the bridge and the river—the graffiti on a girder, a bird flying at the same altitude, sun reflecting off the water.

I replayed the scene when the driver grabbed the shotgun, leveling the double barrel out the truck window. I saw his stubby finger on one trigger. The way he disengaged the safety. Bloodshot eyes staring down the two barrels. Dirty Band-Aid on the left index finger. The sight at the end of the twin barrels—the white bead, a glowing marble perched between two dark, empty eyes of steel. I could tell the shotgun was a vintage model, one I recognized. I believed it was made by the A.H. Fox Company. I reached in my console and lifted up the Ziploc bag with the piece of buckshot. I thought about digging the shot out of the old oak. *Had I found the original shotgun?* To answer that, I'd have to go get it.

FORTY-ONE

I needed to hide my Jeep. I didn't believe the brothers Grimm would be heading back soon. But on the way to the hospital to set the man's fractured wrist, they would calling kinfolks. Maybe a convoy would be in the vicinity like a swarm of hornets. Maybe no one would show up, but I wasn't going to take any chances.

I drove my Jeep down a short dirt trail, parking behind a thicket of trees. I locked the doors, shoving the Glock in the small of my back under my shirttail. I sprinted across the road, climbed the cattle gate, ignoring the sign: *No Trespassing.* I had to find an old school bus somewhere in a pecan grove, and I didn't have a lot of time to look for it.

The air had the musty smell of broken pecan shells and wood smoke from somewhere in the distant fields. I walked down a sandy trail, stopping to look at tire tracks. They were wide. Truck tires. I wondered if Jeremiah Franklin drove a truck. More than that, I wondered how he'd react to me, considering the circumstances. As a homicide detective, I'd interviewed a lot of witnesses. But I'd never spoken to a witness who'd seen a murder as a child and buried it inside for fifty years.

Maybe, somehow he might talk to me, or he might confirm what I was suspecting. I had no illusions, but I had to find him. If nothing else, I had to warn him. The fact that the brothers had slowed down driving by the property indicated that someone had tipped them off. Was it the state attorney, Lana Halley, or the detective—or any number of people connected to them? Who had the most to lose? Who had the most to gain? And who was in bed with whom? To lift the sheets, I needed to raise the stakes.

A gust of wind blew through the pecan trees. I could hear some pecans falling, bouncing off branches, the soft *thud* as they hit the sandy soil. Something moved. In the distance, moving between the trees, there were shadows. I slipped my Glock out and stood near the base of a tree, waiting. Three large sand hill cranes came into view. One crane lifted its feathered head, opened its bill and called out. Behind the echoes of its call, somewhere in the distance, I heard a hound barking. I shoved my pistol back under my belt and followed the trail.

I walked for at least a quarter mile before I spotted a patch of yellow through the rows of trees. It was an incongruous color in a grove of brown bark and green leaves. I walked closer and an old school bus came into view. It was near the end of the grove, anchored close to what appear to be a creek. The area around the bus was landscaped. Azaleas blooming. Potted ferns growing adjacent to the front and back of the school bus. Red roses grew from dark earth in a small area bordered with decorative railroad crossties. Wind chimes hung from the bracket that supported the bus's large exterior mirror.

When I came to within thirty feet of the bus, I stopped. I kept my Glock hidden, hoping there'd be no reason to display it. I could see no indication of movement. The bus door was closed. No car. No truck. No sign Jeremiah Franklin was home. I heard a hawk call out from a pine tree near the property. I shouted, "Jeremiah...are you here?"

Nothing. The red-tailed hawk flew from the tree and a warm breeze blew through the pecan grove, the wind chimes jingling. I lifted the handwritten note from my pocket. I raised my voice. "This was written by Jesse Taylor. He asked me to come here today. In the note he says to let you know that he told me you and your grandpa taught him to fish on the Chipola River."

Nothing. The wind was still. Chimes silent. A honeybee darted in the rose blossoms.

"Why you here?"

The question came from behind me. I didn't know if Jeremiah Franklin was pointing a gun at my back. I lifted my hands and slowly turned to face him. He was a big man. Skin matching the dark color of creosote in the railroad crossties. He held a pitchfork in both large hands. His bib overalls were stained from dirt and field sweat. He wore work boots, the laces made from twine. Perspiration glistened from his chest.

I nodded. "I'm here because of something Jesse said. I'm just a messenger."

He used one hand to thrust the pitchfork into the ground. "What do you mean messenger? What's your name? I ain't never seen you in town."

"My name's Sean O'Brien. I'm from the east side of the state, near Daytona. I'm here because a man who was held in the old reform school, about the time you and Jesse were there, hired me to investigate the murder of Andy Cope." I stopped. Watched his reaction. When I'd mentioned Andy's name, Jeremiah's eyes opened a little more. His right hand gripped the pitchfork's wooden handle. "Unfortunately, my client, Curtis Garwood, was suffering from terminal cancer. He took his own life. And his dying wish was that Andy's killer or killers be brought to justice. I'm hoping what you can tell me will do just that."

He crossed his large arms across his chest. "Nobody's done nothin' all these years, and now on account of a dying man's wish, people be comin' out of the woodwork to see what happened to Andy."

"What people?"

"You and Jesse. After fifty years, that's a crowd, man. Look, I won't ya'll to leave me alone. Andy was just one. Lots of kids never walked outta there. My brother was one of 'em. The difference is I'm alive. And I'd like to keep it that way. Ain't a damn thing gonna change."

"Change begins with you. It begins with anyone who's witnessed someone being hurt or killed. Otherwise they got away with it, and the next generation has a license to repeat it."

"I tol' Jesse I'd call him if I had somethin' to say. But now he sends you."

"He's in jail or he would have come."

"Why's he locked up?"

"Because he shot his pistol in a bar to keep the dogs off him. Jesse will make bond. The charges will probably be greatly reduced. Jesse wasn't read his rights."

"Who'd testify to that? Sounds like somethin' the police can cover up."

"I'll testify. I was there."

He angled his head, as if he was seeing me for the first time, the sun breaking through a pecan tree behind him. He grinned. "You definitely ain't from 'round these parts. I tol' Jesse I'd let him know if I had sometin' to say about Andy's killin,' and right now I don't. My mama wants my brother Eli's body to be laid to rest in a proper burial. But finding him on that school property ain't likely. I got work to do. Unless you got somethin' more to say…"

"Jeremiah, I have to share something with you. You need to be on guard."

"What'd you mean?"

"Jesse made a mistake—an honest mistake. Thinking the prosecutor's office would convene a grand jury, he told them you might be in a position to reveal the killer's identity. He went to detectives, too, trying to get you in a witness protection program—"

He stared at me, stunned. "Jesse might as well have put a bomb under my house."

"Here's how you can take the fuse out of it. If there are kids buried on the school property, the FBI will get involved. You need to tell your story to the FBI. I can make that happen. Once the killer is arrested, a lot of the heat's gone. It'll be all over the news media. When you're that visible, it's less likely someone will come for you because of the much greater police, prosecutorial, and media muscle surrounding you and the case."

He sighed, looked down at his scuffed boots and then raised his eyes to mine. "A trial could be a long time comin'. That'll give 'em more time to take me out. I'm going to my mama's place tonight. She made pork roast and pecan pie. When Jesse's out of jail, tell him to call me. Only Jesse. Nobody else. You think the FBI's got someplace they can let me stay?"

"Depends on what you tell them."

"I got a lot to say, and to be honest wit' you, I'm tired of holding it. When I was up in Michigan pickin' apples last year, I saw somethin' bad. Real bad. A Mexican, a younger fella, we became friends. His name was Carlos Valdez. Had a wife and baby girl in Texas. He was a fast picker, but he'd never pick on Sunday. He was Catholic, and he'd always say *El Domingo es de Dios*...it means Sunday is God's day. We stayed in a rundown old motel outside of Muskegon. One rainy night, Carlos had just come back from some Mexican joint with tacos. We were gonna eat 'em in the room, watch some football on TV, and split a six-pack. I heard the shots in the parking lot. Later, the cops would say it was a case of mistaken identity. I looked out the blinds and saw Carlos lyin' on his back. A guy in a hoodie jumped in a Toyota and took off. I opened the door and ran to Carlos."

Jeremiah paused and licked his dry lips. "He'd been shot in the chest and neck. The night manager had called 9-1-1. Carlos asked me to pray for him. I couldn't remember how to pray, man. I tried to remember the Lord's Prayer. Carlos whispered something. It was first Peter...one...twenty-five. All I could do was hold his head to stop some of the bleeding. But he died as the ambulance was pullin' into the lot. I couldn't sleep the rest of the night...couldn't shower long enough. I sat there in the dark in that motel room. Drank all the beer. About four in the mornin' I lifted the Bible off the nightstand and looked up what Carlos had referred to. It says all people are like grass. Their glory is like the flowers in the field. The grass dies and the flowers fall, but the word of God stands forever. I gotta remember that now more than ever."

I nodded. "When I came out here to speak with you, a couple of roughnecks were casing the entrance to the property. They abruptly left. But they'll be back."

"Did you say somethin' to 'em?"

"I did. But it's a temporary fix. When you visit your mother's house, you might want to stay there until law enforcement can get these guys off the street."

"With all respect, Mr. O'Brien, you might not be who you say you are. I know Jesse. At least I know we came from the same cut in life. If I tell him who did it, if anything happens to me, I don't take it to my grave. Tell Jesse to call me. The sooner the better."

FORTY-TWO

Jesse Taylor followed the guard through the jail's labyrinth, walking down a long corridor, the chants and yells from prisoners reverberating through the bars. The guard, a stoop-shouldered man with a jowly pink face, pointed to a small room. "Lose the orange in there. Your clothes are in this paper bag. You can pick up the other stuff you came in with at the desk."

Jesse nodded, took the paper sack and entered a small, windowless room that smelled of bleach. He put on his jeans, shirt and boots and then followed the guard to the inmate release area—a lobby that had hard plastic chairs and a middle-aged female corrections officer behind a thick glass window. Jesse thought it looked like a place you'd buy movie tickets. He said, "Name's Jesse Taylor. Bondsman's come and gone. It's my turn."

She looked through the glass, expressionless, and said, "I'll get your stuff. You gotta sign for it." She pushed a manila envelope under the slot in the glass.

Jesse opened the envelope, removed his wallet, looking through it. Satisfied, he slipped his watch on his wrist and glanced at his phone screen. "Two calls. Looks like somebody missed me." He signed a slip of paper attached to a clipboard. "It's all here." Then he turned around and walked out the entrance to the county jail, stopping in the parking lot, closing his eyes, tilting his head toward the sky, and bathing in the warm sunlight. He lit a cigarette, walking to the shade of mimosa tree.

He played the first missed call. "Hey, Jesse, it's Harold. I'm calling you from the same booth we sat in just a few days ago when you hit town. Old buddy, you've come in here like a tornado. I heard you made bond for that shootin' at Shorty's. Caroline Harper must really believe in you. A security guard pal of mine says Wayne Johnson brought his brother in to be treated at the county hospital. My friend said Johnson was in a bad damn fight. He had his arm broken in two pieces. Did you hire somebody to do that? Jesse, they're gonna find you burned to death in your car if you don't let up. You're messin' with some mean sons-a-bitches. Call me, okay?"

He played the second message. "Jesse, it's Caroline. Call me as soon as you get this message. I'm hoping you've bonded out by now. I just spoke with Sean O'Brien. He wants you to call him. It's something about the eye-witness to Andy's killing. It's 2:30 now. Meet me at the Alpine Inn for coffee. Thanks, bye."

Jesse slipped his phone into his pocket and walked toward the main entrance to the county jail. He recognized someone coming out the door. It was Ace Anders, the man Jesse had met at Shorty's Billiards. Jesse grinned and said, "Hey, Ace…look, I didn't get a chance to thank you for covering my back the other night. Anyway, thanks."

Ace nodded, looked at Jesse and glanced around the parking lot. "I'm sure you'd do the same for me. It's not something you leave behind at Ranger school. You carry it for life."

"I was hopin' they'd give you a break and cut you loose."

"Cooter Johnson, or his family, filed a trumped up charge of assault and battery. If I'd actually assaulted that freak, he'd be in a cast." He looked over Jesse's shoulder, eyes scouting the lot and the people coming and going from the county jail building. "Look, Jesse, I'm not sure what's happening. Yes, we got into a bar fight with Cooter and his posse, but it's not like we robbed a bank."

"What do you mean?"

"They're trying to say your threatening Cooter with the pistol and firing a live round was more than it appeared, as in assault with a deadly weapon. That can get you fifteen years in prison. That's bullshit. The prosecutor, the woman with the great ass, she might drop charges against me if I'd testify against you. I told 'em I don't negotiate with extremists." Ace smiled. "Something's going on. I gotta believe it's connected to that stuff you said to Cooter in the bar—the stuff about his grandfather being a pervert and shit that happened at the old reform school. Man, you touched a fuckin' nerve. But why would the prosecutor want to dump on you? The Johnson family is pretty much all criminals, especially Cooter's father, Solomon Johnson. And the DA's office knows that. So what the hell's goin' on?"

"It isn't about them. It's about the sale of all that land. If shit starts hitting the fan, if we find a bunch of bodies…kids buried there…it's against the law to build on top of a cemetery."

"You think there are bodies, graves hidden up there."

"Yeah, yeah I do. And I'm gonna find them."

"You think all this makes a full circle back to Cooter Johnson's grandfather?"

"He was there when I was locked up as a kid. The boys called him Preacher. He quoted from the Bible, but he wasn't preaching from the Bible. He was preaching from a damn dark place. It was complete evil—the look in his eyes when he'd sling the belt. It's like he loved the smell of blood. Loved to hear kids cry. It made him beat you harder, 'til there was no crying left, because at that point you were dying. He was preaching from the devil's pulpit. I can't imagine how many lives he destroyed. That kind of psychological abuse gets handed down, father to son, to whoever lights their short fuses."

"He's gotten away with it all these years. What's gonna change that?"

"Because somebody saw him. The witness saw three men who gunned down a boy named Andy Cope."

"What witness? What's his name?"

"I'd rather not say right now."

Ace nodded. "All right then…why didn't the witness say something?"

"Because he was afraid they'd hang him. He's still scared. But I think that's about to change. Ace can you give me a ride back to my car? It's at the motel where I'm staying."

"Sure, but let's take the back roads. I got a strange feeling that we're being watched."

FORTY-THREE

The man's profile was like an image from a dream. No identity, but it was there—under the surface of memory. It floated there. Vaporous. Just out of bounds for reach and clarity. With the exception of Caroline Harper and Lana Halley, I didn't know anyone who lived in Marianna or Jackson County. So why did one of the men in the car next to my Jeep at an intersection look like someone I knew? Maybe the car wasn't from here. Maybe the guy in the back seat wasn't. I had just a few seconds before the traffic light changed. *Who was he?* And why did I somehow feel his identity was important?

I could only catch his profile. Sitting in the rear seat on the right side of the black Mercedes S-Class sedan. Silver hair, neatly parted. Custom suit. Designer shirt. I tried to read the monogram on the cuff, near the gold cufflinks. Too far away. He held a phone in his right hand, talking. He was alone in the backseat. A younger man sat on the passenger side, front seat. Dark glasses. Dark suit. The driver looked Hispanic, dressed in a polo shirt.

The light turned green, and I looked again as the Mercedes pulled away. I memorized the tag number. The car was registered in Dade County, Florida, the county seat for Miami, a place I'd spent more than a decade in law enforcement. I drove behind the car for a block, heading toward the Alpine Inn where I'd meet Caroline Harper and Jesse Taylor. My plan was to let Jesse know that Jeremiah Franklin was ready to talk—to probably name the killer, but he was justifiably afraid of possible repercussions. When Jesse met with Jeremiah, I wanted to be there. Not necessarily physical as in the same location, but somewhere within visual contact. I didn't want them out of my sight. Maybe I was being overly cautious. I didn't think so.

I picked up my phone to call Dave. I wanted him to run the numbers on the license plate. I wanted to know who was riding in the back seat of a chauffer-driven Mercedes and why he was in Marianna, Florida. I remembered the photo attachment Dave had sent—the picture of the man Dave said was the head of Vista Properties, whose subsidiary is Horizon Inc., the multinational corporation with plans to build a country club development to be called Chattahoochee Estates.

It's funny how memory is like a card in a deck. Not always in sequence. But when the luck of the draw puts a picture card in your hand, how will you play it? What risks will you take? Do you fold or stay in the game? I punched up the image on my phone. And there he was, staring at me from the screen. Was the same man in the back seat of the Mercedes?

The way to find out was to come knocking. The driver stopped at the next light. Traffic was picking up, and we were still in a four-lane intersection. I pulled up beside the long black car, windows slightly tinted. I tapped the Jeep's horn and motioned for the man in the back seat to roll down his window. He ignored me. The guy in the front seat didn't. He pressed a button and the window slid about half way down.

I smiled and asked, "Excuse me, I'm a little lost. I'm looking for I-10. Do you know if we're close to the highway?"

The guy behind the dark glasses turned his head and spoke with the driver for a few seconds. It gave me time to look behind him, behind his headrest to catch a partial glimpse of the man in the back seat. *Bingo.* If he wasn't same face in the picture, then they were twins. Sunglasses turned his head back toward me. He said, "About a half mile on the right. You'll see the sign leading to the highway."

"Thank you."

He nodded, non-smiling, the window sliding back up, the men returning to the cocoon of tinted glass, cool air, leather seats, imported wood, satellite phones, and thick-carpeted floorboards. The Mercedes moved on, and I stayed back letting the big car gain distance. Was the CEO of Vista Properties in Marianna to close the deal? Had the deal been closed? Who was he meeting with, or whom had he already met?

I drove slowly, staying well behind the Mercedes. I looked at the data Dave had sent, and then I punched the phone number to Vista Properties. A woman with a slight Hispanic accent said, "Horizon International."

"James Winston, please."

"My pleasure." She made the transfer. I listened to soft jazz playing through my phone. Less than thirty seconds later, another woman picked up. "Boardroom, this is Rhonda, may I help you?"

"Yes, hi Rhonda, this is William Brackston, with the Jackson County Planning Committee way up in Marianna. How are you?"

"Fine, thank you."

"I had a scribbled note, left by my secretary, she was in a hurry to make a doctor's appointment, it's her first baby. Anyway, it looks like James Winston may or may not be meeting with the committee while he's in Marianna. Is a planning committee meeting on his agenda this time?"

"Hold just a minute, Mr. Brackston, I'll pull up his schedule."

"No hurry." I could hear her fingernails tapping the keyboard.

"It looks like Mr. Winston is meeting with the county manager, some people with a real estate firm, and a one o'clock appointment. His schedule doesn't indicate all the names of those with whom he's meeting."

"Maybe it's me. Maybe not." I chuckled.

"I can contact his assistant to find out for you."

"That's not necessary. I have a one o'clock at the courthouse. Is that, by chance, his one o'clock too?"

"No, Mr. Winston's one o'clock is a luncheon at the Jackson Country Club."

"I'd rather be there than at the courthouse. Maybe next visit. Thank you, Rhonda." I disconnected, looked at my phone and keyed in driving directions to the Jackson County Club."

FORTY-FOUR

Jesse Taylor sipped from a cup of coffee, glancing at the front door to the coffee shop, the caffeine entering his bloodstream. He looked across the small wooden table to Caroline Harper and said, "I hope O'Brien shows up."

Caroline smiled. "He will. He's like you, Jesse. He's a good man. Dedicated to doing what's right."

Jesse grinned. "I don't know how good of a man I've been. I'm tryin' to make amends, to make up for time I pissed away, hustling, drifting from job to job. Thanks, again, for makin' my bail."

"Sean told me he thinks the charges will be dropped because they didn't read your rights to you. He'll testify to that. Plus, you have the witness, the other gentleman who helped keep them off of you."

"Ace, the guy you're talking about, has to get through this kangaroo court, too. He refused the prosecutor's offer to drop charges if he'd testify against me." Jesse's phone rang. He didn't recognize the number. He let it ring.

Caroline said, "You can go on and answer it."

"Don't know whose callin' me. I don't answer if I don't know who's knockin' on my door. It'll go to voice-mail, and if it's important, they'll leave a message."

"Maybe it's Sean calling you."

"I programmed his number. It's not him." There was a soft *bong*. Jesse said, "Let's see who's my anonymous caller." He pressed the message button, the caller's soft voice on speakerphone. "Jesse…this is Sonia Acker. I met you that day in the sheriff's office. You were talkin' to the police, the detective. I'm Jeremiah Franklin's niece. I was over at my granny's house last night. Uncle Jeremiah was there, too. Something happened. I need to show you. Call me back, okay. And please hurry."

Caroline looked up at Jesse. "You'd better call that girl. She doesn't sound good."

Jesse nodded and hit the return call button. "Sonia, it's Jesse."

"I need to see you."

"Sure, what's it about?"

"I'll show you when I see you. Where you at?"

"Ruby's Coffee Shop."

"Is that next door to the flower store?"

"Yeah."

"I'll be there in ten minutes."

"Is Jeremiah okay?"

"For now he is. That's what I want to talk to you about."

— ● ━

The Jackson Country Club smelled of old money. I drove through a stately ivy-trimmed, brick entranceway; flickering yellow flames in the center of nineteenth century coach lamps were perched atop the brick pillars. A sprawling golf course was to my left, tennis courts and a massive swimming pool to my right in the distance. The clubhouse beyond the pool and tennis courts was Old World brick, French chateau styling and pitched roofs. Camellias blossomed in fist-sized white blooms. Azaleas popped in flowers of pink and blood red. The scent of the flora mixed with the smells of fresh cut grass and wealth.

The golf pro shop was to the left near the end of the big circular drive. Two men in their fifties, smoking cigars, stood next to a new Cadillac, trunk open, a teenager in shorts and a polo shirt, nametag pinned to his shirt, unloaded golf clubs from the men's car. Another tall, skinny kid in his late teens, red-faced and perspiring, ran to fetch a golf cart as two other men waited.

Fifty yards to the right was the main clubhouse. Ancient live oaks draped in Spanish moss stood on both ends of the massive structure. The verdant St. Augustine grass, much of it cast in deep shade from the oaks, resembled a thick, green carpet bordered with azaleas and yellow and white impatiens.

I spotted the Mercedes moving through the parking lot, which was peppered with a few dozen luxury cars and upscale SUV's. The driver in the Mercedes tapped his brakes, lights flashing on as he pulled up near the front entrance. The driver smiled, waving away the valet guy who trotted up to the car. The driver parked close to the grand chateau. I parked between a Jaguar and an Audi, turned the Jeep's engine off and watched.

James Winston and the man in the front seat of the Mercedes got out, Winston glancing at the gold watch on his wrist. The driver stayed in the car, windows down, and sunglasses on. From somewhere in the cavernous shadows of the Porte-cochere, came a man I recognized. He stepped into the sunlight and grinned, shaking the hands of his newly arrived guests. He wore a light gray suit, deep red tie.

State Attorney, Jeff Carson, slapped James Winston on the back and led his party into the affluent and insular sanctity of the members-only fortress. I remembered what Jesse had told me about one of the reporters at the local newspaper, Cory Wilson. *'He said he really wanted to write a story, but didn't have enough to go on, so he wanted me to let him know if I found something else.'* Maybe I'd just discovered the something else. I called the number to the newspaper and asked to speak with Cory Wilson. When he answered I said, "You told Jesse Taylor you wanted to write a story about the corruption and political graft going on surrounding the sale of the old reform school property, but you didn't have enough to go on. You might now."

"Who's this?"

"That's not important. What's important is the CEO of Horizon Properties, James Winston, is having a private meeting with the state attorney, Jeff Carson. They're at the Jackson Country Club. And, if you leave now, they'll probably be having dessert when you get here."

I disconnected.

— —

Sonia Acker entered Ruby's Coffee Shop, hesitated at the front door, spotted Jesse and Caroline at a back table and walked towards them. Jesse looked up and smiled. He watched her approach, wondering what she was carrying in the paper grocery sack. She stepped up to the table and Jesse said, "Good to see you, Sonia. This is Caroline Harper. It was her brother, Andy Cope, who got shot in the reform school that night. Your uncle, Jeremiah, saw who did it. Please, sit down. You want some coffee, somethin' to eat?"

"No thank you. I can't be stayin' long."

Jesse smiled. "Your eye sure looks better than the last time I saw you."

She was embarrassed, self-consciously touching her eyebrow with two fingers. She looked over her shoulders, glancing around the coffee shop. "What I want to show you is in this bag. My Uncle Jeremiah cut it down early this morning when he saw it hangin' from a cottonwood tree in the middle of granny's front yard." She reached in the bag and retrieved a short piece of quarter-inch rope. The rope had been fastened into a hangman's noose. She set the noose down in the middle of the table.

Caroline sat straighter. "Dear God. This is inexcusable."

Jesse said, "It's got to be one of those assholes in the Johnson family."

Sonia moistened her dry lower lip. She said, "But why now? My uncle ain't never said who done it. He tol' my grandma last night that you'd visited wit' him, and your friend, a tall man, was there. But Uncle Jeremiah said he didn't tell ya'll who was responsible for the boy's death. So why would somebody hang this from my grandma's tree?"

Jesse blew out a long breath. "It's on account of me."

"You? If you don't know who did it, you can't tell anybody."

"And that's why the noose was there. Somebody related to the killer obviously wants the secret to remain a secret. I was stupid in telling the prosecutor and detectives that Jeremiah knew who did it, thinking they'd talk with him and arrest or file charges against the people responsible, assuming some are still living. Apparently, some are still kicking or this never would have happened."

"What you gonna do now? What's my uncle gonna do now? He doesn't want to move away the rest of his life. He's gettin' older. And he's not travelin' too far away no more to pick. And his mama is old. She needs him."

Caroline reached out and touched the young woman's arm. "Sonia, I'm so sorry that some racist did this. Maybe you should report it to the police. At least they'll have a record of it. Maybe there's some DNA there in the knot of the rope. Something physical they'd have to go on."

"With all due respect, Miss Harper, you know they won't do anything. That's the way it is. In some ways, the area has changed a lot for the better. In other ways, it's the same as it was a long time ago."

Jesse stared at the noose and lifted his eyes up to Sonia. "I need to talk with Jeremiah."

"I doubt he got nothin' more to say."

"I couldn't blame him. I need to make it up to Jeremiah, to take the heat off him. If I know who did it...I can go after them, or they can come after me. At this point, I don't much care."

FORTY-FIVE

On the way into town from the country club, I thought about Lana Halley. Not Lana Halley of late, but rather the fearless prosecutor I'd witnessed in the Pablo Gonzalez murder trial. Her tenacity and courtroom savvy was only topped by her adamant judicial moral code. For her, especially in a case as black and white as the Gonzalez trial, there was no gray area. No room for compromise. No pleading to lesser charges. She was textbook. Beyond concession or reproach.

Then why was she willing to drop charges against Ace Anders to nail Jesse Taylor? Maybe what I'd just witnessed at the country club was part of the answer. Maybe Lana had succumbed to at least one of the seven deadly sins. Greed. Was she so power-hungry she would compromise her integrity to get Jeff Carson's job should he be tapped to become the next U.S. Attorney General? And that's assuming Governor Burnett would come out on top in the primaries and go on to win the presidential election.

I needed to talk to her. Not on the phone. Away from her office. Somewhere private. Someplace I could get an accurate reading as to what was or wasn't motivating her. Before that, I had to meet with Jesse and Caroline. I called Jesse's number en route to the Alpine Inn. No answer. Voice-mail. I disconnected and called Caroline. She said, "Sean, where are you?"

I never like conversations opening like that. "I'm headed your way."

"Jesse's gone."

"What do you mean by gone?"

174

"I believe he's gone to find Jeremiah Franklin. Jeremiah's niece was just here. She brought something in a paper bag that was frightening. And she left it here."

"I'm almost there. Stay at the coffee shop, and I'll meet you in a minute."

I was doing fifty-seven miles-per-hour in a fifty-five stretch of county road. I wanted to push the Jeep beyond the speed limit, but I didn't want to take a chance. I had no doubt that the brothers Grimm had called family members and connections within the justice system. Since I'd captured their aggression and language on camera, it wasn't my word against theirs. I doubted charges had been filed.

When I hit the Marianna city limits, I got an insight—a feeling that I often sensed when something ominous was just beyond my peripheral vision. Beyond the blind spots and tucked in dark corners. I slowed to a speed below the posted limit. I checked all three mirrors. There was nothing but sporadic traffic. A minivan with a mother and two children coming in my direction. A semi-truck slowing at a traffic light, the driver on his cell phone, trying to spot landmarks. A beer distributing truck behind me.

And then, like a yellow canary in the wind, a flash of color came up quickly behind the delivery truck. When I checked my side-view mirrors a second time, the yellow was not visible. I assumed it was the 1950's model pickup and the driver was following close behind the beer truck. When the distributing truck changed lanes for a left-hand turn, the yellow pickup was about ten car lengths behind me. I could see the Mohawk haircut, saw Cooter Johnson adverting his head from my immediate direction.

Another person sat in the front seat. I recognized him, too. He was the man with the beard, the guy who held court with his clan outside the courthouse when Jesse was sent to jail. And now his beard was gone, his face hard as stone. And he was the same man who'd debriefed the old man who'd remained in the car while the family attended Jesse's hearing.

Cooter Johnson quickly turned into the lane the beer distributing truck had followed. I turned right at the traffic light and stayed within the speed limit, driving toward the coffee shop. I parked in front of the shop's main window so I could have a view of my Jeep. And I sat there, listening to the ticking engine cooling, the sound of church bells in the distance. I watched all three mirrors. There was no sign of the yellow truck. I shoved my Glock under my belt in the center of my back and got out of the Jeep.

Caroline Harper tried to smile, waiting for me at one of the nine tables in the shop. The smell of fresh ground coffee met me at the door. The place was quaint—hardwood floors decades old that groaned under my shoes, coffee themed prints on the wall, and dozens of ceramic cups for sale on the shelves. Two college kids were sitting at the same table, laptops open, earbuds wedged into their hearing canals. A middle-aged woman, a barista—maybe Ruby, worked the counter, cutting an apple pie while waiting for a cappuccino to finish pouring from the machine.

I took a seat next to Caroline with a view out the window of my Jeep. "I wish I could have been here earlier, but I had to follow a lead that happened as I was driving. What did Jeremiah Franklin's niece show you?"

Caroline leaned closer, her body language stiff, tense. "It's here, in a paper bag. She was going to throw it in the trash." She reached under the table and lifted a grocery bag. "It's a noose fashioned from a small rope."

"You mean a hangman's noose?" I took the bag and peered inside.

"Somebody hung it during the night from a cottonwood tree in her grandmother's yard. Her Uncle Jeremiah was in the house at the time. He cut it from the tree when he saw it this morning. I have no idea where he is now, not after this."

"Maybe he's still at his mother's home. Do you have the address?"

"No, but I can find it for you. I'm afraid for Jesse. And what Mr. Franklin and his family were exposed to…it's unthinkable. We told Sonia to go to the police, but she feels that'll do nothing. She may be right. But I have to believe there are good and decent law enforcement people in the city and county."

I thought back to the night at Shorty's Billiards when one of the deputies told Detective Lee that maybe the Miranda rights weren't read to Jesse. *"Detective Lee, sir, I think he's correct—"*

"Shut up, Parker! When and if you become a detective, your opinion matters."

"Caroline, the night Jesse was arrested at Shorty's, I watched a deputy, his name was Parker—he questioned a detective when Jesse was arrested. This deputy told the detective that the Miranda rights were never read. I believe Parker will do an honest investigation."

"What can we do?"

"I'll call him." I used my phone to find the number to the sheriff's office and hit dial.

A female dispatcher answered the phone. I asked, "Is Deputy Parker in today."

"Hold on." She was gone for a few seconds. "He's on a call. Can I take a message?"

"Yes, please have him call Sean O'Brien. It's in reference to some evidence he's looking for." I gave her my number and disconnected.

Caroline said, "I hope he's fair. You think he'll call you?"

"I think so."

"Maybe he'll investigate. Sean, Jesse was so upset when he left here. He feels guilty and wants to do what's right, to make up for his mistake to Jeremiah. He said if he knows who murdered Andy, that knowledge will take some of the threat off of Jeremiah."

"In the eyes of the law it means nothing. All that counts is the person who actually witnessed the killing. And that was one man, Jeremiah Franklin."

"I don't believe Jesse was thinking about that. He's pretty discouraged about the law. I believe he wants the killer's name for one reason, and that reason is to personally go after him."

"That would be suicide or the death penalty. Either way, the outcome is the same."

"I don't think Jesse cares anymore—at least not about himself or his problems. And that's because, for the first time in a long time, he has something bigger to care about: justice for Andy and the rest of the boys."

"Maybe I can find Jesse and Jeremiah. If I'm lucky, they'll be in the same place, and then I can speak with them both. We have to come up with a game plan. And part of that has to include a prosecutor that cares deeply about justice." Something caught my eye. Outside the window, standing near my Jeep, was a man dressed in a jungle-green camouflaged shirt, matching baseball cap, jeans. He looked directly toward the window of the coffee shop. He held up a key and stepped to the side of my Jeep, face hard as stone. I looked at Caroline and said, "Outside—the man next to my Jeep. Do you know him?"

Her eyes widened. Eyebrows lifting. "That's Solomon Johnson… Cooter's father. He has two other sons. Although I don't personally know him, I've heard he's a man born without a soul."

FORTY-SIX

It was bait. Pure and simple. *Come out into the daylight and let's see what happens.* Solomon Johnson, sporting an attitude along with his hunter's camouflage, stood next to my Jeep with a key in his hand. He was a man ready to cut a scar into the Jeep's exterior paint. I didn't think he'd do it in the light of day, in public, in front of a downtown coffee shop.

So what was his game? Why'd he want me to step outside?

What I didn't know was who might be standing on either side of the shop's front door. Or who might be on a rooftop with a rifle, scope, and the skill to send a bullet through my head from a block away. I looked over to the woman grinding a pound of coffee and asked, "Do you have a backdoor?"

She seemed surprised. "Yes, hardly anybody uses it. It's past the bathroom. Goes into the back parking lot."

"Thanks." I turned to Caroline. "Stay here. If something happens, call the deputy I mentioned—Deputy Parker. Maybe he's off his call by now."

"What do you think Solomon Johnson wants?"

"I'll ask him." I watched the sun come out from behind a cloud. I hoped the light would reflect from the window, making it difficult for Johnson to see deep inside. He lit a cigarette, his eyes looking down. I turned, sprinting down a short hall, past the single restroom, past a small supply closet and out a door into the back lot. I ran about fifty feet to my right, ran by a dumpster that smelled of decaying chicken and shrimp. I reached back and touched my Glock in its holster tucked into the belt under my shirt.

I found an alley and cut down it, stepping over an empty bottle of cheap wine and a Anders beer bottle on its side. When I got to the end of the alley I stopped, warily peering to the left and then the right. There was nothing but a few shoppers. An elderly man sat on a bench next to a barbershop, reading a newspaper. I looked at rooftops. Looked for the yellow pickup truck. Nothing.

I watched Solomon Johnson for a second. He stared into the window. Motionless. A smoldering cigarette wedged in one corner of his mouth. I waited for a propane gas truck to come down the road. As it passed me, I jogged behind it, keeping the truck between Solomon Johnson and me. Then I cut to my left and ran across the street. Johnson was now fifty feet in front of me. I slipped my shoes off, placing them under a park bench, and walked silently across the street. When I got with ten feet of Johnson I said, "If you wanted to talk, you could have come inside."

He lowered his hand holding the key, slowly turning around to face me. I stood at least a head taller than him, even in my socks. He was about sixty. Lean. Ropey brown arms. He stared at me for a moment. No emotion. Deadpan dark eyes. Mouth small. Cleft chin. He was the member of the Johnson family I'd seen walking from the courthouse steps to join the old man in the car. I could see by the slow rise and fall of his chest that he was not nervous, in control. The sun went behind a cloud. He said, "You did a real bad thing to my boys. Broke Earl's arm. That ain't smart."

"It's not too smart to send your boys after me either. One of them pointed a shotgun at me. What would you have done?"

"You started with my oldest boy, Cooter. You stood in a court of law and said you'd testify that Jesse Taylor, a man with some real issues, wasn't read his fuckin' Miranda shit. You come into my town. You fuck with my boys. I read that story in the paper. You're nosing around trying to find dirt about the old reform school, somethin' nobody gives two shits about, and you do bodily harm to my family. I thought it was time you met me."

"There are people who do care what happened inside the reform school, what happened to people like Jesse Taylor when he was a boy. If Jesse has issues, it's because of that. And I'm betting the old man I saw in your car, is probably your father, and he's most likely one of the men who abused boys when they were in the reform school. And you were spawned from the same deviant seed."

He raised his left hand, taking a drag from the cigarette, fingernails long, packed with black dirt. He inhaled smoke deep in his lungs, holding it inside, studying me with snake eyes. He finally exhaled, blowing smoke from his nostrils, lifting his chin, leaning toward me, his black eyes undaunted. "You come looking for my daddy, it'll be your final hunt on earth."

I said nothing, staring down at him. His breathing unchanged, a speck of brown tobacco in the corner of his mouth. A breeze came from behind him. I could smell old sweat and stale whisky on his T-shirt. He turned, placing the end of his right index finger on the hood of my Jeep. He used the longer fingernail to make a smiley face in the road dust on the hood. Then he strolled down the sidewalk to the waiting yellow pickup truck parked near the intersection. I walked back to the park bench, sat down, and slipped on my shoes.

I looked across the street at the coffee shop. Caroline Harper stood behind the window, her arms folded, face worried. Then the clouds slowly parted and the sunlight returned, reflecting off the shop's window. Caroline's troubled face disappeared slowly as if it had been sealed inside a glass time capsule.

FORTY-SEVEN

Jesse Taylor hoped Jeremiah Franklin was still there when he arrived. He thought about the noose and what Jeremiah's niece Sonia had said. Jesse wasn't sure what he'd say when he finally found Jeremiah. *Couldn't blame him if he took a swing at me. Maybe knock some damn sense into my head.* Jesse looked at his cell phone and then glanced up in the car's rearview mirror. He watched a police cruiser a half block behind him. He looked down at his speedometer, easing his foot off the gas.

"Just paranoid," he mumbled, lifting the phone. "Two missed calls." He played the first one through speakerphone: "Jesse, this is Cory Wilson with the Patriot. I've been thinking about what you shared with me. It's caused me to do some digging in files, talking with a few people. You mentioned that I should talk with Caroline Harper. I'll do that. Also, there are some things I need to ask you. So give me a call. You have my card and now my number. Thanks."

Jesse hit the play button for the next message. "Jesse, it's Sean. Call me when you get this. Caroline told me about Jeremiah finding the noose hanging from a tree at his mother's house. If you're trying to speak with Jeremiah, let's talk with him together. I already spoke with him. We can protect Jeremiah in a couple of ways. One is to have him tell his story to the FBI. The second is to get some national news media interest, and that shouldn't be hard. That might lead to the attorney general of Florida calling for an investigation. Call me. Don't do this alone."

Jesse tossed the phone down on the seat beside him, lit a cigarette and slammed his open palm on his steering wheel. "Shit! You get national news coverage when you start diggin' up the bodies of kids. We're not there yet."

He inhaled from the cigarette, blew smoke out the side window and drove toward the home of Jeremiah Franklin's mother.

— —

I walked Caroline Harper to her car across the street from the coffee shop. It was quiet in the afternoon lull, except for the blackbirds cackling from the canopy of a live oak. I carried the rope noose in the paper bag. The physical appearance of an iconic noose cut from a tree had left Caroline queasy. She was worried about Jesse. Worried about Jeremiah Franklin. She said, "I'm going home to read my Bible, to pray, and to hope that this nightmare will end. As much as I want to find Andy's grave and bring him home, to bring people to justice, I can't stand the thought of bloodshed."

"Maybe it won't come to that."

"I'm not sure I can find solace in what I feel you don't really believe, Sean."

"I do believe that sometimes things have to be broken apart to be fixed."

"What do you mean?"

"Overseas, I once met an elderly Japanese man who could repair broken pottery by using a liquid gold or silver powder. He'd painstakingly put the broken pottery back together again, holding each piece by hand next to the other pieces until each one dried, creating veins of gold or silver. This would give the vase or bowl a different type of beauty and strength. The old man said the new bowl or vase was made better by having been broken."

She was quiet a second. "Are you suggesting we should wear our scars with pride?"

"Something like that." I smiled, looking down at her anxious face. "And even if all the king's horses and all the king's men could never put Humpty together again. But at least ol' Hump ventured to the edge of the wall. You just have to learn balance."

She smiled and got in her car, hands gripping the wheel, face reflective. I watched her drive away, walking to my Jeep. I looked at the smiley face Solomon Johnson had left on the hood. I went back inside the coffee shop, bought a bottle of water, returned to the Jeep and poured the water into the center of the smiley face. The image dissolved, the dirt running down the side of the Jeep, tracking toward the curb and vanishing through the grate of a sewer drain.

I sat in my Jeep and picked up my phone to call Lana Halley just as the phone buzzed in my hand. The caller ID indicated it came from the same place I called earlier, the sheriff's office. I answered and the voice said, "This is Deputy Ivan Parker returning a call to this number."

"Thanks for returning my call. This is Sean O'Brien. I was there the night that Jesse Taylor was arrested in Shorty's parking lot."

"You're the guy who told the detective you'd worked homicide with Miami-Dade."

"And you're the deputy who told the detective Miranda wasn't read. I admire your attention to investigative protocol."

"Thank you. How can I help you? You told the dispatcher something about evidence. What is that?"

"You ever see a professionally tied hangman's noose?"

"Can't say I have, at least not in person. TV and the movies, maybe. Where'd you find this noose?"

"I didn't. A young black woman, Sonia Acker, and her family found it. And they found it in their front yard—the yard of Sonia's elderly grand-mother. "

"Why didn't they call it in?"

"They're afraid. I have their address and phone numbers. And I have the noose. It's in a paper grocery sack. Just as the girl delivered it."

"What's your location, Mr. O'Brien?"

"I'm parked in front of Ruby's Coffee Shop. Black Jeep. Are you with a partner? Can you come alone?"

"I can come alone. I'll be there in a few minutes. I'm sure I don't have to tell you not to touch the evidence inside that bag."

FORTY-EIGHT

When he looked inside the paper bag his eyes widened. I stood with Deputy Ivan Parker under the shade of a canvas awning in front of the coffee shop. I guessed his age at about thirty. He had short-cropped dark hair, rawboned face, inquisitive and skeptical hazel eyes. The same eyes I'd seen in dozens of law enforcement officers. Their guard always up. Everyone's a liar. And it's your job to cut to the chase and figure out who *might* be telling the truth. And just maybe, peel the onion of lies back far enough, there's an honest person in there. The perpetrators wear camouflage. The real truth is the real victim.

As a former detective, I had Deputy Parker's attention. Maybe I could gain his respect. I provided him with some of the information that I had. He closed the paper bag and asked, "Did Sonia say who she thinks might have done this?"

"According to Caroline Harper, she didn't. Sonia's a scared kid. Who knows where her Uncle Jeremiah is right now."

"This hate tactic won't fly in Jackson County. I grew up here. My son and daughter are growing up here. This sort of thing ought to be long buried in the past. I'll ride out there and speak with Mrs. Franklin. I know her. She's a fine lady. I'll try to locate her granddaughter, Sonia and Jeremiah, too, if I can find him. Maybe we can piece this thing together."

"How long have you been with the sheriff's department?"

"I'm coming up on my ninth year. I'm applying for detective. I graduated from Florida State with a degree in criminology."

"Put that degree and your experience to good use looking at a cold case."

"What do you mean?"

"The Dozier School for boys...there are people who are convinced murdered kids are buried in hidden graves there."

"I've heard those rumors. Somehow, they don't seem to gain much traction here."

I reached in my shirt pocket and pulled out the photo of Andy Cope. "This isn't a rumor. It's a picture of a boy who was held at the old school. His name is Andy Cope. He went missing fifty years ago." I told him the story and added, "If you want to make detective, investigate that. Unlock the biggest criminal secret in the county, maybe the entire state. I'll help you."

He blew out a deep breath. "I can't work an investigation with a civilian."

"Sure you can. Every good cop in the world does it. It's called working with informants. Can you trust the sheriff?"

"He's by the book. No BS. Tough but fair."

"Good. You'll need him." I told him about Curtis Garwood and how I got involved when Caroline Harper came to me near where I live on the east coast of Florida. "Jesse Taylor and Jeremiah Franklin knew each other growing up around here. Both spent a little time in the reform school. Their alleged infractions wouldn't justify reform school today. But it was very different back then. Talk with both of them. If Jeremiah does tell us who killed Andy, can you get with the sheriff and offer Jeremiah protection? Maybe keep a patrol in front of his mother's house, if that's where he'll be?"

"You really think somebody would take him out?"

"Look again in that bag and tell me what you think."

His jaw-line popped slightly. He looked past me as a diesel truck lumbered by. Then he leveled his eyes at mine, his guard now lowered, replaced by a spark, a sense of justice inside that first drew him to police work. "I don't need to look in the bag. I need to find who did it."

"Off the record, what's your take on Detective Lee?"

The deputy shook his head, blew out a breath and said, "He's old school. Been around a long time. I saw him at a restaurant, off duty a couple of months ago. He was wearing a gold Rolex. I heard he vacationed in the Greek Isles last winter. How's a detective from these parts afford that stuff?"

"He doesn't, at least not on the income he makes from the county. Be careful, Deputy Parker." My phone rang. It was Caroline. She said. "I just wanted to thank you, again, for what you're trying to do."

"It's not just me. I have Deputy Ivan Parker with the sheriff's office here. He's trying to help, too. I told him about Andy. Maybe you can add more information. I'll put him on the phone."

"Okay."

I handed the phone to Deputy Parker. He introduced himself and listened, occasionally jotting down notes, asking a question, more notes. Efficient. Attention to detail.

"Yes, ma'am. I'll give you my number. Don't hesitate to call anytime. We'll see if we can change things."

After he disconnected, he handed the phone back to me and said, "We've got to try to bring closure to that lady."

"That's the plan, Deputy Parker."

He nodded. "If we're working together, just call me Ivan. That'll do fine." He wrote a number on the back of a business card. "This is my mobile phone number. Use it to call me rather than on the office phone."

"Where are you headed?"

"To Mrs. Franklin's house. And to visit a cottonwood tree."

FORTY-NINE

I watched Deputy Ivan Parker drive away in the squad car, the paper bag on the front seat beside him. I hoped by bringing him into the circle that an official investigation would begin. The only problem was that Deputy Parker didn't feel comfortable letting some of his coworkers know he was looking at a cold case. So unofficially he'd investigate. I wasn't sure which is more dangerous, tracking evil in the field or eluding it directly on the force.

I unlocked my Jeep, turned the ignition switch, and heard my phone buzz. I wanted a few minutes to call Lana Halley, to convince her to meet and talk with me. I looked at the caller ID. I recognized the number from the local newspaper. I answered and Cory Wilson identified himself. "I appreciate the tip, although it was anonymous. Can I ask who you are?"

"Did you find the state attorney and the CEO of Horizon Properties, James Winston?"

"As a matter of fact, I did. What's your connection to the former Dozier School property? I assume you have some connection because you mentioned Jesse Taylor's name. When he met with me, the school—what he said happened there, was all he talked about. I'd venture that those fourteen-hundred acres and the buildings would be the only common thread between the state attorney meeting with a potential developer."

"Good deduction. Did they corroborate that?"

"Before we go further, tell me your name."

"I've already been in your paper. Your colleague, Wallace Holland, didn't let the facts get in the way of his story. Name's Sean O'Brien."

There was a four second delay. I heard him tapping a keyboard. "So you're the Sean O'Brien in Wallace's piece on the Dozier School, the paramilitary connection." He continued beating the keys faster. "If you're not here looking to build a paramilitary center on the property, what do you want with it?"

"I want nothing with it. I want to have an independent forensic unit look for unmarked and undocumented graves of children who were held there."

"Since Jesse Taylor was here, I've been doing some digging on that. I was about to dismiss the stuff he was saying for a lot of obvious reasons—the one hundred-eleven year history of the place. Probably some of the coldest of cold cases…but when he saw me noticing the scars on the back of his hands, he shared his story of how he got those scars. I had a hard time sleeping that night."

"It gets worse than scars on hands. Now, it's your turn. Why is the state attorney meeting at a private country club with the CEO of a company wanting to develop that property?"

"Mr. O'Brien, can we meet to talk in person, off the phone?"

"When?"

"As soon as possible. Where?"

"There's an area downtown with a gazebo and a tall monument."

"It's called Confederate Park."

"Meet me there in thirty minutes."

"Mr. O'Brien, based on what I've found and not been able to find these last few days, this could be a very big story. Maybe it's the story of the century in these parts."

FIFTY

Jesse slowed down his car as he drove past the gray mailbox with the red cardinal painted on one side hoping he'd see Jeremiah's old Toyota parked in his mother's driveway. He stopped and turned into the drive, moving slowly, acorns popping under his tires. No Toyota. He pulled next to the home, parked and got out. Taking a deep breath, he walked to the front door and knocked. He could hear a television in the background, the dialogue sounded like someone delivering a sermon. *Was it Sunday?* He wasn't sure. *Days running together. Time a blur.*

The door cracked open a few inches, Jeremiah's elderly mother standing just beyond the opening. In the background, he could definitely hear a TV preacher shouting. She looked up at him, one eye partially closed, as if she'd had a stroke since he last saw her snapping green beans on the front porch.

He cleared his throat. "Good afternoon, Mrs. Franklin. Is Jeremiah here?"

"No, he's not. And you don't need to be talkin' to him no how."

"Yes ma'am, you're probably right about that. Sometimes I put my trust in others that haven't earned it. I'm not makin' excuses, I just want to do what's right."

She opened the door further. Jesse could smell green beans and fatback pork cooking from in the kitchen. She pointed over his shoulder and said, "That cottonwood tree was where he found it, the noose."

Jesse turned. He saw a single piece of rope dangling from a low-hanging limb, the end of the rope frayed from having been cut. He turned back to the old woman. "I'm sorry that happened. We'll find who did that."

"Who's we…you? Little Sonia carried it in to town to show ya'll. I tol' her not to. She find you?"

"Yes, ma'am, she did."

She stared at the tree, her closed eye now partially open—milky, her thoughts someplace else. She looked up at Jesse. "It's been a long time since I seen that. Used to see it some when I was a little girl. Back in 'em days I was always home 'fore darkness of a night set in deep."

"Did Jeremiah go to his home, the bus?"

"Don't know where my boy is. You leave him be. I ain't never gonna bring lil' Elijah home. I just thank God I got a son and daughter left. Leave Jeremiah alone." She closed the door.

Jesse started to knock again, but stopped. He turned, stepping off the porch. He looked back at the single piece of rope as a breeze blew through the trees, the rope moving like a pendulum in the wind. Jesse started for his car, stopping as a deputy sheriff's cruiser slowly entered the driveway. The deputy parked directly behind Jesse's car and got out. He carried a paper bag and walked up to Jesse. He said, "I recognize you."

Jesse nodded. "Maybe it's 'cause ya'll arrested me for doing nothing but trying to defend myself."

"I'm Deputy Parker. I could tell you'd been drinking that night but, if you recall, I'm the guy who agreed with the witness about your Miranda rights."

Jesse turned his head slightly, trying to remember the deputy's face. He sighed. "Sorry, man. There was so much shit goin' down that night, I can't remember who all said what. I do appreciate you bein' a standup guy."

"The witness, Sean O'Brien, gave me this, too." The deputy held up the bag. "I understand you and Caroline Harper saw what's in it."

Jesse pointed to the cottonwood tree. "What's left of it is still hangin' from that tree."

"Mrs. Franklin home?"

"She's in there. She's not too damn happy, though."

"Rightfully so. Is Sonia Acker in there too?"

"Don't know. Last time I saw her is when she left that paper sack on the table in the coffee shop."

The front door slowly opened, the hinges creaking. Deputy Parker and Jesse looked in that direction. The old woman stepped on her porch. She held an open Folgers can. She spit a stream of tobacco snuff into the can and set it on the small wooden table next to plastic flowers in a vase. She stared at Jesse, her mouth pulled down in the corners. "Look what you done. You got the po'lese out to my house. Ya'll both go on…get."

Parker smiled and said, "Mrs. Franklin, you may not remember me. I'm Deputy Parker. I was out here a couple of years ago when your house was burglarized. Your daughter had called us."

She gazed at him a few seconds, the snuff under her lower lip, the neighbor's dog barking from a house directly behind her property. "I 'member you."

"If you recall, I found the teenager who did it. And we recovered the things he stole from you. Ma'am, I'm going to take down what's left of that rope in the tree. And then I'm going to try to find the person responsible."

"Lil' Sonia shoulda never brung ya'll out here."

Parker nodded and looked at Jesse. "Hold the bag for me." He handed Jesse the paper bag and then put on rubber gloves. "Follow me."

They walked twenty-five feet to the cottonwood tree. Parker held his right hand up, signaling for Jesse to stop, and then the deputy looked at the ground just below where the remnant of rope hung. "Wait a second." He knelt down, looking at a barren spot of yard, mostly dirt. He used his cell phone to take two pictures. One was of an impression of a boot print. The other was of an impression bare feet had left in the moist dirt. He looked back toward the old woman.

"Mrs. Franklin, when Jeremiah walked out here to cut that noose down, was he wearing boots?"

She shook her head. "He was in his bare feet. He was so mad when he saw it he ran outside in the early mornin' and cut it down. And he tracked some mud back on my flo'."

Jesse looked down at the ground and said, "Whoever left that boot print was a big fella. There's a pyramid thread shape on the heel."

The deputy said nothing. He looked at Jesse's feet, his slip-on boat shoes. Jesse shook his head. "You really think I could have done this?"

"It's not what I think. It's what I find. Only thing in this business that doesn't lie is the science of evidence."

"Until somebody plants fake evidence."

Deputy Parker ignored the comment, standing to look closely at the frayed end of the rope, and then he untied it. "Open the bag." Jesse did so and the deputy dropped the rope piece into the bag with the noose. The deputy folded the bag and removed his rubber gloves. He said, "I'm riding out to Jeremiah's place down near the holler in that pecan grove. You need to stay out of this. You still have to face the judge on the other charges."

Jesse said nothing. He followed Parker up to the front porch. The old woman looked at the deputy out of her one good eye. He said, "Mrs. Parker, I'm real sorry somebody left that noose in your yard. I have a picture of his boot. With some luck, I just might find him. Why, ma'am, do you think some idiot did this?"

"Mean. People bein' mean."

"There's a lot of that, unfortunately. You think it's because of what Jeremiah might have seen in the reform school when he was a boy…you think that's why somebody did this?"

Jesse stared at the deputy for a second and then looked over to the old woman. She watched them both out of her good eye, silent. A crow called out from a tree line across the road. She spit in the coffee can and looked back at the deputy. "All these years Jeremiah kept that inside of him. Even after all this time, somebody don't want Jeremiah to say who kil't that white boy. My boy, Elijah, never came out of there alive or dead. Somebody kil't him, too."

The crow flew over her home. She watched it disappear. "In my dreams, I see Elijah bein' buried alive. The dark soil movin' 'cause his heart was still beatin' fast, just under the black earth, his little hands clawin' like an animal. I heard him whimper, tryin' to cry out to me…mama. But he couldn't holler much 'cause his mouth was full of dirt. Men fillin' his shallow grave with shovels of dirt. And then he's quiet. His tears got nowhere to go except to make the dirt into mud." She turned and walked back inside.

Before the door closed, Jesse could hear the TV preacher shout, "Redemption! It's in your hands."

FIFTY-ONE

Near the center of Marianna, the gazebo stood close to an obelisk concrete monument to slain soldiers. The top of the monument tapered into a pyramid shape. At the bottom was an inscription. From where I sat in my Jeep I could read the engraving: **Confederate Heroes – 1861-1865**. I glanced at my watch. Cory Wilson was five minutes late. At that moment, a blue Ford Explorer pulled into a parking spot. Cory got out, looked around, and walked toward the gazebo. I followed him. He carried a small notepad in one hand, phone in the other. He stood next to the entrance to the gazebo and waited.

I approached from behind him and said, "Glad you could make it."

He turned around, nodded. "I appreciate you coming, too."

"If you don't mind, I'd like to see your phone."

"Why?"

"I'd prefer not to have my voice or image recorded."

"If I did that, I'd let you know."

I held out my hand. He gave me his phone. There was no indication of a recording. I handed it back. "You saw the state attorney and James Winston at the county club?"

"I approached them in the club's parking lot, right before Winston ducked into his waiting Mercedes. Winston said he was looking to buy a home in the area and was considering applying for membership to the country club, a place where Jeff Carson is a member. Carson said he was introducing Winston to the amenities the club offers."

"What do you know about Carson's background?"

"What do you mean?"

"His history. Education. Where he grew up. Early and current politics. Wives. Girlfriends. Family."

"He's effective as a prosecutor. Wins more cases than he loses. I think a lot of that is because he's hired some good lawyers. The Second District is large. He's divorced a couple of times. Carson's a master politician. When running for office, he touted the fact he came from a hardscrabble, dirt-poor life to achieve the American dream. He still has a house in Jackson County. His father apparently abandoned the family when Carson was a kid. After that, a single parent, his mother, raised him and a brother named Andrew."

"Does Carson have children?"

"One, a daughter who lives in Atlanta."

"Where's his mother?"

"I heard she's at Cypress Grove, an assisted living facility in the county. Her name's Julie Carson."

"Does anyone know you're meeting me?"

"If I said no, is this where you pull a gun and take me somewhere to shoot me?" He smiled nervously. "I did a cursory background check on you."

I said nothing, letting him talk.

"I didn't mention to Wallace Holland that I was meeting you. Not much available on your background. Looks like some of the things Wallace got right in his story. You were the sharpshooter that took out the terrorist pilot with the nuclear cargo. Damn impressive shot. And you were a detective, homicide, down in Miami. But you, apparently, have nothing to do with land acquisition and development. Jesse Taylor had told me about the letter you received. He mentioned the story of Andy Cope…tragic if true."

I reached into my shirt pocket, lifting out the photo of Andy Cope, handing it to him. "This is Andy. It's because of what happened to him that I'm here. And because of his sister."

He held the picture, studying it for a moment. "You think he was murdered and buried on that property?"

"Yes."

Wilson raised his eyebrows. And then I gave him a briefing—my initial outing with Curtis Garwood, the two letters, the spent shotgun shell, the piece of buckshot I dug from the tree, and Caroline's hopes to find Andy's grave.

He handed the photo back and said, "I spent time looking or trying to look at burial records from the old reform school. Not a lot there. The state has records of a couple dozen deaths of kids held at the school. They indicate most died in a fire. Others from diseases. There's a tiny cemetery tucked away on the property. It's marked with headstones made out of plastic pipe." He flipped open his reporter's notebook, leafed through the first few pages of notes. "I didn't see a death record of Andy Cope."

"Murders by the hands of reform school staff aren't recorded. At least the cause of death isn't reported accurately. In Andy's case, and probably more boys, there's not a record of death because the supervisors at the time informed family members their son had escaped—had run away. Jesse Taylor believes there is another cemetery up there, one that's unmarked. And he's convinced that's where Andy Cope and others are buried."

"Do you believe him?"

"I do."

Cory Wilson turned more pages in his notebook. "I checked employee records around the time Jesse Taylor was held there. I checked it against death records. From what I could determine, there are four living in the area that'd worked in the reform school in the mid-to-late-sixties. Those include two men and two women. I'm trying to speak with them. Don't know how receptive they'll be or even what they'll recall."

"Who are the men?"

"Edward Johnson…goes by Hack Johnson. The other one is Zeke Wiley. He maintains a P.O. box. No physical address in the property tax rolls. Johnson lives with his wife on a farm."

"I'm not one to suggest how you do your reporting job, but if you speak with Caroline, you'll have a better grasp on the story. Jesse Taylor, and probably a few others his age, can give you some first-hand information. Also, you'll be entering some dangerous areas of reporting. Know whom you can really trust. Your colleague, Wallace Holland, isn't one of them."

He moistened his lower lip, closed his notebook and slipped it in his back pocket. "I think you're right. I'm the new guy, and this is the first real news story I've seen since I started there. And for the most part, until it's ready to be written, I'm doing it a little covertly. My editor knows, but no one else."

"Once you get enough for the public to see the enormity of it, a century of abuse to kids, your story will go international. Then you can work anywhere, if you want."

"It looks like the sale of the old school is imminent. At the newspaper, we've heard rumors of a press conference soon. If James Winston and Vista Properties buy the place, I wonder if they'll have contingency conditions built into the sale."

"What do you mean?"

"An option for the property to go back to the state, and monies refunded in the event a mass gravesite is found as they start pushing dirt around and building houses."

"If we can find even one of those graves before that, there won't be a sale, at least not for a while, and that'll give forensics people time to look for more graves. Maybe the whole place can be turned into a memorial park."

"You mind if I have copies of those letters that Curtis Garwood sent you? I'll need a copy of Andy Cope's picture, too."

"I'll give you copies of the letters. Caroline Harper has extra copies of the photo. I'm hanging on to this one."

He smiled, teeth showing this time. "Although I couldn't find a lot about you in public records, I'd suspect privately you're highly trained in this sort of thing. I'll keep detailed notes as the story unfolds. Maybe one day you'll tell me why you got out of law enforcement."

"Maybe I'm not completely out. Maybe I've just shifted my priorities."

He nodded. "I'll call you to get copies of the letters. I'd better head back to the office."

I watched Cory Wilson walk away—now walking into what would be the most dangerous story he would cover. My phone buzzed. I recognized the caller ID. I answered and special agent Carly Brown from the FBI said, "Sean, I wanted to get back with you earlier, but when you look for a fifty-year-old fingerprint, it takes time and expertise. We used an electro-static charge and found one print on the brass end of the shotgun shell casing. It looks to be a thumbprint. Now all you have to do is find a match."

FIFTY-TWO

Jesse Taylor felt the demons awakening deep in his chest—the gnawing at his gut. Dry mouth. Rapid heartbeat. The voices telling him one drink would make it all go away. He drove without a place to drive to—no destination, no safe harbor. *Just out here with the sharks circling closer,* he thought. *Got to find Jeremiah.* He wanted to drive out to Jeremiah's bus but he was hesitant. *What if the deputy sheriff was there? Just another shark in a pressed uniform.*

He lit a cigarette and headed back toward Marianna, the late afternoon sun creating deep pockets of shade in the palms and piney woods. Jesse drove by an old barn long abandoned, the words *See Rock City* almost covered in green kudzu vine. The barn, surrounded by dead and broken corn stalks, had lost its form and character, the roof sagging under the thick kudzu, the barn now a humpback leviathan—a fossil in a field of abandoned dreams.

Around the bend he spotted an oasis, or maybe it was an illusion of escape. He didn't care at that point in time. He stopped at a liquor store and bought a fifth of vodka. He returned to his car, sat behind the wheel and unscrewed the cap. He took a long pull from the bottle. His face flushing the color of cherries, eyes wet. He picked up his phone and punched in Sonia Acker's number. When she answered, he said, "Sonia, it's Jesse. Don't hang up, okay?"

"What you want?"

"That's a helluva hello. If you didn't want me to do something about that noose, then you shouldn't have brought it to the coffee shop. The sheriff's office is investigating."

"So you called the police?"

"No, but it doesn't matter right now. What matters is keeping shitheads off your grandma's property."

"She's old. Just leave her be."

"The last thing in the world I want to do is…is to mess with your grandma."

"You been drinkin' or are you on some kinda pills?"

"I have to talk with your uncle. Jeremiah can't keep carrying this weight. If I know who shot Andy Cope, probably the same asshole who shot your Uncle Eli…if know who did it, it's not Jeremiah's cross to bear anymore. They won't come after him—they'll come after me 'cause I'll take the information to all the news media in the state. And that's got them scared because there are lots of roots growin' in this shit. And the state doesn't want the truth to turn fourteen hundred acres into land with zero worth to developers. It's like some poor bastard realtor tryin' to unload a haunted house. Nobody wants somebody else's ghosts."

"I'll give you my uncle's number, and then you can call him. No sense me bein' in the middle. If he wants to talk, to tell you somethin' nobody will do nothin' about, that's cool. But if he don't…just go away. Okay?"

"You have my word."

"What's that supposed to mean?"

"For me, it's all I got left in this shitty world."

She gave him the number and disconnected. Jesse called Jeremiah. It went directly to voice-mail. "Jeremiah…Jerry…it's Jesse. Man, you got to let me try to make it up to you, okay? You have my number. Call me, all right? Together we'll stay strong—for us and all the guys who survived that shithole." Jesse left his number and added, "We got to talk. Call me, okay?" Jesse put the fifth of vodka under the driver's seat, popped a mint into his mouth, and drove toward the place that changed him forever—the Florida School for Boys.

FIFTY-THREE

For the first time since I received Curtis Garwood's initial letter, I thought there might now be physical evidence to connect someone to the murder of Andy Cope. I started my Jeep, Carly Brown still on the phone. I gave her a brief update, told her I was working with local law enforcement, didn't say how many and added, "Well, it's a challenge to find a match, but it's better than not finding a print to match. At least we're halfway there."

She chuckled. "I guess to you, my optimistic friend, that means the glass is half full."

"I never considered the half full or half empty perspective. I'm always curious as to what's in the glass and how it got there—the source."

"That's a different point-of-view. The bureau just eliminated more than seventy million suspects for you. We didn't, of course, get one smidgen of a hit in the AFIS database."

"I wouldn't think so. The print you pulled from the brass head is at least fifty years old. So all I have to do is find out who was working at the reform school in the mid-sixties. Due to time and circumstances, the pool can't be deep."

"But it can be deadly, assuming the perp is still alive. Can't imagine the guy's willing to go to prison to die. You start sniffing around that county, and he could be holed up somewhere. A guy like that could be suicidal and willing to take others out before he saves the final brass nail for his own coffin."

"Or he might go quietly into the night."

"We're back to that perspective thing again, Sean. You want to know what's in the glass? The only way to do that is to search for the source."

"At least I have something to search for now."

"Yes, but keep this in mind, to get prints of some elderly guy, or anyone for that matter in Florida, you'll need to show probable cause. A fifty-year-old print from a shotgun shell, no dead body or indication of murder, is deep into the gray area of probable cause. So you're going to need a lot more to convince a prosecutor to take it to a jury."

"I've got the print, thanks to you. What if I could find the shotgun that fired the shell?"

"After a half-century, doubtful."

"It's all about the source, Carly. I'm not thinking about the perspective, I'm thinking about a firearm I recently saw up close and personal."

"Let me guess…somebody pulled a gun on you."

"A double barrel 12 gauge shotgun. And if I'm not mistaken, it's a vintage piece. The markings are distinctive, made by A.H. Fox Firearms."

"You *were* close. That's a fairly rare shotgun."

"But, yet, two local lads had it in a gun rack in the back of their truck."

"Could have been stolen or sold long ago. If you take care of a classic shotgun like that, it'll last two lifetimes. So if you were close enough to ID the model…want to tell me what the hell happened up there?"

"If I thought it'd bring in the FBI, I would. I'll fill you in when there's more puzzle pieces in this tragic and macabre mystery. And it's only a mystery because it was allowed to happen and then swept under a lot of bureaucratic rugs through people and politics."

"You told me you're working with the sheriff's department. It looks like you and some overworked investigator have your work cut out before he or she asks a judge to haul some elderly person into the sheriff's department to get prints made."

"If I can squeeze out one more favor…send a digital file of the print to me. Please overnight the shotgun shell to the motel where I'm staying. I'll text the address to you. Thanks, Carly. The FBI's always welcome to join the search."

"I wish we had the manpower to chase ghosts and ice age cold cases. Fact is, unless it'll rewrite American crime history, we don't. But if you start finding multiple bodies of kids buried on the grounds of that spooky old place, that will be a green light for us to send in the resources. Good luck, Sean. Next time you're in Tampa, you owe me a cold martini." Carly disconnected.

I started my Jeep and called Caroline Harper. "I wanted to let you know that the FBI managed to pull a print off the brass head of the shotgun shell Curtis Garwood kept all those years. It was embedded in the brass, meaning the print came from the person who fired the gun at Andy that night."

"Dear God…I think I'm going to cry."

"You've earned it. It's my hope you can cry tears of joy when we find a match for the print."

"Sean, thank you."

"You can thank me when I find your brother's killer. A matched print will bring us ninety percent closer. If we find the match, it'll be the last ten percent that will send him to prison, maybe even a penalty equal to what he chose to do to Andy."

"What do you do next?"

"I'm driving to the courthouse. Maybe, just maybe, the assistant state attorney will look at this without clouded judgment. I'll keep you posted. Have you heard from Jesse?"

"No, and I'm worried. His anger is leading him into dark places."

"If you hear from him, tell him to call me. Advise him to stay away from Jeremiah Franklin. Deputy Parker is a good man. I think Jeremiah will be able to sense that. I'll speak with you later."

I headed in the direction of the county courthouse. Maybe I'd call Lana Halley to speak with her in person, or maybe I'd just walk into her office. Because now I had evidence, a fingerprint and the shotgun attached to it. I had cell phone video of the state attorney meeting privately with the CEO of a company ready to bulldoze buildings and land. And it's land that the state attorney said hid no apparent evidence of abuse.

I didn't know whether Lana was in the mud with her boss, complicit in the denial of allegations and quick to prosecute people like Jesse for rocking the boat. Either she opened the closed door to Jeremiah's identity, passing it to someone with a motive, or it was Detective Lee. Whoever did it might as well have tied the knot in the hangman's noose left in front the home of Jeremiah's mother.

I'd soon find out, and the answer would dictate my path. If Lana was involved in this spider's web, I knew how to discover it. And then I'd go to the attorney general of the state. But before that meeting, I'd find as much evidence as Deputy Ivan Parker and I could recover. We'd have to do it before Jesse Taylor crashed and burned, taking Jeremiah Franklin into Jesse's downward spiral.

FIFTY-FOUR

I t was late afternoon and Jesse Taylor didn't remember driving there. It seemed to show up. Sort of how a dream shows up. It just appears. But for Jesse it wasn't a dream, it was graphic proof of a nightmare that never had a third act ending. He slowed his car in front of the main entrance to the former reform school and rolled down his window. A pickup truck was parked near the guard gate. Jesse recognized the truck. Same truck. Same security guard. Johnny Hines sitting in the guardhouse behind the big glass windows.

Jesse drove slowly by the entrance and continued around the perimeter of the immense property. He looked at the chalky-white buildings in the distance, rusted water tower, old brick smokestack, and together they reminded him of something ghastly. The combined visuals, beyond boundaries of the razor wire fence, had the appearance—the grim bits and pieces of a German death camp. He reached for the bottle of vodka and mumbled, "They did everything but put a numbered tattoo on my wrist and turn on the fuckin' gas."

He pulled off the road on vacant pinewoods land across from the property, a thousand yards away from the main entrance. Jesse reached in his backseat, pulled the green Army blanket off his guns, found the .45 caliber pistol next to his shotgun. He set the bottle of vodka on the center console and held the pistol in his scarred hands. Lifting the end of the barrel to his nostrils, he smelled the gun oil. Jesse looked to his left and then right. No traffic. He got out of his car, shoving the pistol under his belt, grabbing the bottle of liquor.

He sauntered across the street, walking up to the fence. He stood on the same property he hadn't walked on in fifty years. His heart beat faster. Palms sweaty. He hiked along the outside of the fence for about one hundred feet, coming to a locked gate. It was a small entrance, barely large enough for a compact car to drive through if the gate was open.

Jesse stood there, looking at the buildings in the distance, remembering the long days and excruciating nights here. His breathing came quicker. He was back inside—transported through a keyhole he could never lock, back to the first night he was marched to the White House. At least five boys were forced to stand in line outside the door to the torture chamber. The fan started. *Whump – whump – whump*. Then the crack of the leather on flesh. The sound was like a firecracker. It was followed by the first scream. Always the loudest scream before the boys lost their voice during the begging, pleading and the crying. Smack of the whip. *Whump – whump – whump*. The screams faded as the crack of leather, chewing into bleeding flesh, seemed to move in sync with the turning of the fan blades. *Whump - whump – whack – scream.*

The boy standing in front of Jesse was probably ten years old. He stood rigid, tears trickling down his pink cheeks, legs shaking. He glanced back at Jesse. The boy turned around, not looking up at the fleshy man whose job it was to send them inside. One-by-one. The youngest boy's shoulders trembled, urine staining his pajamas and pooling between his bare feet.

It was a week later, Jesse's buttocks still covered with open lacerations, when the Preacher came into his bunk in the cottage. It was a hot summer night. No air moving through the screened in windows. The pulse of crickets chirping loud outside. Preacher smelled of tobacco and bourbon. His body stank of sweat, testosterone and diesel grease. He grabbed Jesse by the back of his neck, his strong fingers digging into his tendons, the strength of his grip almost paralyzing. "It's time for your next whupin' boy. Lay across that bunk on your stomach. He pushed Jesse face down onto the cot. "Don't you scream, hear me boy?"

The sound of a semi-truck moving through its gears brought Jesse back to the present. He looked at the bottle of vodka in his hand. It was at least three-quarters full. He held the neck of the bottle and smashed it against one of the steel fence posts, shattering the glass. Then Jesse pulled out the pistol, gripping it with both of his scarred hands, aiming and shooting the padlock off the gate. He picked up the lock and walked back to his car. He sat there, his heart hammering. Breathing hard. Trying to fill his lungs with air. Sweat beading on his brow. Nausea billowed from his stomach like sulfurous gas.

Jesse opened his car door, vomiting on the ground. He leaned back in his seat, his head on the headrest, the lock in one hand. He started his car and drove back toward the main entrance to the school. The pickup truck was still where he'd seen it. It looked like Johnny Hines was watching television. Jesse got out of his car and walked up to the guardhouse.

Hines opened the door, stepping outside, staring at Jesse approaching, not sure what to say. Hines rested one hand on his holstered pistol. "You again, Jesse? You'd think after spending time here as a kid this would be the last place you'd want to visit. Why you back here?"

Jesse said nothing. He looked down at the man's hand on the butt of the pistol. He grinned and said, "What you gonna do, Hines, shoot me for walkin' across the parking lot?"

"What'd you want?"

"From you, nothing. From Hack Johnson, a real sincere apology for being an asshole pedophile."

Johnny Hines' chin jutted out a half inch, his right hand still on the pistol butt. "You look like shit. You been drinkin' or are you truly insane."

"I know you're tight with the Johnson clan. You told 'em when I rolled into town." Jesse reached for the lock in his jean's pocket. "Found this on your south gate. Looks like you got a breach of a previously secure facility on your hands, Johnny. Could be all kinds of vandals on the property fornicating and writing graffiti on these hallowed buildings." Jesse held the lock up to his eye, looking through the hole in the center. He stuck his index finger into the hole, handing the lock to Hines. "It's a souvenir for Hack. Deliver it to him and let him know he's not secure either."

Johnny Hines held the lock in the palm of his hand, staring at it, cutting his eyes up to Jesse. "You did this?"

"I'm flatly denying it."

"You damage state property and there will be consequences."

"When the state damages and kills kids, there should be consequences."

"I can't arrest you, but the sheriff can. I'm calling this in."

Jesse grinned. "Before you do, Johnny, remember this…I used to have fun with your brother Frank. We'd give each other noogies, horseplay, but then one day Frank and two of his buddies decided they wanted to jump me. I had a job. I worked. Made money. They didn't. I'd just cashed my check when they jumped me. Frank was in the hospital for two days. His buddies took a lickin' and barely crawled away."

Hines' eyes narrowed, a vein jumping on the left side of his neck. "*You* did that to my brother?"

"And I'll do it to you. So go on and call the law. It's my word against yours. Nobody saw me shoot anything. I'm gonna turn around and head back into town. You be a good snitch and deliver that to Hack. Tell him to lock his doors and windows."

Jesse turned around, got into his car and drove down the exit toward town. He stopped at the end of the drive, looking into his rearview mirror as Johnny Hines lifted a phone to his ear.

— ▬

I sent a text to Carly Brown at the FBI, giving her the delivery address of the motel where I was staying. I hoped she'd have time to make an overnight delivery for the morning. I'd hit the send button when my phone buzzed. It was Dave Collins. "Sean, I've been doing some gentle poking and prodding, looking for what Jeff Carson did in the prosecutor's office while he was in Miami-Dade."

"What'd you find?"

"Probably the reason you didn't see him in the state attorneys office is because he quit working for the state and went into private practice. He became a defense lawyer for three years before working his way back into the prosecutor's office up in the Second District."

"Who'd he defend?"

"I thought you might ask that. All very wealthy clients, of course. A couple of high stakes divorces. He did a tax evasion and fraud case. The client was Ronald St. Arnold, a guy who owns a cruise line based out of Miami. Looks like Carson saved him a bundle and possible jail time. One of Carson's clients was James Winston. Winston's wife had filed for divorce and hired a big time LA based lawyer to represent her. She was suing him for a substantial share of his assets, a beach house, along with enough alimony money to float a small town's annual budget. Mrs. Winston and three other people, all well-heeled, were on a ninety-foot Ferretti yacht, en route from Ft. Lauderdale to the Bahamas. About nine miles off the western coast of Bimini there was an explosion and fire. No one survived. They didn't even have a chance to get off a distress signal. The channel in that part of the Atlantic is very deep. What's left of the yacht is on the ocean floor, miles beneath the surface."

"I remember that. It was investigated by a half dozen law enforcement agencies. They called it an 'unfortunate mystery,' if I recall correctly. Another casualty of the Bermuda Triangle."

"Jeff Carson, as a defense attorney, is good at maritime law, too. He's so good, in fact, he sued the yacht manufacturer. Nothing could be proved, of course. But the tactic dimmed the spotlight of suspicion as to a deliberate and intentional cause. It took the heat off Winston, and it quickly evolved into a tragic and freak accident to blame on someone else. James Winston collected two million dollars from his wife's life insurance. None of the bodies, even so much as a finger, were ever found."

"That explains a lot."

"So now, fast forward a few years, James Winston and Jeff Carson are reunited. The assurance of a clean bill of sale on the reform school property represents millions to Winston's company, and Jeff Carson is first in line to get a nice bonus for making it happen and for stopping anything to keep it from happening. That last part, Sean, is up to you."

"And now I have a better hand of cards courtesy of my friend, Carly Brown, with the FBI. Her techs completed the electrostatic on the brass head of the shotgun shell. They found a pearl in that oyster. More than fifty years in the making. Nothing matched in their database. I have high hopes my new BFF, Deputy Ivan Parker, can find a match somewhere here in Jackson County."

Dave grunted. "Well, that's better news. Should you and the good deputy be successful—all a prosecutor has to do is prove the perp and the shotgun were at the crime scene the same night when the boy was killed. You're getting closer, Sean. But you're still heading into the woods, not coming out."

"At least I know where the woods are now. I just have to help a deputy find a print."

"Before you left, sitting here at the table with Nick and me, I suggested you'll have to look under a mountain of hay to find the proverbial needle. You said if the hay's burned, the needle will be left, a little charred, but there in the ashes somewhere. I hope you don't have to result to arson to find it. Could be way too much collateral damage."

"I also said a magnet is a good way to find it, to draw out the perp. I just have to get the magnet close enough to start the pull, to lure a spider out of a hole. Give Max a hug for me. Looks like I'll be awhile. And Dave, I'm going to need you to overnight a GPS tracker to my motel."

FIFTY-FIVE

I had one minute to make the call. It was 4:59 on Friday afternoon. Maybe someone would answer the phone in the state attorney's office before the magic hour of five o'clock when all calls were sent to a digital receptionist. I punched the number to Lana Halley's office. The greeting kicked in and, again, it was the baritone voice of state attorney Jeff Carson telling us his office was closed for the day. He or a representative would be glad to help us the following business day.

Friday evening. The next business day—Monday. I didn't have Lana's cell phone number. At least I didn't think I did. I drove through Marianna as fast as I could risk it, pulling into the courthouse parking lot a quarter past five. And, on a Friday evening, the lot was almost empty. Three cars. What were the chances one of those cars would be owned by Lana? Slim.

I parked and waited, taking the opportunity to see if I'd stored her number during or after the Pablo Gonzales trial. Lana wasn't in my contacts. No indication of a phone number. Did she still have the same phone number? I had no choice but to wait.

A woman exited the building from one of three doors in the rear of the courthouse closest to the reserved area for employee parking. She was at least fifty, redhead, and making a fast beeline to a minivan. Two cars left and now it was 5:30 p.m. A man came from the same door. He wore a dark sports coat, jeans, carrying a brief case, a phone held to his ear.

The last car was a Subaru SUV. I tried to picture Lana driving a Subaru. I had no idea if she enjoyed the outdoors, going places an all-wheel-drive like the one in the lot could take her. As a matter of fact, I knew nothing about Lana with the exception of her courtroom performances. And that's what they always were. Not a performance unique to Lana, but rather one unique to the profession of law. Some of the greatest actors aren't trained in drama schools. They're trained in law schools. A jury is a small audience selected to decide who has the better attorney. *If the glove doesn't fit…*

It was now almost six o'clock, the sun getting lower in the west, the Subaru still where someone had parked it when he or she came to work earlier this morning. The door opened and Lana Halley stepped out, purse over one shoulder, briefcase in the opposite hand. I started my Jeep and drove toward her car. She looked up, probably unable to identify me from the angle the sunset was reflecting off my windshield.

I pulled closer to her, my driver's side window down. "I have a feeling you're the last person out of your office."

She stared at me for a moment, shook her head. "Are you stalking me?"

"I'm only wanting a brief and friendly visit with an assistant state attorney."

"Make an appointment."

She started to walk around my Jeep to her car. "Lana, wait a second, please. Just listen." I shut off the engine and got out.

"Sean, just go take your conspiracy theories someplace else, okay? It's been a long week. I'm going home."

"Your boss is a crook. I don't know a better way to say it."

"I'm not going to justify that asinine comment by responding. So get out of my way before I file a restraining order against you." She walked around me, pointing her remote key at the Subaru, the locks popping open.

"Four people were murdered in a boat explosion and Jeff Carson helped cover it up through maritime legal maneuvers. The person who owned the yacht was James Winston, the same guy whose company is bidding on the reform school property. Carson was his attorney in Miami. Winston's wife and three others died in the explosion. And now Winston wants to turn the reform school property into a posh Florida version of Beverly Hills. He's paying Carson to make it happen. I have video on my phone of Carson meeting privately with Winston at the Jackson Country Club."

She leaned against her car, face flush, eyes searching for nothing that was visible. Her mind seemed to be replaying events of late. She looked at me. "Are you sure? Are you positive?"

"Yes." I pulled my phone from my pocket and hit the button to play video. I held the screen so Lana could see it but away from what I thought would be camera angles poised on the buildings. I watched her eyes absorb the moving images, watched the misplaced trust in her boss bleed from the corners of her soul. She moistened her lower lip, a dry swallow, inhaling deeply through her nostrils.

"I don't even know what to say."

I studied Lana's eyes, looking for traces of deception, looking for clues of a refined performance. There were none. "Here's the challenge: Carson will try his best not to leave an electronic trail. He's either had payments wired into an offshore account, or he's been paid cash. You need to set a trap for him."

"Me? How?"

"Catch him in lies. To get a grand jury indictment against Carson, to find probable cause, as a prosecutor you can—"

"Wait! Okay? I know what I can and can't do in my job. You're asking me to go behind the state attorney's back, behind the backs of the other assistant SA's in the district, and present enough evidence to a grand jury— people from here, with the result to have an arrest warrant issued for Jeff Carson."

"The result would be prison time. Lana, it's not just about a massive development on property that probably has a hidden cemetery and should be sanctified, it's about murder or murders and the abuse of kids through the years." I reached in my pocket and pulled out the picture of Andy Cope. "It's about him and others like him. He never walked out of that school. His sister believes his body is still there. Others, people like Jesse Taylor, believe more kids are buried there. Some children killed by people assigned to their welfare. It's about doing what's right, regardless of the time that's passed." I told her about both of Curtis Garwood's letters.

She reached for Andy's picture, holding it in her hand. "He looks like my sister's son. Sean, to present to a grand jury, I will need a lot more than cell phone video of Jeff Carson walking into the country club with James Winston. Even though Jeff may have been Winston's lawyer before, it shows no wrongdoing. It implies the possibility of improprieties, but that can't be prosecuted. I need proof. This is overwhelming, to say the least. I didn't have time for lunch and I'm a little lightheaded. I need time to process this."

"We don't have a lot of time. Maybe you can begin processing over dinner. My treat. It'll give me a chance to show you more evidence I have, what I have coming, and a further connection I might be able to prove. And then you'll have something to take to a grand jury."

She looked at the photo again. "What was his name?"

"Andy…Andy Cope."

She held the photo closer, her eyes boring into the image. "This is Andy Cope?"

"Yes."

"This is the boy that Jesse Taylor talked about. Even though it's black and white, I can make out the freckles across his nose and cheeks."

She handed the photo back to me. "Lana, this is an opportunity to right a long overdue, horrible wrong and injustice. Will you help? Will you do something no one else has done in decades?"

She looked beyond the courthouse, beyond the gnarled old live oaks, the last traces of a setting sun warm against her face. "I want to believe this is why I became a prosecutor—to give the dead, the murder victims, a voice. Maybe we can find Andy. In this small town, it's going to be hard to conduct an investigation from the state attorney's office. If this is a farce and it doesn't pan out, if I screw up, I'll be out of a job. Maybe out of a profession if I'm disbarred for conducting a witch hunt. But if what you say is correct, it's worth the damn risks."

"Did you tell Jeff Carson that Jeremiah Franklin is the only living eyewitness to the shooting of Andy Cope?"

"I didn't put it quite like that. In my briefing report, I listed it. So now, much to my chagrin, I told him."

"Who did he tell? That person could be responsible for leaving a warning, in the form of a hangman's noose, in the front yard of an elderly black woman, Jeremiah Franklin's mother."

Lana pointed to one of the largest live oaks. "That tree, the biggest, I'm told it was the tree they used to hang a man in 1934. Was he guilty of murder? Maybe. Was the mob, people who ignored due process of the law, guilty of murder? Yes." She turned her head toward me, her blue eyes soft in the setting sun. "I'd like to think, to hope, those days are deep in the past. But the longer I'm in this job, the more certain I am that isn't so. I'll do what I can to help you find Andy Cope, and maybe we'll find his killer."

FIFTY-SIX

A full moon punched its way through swirling dark purple clouds, the moon rising in the distance behind the Jackson County water tower. The tower was suspended more than one hundred feet in the air, supported by four steel girders. Jesse Taylor glanced at the tower as he drove slowly through the night, the moonlight casting the massive tank in silhouette. He remembered long nights in the reform school, looking out the bedroom window, watching the moon rising above the old wooden water tower. He remembered the smell of sulfur in the water, the taste gritty, as if tadpoles had been swimming in the well water.

—◀━

On the drive back to my motel room, my phone vibrated. I recognized the number. Deputy Parker. I answered and he said, "O'Brien, I just wanted to let you know that I rode out to Jeremiah Franklin's place. He wasn't there. I spoke with his mother. She has no idea who hung the noose in her yard. I found a solid boot imprint next to the tree. Took some close-up photos of it. If we find a suspect, we might get a match."

"Good, and speaking of matches, a friend of mind in the FBI used an electrostatic process to lift a print from that shotgun shell I told you about. All we have to do is find a match today and we'll connect fifty years of a neglected cold case into the moment. I'll copy you on the print. FBI ran it through all known databases. Got nothing."

"That means I have to put some boots on the ground. Start pounding on doors."

"Who can you trust in your department?"

"A few guys."

"You might want to ride with a trusted partner when you start pounding on locked doors. I believe this thing is a lot deeper than I originally thought."

"Yeah, I'm starting to feel that in my gut."

— —

Jesse pulled his car into the Heartland Motel parking lot. He parked a few spaces away from his room, number 29, wrapping the Army blanket around his shotgun and pistol. He pulled the door handle release, about to get out of his car when he noticed someone in the side-view mirror walking across the lot. A woman, bottle blonde, short brown leather skirt, stacked high heels, and a low-cut blouse, ambled down the outside walkway, glancing at the numbers on the doors. She stopped at number 17, looked at something written on a folded cocktail napkin and then knocked.

An unshaven man opened the door, standing in the threshold. He wore a white T-shirt outside his blue jean shorts. No shoes. Baseball cap on back-wards. He gestured for her to come in. She glanced over her right shoulder toward a pickup truck in one corner of the lot, the yellow parking lights on.

Jesse looked back at the truck, barely making out the profile of a driver—a man, the orange glow of a lit cigarette bending back and forth as the man smoked. Jesse locked his car and walked around some shrubs, avoiding the overhead lights down the strip, quickly entering his room and locking the door.

He set the pistol on the dresser, shotgun on the bed. He sat on the edge of the bed and called Caroline Harper. "Jesse, where are you?"

"Back at this fleabag motel. Who would have thought this little town had hookers crawlin' out like roaches?"

"Have you been drinking?"

"A little."

"There's no such thing as a little for someone who has a problem with alcohol."

"Maybe, Caroline…just maybe the problem isn't with alcohol…maybe the problem's with me. If I could fix me, and stay fixed, I could follow the yellow brick road. Maybe ol' Oz has a heart for me, too."

"Jesse, stop it. There's nothing wrong with your heart. You can get help. I'll help you if you let me."

"I drove out to the old school. Don't know why, really. Just started drivin' and next thing I know, there it is—like some damn ghost town. I parked across the road and just sat in my car, lookin' through the fence and razor wire to the buildings and the old water tower. The place reminded me so much of the pictures and old film of the World War Two death camps. Something snapped, Caroline."

"What happened?"

"I got outta my car and crossed the street right up to the damn fence. And then I walked along the fence. Every time I stopped to touch it, I thought electricity was shooting through my fingertips, up my arm, and shocking my brain. When I came upon a locked gate at the south end, I pulled my pistol and shot the lock off the gate."

"Jesse, you're out of jail on bond. They'll throw you back in and forget you exist."

"I picked up the lock and stopped by the gate at the main entrance. Johnny Hines was there in his neatly pressed rent-a-cop uniform."

"What did you do?"

"I told him I found the lock that way, all shot to hell and back. I told him to deliver it to Hack Johnson with a warning—advising him to lock his doors and windows 'cause something bad is comin' to visit him."

"Jesse, I know how angry you are coming back here, the state about to turn the school into a neighborhood with houses and tree-lined sidewalks, but you're letting your anger drive you to do things that will land you in prison, or worse. If you can find it in your heart to forgive those men who did those horrible things to you, then you no longer allow them to hold a dark place in your heart. You free yourself by not being chained to their evil."

Jesse said nothing, sliding the blanket off his shotgun, cradling it across his lap.

"Are you there, Jesse?"

He looked out the window in the darkened room, moonlight coming through the slats in the blinds. "I'm here."

"Have you spoken with Sean?"

"Not since I was locked up when he came to the jail before you made bond. I have to find Jeremiah, and I need to do it alone. That's the only way he'll talk, and maybe now he won't say anything. I don't know. I messed things up and now I have to get right with him to gain his trust. Sean can take it from there. Bring in the fuckin' troops at that point. Give Jeremiah a safe hideout, and we'll get through this."

"Sean and the FBI found a fingerprint embedded on the brass part of the shotgun shell Curtis found the night they killed Andy. Jesse, they're trying to locate a match."

"I bet I know where to find it."

"Let them find it, okay. Sean has spoken with Jeremiah, too. So it's not like Jeremiah doesn't know him."

"I've always cleaned up my own mess. I have a history with Jeremiah, just like I do with you. We all came from the same dirt-poor families. In a strange kinda way, we tried to take care of one another. I want to do that today for you, okay. It's not just about Andy, it's about you."

She was silent for a moment. "Thank you, Jesse. That's very kind."

He watched a shadow move outside in front of his window. It looked like the profile of the woman, the prostitute who was doing her thing two rooms down.

"I mean it, Caroline. To bring closure to you is what I think the man upstairs wants me to do. Look, I broke a bottle of vodka across a fence post at the school. The bottle was almost full. I didn't *need* it. Somehow, that released something disgusting inside me. I don't want to drink, don't want to go down that rabbit hole. I'm gonna take a quick shower, and if you haven't eaten, I'd like to buy you dinner."

There was a knock at his door.

Jesse stood from sitting on the bed. Caroline said, "Are you there."

He spoke in a whisper. "Yeah, somebody's at my door."

"Don't answer it."

"I think it's the prostitute. I'll get rid of her."

Another knock. Slightly louder. "Special delivery for anybody lookin' to get lucky." It was a woman's sultry voice. Jesse set the shotgun down on the bed and walked to the door.

FIFTY-SEVEN

Lana Halley silently read Curtis Garwood's two letters, her eyes moving across the page. We sat in a back booth in an Applebee's Restaurant. She looked up at me. "This is so sad. The post-traumatic stress that men like Curtis, Jesse Taylor, and others have suffered with and are probably still suffering from is appalling. And this has nothing to do with corporal punishment in Florida before the state banned it. This kind of abuse has everything to do with torture, pedophilia and murder."

"Those crimes are horrible by their very nature, but morally bad behavior is compounded by allowing it to continue. And that's what happened even when allegations of repulsive crimes were brought to the attention of people who oversaw the state's reform schools."

Lana lifted her cup of coffee with both hands, looking out the window, a light rain falling across the parking lot. She turned back to me. "I'm not sure what to do, Sean, and that sounds so damn weird coming from me. That's only because I use the letter of the law and the tools the office has to prove and convict those guilty of crimes. But when the crimes are almost historical in time and when my boss appears complicit, I have to become a spy to do my job in a covert world. That's not where I'm comfortable."

"The facts, the physical evidence—once it's gathered, will level the playing field for you somewhat. Who can you trust?"

"There is one assistant SA that I know I can trust. His name is Alex Bell. I used to trust Detective Lee, helped to prosecute at lease a dozen of his cases. You think this senior deputy you mentioned, Ivan Parker, is one of the good guys?"

"Yeah, I do."

She inhaled deeply and sat straighter in the booth. "Okay, let's do this. Parker needs to find a matching print. Maybe it's from the patriarch of the Johnson family. Maybe it's someone else. We won't be able to drag an old man into an investigator's office for fingerprinting. But, if I can get a court order, Deputy Parker can take the prints in the field. The question boils down to probable cause, and that's not a half-century old print on a shell casing when we don't have a body."

"The double barrel shotgun I told you about would narrow the gap."

"If it was the gun that fired the deadly blast, that would be a chess match movement that's hard to counter."

I reached into my shirt pocket and lifted out a small Ziploc bag, the piece of buckshot inside.

Lana leaned closer. "What's that?"

"Buckshot, double aught, to be exact. Fired from a 12 gauge. I dug it out of an old oak tree on the reform school property. It's the tree Curtis describes in his letters. If the gun in the back of the Johnson brother's pickup truck is the 12 gauge, bingo. And if we find Andy Cope's grave, locate his body on that property, and if forensics testing uncovers buckshot like this in his body…our perp is nailed."

"That's a whole lot of ifs, Sean."

"They're all connected problems. All we have to do is solve one, then another, and suddenly we're about to cause a house of cards to fall flat."

"You have to promise me something?"

"What's that?"

"You can't go all cowboy on me. You can't go in places with guns blazing and people dropping like flies. There has to be a system, if not, why have a system? No vigilante shit, okay O'Brien?"

"In this case, the criminal justice system failed, it failed in a lot of ways. I'm always willing to work within the system as long as it's working. But when there are criminals within the justice structure calling the shots, I'm forced to change strategy."

"Just no body count on my watch. What do you do next?"

"You need to take evidence to a grand jury. I need to go find it for you."

— —

Jesse Taylor stood next to his room door for a second, listening to the rain falling in the parking lot. He held his phone to one ear.

Caroline said, "Are you okay, Jesse? What's going on?"

"I'm gonna tell her to go away." Jesse looked through a slat in the blinds. It was the same prostitute he'd seen earlier. He couldn't see anyone else. "Hold on Caroline." He set the phone down on a table and slid the chain lock off the door. The woman looked younger up close, her red lipstick smeared, sheen of perspiration on her breasts.

She smiled and said, "Saw you sitting in your car. You looked a little lonely. Thought I could cheer you up. A lollipop is only fifty bucks."

Jesse nodded. "If you saw me sittin' in my car, you didn't see me go into this room. How'd you know this was my room?"

The shrubs moved. Jesse could feel no wind blowing. Her smile dropped, eyes dead. "Fuck you, old man." She bolted away.

Before Jesse could slam the door, two men pushed through the shrubbery, wearing ski masks, black T-shirts, jeans. They attacked. Jesse managed to connect his right fist into the side of one man's head. The larger of the two, more than 250 pounds, rushing Jesse like a linebacker, slamming him against the dresser, the TV falling to the floor.

The blow knocked the air from Jesse's lungs. The big man drew back and smashed his fist into Jesse's mouth, the hard punch loosening teeth, blood filling into his mouth. He lifted Jesse to his feet, the second man pounding Jesse's stomach, cracking ribs. Then the smaller man drove his left fist into Jesse's forehead, opening a deep cut, a flap of skin dangling over Jesse's eyebrow, blood pouring down his face.

The big man backhanded Jesse, knocking him across the bed. He picked up the shotgun, pressing the end of the barrel into Jesse's nose. He said, "Listen up, cocksucker. This is your last chance. You clean your sorry ass up and drive outta here before first light. Most of us voted to kill you. You got real damn lucky on this draw."

The second man pulled the padlock from his pocket. He ignited a lighter, butane gas hissing in the blue flame. He held the flame to the center of the lock, moving the fire around the perimeter of the bullet hole. The man's eyes were wide, animated through the opening in the ski mask. He held the lock by the curved shackle, stepping next to Jesse, grabbing his wrist and pressing the hot side into Jesse's forearm. Smoke rose from singeing hair and burning flesh.

Jesse clinched his teeth, closed his eyes, refusing to scream.

The man lifted the lock, satisfied with his work. "Now that's a tat. It's really a brand. We branded your ass like an animal. Looks like a square doughnut." He laughed.

The two men backed up a few feet. The big man emptied the shells from the shotgun, scooping them up and setting the gun against a wall. They left leaving the door wide open. Jesse tried to stand, tried to fight the darkness descending, tried to keep the bile from boiling out of his stomach.

He could hear the wail of sirens in the distance. *Caroline must have called 911,* he thought. He attempted to sit up, looking out the open door to the parking lot. Through the blood running into one eye, through the smoke in the room from his scorched flesh, he saw the same pickup truck. A man in silhouette sat behind the wheel, the orange glow of a burning cigarette like a distant planet in the dark universe.

Jesse leaned back across the bed, the stink of his burnt skin and hair hanging in the air, the room filled with the coppery smell of blood—the odor of a slaughterhouse.

FIFTY-EIGHT

I was paying the check at Applebee's when Caroline Harper called. "Sean! Jesse's been hurt! I don't know how bad he's injured. They came in his room and beat him. I heard it on the phone. I called 9-1-1. Dear God it was awful. He's at the hospital—"

"Caroline, slow down a second. What happened?"

"I was talking to Jesse on the phone. He was in his room at the Heartland Motel, and men burst in and attacked him. They were beating him horribly. I hung up and called for help. I don't know if they found the men who did it to him."

"I'm on my way. I'll call you when I know something." I disconnected and turned to Lana. "That was Caroline Harper. She said Jesse Taylor was attacked in his motel room at the Heartland Motel."

"That's in the city limits. Is he alive?"

"I don't know. I'm going to the hospital."

"Please call me, okay? Let me know."

"Okay."

"Thank you, Sean."

"For what?"

"For trusting me."

I drove toward Marianna, used my phone to find the address to the Jackson County Hospital, but decided to head toward the motel first. There would be little I could do immediately at the hospital. Maybe there was something I could discover at the crime scene, assuming I could get access

TOM LOWE

to it. A fight, unless it was a stabbing or resulted in a homicide, often didn't warrant an investigation beyond interviewing witnesses, if there were any.

Driving to the motel, I thought about how, in the moment of trauma, a wrong decision can have a negative domino effect. As a detective, I used to work backward to find the source, the thing that caused the chain of events, looking for the origin, the first blow of kinetic damage. This would sometimes lead me to arrive before the last domino fell—before a serial killer took his next victim. A two-by-one-inch domino can knock down a domino fifty stories high if the moving energy and mass builds between the sequences of falls—the order of events. Lynch mobs can be the result of one person pressing the collective buttons of like-minded people causing a human tsunami to roll over reason.

Jesse was his own worst enemy, pushing the wrong buttons.

I spotted a Marianna police car in the parking lot of the Heartland Motel, an officer in the driver's seat speaking into the mic. A second officer stood near the open door to a room, notepad in hand, interviewing a guy in a white short-sleeve shirt and a red polka-dot tie. I assumed he was the night clerk. A man in a bathrobe stood outside one room, smoking. The other guests were either oblivious to the fight or had gone back in their rooms and bolted their thin doors. I parked in a far corner of the lot and followed the long walkway in front of the rooms.

I could smell burning marijuana coming from the threshold of one room, the throb of country music behind the door. When I approached the officer, he'd just finished his interview with the skinny man wearing the wide polka dot tie. The man flashed a nervous smile at me, walking back toward the office, a key ring hanging from his belt and clanking like a sidewalk Santa.

The officer was in his early twenties, rangy jaws, and thick black eyebrows. He closed his notepad as I approached, the clipped verbiage and static of a police radio on his belt. He stood square to me, feet about eighteen inches apart. I smiled and said, "How's Jesse?"

"How do you know him?"

"We're friends. A mutual friend called me. She was on the phone with Jesse when it happened."

He started to reach for his notepad, hesitated to appraise my intentions. "What's this friend's name?"

"Caroline Harper. I'll give you her number. She called you guys when she heard the fight going down. I used to work homicide at Miami-Dade. Fights, especially domestic, often resulted in homicide." I could see him relax a notch. He reached for his notepad and pen. I asked, "How was Jesse when you found him?"

"Paramedics got here first. They had him stabilized. A witness said two men in ski masks jumped in a black or dark blue truck and peeled out of the parking lot. What's your name?"

"Sean O'Brien. The description of the getaway vehicle matches about half the trucks in Jackson County. Does it appear to be a robbery?"

"The room is trashed, and that's probably because of the fight. When the hospital releases him, he'll have to tell us if anything is missing. His wallet was still on him when they rolled Mr. Taylor out of here. There's a shotgun and pistol in there. It's odd why he wouldn't use one of the firearms to defend himself."

"That often means the victim knew the perp or perps. Or Jesse might have been surprised and jumped. Are you stringing up crime scene tape?"

"No. The manager is keeping the door locked. He's keeping the help away in the morning. Apparently Mr. Taylor prepaid for another few days, so the manager is leaving it like we found it."

"Mind if I take a quick look? I might be able to tell if something's missing."

He glanced toward the lot and the squad car, the dome light on, his partner filling out a report. "Since you were a cop, I'll extend a professional courtesy, but I'll go in with you. Don't touch anything. If, for some reason, your friend doesn't make it, this does become a crime scene."

"I understand." I walked into the room, the officer close behind me. The smell of alcohol and charred skin clung to the stained carpet and bedding. Blood had soaked into the sheets on the bed. "Did you notice whether he'd been burned?"

"We smelled something. Wasn't sure what the hell it was. Burned skin, maybe. There was nothing obvious. He had blood all over his shirt. I could only see lacerations to the face. Knuckles on his right hand looked swollen. We'll check with him at the hospital for further damages and to see if he wants to press charges. But with the perps wearing ski masks, that's unlikely."

I said nothing, looking down at the worn beige carpet. There were two shoeprints, one more discernable then the other. I could make out a slight pattern on one print. It appeared to be a boot imprint left from dark brown mud. I pointed to the print. "I wonder if that was left by Jesse or one of the bad guys."

He stared at the pattern a moment. "Couldn't tell you. We'll check on it down at the hospital."

"Sounds like a plan." I pulled out my phone, leaned in close to the print and snapped a picture, the flash illuminating the room for a second.

He said, "I think I'll get a photo, too. I'm not sure if we'll need it in the long run, but better safe than sorry."

After he took the photo, I walked back to the door and outside, the night air still cool from an earlier rain. I followed two more muddy prints indicating the man had stepped on the concrete walkway from behind a small row of border grass and shrubbery. I used the flashlight on my phone to illuminate tracks, boot tracks. They seemed to match the pattern left on the carpet. There was a small pyramid shape at the heel. The officer appeared behind me. I motioned to the prints. "This is where one of the two guys stood. He may have become a little wet if he waited long in the rain."

The officer examined the prints and snapped a second picture. "Hope we can use these. It all depends on whether or not your friend wants to get further in the mud with these guys. No pun intended." He grinned.

"Yeah, the thing about pressing charges is someone has to find the guys who did this so my friend can have the option to press charges or not."

He nodded. "We'll do our best. There aren't any security cameras pointed directly at this area. The one witness said he saw the perps from a distance. The masks make an ID impossible. Maybe your friend has an idea who did this to him."

I reached in my wallet and found Deputy Ivan Parker's card. "Here, take this. This deputy is working a case in the county, and he found a clean boot print near the crime scene. Maybe it'll match. You can make a cast and compare."

"What kind of crime is he working?"

"Hate crime. Someone left a hangman's noose in the yard of an elderly black woman."

The officer glanced back down at the patterns left in the mud. "I heard about that. Something like that is an indication of a real nut. I don't know much about your friend, but if the prints match, I'd say he's lucky we didn't find him dead in that room."

I nodded, turned and walked onto the parking lot, stepped a few feet beyond the parked squad car, the second officer looking up and nodding. There were two open parking spaces next to his car. I saw a fresh oil stain on the asphalt. Whatever car or truck had left it, hadn't been gone too long because the stain, about the size of a small pancake, wasn't diluted by rainwater. I squatted down and touched it with my fingertips, the dark oil still warm to the touch. I spotted four cigarette butts near where the driver's side door and window would have been. I looked at the butts, unfiltered cigarettes. Someone had been here waiting…watching. Chain-smoking unfiltered cigarettes while his goons beat Jesse, and by the smell in the room, one of the marks left on his body didn't come from a fist.

I walked quickly toward my Jeep, hitting the GPS on my phone for the best route to the hospital.

FIFTY-NINE

I could never shake the apprehension. I felt it each time I walked through the doors of an emergency room. Often it was here where the results of an attempted murder, in spite of heroic efforts of medical personnel, flat-lined into a homicide. It's where I used to speak with distraught family members, trying to make sense of the senseless, trying to find who tipped the first domino and which tumbling tile caused the unalterable consequence of death.

I thought of that when the glass doors automatically opened and I smelled the whisper of bleach, adhesive, and the elusive trail of human despair, looking across the waiting room into anxious faces struggling for courage.

The admitting receptionist was a middle-aged woman in a blue uniform. She sat in an open cubical in front of double closed doors that read: NO ADMITTANCE. She looked up from her computer screen as I approached, her alabaster face cast in bluish light from the screen. Her nametag: Gail Stevens.

I smiled. "Hello, Gail. Looks like the nasty weather is keeping your team busy tonight."

"It's not helping anything. Glad the rain finally stopped. Can I help you?"

"I'm here to see how Jesse Taylor's doing. He was brought in a couple of hours ago."

"Are you a member of his family?"

"Maybe better than family…I'm a close friend."

She almost smiled. "Then you can't go back. Sorry. You can take a seat in the waiting room."

"I understand. Maybe you can check to see how he's doing. I'd hate to call his elderly mother with inaccurate information. No sense in putting her through stress she doesn't need."

She looked at me a second and then picked up a phone and hit three buttons. "Hey, Barb. Can you check on Mr. Taylor? Is Doctor Paxton done with him?" The woman nodded, listening. "Thanks." She disconnected and looked up at me. "You can give Mr. Taylor's mother some good news. He'll be released. He had stitches and was treated for cracked ribs. He's had some medication. If he's released tonight, he could probably use a good friend to drive him home."

I smiled. "Thank you." I entered the adjacent waiting room and took a seat in the corner so I could see who was coming and going. The first to arrive were the same two officers from the motel investigation. The officer I'd spoken with nodded as he and his partner were allowed in the patient treatment area. One of the officers carried a notepad, the other an iPad. I hoped that whatever medication Jesse was on wouldn't cause him to say anything beyond the details of his assault.

The automatic glass doors opened with a *whoosh* and Caroline Harper stepped inside the emergency room. She wore jeans, white blouse, a shawl, her face tight, hair hastily pinned up. She looked at me, her mouth forming an O. She held a closed umbrella and stepped into the large waiting room. A half dozen people looked up from turning pages in magazines, texting, watching CNN news on a muted TV screen, pictures of a forest fire in the background.

I stood and walked to her, ushering her into one corner of the room. She looked up at me and asked, "How is he? Have you heard anything?"

"It looks like he'll be okay."

"Oh, thank God. I was so worried. Jesse thinks he's a knight, and he's really more like Tin Man in Wizard of Oz, but in Jesse's case he does have a big heart." She smiled, her eyes drained. "Did they find the men who did this to Jesse?"

"Police are back there with him now. Apparently the men who attacked him wore ski masks. Looks like he has cracked ribs and facial lacerations." I didn't mention the odor of hair and flesh I'd detected in Jesse's room.

She crossed her arms, purse hanging from one small shoulder. "The police are here."

The two officers came from behind the main doors and walked over to us. The officer I'd spoken with in Jesse's room sighed and said, "He has no idea who did his to him. Said he'd press charges if we picked up the guys who beat him. He does have a permit to carry those two firearms in his room. If I were he, I'd go back there just long enough to pack my bags. Looks like what they gave him was a painful warning. He says he doesn't know why he was attacked."

The other officer shook his head a bit and said, "But I think he does know. He's just not too eager to say anything. Now that Mr. Taylor's cleaned up, I recognize him. He's the same guy who was arrested in that fracas at Shorty's Billiards." He looked up at me. "You a friend of his?"

"Yes."

"You might want to give your friend some sound advice and tell him to stop doing whatever he's doing to piss certain people off. I'd guess that whoever roughed him up is probably connected to the Shorty's incident. There were more than thirty people in that joint when the fight went down. That's a pretty big pool of suspects."

Caroline said, "At least you have somewhere to start."

The officer nodded. "Yes ma'am, we just have to eliminate twenty eight of 'em. And we're still not positive the perpetrators that beat up Mr. Taylor came from the brawl in the pool hall."

I said, "You have the boot prints in the room and in the mud."

"Forensics investigators would pour a mold in a homicide. His isn't that, and Mr. Taylor tells us he's moving on."

I smiled. "Is that what he said?"

"Go ask him. You two have a good night." The officers left.

Caroline turned back to me and started to say something when the NO ADMITTANCE doors opened and Jesse Taylor stepped out.

SIXTY

A nurse came from behind Jesse as Caroline approached. The nurse smiled. "Are you his wife?"

"No, I'm a friend."

"He'll need to be driven home. He's had a low dose of Vicodin. Here's his paperwork with a prescription. He has two cracked ribs, sixteen stitches, and a burn. He's going to be sore." The woman glanced at the people in the waiting room. "I hope you feel better. Take care." She gently touched Jesse on his shoulder and then went back into the treatment area.

Jesse just stared at us for a moment, somewhat perplexed. There was a large adhesive bandage above his left eye, his shirt partially unbuttoned, a binding wrapped around his middle, the bandage visible under his shirt. Caroline bit her lower lip and walked up to Jesse. "Are you okay? Should you be leaving? Maybe you should stay overnight in the hospital."

Jesse slowly inhaled deeply, a slight flinch in his eyes. "Doc cut me loose. Besides, my insurance is runnin' on empty." He took a step, his jawline popping.

I moved up to him and said, "Let me help you to my Jeep."

He nodded. "I always wanted a Jeep. My car's at the motel."

Caroline said, "Jesse, you can't go back there. Not after what they did to you. Stay at my house. I have plenty of room. You'll have privacy and even your own bathroom." She smiled.

"That's real sweet of you, Caroline, but—"

"I don't want to hear it. We can go by the motel for your things, and then I'm taking you home." She looked up at me. "Sean, can you help him to my car?"

I reached for Jesse's arm. He winced in pain, pulling away. "Sorry, man. You just touched a spot that's on fire." He rolled up his sleeve. There was a dark red mark on his forearm, a burn mark. It resembled a square with layered serrated pieces, a splintered hole in the center. I knew immediately it came from a round shot through a padlock. A clear ointment had been applied over the burn.

Caroline gasped. "Dear God...what'd they do to you?"

He looked up from his wound, his eyes filled with darkness. "I'd been drinkin' and sort of lost it. This burn came from the lock I shot off on the south gate to the reform school. After I shot if off the gate, I went around to the front entrance and handed the lock to the rent-a-cop guard, Johnny Hines. I told him to give it to Hack Johnson to remind him he's never gonna be safe. He gave it to somebody in their family, because after they jumped me, one of 'em heated it with a butane torch."

I said, "When you asked to have it delivered, that's waving a red cape in front of the bull, or in the case of the Johnson family, a herd."

He started to grin, his mouth more crooked, his eyes now heavy. "You got to get in the ring to fight. I figure I can't find the bastard back in the swamps...so I'll draw him out."

"Jesse, it's not an eye for an eye," I said. "It's trying to prove Johnson or someone else killed Caroline's brother. That's what'll stick. Nothing else. Do you understand me?"

He lowered his eyes back to the burn on his arm. "When I was a kid, I was scarred for life. Now the bastards have branded me. Branded me like a rancher brands his cattle, his property." He looked back up at me, water welling in his eyes. His voice was raspy, now barely above a whisper. "I'm no one's property. I am a man!"

I nodded, lifted Jesse's arm to my arm to steady him and gently helped him walk outside, Caroline following. She opened the front passenger door to her car. I lowered him onto the seat. He leaned his head against the head-rest, eyes closing. I shut the door and turned to Caroline. "He's out. Follow me to his motel room. I'll get his stuff and then follow you to your house to help get him inside and into bed."

She looked up at me, the ruddy light from the illuminated EMERGENCY sign falling across her face. "Thank you, Sean. When I first contacted you, when I spoke with you at the marina…I didn't know things would turn out this way."

"Things haven't turned out yet, not completely. It's a process of discovery and elimination. Some doors are opening. Others are still closed and locked. All we can do is track down leads, go backwards in time to the source. You need to know what happened to your brother. Men like Jesse need to know they may have been warehoused and abused as kids, but their pasts and futures matter."

— —

It was close to one o'clock in the morning when I finally got to bed. I lay there in my motel room, the worn mattress lumpy, thinking about the past twenty-four hours. I played back conversations, events—looking for patterns, links, looking for vine-covered and rusty closed doors. Places with twin routes to the past and present. Tomorrow I'd receive the package from FBI agent Carly Brown. I'd get the GPS tracker from Dave. I hoped the shotgun shell and the print would open a crucial door into the past. And I wanted to see if the tracker would lead me to someone currently trying to keep that door shut and locked.

Sometime tomorrow I'd visit Cypress Grove, an assisted living facility. Maybe I could talk with one of the people that reporter Cory Wilson said was a resident there, Julie Carson, the mother of the state attorney, Jeff Carson. I didn't know if she had dementia or some other mental condition. But I did know what I wanted to ask her. And her response just might get me a little closer to finding Andy Cope.

SIXTY-ONE

Jesse Taylor scooped up a final spoonful of grits and scrambled eggs from his plate. He sat at the kitchen table in Caroline's home, the smell of bacon and coffee in the air. He sipped black coffee from a small white cup, Jesse's index finger almost too large for the handle. He set the cup back on the saucer and said, "Can't remember the last time I had a breakfast this good. Thank you, Caroline."

She smiled, the light from the morning sun coming through the tall glass windows in the Florida room, yucca and ficus plants growing from earthen pots in each corner. "I'm just so happy you're eating. I know it's not easy with loose teeth and cracked ribs. How's the burn on your arm?"

Jesse glanced at the wound. He wore a fresh white T-shirt and jeans. "It's painful, but I'll live. I'm hoping that when it heals there won't be much of a scar."

"Did you take your medicine?"

"Took the antibiotic. I'm tryin' to hold off on the painkillers. When I cough, though, my ribs feel like somebody's pullin' them apart with a crowbar. But I don't do well with narcotics; they make me tired and nauseous."

"Do only what you feel you need to do. I'm hoping you'll have a speedy recovery and they'll catch the men who did this to you."

"All I want is a speedy recovery of Andy—at least finding his whereabouts. The word speedy sounds damn weird after all these years. I need to get my car outta that motel lot before they tow it. Can you run me over there?"

She got up and stepped in the kitchen. "Can you drive?"

"No problem with that." His phone buzzed. Jesse looked at the screen. He recognized the number. It was Jeremiah Franklin. "Hey, Caroline, do you have the newspaper?"

"It's on the front porch. I'll get it for you"

"Thanks." He answered his phone and whispered, "Hey, Jeremiah, where are you?"

"Heard what happened to you. Sonia works up there at the hospital. She saw a report on what they done to you, Jesse. Are you hurt bad?"

"I'm all right. The important thing is we got the bastards scared. They're scattering here and there like cockroaches in a kitchen drawer."

"Can you walk?"

"Damn sure I can walk."

"Meet me at the old place we fished as kids."

"You mean Bellamy Bridge on the river?"

"Yeah, that old fishin' hole brings back warm memories for me. You too, I suppose. Meet me there at noon. When I see you I'm gonna tell you what you want to know. I'm gonna tell you who it was that killed Andy Cope.

— —

Both Fed-EX packages were waiting for me at the motel office. I signed for them, bought a large black coffee at a convenience store, and drove to the Heartland Motel, hoping Jesse's car was still there. It was. I parked next to it and opened the small package Dave had sent. There were two state-of-the-art GPS trackers. Last night, after packing Jesse's stuff into Caroline's car, I made sure one of the doors to Jesse's car was unlocked.

I put a battery inside one tracker, got out of my Jeep, opened the front passenger door to Jesse's car and slipped the tracker under the seat. At the hospital, Caroline had said Jesse wanted to be a knight—maybe he wanted to be her white knight, but he had the rust of Tin Man and no elixir, no can of oil in sight. I couldn't keep him on a leash, but I could keep tabs on him. And if he ventured too far from Marianna, too deep into the abyss, I could bring him back. Or I'd at least know where to look.

I got back in the Jeep and opened the package from Special Agent, Carly Brown. She had enclosed a handwritten note. I silently read it. *Sean, here's your fifty-year-old print and the shell. Let me know if there's a police agency you want me to send a digital copy to. Enclosed, you have an enlarged copy to use. If you find a match, you might be studied at Quantico in the future. And you might want to play the lotto, too. Good luck with everything. Carly.*

I started calling Deputy Ivan Parker when my phoned vibrated. It was reporter Cory Wilson. He was next on my to-call list, and now he was saving me time. I answered. "Mr. O'Brien, I have some bad news."

"I never like conversations to begin like that." I looked at the shotgun shell in the box, closed the cardboard flaps and asked Cory Wilson to deliver the news.

SIXTY-TWO

There was a long pause on the phone. I could hear Cory Wilson take a deep breath. I could hear the motors groan as a garbage truck lifted a faded green dumpster in the far corner of the Heartland Motel parking lot. Cory said, "I know, sorry. I just wanted to let you know that someone stole my notes. Although I'm relatively new in this career, I take notes—as you saw, the old fashion way, by hand. A lot of the guys use tablets, recorders, whatever. But I find when I physically write down something, I better remember it. I write down the key parts of the interview when I'm questioning people. For me, it sticks. I keep my notes locked in my desk drawer. When I came to work they were gone."

"Was the lock broken?"

"No. And I'm sure I locked the drawer before I left."

"Maybe whoever did it has a key. Wouldn't be too hard to find one in your office."

"No, it wouldn't. But what's really bothering me is *why* would anyone bother? Also, a lot of what I had in there is what we discussed and much more. I'm thorough. I've done research, made extensive notes about Vista Properties, James Winston, state attorney Carson, some of the principals with Horizon and even senior management within the department of law enforcement. I've been tracing as much of their personal and professional connections as I could find. I also had notes about you."

"What do you mean, exactly?"

"Your background, much as I could locate. It looks like you had quite a confession and conviction rate with suspects when you worked Miami-Dade homicide. But your military service record is a blank slate. The stuff about you taking down the plane with one shot and how that level of covert savvy could lead to the unearthing of Jackson County's most heinous secret—the possibility of a hidden cemetery filled with the bodies of boys. That's a story. I wasn't going to press, of course, until I had more, otherwise its mostly supposition, at least the parts about the cemetery."

"Who do you think might want to steal your notes?"

"Wally Holland, maybe."

"You think it's professional jealousy or could it have an ulterior motive?"

"The latter. I think he has an allegiance to some powerful people. Maybe he's on their payroll. I don't know. But I do know that if he's some kind of an informant, your cards have just been exposed. And I feel bad about it. That's why I'm calling you. Watch your back. If Wally's in cahoots with people like Detective Lee, James Winston, or Jeff Carson, you may be arrested for jaywalking. Marianna is a surreal kind of Mayberry. Rumors move at Internet speeds. Just be careful."

"Did you visit Cypress Grove?"

"No, not yet. Why?"

"Did you reference that place in your notes?"

"Only once. And I remember I wrote a note to myself to check at CG, but I didn't spell it out and I didn't list a name of a potential interviewee. So I seriously doubt if anyone could decipher those initials."

"Do me a favor, okay?"

"Sure. After compromising your investigation, that's the least I can do."

"Don't visit Cypress Grove just yet. Give it a couple of days."

"All right. Can I ask why?"

"Sure. But I can't answer you. All in good time, though. I have to go."

"Oh, one other thing. There's going to be a news conference Friday morning. The department of law enforcement is calling it in reference to the reform school acquisition. It's expected that the big announcement will be the sale of the property and exactly what it is that Vista plans to build there. I was hoping to have my story in the can before the announcement."

"That gives us four days. In the meantime, especially since your notes were compromised, write a story about me."

"What do you mean?"

"You can write that I'm in town to unearth the truth about the history of the Florida School for Boys and the possibility of multiple hidden graves. You can quote me by writing that justice for Andy Cope and others is long overdue. That will do two things. First, it'll open a Pandora's box of news media questions as Vista Properties and Horizon make their acquisition announcement. They won't be happy about that. Second, it'll draw out those who've seen your investigative notes and give them a target—me."

"Why would you do that?"

"It takes the dangerous heat off you as a journalist and gives them a real threat—and that's me."

"But you're putting yourself at risk."

I smiled. "Sometimes you just have to enter the cave and poke the dragon. Often, what you seek is just on the other side of the dragon. Gotta go." I disconnected and called Deputy Ivan Parker. When he answered I said, "I have the print I told you about. The spent shell casing, too. Where can I meet you?"

"I'm leaving the office now, en route to the courthouse. Meet you on the square, south entrance to the courthouse. Ten minutes."

"Ten minutes. See you then."

"Oh, O'Brien, don't know if you heard, but yesterday there was a lot of movement on the reform school property. There were a few white, unmarked vans and a moving van. A half dozen black luxury SUV's, too. No one asked for any assistance from the sheriff's office. But somebody was up there doing something. I just hope they weren't moving bodies." He disconnected.

SIXTY-THREE

Caroline Harper pulled her car into the lot next to Jesse's car and said, "Here we are. You sure you're going to be okay to drive?"

Jesse unbuckled his seatbelt and looked over at her. "Absolutely. You worry too much. You don't need any more damn worrying. You served your quota of fret time." He tried to smile.

"I'll follow you back home."

"You go on without me. I need to check in at the front desk, settle up, and get a receipt. I'll be back 'fore long."

She sighed, watching a Hispanic maid push a cleaning cart down the walkway in front of the rooms, one of the wheels on the cart squeaking. Jesse got out of Caroline's car. "No more fretting, okay." He nodded and walked toward the front office. Inside the office he waited until Caroline had left, then he poured black coffee into a paper cup at the coffee stand. The clerk was on the phone confirming a reservation, a Fox News commentator talking loudly from a TV mounted to the wall.

Jesse exited, walking as fast as he could to his car. He could feel the throbbing in his fractured ribs, the pulse of pain in the wound over his eye, and the fiery sting from the burn on his arm. He got into the car, turned the ignition, and started for a place he knew well…a spot on the river where he'd fished and swam with other boys. One of them was Jeremiah Franklin, and even after fifty years, Jesse remembered catching fat bluegill in the clear waters of the Chipola River below the dark shadow of the Bellamy Bridge.

— —

I parked my Jeep in the shade of a live oak on the south side of the court-house square and shut off the engine, the motor ticking as it cooled. Deputy Parker wasn't here yet. I called Dave. "Thanks for the trackers. I placed one in Jesse Taylor's car. He's on a dangerous mission. Keeping tabs on him could do two things: possibly save his life and, hopefully, lead me into the lion's den."

"If the perp or perps are distracted because they're dealing with Jesse, it might give you an opportunity for easier penetration in hostile territory. Where's the other tracker going?"

"A detective's car."

"There is something about investigating the investigators that offers a satirical irony in the footnotes of the justice system."

"File it under poetic justice system."

"Indeed. I'm looking at my computer screen and I can see the one tracker that's still with you. They other one is on the move, heading north out of Marianna."

"That's Jesse. I'm hoping he's driving back to Caroline Harper's place. Her address is Woodland Road, in Jackson County. Can you see if Jesse's heading in that direction?"

"Come on, Sean, give me something a little more challenging. Of course I can."

I spotted the deputy pulling into a parking place. "Got to go, Dave. Don't let Nick spend too much time with Max. Nick doesn't stick to the Mediterranean diet. He calls Max hot dog. If she eats three meals a day with him, she'll turn into a kielbasa sausage."

Dave chuckled. "I'll take her for a long walk." He disconnected.

I picked up the package I'd received from FBI agent Carly Brown, got out of the Jeep and walked over to Deputy Parker's squad car. He lowered the window. I could see my reflection in his dark glasses. He said, "I had the lab take a close look at the boot prints. They enlarged them about the size of your Jeep. The image you sent me matches the print in Mrs. Franklin's yard right down to the design on the sole and the unique wear on the boot. Sort of like looking at fingerprints with scars. So all I have to do is find the guy walking around with those boots."

"We got a match on boot prints. Now let's see if we can do the same with fingerprints, scars and all." I opened the envelope and lifted out an 8x10 enlargement of the print lifted from the shell casing. I handed the enlargement to him.

"So the feds lifted this from a shotgun shell fired a half century ago." He removed his sunglasses to inspect the image, releasing a low whistle. "If he's alive, the shooter is definitely up there in years."

"That night at Shorty's when Jesse Taylor was arrested...the guy he fought with, Cooter Johnson, his grandfather is still alive. Goes by the name of Hack Johnson. Do you know him?"

He looked up from the print to me, his eyebrows rising. "I know of him. They say he's a mean ol' bastard. I heard, years ago, when his family was even more prominent, if somebody crossed him—if they really pissed him off, he'd say 'I smell smoke.' Maybe a week later, maybe a month later or even longer, the person's business, house or even their car would be torched. Two people died in one of those fires. They were just kids. I was in middle school at the time."

"Through the years, with multiple arsons, couldn't your investigators connect the dots to Johnson?"

"Not without physical evidence. He was just too good, or they were not that good, or maybe a little of both. But that kind of strong-arm bravado made people afraid of him, even some of the police. I'd heard that no one, including Cooter, ever has received a speeding ticket or even a parking ticket because of possible retribution. It's like our town had its own country mafia."

"*Had*...you mean they're not a factor now?"

"Not as much. The old man keeps a low profile. You'll see him occasionally. He still drives, but most of the time one of his sons or grandsons is doing the driving."

"I think that family is still a force around here today. The photo of the bloody boot print I got after they beat Jesse Taylor senseless, the print that matches the one you found in the elderly woman's yard, most likely came from them. And they left something else on Jesse…a brand."

"You mean as in branding an animal?"

"Jesse had been drinking when he drove out to the reform school and shot a padlock off a remote gate. He'd left the lock with the security guard, and a left a message for Johnson. Looks like the guard delivered both. Later, the two guys that attacked Jesse used a lighter to turn the lock red hot and held it against Jesse's arm, leaving a brand."

"Shit. That's sending one hell of a message—as in you're marked, leave town. Maybe one of the two guys who jumped Jesse Taylor was that security guard."

"That's a possibility. Run the forensics on his boots and you'll know."

"If it's some of the Johnson clan, most likely that message was meant for you, too, because you stood up to them with the Miranda issue." He ran his wide thumb across the top portion of the steering wheel, flecked sunlight falling though the oak branches and across the car's window. "And you think this fingerprint came from Hack Johnson fifty years ago?"

"Maybe. There's only one way to find out."

"It'll take a court order to go back in those damn swamps and print that old man. Just because he worked there doesn't mean much. Hundreds of people from Jackson County have worked at the reform school through the years. Unless we can speak with Jeremiah Franklin and unless he ID's Johnson, we're pissing into the wind. And when I rode out to Jeremiahs place, his converted school bus, it looked like no one had been there in days. No garbage in the container. No fresh tire marks. Nothing. He might be out of the state."

"How well do you know the state attorney?"

"Carson?"

"Yep."

"He's a politician. I don't see him personally take many cases to trial in the district, unless they're high profile cases. He has a lot of competent assistant SA's who are sharp. Probably one of his best is Lana Halley."

"You trust her?"

"Don't have a reason not to."

"Then whatever evidence we can obtain needs to be evaluated by her because the way to obtain that court order you mentioned, the way to get a backhoe on the reform school land, is for Lana to convince a grand jury that the preponderance of evidence opens those long closed doors. If your sheriff is as by-the-book as you said, bring him in the loop after the physical evidence is accrued. In the meantime, you'll have to be even more covert around people like Detective Lee. Are you good with that, knowing what you know now?"

"Absolutely. Let's do this."

As he studied the print, a Marianna city police squad car pulled into the parking spot next to Deputy Parker's cruiser, the sound of the police radio coming from the squad car. The officer got out, a thick file folder in one hand. He locked his car and glanced in my direction, doing a slight double take. He recognized me and I recognized him from the investigation into the attack on Jesse. The officer walked toward us, a twisted smile working at the left side of his mouth.

SIXTY-FOUR

Jesse Taylor drove with one hand, using the other hand to search for aspirin in his car. He found the aspirin bottle in the middle console, shook out two extra-strength pills, lifting a water bottle from the drink holder. Empty. Not even a mouthful left. He tossed the bottle onto the adjacent seat, popped the aspirins into his mouth and chewed them, dry swallowing, the bitter taste of crushed charcoal on his tongue.

He touched the four-inch bandage above his eye, a dried blood spot about the size of a dime in the center of the dressing. He rolled his shirtsleeve up so air could circulate around the burn, glancing down at the image singed into the flesh and muscle on his forearm. He looked at his watch. Fifty minutes and he'd be meeting Jeremiah Franklin on the riverbank. Fifty minutes and he'd know for sure who killed Andy Cope. Fifty years and fifty minutes later he would hear the truth and then have the chance to face his demons head on, in the daylight. No longer would he be wedged in the dark quicksand of a nightmare.

Jesse sneezed, the exertion causing immense pain from the nerve endings attached to his shattered ribs. His hands shook, a chemical taste deep within his gut. He felt the flames fanning in the core of his chest. "Screw it! Gotta dull this." He searched his pockets, lifting out the small plastic prescription bottle. He mumbled. "Need water." Jesse lifted his phone to his lips. "Find the nearest store."

The artificial intelligence, a woman's voice said, "Crawford's Corner, convenience store is nine point three miles east on U.S 121."

"Thank you, darlin'."

Jesse made a U-turn on the county road and headed southeast—headed to a store to buy water for washing down narcotics to launder psychological and physical pain. He looked at his watch, stepping on the accelerator.

His phone buzzed in one of the drink holder pockets. Jesse picked it up and squinted, trying to see the caller ID screen. It was Caroline Harper. He answered. "Caroline, I'll be home shortly."

"Where are you? You should be getting rest."

"I'm meeting Jeremiah at the old Bellamy Bridge. Listen Caroline… he's gonna tell me who shot Andy. Then we got to get him into witness protection."

"You need to slow down, okay. I want to know who killed my brother more than anybody living. But I want to do it right, to bring justice for Andy. Call Sean. Tell him where you're going. He'll meet you and help you and Jeremiah through this."

"Jeremiah doesn't trust anybody but me. He lost a brother in there, too. I gotta go." Jesse disconnected. His face was flush, hot. Sweat trickling down the center of his chest and into the bandages binding his cracked ribs together. He coughed, the taste of blood replacing the bitterroot of aspirin on the back of his tongue.

— —

I watched the subtle undercurrents between Deputy Ivan Parker and officer T. Garret. It seemed to be slightly beyond judicial turf. More personal. More abrupt than what officers from counterpart agencies needed to be. Officer Garret looked at me. "Mr. O'Brien, you get around. So you're meeting with the county boys too."

"This is Deputy Parker."

"I know ol' Ivan. What's happening, Parker?"

"Always trying to keep the crime stats low here in the city of southern charm." He smiled.

"We'll that's part of the problem. The city's ours. The county's yours." He grinned.

"The city lies within the county."

I nodded, trying to add some levity. "In South Florida, we just called it Miami-Dade. Solved a lot of turf issues doing that. It was Deputy Parker's card that I gave you after you'd photographed the bloody boot prints in Jesse's room. I'd mentioned that Deputy Parker had photographed a similar print."

His grin dropped, pupils narrowing a notch. "Wasn't a whole lot of reason to compare boot prints when your pal, Mr. Taylor, wants to move on. And we have no ID and no surveillance camera video on two guys in ski masks. It is what it is. If something comes up, we can always see if the boot imprints match. But right now, I have more important stuff to do like to testify in a rape trial in a half hour. So if ya'll excuse me, I'll be heading inside the courthouse." He grinned and left, walking down a concrete path to the steps of the courthouse.

Parker watched him walk away and said, "Terry was a couple grades behind me in high school. He has some kind of insecurity going on in his big head."

"I hear there may be a news conference this Friday. The company trying to buy the reform school property may be making a formal announcement. It'll no doubt involve a lot of heavy hitters—city and county politicians, the state attorney, people from the Florida Department of Law Enforcement, and maybe even someone from the governor's office."

"I've been hearing those drums beating too. Didn't know Friday was the day. How'd you get wind of it?"

"Some of the principals from Vista Properties are in town. I've noticed a few more dark suits here than when I first arrived."

"You always this observant?"

"Not always. This would be a good time to let Lana Halley know about the matching boot prints. Let her know you have a fingerprint or a thumb-print from the shotgun shell and you're searching for a match. Something else, too."

"What?"

I reached into the package and lifted out the second GPS tracker, leaving the shotgun shell in the box. "Do you know what car state attorney Jeff Carson drives?"

"Yeah, it's a BMW. Black. Late model."

I handed him the tracker. "You might want to slip this on the underside of his car. I have a feeling he's meeting with some people who would be a direct conflict of interest if it came to an investigation into former criminal activities at the reform school."

He studied it, his doubts coming to the surface. He looked up at me. "Who might those people be?"

"Anyone who would leverage a property sale with that kind of black cloud hanging over it. Unless the haze was lifted by an impartial investigation, their activities are suspect...so far any request in that direction is an immediate shutdown."

"Man, you know what you're asking me to do? Run a stakeout on the highest-ranking prosecutor in the Second Judicial District of Florida. If I get caught, I'd be damn lucky to get a job as a dogcatcher. I couldn't get far enough from Jackson County, and with a wife and kids, that's not an easy option."

I held out my hand. "I understand. Give it back to me and I'll do it."

He blew out a long breath, staring at the black tracker with a suction cup mounted on the top. "I might be able to slap this on the underside of his car, but there's no way I could follow him in a marked sheriff's vehicle."

"You don't have to. Just download the app and you can track him from your phone. You'll have exclusive access to the GPS signal when you enter the tracking code after you activate it. It's just another tool at our disposal. I may be shooting blanks and possibly wrong about Jeff Carson, but after I spotted him lunching with one of the executives with Vista Properties, he entered my radar."

He nodded slightly, his facial muscles relaxing. "Yeah, I can sure as hell see why. I'll do it. Who knows, we might stumble across the crime of the century."

"Let's hope, at least the last half of the century. Right now you need to find a black BMW parked in a reserved spot behind the courthouse."

"Got it."

I nodded and stepped back toward my Jeep as he started the cruiser and drove away. I would head to a senior care center. Maybe Jeff Carson's mom would enjoy a chat.

SIXTY-FIVE

I f there's a visual reminder of just how short our time is on the planet, it's played out daily on the stages of assisted living facilities across the world. It's the slow-motion final act—the epilogue in lives that were often fully led. Some people have referred to them as 'God's waiting rooms.' For certain residents, they're places where the body has outlasted the mind. For others, the upholstery is frayed but the elderly man or woman is still sound in mind and character, yet they sit in corners like human antiques with dust on their shoulders.

I thought about that as I parked in the visitors' area for Cypress Grove Senior Care Center, watching an attendant in a white uniform pushing an elderly woman in a wheelchair. The center was a large, one-story building with more of a hospital feel than a retirement home. The center was surrounded by old live oaks. Azaleas and petunias bloomed around the perimeter. Red and yellow impatiens blossomed on both sides of the shady walkway leading to the glass front doors.

On the passenger seat next to me was a wrapped bouquet of roses I'd bought on the drive over to the center. I picked up the roses and walked to the entrance. Sprinklers on the east side of the manicured lawn were spraying water across the dark green St. Augustine grass, some partially hitting the left corner of the sidewalk.

Inside, there was the slight odor of bleach and human waste—urine trapped in the equivalent of diapers. A dozen or so residents were in the lobby, which resembled a large living room with a slate rock fireplace, framed oil paintings, two sofas, a dozen overstuffed chairs, potted plants, tables and chairs. Some of the elderly were in wheelchairs, others clinging to shiny metal walkers, shuffling across the tile floor.

I approached the receptionist, a twenty-something woman wearing glasses, blonde hair in a ponytail, chipped red fingernail polish. She looked up from her computer screen, the reflection of a game of solitaire off her glasses from the screen. "Can I help you?"

"I hope so. And I hope she'll like these. These are her favorite."

"They're beautiful. I love red roses. Who are you here to see?"

"Julie Carson."

"Miss Carson is probably done with her lunch. Let me get someone to show you to the dining room." She lifted her phone and punched four numbers. "James, Julie Carson has a guest. Would you please escort him to the dining room? Yes, thanks." She looked up at me. "James will be up in a sec to take you to her."

"Thank you." I stepped away as she lowered her eyes back to the screen, her fingers returning to the electronic card game. I watched the residents in the lobby, some sitting at tables playing board games, others parked in comfortable chairs reading, napping, and some staring through the large bay windows at squirrels frolicking across the lawn.

A hefty black man in a white uniform came through the double doors leading from the lobby to the other areas of the facility. He had a large shaved head, shiny scalp under the florescent lights, double chin and thick arms. His eyes were wide and playful. "Hi, I'm James Shepard. You here to see Miss Carson?"

"Yes, how is she today?"

"She's always good. Some days are better than others. She might recognize you today, and then she might not. You never really know. One fella who works here says human memory is like a radio signal. Sometimes you hear it clear enough to dance to the music. Other times it's fading and then nothing but static."

"Maybe Aunt Julie is tuned in today."

He grinned. "C'mon back, we'll see."

I followed James through the double doors, down a hallway, the smell of meatloaf and mashed potatoes coming from around the bend. We entered the dining room. There were at least thirty tables with four chairs to each one. Red-checkered plastic tablecloths. The dining room was half filled with residents, most slowly eating, some very animated and chatting. Some quiet, faces empty. Wait staff carried plates of food to the elderly, bussed tables, and generally seemed to be engaged with the people they served.

James stopped and pointed to a table near an exit door. "Looks like she's done eating." One woman sat alone in a wheelchair. She was slender, dressed in pajamas and a dark blue robe, silver hair brushed and down the center of her back. I looked at her plate as a male attendant with dirty blond hair parted down the center of his head spoke with her. He nodded, smiled, and bussed the table. The meatloaf hadn't been eaten, maybe two bites gone from the mashed potatoes. Green peas seemed untouched. A glass of iced tea was full. James said, "She looks tired. You might not want to stay too long."

"Is there somewhere a little less noisy that I can visit with her?"

"Sure, we have a living center right through the exit doors. We have patios and gardens. Indoors or out?"

"Whatever's closest will be fine."

"That'd be the living center. You want me to wheel her in there for you?"

"Sure. You know the ropes."

"That I do." He smiled and walked to the table. "Miss Carson, you got a visitor, ma'am."

She glanced at him. No expression on her face. I could tell at one time she had probably been a lovely woman. Nice cheekbones, slender nose, long neck. Wide eyes. James touched her gently on the shoulder. "We gonna go for a little ride so you and your guest can visit with one another."

She looked up at me and said nothing. James glanced at me, grinning. "Maybe the radio signal will be a little clearer when ya'll have time to chat." He unlocked her wheelchair, removed a white napkin from her lap and dropped it on the table. I picked it up as he rolled her from the dining room through the open door and into a large room that had more tables, wide-screen TV mounted on a far wall, and more board games stacked on one table. A female attendant on one side of the room read from a book to a half-dozen residents, most were attentive. One woman was fast asleep, her mouth open.

I followed James as he strode by a few residents, some reading magazines or playing checkers. Two residents were engaged in a game of backgammon.

One man sat alone. He was staring at flickering images on the television, the sound muted. James looked at him and said, "Mr. Wiley. You don't forget to tell me when you got to go pee, okay. No accidents today." The old man had a pinched, unshaven face, narrow eyes behind wire-frame glasses, brown age spots the size of dimes on his hands, fingernails longer than they should have been. I could tell he wasn't getting the care most of the residents seemed to be getting. He didn't acknowledge James.

When we passed his table, I said, "That gentlemen looks like he could use some company, too."

James shook his head. "He's what you'd call a loner. Always keeps to himself. Takes a couple of us to give him a bath, and that's when he gets too ripe to be in the same room."

"Where's his family?"

"He's got a daughter. She comes by for a few minutes at Christmas."

"You don't hear the last name…Wiley very much. What's his first name?"

"You don't hear that much either. It's Zeke…Zeke Wiley."

I looked back at the table, back at the man and remembered what reporter Cory Wilson had said, *'The other one is Zeke Wiley. He maintains a P.O. box. No physical address in the property tax rolls.'*

I stared at the old man, ignoring my phone vibrating. The man was employed at the reform school when Andy Cope was killed. Could Zeke Wiley have been there that night…and was he possibly the man who pulled the trigger?

SIXTY-SIX

J ames parked Julie Carson next to one of the tables. He locked her wheelchair in place, looked at me and said, "Ya'll have a nice visit." He smiled
and left.

"Thank you." I sat across the table from the old woman and set the
roses in front of her. She lowered her head, eyes moving from the stems to
the dozen red blooms. She slowly reached out, extending one finger bent
from arthritis, the tip of her trembling finger touching the petals of a rose.
A smiled worked at a corner of her mouth. She looked up at me, her damp
eyes curious—confused.

"The roses are for you, Julie. I hope you like them. I'll ask James to put
them in a special place in your room."

She said nothing, staring at me, waiting for something to form in her
memory. "My name's Sean O'Brien. I'm a friend of Jeff."

She turned her head slightly. Her son's name made a distant penetration.
She looked back down at the roses. Someone unmuted the sound on the
TV across the room, *Jeopardy* coming from the speakers. I leaned in a little
closer to her.

"Jeff sends his love. He stays so busy with his job in the state attorney's
office. You must be very proud of him."

She lifted her eyes up to me. "Ja…Jeffery." Her voice sounded distant,
as if it came from the bottom of a deep well.

"Jeff Carson, your son. He sends his love."

"He's a good boy…Jeffery." Her voice was a little stronger, a tenor of recognition in the rasping delivery.

"Yes, Ma'am. You raised him well. It's hard to raise a boy alone."

She stared at me, her head barely nodding. I opened the white napkin and spread it out on the table. I took out my pen and drew a cartoon face, the face of Minnie Mouse. Julie looked at it a few seconds and smiled, her eyes a littler brighter. She raised her eyes up at me, her head tilting a bit.

Then I turned the napkin over and drew on the opposite side. She watched my hands move, the bold dark ink strokes appearing across the fabric. Each time I made a stroke, I glanced at her before continuing the sketch.

When I drew the last lines, she looked away, her eyes reflecting dread. "It's okay, Julie. He's not here. He won't hurt you. Think back Julie…when you worked for the Florida School for Boys…he worked there too. Nothing was your fault." I reached across the table and held her hand. She looked at me, the presence of terror draining from her eyes. "You don't have to say anything, Julie. Just nod your head. Hack Johnson hurt you didn't he, Julie. He attacked and hurt you."

Nothing. Staring. Eyes wider. Her nostrils flaring slightly.

"It's okay. He's been gone from your life many, many years. But one good thing did come from a very bad thing. You had a son from that attack. Jeffery is Hack Johnson's son isn't he?"

She stared at me a few seconds, nodded and closed her eyes, a single tear spilling from one eye. I looked down at the napkin, the Southern Cross drawn across it. I picked up the napkin, folded it and put it in my pocket. I stood and stepped next to Julie. Then I placed my hands on her frail shoulders, bent down and kissed her on the cheek. "You were a good mother."

I turned and went across the room to find Zeke Wiley.

SIXTY-SEVEN

The closer Jesse Taylor came to the Bellamy Bridge, the more he thought about Jeremiah's mother. He thought about the boot print in her yard when Jeremiah cut down the noose from the tree. He could suddenly see every tread on the print with the pyramid on the heel. He could hear the old woman's words reverberating around the inside his skull. *In my dreams, I see Elijah bein' buried alive. The dark soil movin' 'cause his heart was still beatin' fast, just under the black earth, his little hands clawin' like an animal. I heard him whimper, tryin' to cry out to me…mama.'*

Jesse's thoughts were interrupted by the sounds of something slamming against the undercarriage of his car. He was off the pavement, driving along the shoulder of the road, fallen tree limbs, loose rocks, and dirt hitting underneath his car. The sound jolted him back onto the highway asphalt. "Shit!" His heart hammered. Sweat popping on his brow. Hands shaking.

He looked at his watch. The stop by the convenience store for water cost him more time than he had to spare. He accelerated, heading on a mission to the Bellamy Bridge, the bottle of Vicodin opened on the seat next to him, white pills spilled onto the fabric.

——

Walking to where Zeke Wiley sat, I stopped to read a text on my phone. It was from Caroline Harper. *Sean, I left you a voice message. Jesse's on his way to meet*

Jeremiah Franklin at a place called Bellamy Bridge. I'm worried for them. Jeremiah's going to tell Jesse who killed Andy. Please go there.

Zeke Wiley didn't move his head when he cut his eyes up at me. He'd finished his lunch, most of the food on the plate gone. Pewter whiskers around his small mouth and chin were glossy with grease from fried chicken. He lifted a glass of water to his lips, sipping. Then he gingerly set the glass down, aligning it to the same water-ring left on his tray.

I smiled and said, "Everything in its place, right? Details matter, don't you agree? Are you done eating?"

He nodded.

"I'll take that out of your way." I lifted his tray and set it on a vacant table next to us, and then I sat down across from him. "How are you, Zeke?"

He stared, trying to place me. He cleared his throat and said, "I'm okay. Do I know you, sir? Are you the new doctor?" His voice was croaky.

"No. And you don't know me."

He stared at me, his tea-colored eyes slowly blinking behind the glasses.

"But I know you, Zeke."

"You do? How in the hell would that be?"

"I'll show you." I looked into his eyes, lifting the photo from my shirt pocket, keeping the image toward me until my hand got within two feet of his face. Then I turned the picture toward him. "I know you were there that night when Andy Cope was killed."

The blinking behind his glasses became more rapid. He tried to swallow, a clicking sound in the back of his throat. His lower jaw quivered, lips pursing, air coming from his mouth. I could see the carotid artery flutter under his sagging turkey neck skin.

"After all these years, you do remember Andy. Do you ever think about him, Zeke? Do you ever think what he might be doing today had he lived? Maybe he'd have been an engineer. Maybe a scientist—someone who cleans up the oceans. Maybe a doctor—someone who finds a cure for cancer. But we'll never know what Andy could have been because he was never given the chance. Why'd you kill him? Was it because he was running away? Were you trying to stop a prisoner from escaping? Why'd you do it, Zeke?"

"No...no...I didn't do it. I didn't shoot that boy."

"I never said he was shot. How'd you know he was shot?"

He wiped the grease from his thin lips with the back of his left hand, the narrow yellow wedding band worn dull.

"Did you ever tell your wife what happened?"

"She'd died…long ago."

"So did Andy, longer ago. If you didn't do it, who did? Who pulled the trigger that night, Zeke?"

He said nothing, staring down at his hands—in the background, a contestant on *Jeopardy* answering a statement with a question in the background, a dining room server bussing tables behind us.

"Zeke, it's time that Andy and the others boys had two things: recognition and justice. You can give it to them. At this point in your life, you can change things—make a difference. Help close old wounds. Not only for the families who never saw their children, again, but for the grown men living today who still carry those emotional scars."

"Go…go…away!" his voice a littler higher, his left hand trembling.

The attendant bussing the tables, a middle-aged Hispanic man, approached us. He had a round face, a diamond in one earlobe. "Ever'thing all right?"

I smiled. "I should learn never to talk politics with family. Even after all these years."

The man shrugged. "We are who we are." He grinned, patted Zeke on his back and pushed a cart filled with dirty dishes out of the room.

I leaned forward, closer to the old man who folded his thin arms across his chest, harboring a conscience of deception. I lowered my voice. "Zeke, you may be in a senior center now, but if you don't help bring closure to the deaths of Andy and the others, you'll live your final days in a cell. And even at your ripe old age, the inmates pay closer attention to pedophiles and child murderers."

He reached for the remote control to his wheelchair. I lowered my hand across his hand—bones like wooden pencils, skin malleable and crusty. "Zeke, I'm going to leave an envelope and a sheet of paper with you. You've got a choice. You can write down the name of the person who killed Andy…or you don't. If you feel in a talkative mood, you can write down what happened. If you do nothing, if you continue your silence, then you're an accomplice to a child's murder. And when I come back, it will be with the police and a warrant for your arrest. If you do the right thing, make sure you sign your name, seal the envelope and give it to the receptionist. "

I reached in my coat pocket for the envelope, paper and pen, setting them on the table. I wrote across the envelope. "My name is on the front of the envelope. They'll hold it at the desk for me."

I stood. He looked up at me, an opaque liquid dripped once from his right nostril. I stepped to the table with his dirty dishes, lifting the glass by the bottom, pouring the remaining water into the shallow rubber tub with other dishes. I walked away with the glass and the greasy fingerprints on it, looking back at Zeke Wiley who stared at the paper and pen in front of him, the haggard and frayed appearance of a man about to write his last will and testament.

In the parking lot, as I was unlocking my Jeep, the phone in my pocket buzzed. Dave Collins said, "I thought I'd give you a heads-up on the GPS tracker with the most movement—the one you hid in Jesse Taylor's car."

"What do you have?"

"I can calculate time and space with his movements. He's driving fast, I'd estimate close to ninety. He's on Highway 276 or Bump Nose Road—and that is the name. He's headed north, almost running parallel to the Chipola River."

"He's going to meet the only eye witness to Andy's shooting. He's in a race to meet with Jeremiah Franklin. And I have a late start."

SIXTY-EIGHT

J esse glanced down at the speedometer, the needle below the ninety MPH mark. He eased up on the accelerator just as blue lights flashed in his rearview mirror. He looked into the mirror. A state trooper was not far behind, gaining. "Shit! Shit!" Jesse pounded the steering wheel with an open hand. He slowed down to the speed limit, sweat popping on his forehead, heart pounding. "I don't need this crap now." He scooped the spilled Vicodin pills off the seat, palming them back into the prescription bottle.

He tossed the bottle of pills under his seat, looking up into the rearview mirror at the trooper's car. It was less than two hundred feet behind him. Instinctively, Jesse touched the pistol strapped and holstered above his left ankle. He pulled off the highway, slowing and stopping in a small clearing next to the road. The trooper pulled behind him.

Jesse could see the video camera mounted on the car's dash. The shotgun barrel vertical next to the trooper. Road dust settling. The trooper put his hat on, opened his door cautiously. He had the lanky body of a pro basketball player. Long arms. Long neck. He walked up to Jesse, the trooper's right hand very close to his holstered pistol. He said, "What's your hurry?"

Jesse looked up, sweat trickling into the bandage on his forehead. "I got a bad damn prostate. Gives me fits. Gotta pee real bad."

The trooper stared at him. "Plenty of woods around here. What happened to you?"

"Got jumped in Marianna."

"They catch the guys who did it?"

Jesse said nothing for a few seconds. "You said guys. How'd you know it was more than one?"

"I didn't. Lucky guess. You been drinking?"

"No."

"You smokin' weed?"

"No."

"I need to see your license and registration."

Jesse nodded. "In the glove box."

The trooper rested his right hand on the butt of his holstered pistol, watching Jesse lean over to the glove box, opening it and fishing around loose papers. "I know it was in here before I left from home."

The trooper pulled his pistol and aimed it at Jesse. "Get out of the car! Now!"

"What's the matter with you? Why'd you pull a gun on me"

"Out of the car!"

"So you can shoot me?"

"I'm not telling you again!"

Jesse slowly opened his car door and got out. He raised his hands. "What do you want? Who you workin' for? Is the whole damn county on the take?"

"Shut up! We're gonna go for a little walk into the woods. Move!"

Jesse glanced back at the trooper's car. "On video, they're going to see you pulled your gun for no reason, drew down on an unarmed man."

"Not if my dash-cam has a loose wire. Picture comes and goes. Move!" He grinned.

Jesse walked around the back of his car. In the distance, a truck filled with logs was coming down the highway. The trooper lowered his gun, moving his body between the approaching truck and Jesse. He said, "You act normal."

"What's that supposed to mean when you're holding a pistol on me?"

The trooper said nothing, waiting for the truck to pass. As it blew by, he watched it for a second, looking at the truck's side-view mirrors. Jesse lunged for the trooper's pistol. He used both his hands. Grabbing the man's wrist. Twisting hard, tendons popping. He dropped the gun, Jesse picking it up and rolling to the ground. The trooper charged. Jesse raised the pistol, aiming at his chest. "Stop! Another step and you'll die. Hands up!"

The trooper slowly raised his long arms. "You broke my wrist."

"You're damn lucky I haven't broken your fuckin' neck yet. Walk to your car. Now!"

The trooper turned and walked to his car, Jesse following. "Open the door. Get inside." The trooper did as ordered. "Toss the keys out the door."

"They'll hunt you down."

"The keys!"

The trooper removed the keys from the ignition and threw them to the ground. Jesse picked up the keys, never taking his eyes off the man. "Now, take your cuffs and slap one on your left wrist first. Then you're gonna stick your right hand through the steering wheel and you're gonna cuff yourself to the wheel."

"You're a dead man. You're just too dumb to know it."

"Do it!"

The trooper complied, mumbling under his breath.

Jesse jogged to his car, pain shooting from his rib cage. He tossed the trooper's gun on the seat beside him, started his car and squealed tires, pulling away. He was less than ten miles from the Bellamy Bridge. And at that moment in time, with a trooper's car in his rearview mirror, it felt like he was a hundred miles from the old bridge and old friend.

SIXTY-NINE

I followed the directions Dave gave me, heading for someplace on the Chipola River, somewhere I hoped to find Jesse and Jeremiah. I called Lana Halley. She answered, her voice just above a whisper. "Sean, I have a deposition in five minutes."

"It won't take me that long to tell you something about your boss."

"What?"

"He's mother is confined to the Cypress Grove senior care. Her name is Julie Carson. She worked at the reform school the time Andy Cope was killed. Hack Johnson was working there at the same time. I believe he raped her. I believe Jeff Carson is his biological son."

"What? You say you *believe*. What do you mean?"

"Johnson has a tattoo on his right arm in the shape of the Southern Cross. I drew the cross on a napkin and showed it to Julie. She had a very adverse reaction, like a PTSD flashback when someone holds up a frightening picture of your past. If Jeff Carson is Johnson's illegitimate son, and if he knows it, maybe that's one of the reasons the Johnson clan gets away with...murder."

"But if Jeff's mother was raped by Johnson, why would Jeff do anything for them?"

"We don't know the history—the dynamics, the lies, the greed."

"What led you to approach her?"

"Jeff Carson's chin."

"His chin?"

"The cleft is unique—sort of makes a slight upside down Y pattern. When Hack Johnson's son, Solomon, approached me in front of Ruby's Coffee Shop, I saw an almost identical cleft in his chin. It was so similar it made me wonder if there could be a blood relation. Considering the circumstances—an apparent rape, Julie Carson may never have told Hack Johnson he'd fathered her child. Maybe she did years later. I don't know. I do know that the clan gets preferential treatment in Jackson County. I saw it the night the grandson, Cooter Johnson, tangled with Jesse Taylor at the bar. Detective Lee had no interest in Jesse's story."

"A DNA blood test with the old man will speak volumes."

"And if one of his fingerprints match that from the shell, I'd say you have more than enough for a grand jury. Speaking of prints, I lifted one from a guy named Zeke Wiley. He's a resident of the senior center too. He was working at the reform school the time Andy was killed. He says he didn't do it, but he does know Andy was shot, something I didn't tell him. I'm going to give the print to Deputy Ivan Parker. If it matches the one from the shotgun shell, Deputy Parker will have an easier arrest. If not—he might need some help."

— —

Jesse drove north, heading for Jacob Road—the road that would take him to an old trail leading to the Bellamy Bridge. He punched in the numbers to Jeremiah Franklin's phone. After six rings and no answer, Jesse disconnected. "Hope you're still there." He tossed his phone on the passenger's seat and drove faster. The road wound through thick forests, oak and pine trees. He turned right onto Jacob Road. He remembered the old trail through the woods that would lead him down to the river and the bridge. He hoped that he could still find the entrance to the trail.

After another mile, something positive. Jesse mumbled, "I'll be damned. A sign of the times." The state has erected a sign marking the head of the trail. Jesse pulled off the road, driving behind a thicket of trees on the opposite side of the road, the undergrowth hiding his car from passersby. He picked up the trooper's pistol, sliding it beneath his belt, trotting across the road, one hand pressing against the binding around his ribcage.

He followed the path into the woods, thick trees on both sides, birdsong coming from beyond the perimeter of foliage. The humid air smelled of pinesap and wet moss. Clumps of ferns grew along the edge of the trail. He wanted to run, to jog down to the river to meet Jeremiah. Mosquitoes orbited his head, whining in his ears, probing his neck. He swatted them, rolling down his sleeves, the burn on his arm stinging.

Jesse walked as fast as he could on the path, sweat rolling down his back, the taste in his throat was like gunmetal. He passed two rustic benches, longing to sit for a few seconds to catch his breath. He continued. Around the final bend, the trail opened up to a bridge he remembered as a boy. The Bellamy Bridge always had a spooky look, he thought. Rusted iron and cables straddling the Chipola River. The floor had rotted away long ago. He remembered one of his teachers telling the class it was the oldest bridge of its kind in Florida. It replaced wooden bridges that had carried settlers and soldiers from one side of the river to the other. The old metal bridge still stood, crippled but a testament to another era.

Jesse stopped at the bridge, looked down at the slow moving river, cypress trees lining its banks, a white heron hunting in the shallows of cypress knees poking above dark water. He couldn't see Jeremiah anywhere. Not by the old bridge, underneath it, or along the riverbank. *He's gone. Too damn late.*

"Hey, man…what took you so long?"

Jesse turned around. Jeremiah stepped out from the thicket, smiling. "Skeeters would eat me alive if I hadn't brought some spray. Looks like you could use some too. Jeremiah pulled a small bottle of insect repellent from his pocket and handed it to Jesse.

Jesse sprayed his hands, face and neck. "Thanks. I forgot how bad the bugs could be down here."

"They ain't bad on the river, wind and whatnot. Just walkin' through the woods is a bug love fest." He grinned.

"I didn't see your car. Where'd you park?"

Jeremiah pointed to the right of the bridge, to the water. A johnboat with a small outboard motor was tied to a cypress tree. "I came in my boat. I always preferred rivers to roads, anyhow. Caught me two fat catfish while waiting for you."

"I'm damn sorry I'm so late. Lot of shit happened on the way here."

Jeremiah nodded. "You look all tattered and tore, Jess. Like a scarecrow got a thumpin' by the crows." He smiled.

"Have sure as hell been better. I'm hoping what you tell me will make a lot of folks better. Caroline Harper…your mother…and a lot of guys like us who've been carrying this weight far too long."

Jeremiah blew out a long breath. "I hope so. Maybe that former policeman friend of yours, Mr. O'Brien, can do something. He seems the real deal." Jeremiah looked at the river, the cry of a limpkin coming from across the water, an anhinga standing on a cypress stump, wings extended, drying feathers in the warm sunlight. "Jesse, I think you know who it was that kil't Andy. I used to see him occasionally when I'd go in to town for things. He'd always give me a hard stare. If pure evil can be seen in a man's eyes, you can see it in his. Windows to hell, I call his eyes."

"Who was it, Jeremiah? Who shot Andy?"

Jeremiah swatted at a mosquito in the air, looked up at Jesse and said, "It was—"

His shirt exploded in a bright red flower of blood. The sound of the shot came a millisecond later. Jeremiah fell to his knees.

Jesse ran to his fallen friend, taking him under the arms and dragging him behind a tree. A second bullet echoed through the forest. Jesse pulled out the pistol, firing once in the direction of the shot. The forest was quiet. He could hear the trickle of eddies swirling around the cypress knees. A fish jumping in the river. There was no human movement. Nothing but the sounds of Jeremiah trying to breathe. Jesse knelt beside him, pressed his hands to the bloody wound. "Hold on! Just breathe. We'll get through this together."

"It's…it's…okay…"

"Don't talk. Rest. I'm callin' 9-1-1. We'll get you to a hospital." The sweat loosened the bandage on Jesse's forehead, the bandage flapping. Jesse tore it off.

Jeremiah coughed, blood trickling out of his mouth.

"Hold on! Don't you think about dyin' on me. We've been through too much. You'll make it." Jesse tried to smile. He found his phone, hands bloody, shaking. He was trembling so bad he could barely hold the phone. He punched the numbers 9-1-1. No signal. "Fuck!' No!"

Jeremiah coughed again, his chest rising and falling. "Hold on buddy. I'll carry you outta here." Jesse wiped the blood from Jeremiah's mouth.

"Come closer."

"Please…hang in there." Jesse looked in his old friend's eyes, the light leaving, death approaching. Jesse's eyes welled with tears. "No…

"Closer…"

Jesse lowered his head, turning his ear to Jeremiah's lips, a rustle of breath, like the sound from a seashell, coming from his lips and in the whisper came the name of the man who killed Andy Cope. And then Jeremiah let out his last breath on earth.

Jesse sat up, holding his old friend's head in his hands, tears spilling down both cheeks and dropping onto Jeremiah's face. Jesse looked up through the outstretched limbs of ancient cypress trees, patches of blue sky in the distance, feathers of white clouds floating in the sky. He screamed to the heavens. "Nooooo…"

His voice traveled over the old bridge, into the deep woods, echoing and fading, the sound of a woodpecker drilling into a dead tree across the river.

SEVENTY

I calculated that I was less than ten miles from Jesse's location when Deputy Parker called. "Sean, we found Jesse Taylor. It's bad. Hikers in the vicinity of the old Bellamy Bridge heard shots. They flagged down one of our units in the area. The deputies found Taylor walking out of the woods covered in blood. He was carrying a pistol. Taylor was arrested for murder."

"Murder?"

"Details are sketchy. We have units on the scene. Detectives and forensics en route."

"Who did Jesse allegedly kill?"

"He told the arresting deputies that Jeremiah Franklin was shot. Says he didn't do it. Who the hell knows anymore? I'm headed that way."

"I'll meet you there."

"You might want to keep your distance. Detective Lee is there or he soon will be. He won't tolerate you near a crime scene, not after you calling him out that night at Shorty's. Gotta go."

He disconnected. I slowed my Jeep, thinking about what I just heard. *Jeremiah Franklin dead.* I knew Jesse would never kill Jeremiah Franklin. And I knew, with Detective Lee investigating the killing, Jesse probably would be railroaded and found guilty for a crime he didn't commit. I continued driving to the Bellamy Bridge area, thinking about the killing of Andy Cope, knowing that it was connected to the killing of Jeremiah Taylor. Fifty years apart, bullets propelled when pulled by the same trigger of hate and human prejudice. I didn't know for certain who killed Andy. I didn't know who killed Jeremiah, but I did know that now I had two murders to solve—and solving one would, no doubt, bring closure to the other.

I spotted the flashing blue lights down Jacob Road. A battery of sheriff's cars on both sides of the road—deputies waving motorists through the profusion of flashing lights and the staccato blasts of police radios. I saw the white ubiquitous van—the vehicle that's sent in lieu of an ambulance. It was a nondescript coroner's wagon.

And then I saw death concealed.

They rolled Jeremiah on a gurney from a trailhead leading into the woods. A white sheet draped over his body, a dark red stain near the chest area. They lowered the gurney to the ground, collapsing the legs, then lifting it up and rolling it into the stark metallic grotto of the van. A plump man with a white moustache, wearing a dark blue shirt with the word CORONER across the back, supervised the loading of the body.

I thought about the day I met Jeremiah on his property, the old school bus his converted home. I remembered the story he told me about his migrant friend shot and killed in a motel parking lot somewhere in Michigan. *'I sat there in the dark in that motel room. Drank all the beer. About four in the mornin' I lifted the Bible off the nightstand and looked up what Carlos had referred to. It says all people are like grass. Their glory is like the flowers in the field. The grass dies and the flowers fall, but the word of God stands forever. I gotta remember that now more than ever.'*

A tall deputy standing in the center of the road looked at me and yelled, "Let's move! Nothing to see people." I drove around him, looking at the various squad cars, trying to spot Jesse sitting handcuffed in the back of one. I saw Deputy Parker talking with a man in plainclothes, someone I assumed was an investigator. I drove another one hundred feet, pulling off the road, beyond the last parked squad car. I carefully lifted the glass with Zeke Wiley's prints on it and placed it in a small paper sack.

And then I walked back toward Parker.

He ended his conversation with the man, both nodding and going separate ways. I approached Parker. He looked at me, a frown on his face. He said, "You shouldn't be here."

"I'm not at the crime scene. I assume it's back in the woods. Where's Jesse?"

He gestured to a sheriff's car parked in the middle of the pack. I could see Jesse staring out the window, his face looking in the opposite direction from where they were loading the body into the van. I thought of that night at Shorty's when he was placed in the back of the deputy's car and driven away. I looked at Parker and asked, "What'd he say when he was arrested?"

"I hope you're not referring to Miranda rights."

"No."

"Says he didn't do it. He says someone from the brush shot Jesse. He's not sure where. He says he returned fire. One shot. And guess where he got the gun?"

"Where?"

"From a state trooper. He stole it."

"Stole?"

"The trooper had stopped him for speeding. He's saying that Taylor jumped him, stole his gun and cuffed him to his steering wheel."

"Why would Jesse jump a trooper for giving him a speeding ticket? That doesn't make sense."

"I don't know. Forensics apparently lifted gunshot residue from his right hand. The pistol is the trooper's so this is quickly looking real damn bad for Jesse."

"Can you speak with him? Ask him what happened before he gets orally pummeled by Lee and others."

Parker looked around, eyes anxious. "I can give it a try." He walked quickly to the sheriff's car, opening the front door, leaning in to speak with Jesse. After less than thirty seconds, Parker stood, closed the door and walked back to me. "He said emphatically that he didn't do it...but he knows who did and said he'll only tell that to you. He said get me Sean O'Brien. So that ball's in your court. I'm the unlucky deputy who has to tell Mrs. Franklin that her son, Jeremiah, isn't coming home. It never gets easier."

I looked back toward the squad car, a deputy now standing next to it and talking with Detective Lee. The deputy nodded, got into the car, and drove away, Jesse turning his head, looking out the rearview mirror. I lifted my hand in an awkward wave.

Deputy Parker said, "He's going to need a damn good lawyer."

"It's all about the physical evidence. I have a glass for you."

"Glass?"

I handed him the paper sack. "I was visiting the Cypress Grove senior center and happened to meet a fellow named Zeke Wiley. He was working at the reform school when Andy Cope was killed. Wiley drank from the glass. Good prints. Even visible with the eye. Maybe you can have your lab take a look. If one of the prints matches the one the FBI lifted from the shell, we have more of that physical evidence."

He nodded. "That'll be great for the Andy Cope case, but we'll need something a little more current for Jesse Taylor."

"They're the same case, just a half-century apart. All we have to do is connect the dots."

I turned and walked back to my car, feeling the heaviness, the weight of two murders on my shoulders. The white van with Jeremiah's body drove by me, the driver in dark glasses, brawny hands gripping the wheel. I looked at the Bellamy Bridge sign on the side of the road, knowing that the old bridge was more than a modern crime scene. It was the bridge over trouble waters in the area. I thought about the press conference in three days. I had less than three days to find enough evidence to stop the sale of the property.

And that meant I'd have to find something physical connecting decades and people, somehow exonerating Jesse while convicting someone else. I had about two hours before dark. I was sure the crime scene would be processed in less time than that. They already had "their man." Maybe it would give me time to return. Time to look for something Detective Lee may have missed...or tried to hide.

SEVENTY-ONE

It was a call I didn't want to make. I sat in a McDonald's parking lot, a cup of black coffee in one hand. I punched in Caroline Harper's number. When she answered, I told her what happened to Jeremiah and Jesse. There was a long pause. When she spoke, her voice was strained, drenched with sorrow. "I don't know Mrs. Franklin well, just in passing. I want to visit with her. I'm not sure what I can say. There are no words, really. Maybe I can just be there to offer support. What can we do for Jesse?"

"He needs an attorney immediately. They've booked him in the county jail on first-degree murder charges. Can you have your lawyer go there as soon as possible?"

"I'll call him when we get off the phone."

I heard her exhale. "Sean, no one would ever fault you if you decide to walk away from all of this. All I was hoping to do is somehow get a court order to hunt for my brother's grave. God forbid did I ever think others would die in the process. I'm at a loss. I don't want you to—"

"Hey, wait a second. I didn't sign on for the first half only. I'm here for whatever it takes to start digging out there. Sometimes it takes a few charges to get over the castle wall. If I can't climb the wall or penetrate the gate, I'll figure a way to build my own Trojan horse."

"Thank you, Sean." I heard a sniffle in her voice as she disconnected.

My next call was to Lana Halley, and I told her what had happened. She said, "And you're convinced that Taylor didn't pull the trigger."

"Yes."

274

"What if he got into a heated argument with Jeremiah Franklin. What if Taylor, who has had a drug and alcohol problem, ostensibly from PTSD, just flipped and shot Franklin?"

"He didn't."

"But you can't be sure of that."

"They met because Jeremiah was going to tell Jesse who killed Andy Cope."

"And did he tell him?"

"I don't know. Jesse wants to speak with me. I'll know soon. I wanted you to have a heads up because you now know the history of all this and Carson's role as the state property is about to change hands."

"Sean, this whole thing is so beyond legal ethics. I'm now trying to have a grand jury investigate my boss, and I'll no doubt be assigned Jesse's case because I had his first case when he hit town."

"It's beyond legal boundaries because Jeff Carson decided to take it in that direction. You're within your jurisdiction to find the facts, find the evidence, wherever or to whomever it points. And that includes Carson."

"Then you find something with teeth in it that I can take to a grand jury. I'm certainly not going to get it any other way."

"You may not be able to get a court order to excavate the reform school property for graves, but if you can get a judge to sign an order to acquire fingerprints from Hack Johnson, I think you'll have all you need to interest a grand jury. Why? Because now you have a preponderance of circumstantial evidence that gives you probable cause. Similar to how a police officer can search your car without a warrant. While you're at it, you can DNA test him and prove or disprove if he fathered Jeff Carson."

There was a long pause. "It can be done. If they get pissed, let them sue. Give me a few hours."

"I'm here. Deputy Parker will have to facilitate the order. I'm sure he can find backup he can trust."

"Good, Sean. You can sit tight."

"Somebody will need to backup the backup."

She disconnected and I drove to the county jail.

—▪ ▬—

Jesse's attorney, Daniel Grady, had just met with him when I arrived. I spoke with Grady in a corner of the public waiting area, a half dozen people sitting in hard plastic chairs, all there to speak with family members awaiting bail. Grady looked at me through tired eyes and said, "Jesse has a compelling case. Unfortunately, compelling doesn't win juries. Evidence and motive do."

"I know you can't discuss the details, but do you believe he's innocent?"

"Yes, I do. My problem is the state has a dead body, the victim's blood apparently on Jesse's hands, gunshot residue, and a gun."

"Doesn't mean it's the gun that fired the shot."

"That's true." He looked down at his laced-up brown wingtips and then his eyes met mine. "I need to be going, to prep for an arraignment hearing. Bond may be difficult. He wants to speak with you, Mr. O'Brien."

"This is where I need your help."

"Me?"

"You need an investigator, and I'm the closest thing you've got. As your investigator, I need to speak with our client."

He smiled. "I'll see what I can arrange." He walked away, heading for the jailer's area. My phone vibrated. It was Dave Collins. "Sean, your second appearance in the local newspaper is quite different from the first. The reporter, a Cory Wilson, writes that you are convinced there are bodies of children buried on the old reform school property and how you believe any and all sales of said property should be indefinitely postponed until excavations can prove otherwise. He further indicates that you are aggressively pursuing evidence to substantiate that. The article quotes state officials saying those allegations are unfounded and a gross misrepresentation of the reform school's history. Did you actually do an interview with him?"

"Yes. Did he use a picture of me?"

"Indeed."

"Good. Now those who are moving this thing at warp speed have a speed bump—me."

"There's no gallantry found in the antics of the sacrificial lambs. They only get slaughtered."

"Maybe I can avoid the swords." I told Dave about Jeremiah Franklin's death, Jesse's arrest, and the possibility of family connections I'd found between Jeff Carson and the Johnson clan. When I finished I heard ice clink in Dave's drink.

He cleared his throat and said, "I once knew of a young man who discovered he was conceived from a brutal rape of his mother. He hunted down the man, his biological father, and killed him. There's probably an allusion to Greek mythology found somewhere in there. In the case of Jeff Carson, either he doesn't know that Hack Johnson raped his mother, Julie, or he knows and doesn't care. He's manipulated it to his advantage. He becomes a state attorney with an entourage, a posse to carry out, shall we say, deeds in which he prefers not to be associated. In the meantime, he keeps the proverbial blinders on lady justice. But that, of course, is purely speculation. What do you do next?"

"Talk with Jesse. If Jeremiah told him who killed Andy Cope before the fatal shot was fired, we have an ID."

"But you no longer have an eyewitness, Sean. And that will take a lot of wind out of the prosecutor's sails."

"It will, but if we have a name, we have a reason to get a court order to print and run DNA tests on Hack Johnson. And if it matches the print on the shotgun shell…it's a whole new chapter."

"That's a lot of supposition. However, I must admit, you're damn closer to burning down that haystack.

SEVENTY-TWO

Within days, history was repeating itself. Jesse Taylor back in police custody, back at almost the same visitor's window where I'd first met him. An indifferent deputy stood on one side of the small room, giving Jesse little, if any, privacy. He picked up the receiver, looked through glass smeared with fingerprints and said, "O'Brien, you gotta get me out of this shithole."

"And the way I'm going to do that is to take evidence to a grand jury that will turn this completely around. What have you told investigators?"

"Told them exactly what happened. The same detective, Lee, doesn't believe a word I'm saying. All he's saying is they have a murder victim, gunshot residue on my hand, Jeremiah's blood on my clothes. I told him that's what happens when you fire back at a shooter and you try to save a bleeding man's life—you get blood on your clothes." Jesse told me everything that led up to his trip to meet Jeremiah.

I nodded. "Did you see the shooter?"

"No. I think he was just across the river. He fired three times. I returned fire. One shot. Don't know if I hit him. Man, I was just tryin' to keep Jeremiah alive. Jeremiah and I were standing there at the entrance to the old bridge. He was about to tell me who killed Andy. They cut him down right at that moment. I had to carry Jeremiah behind cover to keep us both from being shot. Although I didn't see the triggerman, I think I know who ordered it."

"Who?"

278

"The same sick son-of-a-bitch that killed Andy...Hack Johnson. With Jeremiah's last breath, he told me it was Hack Johnson who pulled the trigger that night. I always thought it might have been him. And now I know. O'Brien, somehow you gotta get to him. I don't know who you can trust in this county. Somebody's got to drag that old man and half his sorry-ass kin outta those swamps to face the music."

"They say you stole the pistol from a trooper."

"Bullshit! He'd pulled me over, but rather than give a speeding ticket, he was about to march me into the woods and put a bullet through my head. Somehow he knew I was gonna be on that road. He knew I was heading out to meet with Jeremiah. Unless he was just a twisted psychopath in a cop's uniform, somebody hired him. I wrestled the gun from him and handcuffed the asshole to his steering wheel. When he first pulled me over, I hit the audio record button on my phone. I got it all. Least I think I did." He whispered. "I hid it on the left side of the Bellamy Bridge, right under the very first half-rotted plank. If you can get it, the recording will prove I was about to be shot."

"They're getting desperate. The shooter near the bridge could have presumably hit you and Jeremiah, but yet they wanted to try taking you out first. I don't have a lot of daylight left, but tell me exactly where you two were standing, the direction Jeremiah was facing before he was hit. Try to remember details."

— —

When I arrived back at the Bellamy Bridge area, it seemed deserted. No squad cars. No sense of chaos and emergency that was here three hours earlier. I looked at my phone. Sunset was in less than thirty minutes. The small parking lot was hard-packed dirt and gravel bordered by thick woods. I called Lana Halley and said, "I talked with Jesse Taylor. He said that Jeremiah Franklin told him that the man who shot and killed Andy Cope was Hack Johnson. And Jeremiah told him that right before he died. Who'd want him dead, Lana? And why? The Johnson family is inextricably woven into the old quilt of this community. Who's hiding under that quilt...and how can you prosecute them?"

She said nothing for a few seconds. "Maybe it's Jeff. We'll get Hack Johnson's prints, and we'll test his DNA. Where are you?"

"Bellamy Bridge. Looking for evidence."

"Be careful, Sean. Call me. Bye…"

I locked my Jeep, slid my Glock behind my belt in the small of my back, under my loose-hanging shirt, and started walking down the Bellamy Bridge trail. The setting sun was already casting dark shadows across the trail, cicadas beginning night chants in the murky recesses of the forest.

I picked up my pace—walking fast, moving toward the place Jeremiah Franklin had died. Mosquitos followed me, high-pitched droning near my ears and neck. I turned up my collar and jogged the remaining one hundred yards to the bridge. It was an odd silhouette in the sunset. Steel beams, broken cables, girders missing—the ribs of an old bridge straddling the slow-moving river. The remnants resembled pieces from a giant erector set long ago abandoned. Left to rust. Left to give witness to a road less traveled.

I stepped up to the entrance to the bridge, most of the wooden planks long since rotted away. Two were still there, at the very lip of the bridge. I knelt down and searched the first plank. Jesse's phone was in the spot where he'd left it. I stood, slipping the phone into my back pocket.

Yellow crime-scene tape cordoned off a triangle section about seventy feet in dimension. I ducked under the tape and played back the details Jesse had given me. Where they were standing when the first shot was fired—the position of Jeremiah's chest, his stance. Wind movement in the leaves. Whether Jesse recalled the sound of a bolt-action between shots. I knelt down and studied the tracks, boot and shoeprints, the trodden area left behind from an earlier investigation.

I walked toward an ancient oak, wide knotty trunk, the tree Jesse had described. It was the place he'd carried Jeremiah and tried to take refuge, the place where he returned fire. I spotted specks of dried blood on fallen oak leaves, dark red spots of blood on ferns near the base of the tree. It wasn't the season for the oaks to loose leaves. There were more than a dozen, green leaves on the ground. I remembered Jesse saying he heard a bullet rip through the branches. And then he heard one make a thud.

I walked closer to the tree, looking at the trunk from its base up to one of the first mammoth limbs. And there it was—a bullet hole. Fresh. The old tree was oozing a trace of sap from the hole. It was as if the tree had been wounded. I thought back to the night I'd dug the buckshot from the tree on the reform school property. It was an oak very similar to the one I was standing beside. One was shot fifty years ago, and the other a few hours ago. Both rounds, no doubt, coming from the same seeds of anger with roots probably as deep as the tree in front of me. I could tell from the angle of impact the general direction where the shot had been fired. I knew the round could be dug from the tree and, depending on its condition, used for ballistics.

Now to find the spot where the shooter stood.

I turned and looked across the Chipola River, through the black silhouette of the old bridge, near a very small clearing on the riverbank, to the left of a bald cypress tree. It was a perfect trajectory. But I needed a closer look. The only way to get there was walk across the bridge. The wooden floor was gone, crossbeams mostly gone. I stepped up on one of the rusty girders, walking heel-to-toe over narrow cables and beams that straddled the river. I looked at the water maybe fifteen feet below me, moving slowly, the current causing the slight spinning vortex of an eddy off the riverbank. I could see a large alligator in the water, its knobby eyes and back protruding from the surface.

I approached the halfway mark, my weight causing the rusted joints to creak, a slight breeze across the river delivering the scent of schooling fish and damp moss. I heard the long hoot of an owl. It was getting darker. And somehow the rusted old bridge felt like a bridge to nowhere, connected to a road never traveled.

But I had to cross it.

SEVENTY-THREE

I was almost across the old bridge when my phone vibrated. I walked the last few steps, trying to get off the rickety bridge before reaching in my pocket for the phone. It went to voice-mail as I stepped off the last corroded beam. I was now on the opposite side of the river from where Jeremiah was killed. The call came from Deputy Parker. I played the message. "Sean, the lab ran the prints from the glass. There isn't a match to the print from the shotgun shell. So it looks like Zeke Wiley wasn't the shooter that night when Andy Cope was shot, or at least he didn't load that particular shell into the chamber. Where are you? Call me."

The sun slipped behind the western edge of the forest leaving beads of daylight that were dissolving into shades of gray. It was the final ten minutes or so between the afterglow of day and the stark darkness of night—a twilight world of no shadows. Fireflies rose up from the ferns, the portable lanterns in their bellies pulsating with a color that matched the swaths of sunlight reflecting from low hanging clouds. It was all the nightlight I needed to make my way to the clearing by the massive bald cypress tree that I'd spotted when I stood in the same spot Jeremiah stood right before a bullet went through his body.

I swatted a black haze of mosquitoes and walked through thick underbrush in the direction of the cypress tree. I glanced down at the river, the dark water reflecting the deep blood red hue from the clouds. A water bug moved in a clockwise rotation on the surface of the river. The gator was gone. I walked another hundred feet and came near the cypress tree.

I circled the tree, coming closer on each rotation, examining the dark muck soil for traces of an assassin. I didn't have to look long. The first thing I spotted was the dull glint of a brass casing. I knelt down and used the tip of my pen to lift it from the weeds. The casing was a .308. I sniffed the open end, the fresh odor of burnt gunpowder. Jesse said he remembered hearing three shots fired. I found evidence of one. The shooter probably picked up the other two casings, missing the one I found in the weeds.

I set the casing down exactly as I found it. Deputy Parker could officially bag and tag the evidence. I just needed to see it, to smell it. I looked to my right, to within a couple of feet from the base of the tree. Human tracks. Boot prints. I stepped next to the prints and knelt. Even in the diffused light, even in the sepia tone brown pigment of the forest, the print was distinct. There were at least a half dozen. Most positioned as the shooter would have stood, braced against the tree, facing the direction where Jesse and Jeremiah were standing next to the bridge.

I stared at one boot print, the unique tread design right down to the pyramid shape on the heel. I touched the tread pattern with the tips of my fingers, the black soil cool. I looked up at a full moon rising over the river, the clipped hoot of a great horned owl coming from deep in the woods. A breeze came through the cypress tree causing the ashen beards of Spanish moss to sway. I looked back down at the print. I knew the design came from military combat boots. And I knew that whoever wore them had hung the noose from the tree in Mrs. Franklin's yard. He was one of the two men who entered Jesse's room, severely beating and branding him.

And now he'd been here. He'd murdered the only living witness the prosecution would have had to testify in court as to who killed Andy Cope. *How did he know Jesse and Jeremiah were going to meet here? What was I missing?* I returned Deputy Parker's call. When he answered I said, "Got your message about the print. Although Zeke Wiley didn't load the shotgun, he was there that night. He was part of the posse, men hunting a boy."

"That's a horrible visual. Well, at least our search is becoming narrower. Not a whole lot of suspects remaining."

"There's at least one. And his time is coming."

"We'll get him."

"Ivan, before Jeremiah died he told Jesse who killed Andy."

"He did? I'm sure he didn't share that with Detective Lee. Who did it?"

"Hack Johnson. Although we've lost Jeremiah, we have a name and it's the last words Jeremiah uttered before he died. So you can take that information to Lana Halley, take it along with the print the FBI pulled from the shell, the boot print pattern, and the fact that state attorney Carson may be related to Johnson, and you've got enough to get a court order to obtain Johnson's prints and his DNA."

"Whoa...run that by this ol' country boy a little slower. You believe the SA, the highest ranking prosecutor in the district is blood kin to one of the most corrupt families in the Florida Panhandle?"

"Yes. And the sooner you can meet with Lana, the quicker she can get a judge to sign an order for you to pick up Hack Johnson. Who in the department can you trust?"

"The sheriff's a stand up guy. There are plenty of deputies there who'd take a bullet for me and vice versa."

"You might want to pick your best backup when you take him in. If his print matches, you're on your way to solving what is definitely one of Florida's coldest cases."

"Where are you?"

"Bellamy Bridge. I found the spot where the shooter stood. It's across the bridge, down the riverbank, a large lone cypress tree next to the river, maybe eighty yards from where Jesse and Jeremiah stood. I left for you a .308 cartridge on the ground near the tree. It came from the shooter's rifle. And the boot prints here match the prints at two crime scenes."

"So they have the pyramid in the heel?"

"Yeah."

"This guy gets around. We gotta stop the crazy bastard. I'll correlate all the evidence and take it to Lana Halley in the morning. Maybe it'll be enough to get Jesse a bond and give us a ticket to take ol' man Johnson directly to jail. O'Brien, when we wrap this, I owe you the coldest beer in town."

"I'll hold you to it. Look, you can reach Lana now. She can get the judge to sign an order when you give her what you have."

He was quiet for a few seconds. "No better time than the present. I'll keep you in the loop." He disconnected. I stood next to the cypress tree, soft moonlight coming between the whiskers of moss, the chant of bullfrogs on the riverbank. I looked at the Bellamy Bridge, the moonlight casting the vertical beams and cables in dark silhouette. Something about the old bridge suddenly felt ominous, as if it were a bridge to tragic times.

I looked away, back to where I'd left the rifle casing. I could see the glimmer of moonlight off the casing less than ten feet away. What I couldn't see was what I just *felt*. Something was wrong. Very wrong. The inertia pushing the dominoes had ceased somewhere, and I hadn't seen it coming. *How could I have missed it?* I called Caroline Harper. When she answered, I said, "When you spoke with Jesse…when he told you he was going to meet Jeremiah… you tried to reach me, right?"

"Yes. Why?"

"When you couldn't reach me immediately, did you call anyone else?"

"Yes. I was so worried that I called the young man we met at the coffee shop. Deputy Parker. He'd given me his card that day. I know you trust him so I wanted to see if he might help Jesse, maybe bring him home if he'd used painkillers and shouldn't be on the road. Is everything okay, Sean?"

Someone was beeping into my phone. Dave Collins calling. "Caroline, I have to go. Everything will be fine." I disconnected and took Dave's call. He said, "The tracker on Jesse's car has been in the same position, of course, since he was arrested. His car was probably impounded. However, the second tracker, I'm seeing some very fast movement right now. Did the deputy ever place it on the DA's car?"

"At this moment, I doubt it. I'm pretty sure it's still in his car because he's either working for Jeff Carson or the Johnson family, and right now they're all the same."

"As the haystack burns the rats run. He must be one hell of an actor to fool you."

"Sociopaths can do that, sometimes. Maybe I wanted to trust him too much."

"Don't beat yourself up over it, Sean. It's fixable. I don't hear that tone in your voice often. Maybe in a blue moon when something's backfired, and that doesn't happen often."

I stared up at the moon over the tree line. "It's happened now. Deputy Ivan Parker, the man I saw as trustworthy, has to be involved in this. I'm not sure to what level, but I know he alerted the trooper, probably a pal of his, when Jesse was en route to meet Jeremiah."

"Where are you?"

"Bellamy Bridge area. The place where Jeremiah Franklin was murdered."

"If the tracker is in the deputy's car, as you believe, he's coming toward you and he's in one hell of a hurry to get there. Be ready, Sean. Looks like you're about to have a dangerous fight on your hands."

"You have the app to follow the GPS signal from my phone. Now is a good time to turn it on. If you don't hear from me, if the signal stops or if it goes stationary, send in the troops. Call Carly Brown with the FBI in Tampa, maybe the U.S. Marshal's office in Tallahassee or the Florida Department of Law Enforcement. I have no idea what I'm about to face. It could be half a dozen deputies who might believe anything Parker tells them."

SEVENTY-FOUR

I didn't use the flashlight on my phone as I crossed Bellamy Bridge. I needed to save battery power, and I didn't want to be a moving target in the event Deputy Parker had a scoped rifle trained on me. I walked across the cables and beams using the moonlight as my guide. I stopped, gripping onto one of the vertical beams to steady myself. I looked down at the river, the bright light from the moon reflecting in red dots. Some were moving slowly. Some stationary. Most about half a foot wide—the space between alligator eyes just above the river's surface.

I walked slowly across the twin cables. Like a duck on land. Halfway there. The thick cables wobbling each step I took. A breeze from the west brought the scent of wood smoke somewhere in the forest. My phone vibrated. I couldn't answer and maintain a surefooted balance. I was less than fifteen feet from the other side when it happened. One of the cables dropped out from under me. I went down, catching myself. Grabbing the other cable with my hands. I dangled just a few feet above the dark river. Mosquitoes alighted on my neck, drilling into my bloodstream.

I held on, moving hand-over-hand toward the riverbank. Sweat dripping down my back, a sulfur smell coming from the water. Ten feet more. I gripped the rusted cable, shards of rust and metal falling on my face. I continued the climb. The thick wire groaned like mooring lines on a dock in a rising tide. And now the cable felt like a macabre trapeze with no safety net.

Five feet to go.

I swung my legs up to the riverbank. I pulled myself out from under the bridge, standing on land. My hands bled. Sweat in my eyes. I ran down the dark trail, patches of moonlight squeezing between the trees. I listened to a voice message from Dave. "Sean, he's just pulling into the trailhead parking lot. No movement from the tracker, so I'd say he's parked and out of the car. Wish I knew if he came alone or with others. Prepare for the latter."

I calculated the time and distance. Dave left his message three minutes ago as I was dangling from the bridge. I knew that the trailhead parking lot was approximately a twenty-minute walk to the bridge. Parker, if he wasn't waiting to ambush me in the parking lot, had been on the trail for roughly two and a half minutes, assuming it took him thirty seconds to lock and load. I didn't know if he had night-vision glasses or an infrared night scope on a rifle or shotgun.

I stepped behind thick undergrowth and called Lana. Got her voice-mail and whispered, "Lana, it's Sean. At the Bellamy Bridge I found evidence that someone other than Jesse shot Jeremiah Franklin. On the north side of the river from the bridge, at the base of a huge cypress tree, is a spent rifle casing. Boot tracks at the site will match those left in Mrs. Franklin's yard where the noose was found. The tracks will match the same found on the blood in Jesse's room when he was attacked. They're very distinct, a pyramid shape at the heel. I have an audio recording of the trooper ordering Jesse into the woods. Deputy Ivan Parker is complicit in this. He knows I'm here, and he's on his way to stop me. So if you have someone in law enforcement you can trust, you can send him or her my way. Just tell them to say Lana sent me."

I walked quickly, keeping to the shadows. Looking for a tree to climb. One of the things I learned in the military was the psychology of the human hunter. Maybe, in the day of giant pterodactyls sailing down to grab prey, our relatives looked up when hunting. But today, when armed with high-powered assault rifles, the hunters usually kept their eyes sweeping the ground in front of them. Not above them. As a sniper, I used high elevations for a trajectory advantage. Tonight I had to use it as a tactical advantage, especially if Parker brought another hired gun.

The breeze became still. I stopped on the edge of the trail, standing in silence. I cupped both hands behind my ears, listening. Trying to pick up any noise that was inconsistent with the night sounds of the forest. Crickets chirped in the dark crevices. Cicadas chimed in for a short stanza and then ebbed, as if nature played two notes from a harmonica, pausing to take a deep breath before the next performance. It was when the crickets and cicadas stopped in mid-song that I knew it was because they sensed danger. And that danger was usually manmade.

I spit on both hands, rubbing saliva on my face and forehead. Then I knelt down, finding loose dark soil, rubbing the dirt on my face and the back of my hands. Listened once more. Nothing. Then I walked quietly, hunting for the right tree.

I found an ancient live oak with an immense girth, the trunk knotty and expansive. There were plenty of hand and footholds. It's thick limbs extended well beyond the width of the trail. I climbed. Silent. Controlling my breathing. Listening. The whine of mosquitoes followed me up the tree and into the branches. I steadied myself, holding onto smaller branches. I walked along one of the limbs that crossed the path. The trail, the direct pathway, was now fifteen feet below me.

I squatted on the limb, ninety-five percent of my body hidden from anyone on the trail coming from either direction. I waited under the light of a full moon. Ignoring the mosquitoes. Watching shadows in the moonlight.

Waiting for the first shadow to move.

SEVENTY-FIVE

I lifted my Glock, holding it. Waiting. The moon was directly over me, soft light coming through the branches and leaves. I could see well. Maybe one hundred feet down the trail. I spotted a fat raccoon waddling across the path, stopping to sniff something, and then vanishing into the undergrowth. From somewhere above me came the quaking sound of a nighthawk diving for insects. I didn't look skyward, keeping my eyes on the trail.

And then a cloud crept in front of the moon.

Total darkness. My phone vibrated in my pocket. It stopped after two vibrations. I waited for the cloud to pass. Would he be on the trail near me? Would he have passed me? Or would he be directly under me?

The crickets stopped first—all at once. They stopped chirping. Within three seconds, the cicadas became silent. And then the cloud ebbed away. Moonlight again drenching the trail. A man was coming. Slowly. Stealthy. Maybe seventy-five feet away. He held a rifle. One hand near the trigger-guard, the other hand gripping the forearm. The tip of the barrel pointed ahead of him.

By the time he walked ten feet closer, I could tell he was wearing a deputy sheriff's uniform. Deputy Ivan Parker was hunting me. He appeared to be alone. His radio was either turned off or disconnected. A twig popped under his feet. He stopped. Waited for a few seconds and then proceeded.

I had to time it perfectly for maximum shock. I was approximately fifteen feet above the trail. He stood close to six feet. When I jumped, I needed to hit with both feet on his shoulders, about a ten-foot jump. Gravity and my 210 pounds would bring him to the ground. I was betting he wouldn't hold the rifle with a hit that powerful.

He was less than twenty feet away. Walking slowly in the dead center of the path. *Come on…a few more steps.* Five feet. I stood. Waiting for the exact second. Then I jumped. In the moonlight, I aimed for his shoulders. My boots made square impact. I heard a subtle *pop.* He hit the ground hard. Face first. A *whump* sound when his chest slammed into the dirt. The rifle flew out a few feet in front of him. He crawled to it. I charged him, grabbing his shoulders, pulling him back. He turned in my grasp, landing a punch to my mouth. He pounced, pulling a knife from his belt, rushing me. I sidestepped, blood dripping from my split lip. He dove at my legs, trying to tackle me. I brought one knee up into his face. His nose snapped, blood pouring from ruptured skin and cartilage.

Parker glared at me, reaching for his knife. "Fuck you and the horse you rode in on!"

"Drop the knife!"

"Sure!" He threw the knife hard at me. I turned, the knife vanishing in the thicket. I reached for my Glock just as he scrambled and grabbed his rifle.

"Don't do it, Parker!"

He hesitated a half second, turned and raised the barrel in my direction. I fired once. The round hit him in the chest. He shot again, the bullet just missing my left ear. I knew now that he was wearing a bulletproof vest. I aimed in the moonlight, firing a second round. This one hit him in the center of his forehead. He fell back, dead—the moon iridescent, reflecting from the dark pool of blood forming next to his open mouth.

I lowered my Glock, a mosquito whining in my ear. I thought of how wrong I'd been about the man I just killed. Remembering the day I spoke with him in front of the coffee shop.

"We got to try to bring closure to that lady."

"That's the plan, Deputy Parker."

"If we're working together, just call me Ivan. That'll do fine."

I held two fingers to my lip, slowing the blood flow. I remembered the incoming call I'd received while squatting on the tree limb. I looked at my phone. Lana Halley. I pressed the redial button. "Sean, I got your message. Are you okay? Did Deputy Parker arrive?"

"He did. But he'll have to leave in a gurney."

"You killed him?"

"He left me no choice. He was *hunting* me. Hunting me with a high-powered rifle. He shot at me twice. Close range with the rifle. I returned fire. His body is on the Bellamy Bridge trail, about half way down the trail."

"I understand. Are you okay?"

I pressed the back of my hand against my bloody lip. "Define okay."

"I'll call Sheriff Monroe. He's fair and he exemplifies integrity."

"I'll wait for the cavalry at the trailhead parking lot. Lana..."

"Yes?"

"Thank you."

"See you soon. I'm working on getting Jesse released." She disconnected.

I walked under the bright moonlight toward the parking lot, thinking about the conversations I'd had with Parker. Trying to replay verbal or visual clues that would have made me suspicious. There were none, at least I didn't see them. Maybe I'd let my guard down too quickly, wanting to believe in his honor, his honesty, before seeing proof that it was ever there.

I'd walked back to the trailhead parking lot sooner than I anticipated. I figured I had maybe a fifteen-minute wait until the sheriff's deputies and investigators deluged onto the lot. There were no streetlights, only the light from the moon. I'd put my Glock on the front seat of the Jeep and stand outside, unarmed, when they arrived. They'd demand that I put my hands on my head and spread my legs. Then they'd probably cuff me.

I anticipated that Detective Lee would lead the posse. I hoped it was Sheriff Monroe, assuming Lana got through to him. Either way, there was nowhere I could go. I'd effectively reported the incident to one of the district's lead prosecutors and had asked her to notify law enforcement. Done. For now.

I opened the Jeep door, placing my Glock on the seat. I closed the door and looked across the lot at the sheriff's car left there by Deputy Parker. I stepped to the front of my Jeep and leaned against it, waiting. I could see deer tracks in the soil a few feet away. Wide-spaced. Probably a buck. The tracks looked fresh. The front tracks and the back far apart. It looked like the deer had been running across the lot. Maybe spooked by the sounds of gunfire. I stepped up to them, hit the flashlight app on my phone and knelt down to examine the tracks.

There were others. Tracks from man. Imprints from a boot. A boot with a pyramid shape on the heel. It was then I heard the sound of a pump shotgun, followed by a low voice. "Lemme see your hands! Turn around slowly, O'Brien."

I stood, raised my hands and turned around. The man had the 12 gauge pointed at my chest. I recognized him. Military haircut. Gym body. He wore a jean jacket with cut-off sleeves. I could make out the tattoo. Army Rangers. I remembered Jesse had said the man's name was Ace something… Ace Anders.

He looked at me with no expression on his face. "Give me your phone."

I reached in my back pocket, lifting out Jesse's phone, handing it to him. Anders tossed the phone into an open trash barrel. He grinned. "Now it's just you and me. Get in your Jeep. There are some people who want to meet you."

SEVENTY-SIX

Ace Anders held the 12-gauge on me walking back to the Jeep. He stepped to the passenger side and said, "Get in."

I knew I had no more than two seconds to pick up my Glock and get off a round before he fired the shotgun. At this range, it didn't make any difference what was in the shells—buckshot or slugs, I would be cut in half. When he opened the door the dome light turned on. He spotted the Glock and said, "Don't even think about it. Back up!"

I stepped back and he reached across the seats, lifting the Glock. He looked up at me and gestured. "Let's go! I'm assuming you killed Parker or he'd be standing here instead of you."

I said nothing. But now I knew Anders had ridden here with Parker.

I sat in the driver's seat. He sat on the passenger side, holding the Glock on me. "Drive."

"Where we going?"

"Leave the lot and turn right. I'll give you directions as we drive."

I started the Jeep, put it in gear and drove by the abandoned sheriff's car, turning right onto the highway. He didn't take his eyes off me. His breathing was steady. Unruffled. Changed from the shotgun to the pistol with ease. He had the moves and demeanor of a pro—a mercenary. A hired gun. I said nothing for the first mile. I figured he would speak only when he was giving directions or orders. I said, "You wear some nice boots. Expensive. Made for jungle combat. If I recall, only one manufacturer makes that boot.

The pyramid on the heel is sort of like the Nike logo, but you only see the pyramid when the person wearing the boot leaves tracks. You get around."

"Shut up!"

"Sure, as soon as you tell me why you sold out Jesse. Takes a big man to hang a noose from a tree in the front yard of an elderly black woman. Takes a helluva man to burst into Jesse's room, a Ranger brother, and beat and brand him while you and your pal are hiding behind masks. And it really takes a tough guy to assassinate Jeremiah Franklin, an innocent unarmed man."

"Fuck off. I'm a soldier for hire. We got a war on our hands here. I've seen it across the world. Now it's here, more than ever."

"Who do you work for?"

"Myself. I do free-lance contract work. Make a right at the cattle gate."

I slowed and turned right, driving down a dirt road. No sign of farms or people. Just thick woods on either side of what felt like an old logging road. After a mile and a quarter he said, "Take the next left."

"Do you work for Jeff Carson?"

"None of your fuckin' business."

"Or maybe you work for the whole Johnson family. Maybe you have your favorites and Cooter isn't one of them. Maybe he's a little too liberal for your tastes. That it?"

"Might as well run your mouth while you still got a voice box. These ol' boys back here do stuff that makes ISIS look like a bunch of pussies. You'll see."

We drove to what appeared to be a ramshackle farm setting with trailers and out buildings. I remember what Dave had said after pulling satellite images: *Looks like some kind of compound back in the swamps. Lots of fencing. Some wetland. In the dry area, I'm counting five trailers…something that resembles a farmhouse, a couple of barn-like structures.* I could see an old farmhouse to the far right, a single bare light burning from the front porch. Various barns and portable garages scattered about the property.

I counted three doublewide trailers. Rusted cars were on blocks in the front yards. A trampoline ripped and sagging. An antique tractor, paint long faded, was parked in one yard. Weeds grew tall around the tires. There were broken barbecue grills, faded wooden picnic tables, four-wheelers with flat tires. White smoke twisted from an opening in a trash barrel with holes drilled near the base. The smell of charred garbage hung over the place.

I counted seven pickup trucks. One was the yellow late fifties model I'd followed the night Cooter Johnson left Shorty's and took a girl to a motel near the Interstate intersection. Any plans I'd been thinking about to infiltrate this compound were now out the window. The biggest advantage you get facing an enemy is the element of surprise. Remove that, especially when you're vastly outnumbered, and the odds of survival go exponentially down. The logarithms of living can only be counted in milliseconds of timing, luck and cunning. I knew, that in just a few minutes, I'd need all that and more to walk out of here.

Anders said, "Drive to the left and head toward the big barn."

I drove up to an old barn that was in bad need of paint. The boards had long since turned ashen gray from years of Florida sun and rains. There were no pickup trucks in the immediate vicinity of the barn. Maybe the clan was still asleep and Anders would have to wake them to come see the trophy he'd captured in the woods.

Anders continued holding the Glock on me, reaching for the shotgun next to him. "Park it, turn off the motor and give me the keys. Then get out."

I handed him the keys and opened the Jeep door. He did the same, putting the Glock under his belt and cradling the shotgun in his arms. He said, "Stand next to the door."

I stood there while he used the barrel of the shotgun to tap four times on the large wooden door. I heard walking coming from inside, the sound of metal scraping, a sliding bolt unlocking. The massive door swung open, rusted hinges squeaking.

Light poured out. The interior was lit from a half dozen bare bulbs hanging by cords from the rafters. Seven men stood inside the barn. Most unshaven. All carrying guns and bad attitudes. Some with pistols. Others with sawed-off shotguns. Two with assault rifles. I could smell burning marijuana, whiskey and body odor. Not a good combination.

In the center of the group, sitting down, was an old man. He wore a Stetson, gaunt face with white whiskers. His blue denim shirt was buttoned to his neck. Sleeves rolled to his scrawny elbows. He raised his right hand, pointing at me. I could see the tattoo on his forearm—the Southern Cross. In a rasping voice, Hack Johnson said, "I hear you been lookin' for me, son. Now that you found me...what you gonna do?"

SEVENTY-SEVEN

The small crowd parted, men shuffling out of the way as another man came from somewhere in the recesses of the barn. It was the same man I'd met the day in front of Ruby's Coffee shop. Solomon Johnson wore jeans, shirtless. He was barefoot. Toenails long. Chest filled with ink. A large tattoo of a Nazi swastika, a shamrock with the letters AB, an image of a human skull with deer antlers coming out of the sides and twisting into the numbers 666. There was a gloss of sweat over his body. He wore lightweight training boxing gloves.

He walked up to within three feet of me, his eyes flat. "I warned you that day. But you didn't listen. You come here and stir up trouble." He gestured back to the old man in the foldout metal chair. "You tryin' to have the law mess with daddy. That won't fly in Jackson County. Our family is the law…sometimes that's the lawless." His men snorted and chuckled. "Earl, Cooter, ya'll hold onto this dumb fucker."

Cooter, and another man walked toward me. I recognized the other man, Earl, as one of the two men I'd encountered when I was looking for Jeremiah Franklin's property. His right wrist was still in a cast, which meant he'd be a little slow to lift the pistol he slid under his belt. Earl leaned in my face and said, "Hey asshole, remember me. Before the night's over I'm takin' a baseball bat to your arm. Eye for a fuckin' eye."

They stepped behind me, each man grabbing my arms by the wrists. Solomon Johnson swung hard. I turned quickly, trying to avoid a direct hit.

His gloved right hand connected with my right cheek. Then he used his left to slug me in the mouth. I felt the taste of blood, spots floating in front of me for a second. I feigned weakness, a wounded soldier. I didn't have the element of complete surprise, but I might be able to fake just enough physical signs for the men to lower their guard.

He grinned, massaged the knuckles on his right hand. Then he hit me square in the gut. I'd tightened my stomach muscles to deflect as much of the impact as possible. I doubled over, blood dripping from my mouth onto the hard-packed dirt floor. He drew back and delivered a hard hit to my forehead, the blow causing two seconds of total black before my eyes.

He slapped me playfully on the right side of my face, bent down and said, "I'm lovin' this. It's better than the best video game."

I looked up at him and smiled.

He said, "What's so fuckin' funny motherfucker?"

"You are."

His gang laughed. He paced in front of me and said, "Here's a punch line." He drove his fist into my ribs. "I don't see you laughin'."

I stared at him a moment. "This is your last appearance before your handpicked followers."

"Why's that ass wipe?"

"Because I'm going to kill you."

He laughed, his laughter sounding like a jackal howling. And then he hit me in the jaw, the blow causing a few seconds of vertigo. I let my legs go slack.

He looked at Cooter and Earl, smiling. "Ya'll can cut him loose. He can barely stand up."

He turned and looked back at the others. "Who wants to skin him?"

All the hands shot up. Excitement of a kill in the eyes of wolves. I continued bending over, pretending to cough, spitting blood, looking back at Earl who was laughing and grabbing his crotch.

"Who wants to cut his balls off and feed 'em to the pigs?"

The same number of hands shot up, two men passing weed and sipping from a bottle of Jack Daniels.

Timing and luck. I had to cut the head off the snake.

TOM LOWE

I reached back fast. Less than a second, jerking the pistol from Earl's pants. I shot Solomon in the center of the Nazi swastika. Ace lifted the shotgun. I shot him in the throat. I grabbed Earl by his beard, pulling him in front of me and shoving the barrel into his ear canal. "Lay down your guns! Now or he's the third that'll die here tonight."

Solomon glared at me, falling onto his knees, blood pumping from the middle of the swastika. "Turn my boy loose!"

"He'll be your dead boy in three seconds. Lay down the guns!"

Solomon gestured to his men. "Set 'em down boys. Ain't no way he's gettin' off this land alive." Then Solomon toppled over, his dead eyes locked on my position, right arm extended, his middle finger pointed.

In the distance came the sweetest sound I'd heard in a long time. A helicopter incoming. I could tell by the rotor sounds that it was two choppers. Within seconds they were over us, powerful spotlights crisscrossing the compound. I could hear sirens, the advancing pulse of blue and red lights. It looked like the cavalry was finally coming. I backed out of the barn, dragging Earl with me. I pushed the barrel in farther. "Walk backwards!"

I held Earl hostage in front of the barn so the police pilots could see us. The squad cars were pouring onto the property. Lights in the double-wides turning on, dogs barking. I looked over my shoulder. Some of the cars were from the Jackson County Sheriff's department. Some from the Florida Department of Law Enforcement. Others from what I assumed was the U.S. Marshal's office.

Both choppers flew stationary, hovering at forty-five degree angles in the air away from the barn. One of the spotlights was trained on me, the other light illuminating inside the barn. Dozens of men in uniforms, badges and guns descended around the barn. Someone on a PA system said, "Everyone out! Come out with your hands on top of your head. You are completely surrounded."

The men inside the barn hesitated. Some looked at the old man for guidance. Others looked at Solomon Johnson's dead body.

The voice on the PA came again. "You've got ten seconds to surrender. You are outgunned ten to one. The man holding the hostage…drop your gun."

300

I looked at Hack Johnson and the rest of the gang. If the old man signaled for an assault, all hell would break loose. I'd take twenty bullets before the count of two. I kept the barrel in Earl's ear—the ear now bleeding.

The next voice on the PA came from a woman. "Sean, it's Lana...put down your weapon. We know what happened on the trail and how that trail led you here. Please put down the gun."

Hack Johnson stared at me. His grandson, Cooter, was about to come out of his skin. They both looked beyond me at the firepower all pointed at them. Hack cut his eyes back to me. "I might be old, but we ain't done... you and me." To his men he said, "Fold 'em boys. Ain't no use in gettin' all shot up in a barn when we can beat this shit in a courthouse. It's all about family law, brothers."

Slowly, I withdrew the pistol. I held it out by my side for a second before dropping it to the ground. I kept my grip on Earl, now using both hands. His body in front of me was my only form of life insurance.

Each man laid his gun on the ground. The voice on the PA was one of the officers. He said, "Place your hands on top of your heads, fingers interlocked, and walk out single file, one-by-one and keep your hands on your head."

I released Earl. He interlocked his fingers together, hands on his head, joining the others in line, walking out into a blaze of white lights. I watched Hack Johnson slowly stand, his face tight, defiant. He took his place last in line, laced his arthritic fingers together on his head and shuffled outside. I stepped over to him. "You asked me what I wanted." I reached into my shirt pocket and lifted out the picture of Andy. I held it near the old man's face. "This is why I'm here. Justice for a little boy that's long overdue. Justice for a boy named Andy Cope. A boy you shot in the back."

Hack Johnson looked at me through his smudged glasses, his eyes wide and filled with hate and denial. Remorse wasn't in his DNA. I slipped the photo back in my pocket, careful not to get blood on it. I watched as law enforcement processed each man, arresting and reading rights before they were loaded into sheriff's vans. I looked at the plain-clothes investigators. There were a half dozen. Detective Lee wasn't in the mix.

From my left, two people ran up to me. Paramedics. One man and one woman. The woman said, "Sir, you need medical attention."

"What I need is ice."

The man said, "Sir, please step over to the ambulance. You don't have to go to the hospital if you don't want to, but we need to take a look at your injuries in better light. Give you something to stop the bleeding."

I nodded and followed them, investigators following me. The paramedics cleaned me up as one detective from the sheriff's office questioned me. Another investigator from the Florida Department of Law Enforcement took notes and asked a dozen questions. A few minutes later, Lana Halley and a man I didn't recognize approached. He was dressed in a uniform, an older man with silver hair, wide shoulders and accepting eyes. Rare considering the occupation. Lana said, "Sean, thank God you're okay."

"How'd you and the troops get here so fast?"

"Your friend, Dave Collins, you have someone with excellent communication skills."

"Dave's a talker." I tried to smile.

"He's also great at recon and strategy. He could tell us exactly where you were, and he could tap into the microphone on your phone. He'd alerted the FDLE, U.S. Marshal's office and the FBI before I could. He was like a movie producer bringing all the components together, literally under the gun. Sean, I'd like for you to meet Sheriff Mark Monroe."

The sheriff nodded. "Pleased to meet you. I want to thank you for going out of your way to help. Looks like you've been through one helluva fight. I'm deeply sorry one of them was my deputy."

I shook my head. "That's not your fault. Parker fooled me, too. The guy who shot Jeremiah Franklin is in the barn. He's dead. Name's Ace Anders. He's the one to the right. The other is Solomon Johnson. Anders rode with Deputy Parker to the trailhead. Stayed behind for some reason. I guess Parker thought I was easy prey. He shot at me twice, close range with his rifle. I had no choice but to stop Parker. How and why he's associated with a radical hate group, I don't know. But he was."

The sheriff grunted, looked away for a second and then looked at me. "Ivan was a complicated man. A stern granddaddy raised him in some of the strict and bygone ways of the Old South. I'm afraid Ivan took a few of them to an extreme. He was dedicated to uncover justice, mostly his interpretation of it, as I'm beginning to discover. My men found a big damn meth lab in one of these buildings. We suspected it. Now we know it."

"I've suspected Hack Johnson was a pedophile and a child killer. Now I know it. I'm betting his prints will match the one the FBI found on the shotgun shell. Sheriff, your team just might solve one of the coldest cases in Florida. And in doing so, maybe it'll curb this kind of child abuse in places where kids are supposed to be helped, not raped and killed."

"Let's hope. Much obliged, Mr. O'Brien. We'll get all of your statements in detail."

"Something else, Sheriff. That black Ford pickup to the right has a shotgun in the rack. I can see its silhouette through the windshield. It's an old gun. I know because a couple of the Johnson boys pulled it on me. I'd be willing to bet it was the gun Hack Johnson used at the reform school when he was hunting kids."

Sheriff Monroe looked toward the pickup truck. He turned to one of his deputies. "Don, take that shotgun and tag it as potential evidence." The sheriff tipped his hat and left, issuing orders to deputies, the stammer of police radios sounding like music to my ears.

Lana turned to me. "We'll get Hack Johnson's prints and expedite his DNA. I'd get his blood, but I think ice water runs in his veins. If he's Jeff Carson's father, and if we can get one of the guys arrested to turn state's witness detailing Carson's complicity in any of these crimes, Carson can share a cell with them for all I care. We'll have a read on the old man's prints by midday tomorrow. After they're done with you here, where will you be?"

"Swallowing aspirin, using ice, knocking back a scotch and counting the hours until midday tomorrow."

SEVENTY-EIGHT

I was on my second cup of black coffee at the Blue Plate Diner, reading the latest news piece Cory Wilson had written for the Jackson Patriot, when the call came. He'd been writing a series of articles, each probing the Johnson family and their connection with state attorney Jeff Carson. He also detailed Caroline Harper's hunt for her brother's grave. I answered and Lana said, "I bet you could use some good news."

"I like conversations that begin like this."

"You'll like the fact, did I say *fact?* The fact that Hack Johnson's right thumbprint matches the print lifted by the FBI from the shotgun shell. He can lie, he can cheat, terrorize kids and deny it all…but he can't refute his own print. You got him, Sean."

"It wasn't just me. It was the evidence and the help of others like you… and in the end it was Hack Johnson who got himself."

"I'm in the sheriff's office. They had more questions to ask you, but this revelation seems to have stymied that. I'm going to a grand jury immediately. We'll get a court order to begin looking for bodies on the reform school property. That will stop the sale of the property, at least temporarily."

"Permanently if we find mass graves. And we begin with the grave of Andy Cope."

"Hack Johnson won't talk."

"He's not the only person alive who knows were Andy is buried."

"Who else?"

"Zeke Wiley. He's at the Cypress Grove Senior Center. If you or the sheriff can take him to the school property, have him lead you to the grave. And we might find more graves."

"I'll see what I can do. Oh, one more thing. Cooter Johnson is turning state's witness. He say's he'll testify that his father and grandfather had a long, personal, and on-going relationship with Jeff Carson. Carson was paid to look the other way in cases involving the family's manufacture of meth. He turned a blind eye to the sale and distribution of pot and cocaine in cases that could have implicated the family. Cooter refers to Carson as 'Uncle Jeff.' I'm almost shaking telling you this. Not in a million years. Gotta go."

I called Caroline Harper and told her what had happened. She listened quietly. I said. "We're getting a court order to look for Andy's grave."

"Oh thank God above! I never thought I'd live to see this day."

"It may take a while, but if Andy's buried there, he can be found."

"Sean, I don't know what to say except thank you."

"Hold any thanks until we find your brother. In the meantime, someone else who's been lost for a long time is about to be set free. The state attorney's office is releasing Jesse. This is the time, maybe more than anytime since he was in the school, that he could use a friend."

"I'll make arrangements to pick him up and we'll go to dinner. Thank you." She disconnected.

I sipped lukewarm coffee and called Dave. "Well, hello Sean. Anything new to report from Jackson County."

"Just the fact that I'm alive, thanks to you."

"All in a day's work. Actually, all in a couple of hours work. But it's never a job when you're having fun."

"Can't say getting my jaw fractured and a couple of ribs cracked was a lot of fun." I told Dave what happened and added, "We have a match on the thumbprint found on the shell—it's Hack Johnson's print. Lana's getting a court order to find Andy's grave, and the graves of others believed buried on the property."

I heard Dave sigh. A second later he said, "If there are dozens of graves, and that's an if—then this could become a case of serial killings handed down through the generations of guards who worked there. This could become one of America's greatest tragedies—one that has taken place for one hundred and eleven years. If this leads to mass unknown graves, you're walking a long and frightening path, Sean. Presumably, because at the end of it, are the graves of innocent children—victims of those entrusted to help them."

SEVENTY-NINE

They brought Zeke Wiley to the reform school property in a sheriff's car. And the sheriff himself was driving. Other police agency vehicles were already there. Cars and people from the Florida Department of Law Enforcement were there, too. Forensic workers. People from the coroner's office stood by, waiting. I counted seven TV satellite trucks and a half dozen small microwave news trucks. National and regional media jockeyed for best positions. Reporters and camera operators set up tripods. A man in jeans and a black T-shirt sat on a backhoe, the engine turned off. Other men from the sheriff's office had shovels and evidence bags.

Caroline Harper and Jesse stood under the shade of an oak, Jesse comforting her. I watched Jesse study Zeke Wiley's every step and physical nuance. Even from fifty feet away, I could see the disgust on Jesse's face. Caroline patted her eyes with a handkerchief. Jesse placed an arm around her shoulders and watched a squirrel bury an acorn. The sky was hard blue, a light breeze from the east. A mockingbird cackled from one of the big oaks.

I stood next to Lana Halley as the sheriff walked slowly with the old man. Neither man spoke. Everyone followed, walking from the main parking lot, between two buildings, past a cottage and toward the small cemetery with plastic PVC pipe as grave markers. No names on any of the graves. Nothing but faded plastic pipe and grass choked with weeds.

Reporter Cory Wilson, with a photographer, snapped pictures of Zeke Wiley leading the procession across the property. The other reporters and videographers followed for best spots to catch the old man and the sheriff in search of a hidden grave—maybe more. The national media picked up Cory Wilson's series of stories. They were all here. CNN, Fox News, the TV networks. Major newspapers. And everyone watched the slow processional to search for a shallow grave with very deep consequences. The expression on the old man's face looked redemptive, somehow at terms with what he was about to do—what he was about to reveal after so many decades of hidden secrecy.

Lana glanced up at me and said, "So, just maybe Andy was buried in that small cemetery with the rest of the boys. Some were said to have died in a fire during the twenties."

"We'll soon find out."

Wiley walked past the marked cemetery, more than two hundred feet to a more remote, secluded area. He stopped at the base of a large pine tree, looked to his right and then to his left. He stepped to the center, in a north- ward direction. It looked as though he was counting silently, his lips moving, calculating distance with each small step he took. When he was about fifty feet north of the lone pine, he stopped and pointed to the ground. "There. He's buried somewhere right in this immediate area. I need to sit."

I heard Caroline sob. The sheriff turned and signaled. "Set up the tape here, Brad and Tucker. Everyone else, please keep your distance." Two men rolled out the yellow crime scene tape, cordoning off a square about fifty feet in four directions, pounding in stakes and wrapping the tape around the top of each stake. Then the sheriff motioned for his team to dig. Everyone formed a semicircle outside the tape, watching the body recovery and foren- sics teams. The sound of shovels removing topsoil, the click of cameras, a news videographer raising his tripod and camera. Caroline looked away for a few seconds. A female deputy escorted Zeke Wiley to the shade of an oak. He sat in a foldout chair someone had brought.

A tall man, wearing a shirt with the word FORENSICS on the back, stopped digging with his shovel and knelt down, now using a hand trowel, "Found something. Very shallow."

There was a murmur in the crowd. More camera clicks. The mocking-bird stopped chortling. The sheriff walked up to what now appeared to be a gravesite. He observed as the team used trowels to excavate the soil. The coroner, an older man with a neatly trimmed white beard and bifocals, squatted beside the excavation. He spoke softy with the investigators, nodding his head and pointing to different areas of what appeared to be human skeletal remains.

The sheriff shook his head, swatting a fly, and walked over to speak with other members of his team. After a few seconds, he cleared his throat and spoke to the media and anyone else within earshot. "Folks, this is now a crime scene. You people in the news media, we'll answer your questions as soon as we can get some definitive results. In the meantime, our investigators and forensics folks will go about their jobs in an expeditious fashion. Seems to me too much time has already passed. There appears to be human remains in that grave. Most likely from a child, considering bone and skull size. We'll remove the body, and along with the FDLE, conduct DNA and dental tests. We'll have a news briefing as soon as we know something."

One network reporter, a lean man with close-cropped white hair asked, "Sheriff, can the coroner estimate how long the body has been there?"

"No, not at this time."

Another reporter, a woman from CNN asked, "Are you going to search for additional graves?"

As the sheriff was about to answer, Zeke Wiley stood, raising his hand in the air. The sheriff looked at him. "Yes, Mr. Wiley?"

"There are more graves…more are in this area." His face was flush, his eyes wide, lips pursed, his chest rising and falling quickly.

Reporters circled Wiley, peppering questions. He held up his hands, closing his eyes for a moment, and then looking toward the blue sky, folding his hands as if in prayer.

The sheriff motioned to three deputies. "Ya'll get him into a squad car. Get the air conditioning running. Give him some water."

The deputies nodded, walking up to Wiley, one deputy saying to the media, "That's it for now. Please give this man some room. Show some respect, okay? Mr. Wiley let's get you in the cool of an air-conditioned car."

One of the forensic workers, a woman, sleeves up, rubber gloves on, knelt over the grave and used a small brush to remove debris. I watched her. Stop and start. Brush and examine. The expression on her face was intense. Curious. Thorough. Professional. She lifted a long pair of forensic tweezers from her kit. Prodded. Then she lifted something from the hole. It was small, the size of a peanut. She examined it and signaled for the sheriff. He walked over, spoke with her, looked at the object and watched her place it in a small plastic bag.

The sheriff stepped over to the news media. He paused, choosing his words carefully. "One of our investigators located an object lodged into a pelvic bone. We'll look at it in the lab, but I've been around long enough to know double aught buckshot when I see it. Whoever's in that shallow grave was apparently shot."

A reporter started to ask a question. The sheriff raised one hand. "We'll take questions later."

I watched a Florida Department of Law Enforcement investigator approach the sheriff, talking quietly, the sheriff nodding. The investigator, early fifties, a face that indicated he's seen some of the worst of the worst, turned and looked at the media. His jacket was off. White dress shirt, sleeves rolled up. Tie down a notch. He said, "In view of what we've just found, and for a number of reasons…we need to thoroughly excavate this property. A forensic anthropology team with one of the universities has been following the news stories. Our office received word that they've requested permission to come on the property, using ground-penetrating radar to search for anomalies, or skeletal remains. We see no reason to deny their request as long as they work within law enforcement parameters to find and excavate other human remains, should they find them. This might become an arduous process, considering the size of the property, but we extend the invitation for the professor and her graduate students to help us locate more graves, God forbid that they're really out here."

A reporter shouted, "Do you think that's Andy Cope's grave?"

I looked toward Caroline. She stared stoically, watching the forensics staff continue sifting through dirt and bones.

The investigator said, "We don't know that. In view of what Mrs. Harper has gone through the last fifty years, if this is her brother's grave, we hope it'll help bring closure to her and her family. As you know, we have a suspect in custody. And now we have a body. Is it that of Andy Cope? We don't know, but you can quote me on this…we'll find out, and we'll do it quickly. The state will rush DNA testing to determine if these are his remains. And if so, I've been authorized to let you know the state will pay all costs for removal of the body and a new burial, wherever Mrs. Harper requests. At this time, we'll conclude the news conference. Thank you."

I glanced over to Caroline Harper, reporters forming a semicircle around her and Jesse. One reporter asked, "Mrs. Harper, if this proves to be your brother's remains, what will that finally mean to you?"

She inhaled deeply, looked toward the excavation and turned her head to face the reporter. "It'll mean that my brother was murdered. And if he was, how many more are buried in here? And whom do we hold account-able for allowing that horrible situation to go on so long and no one to step in and stop it. In my brother's memory and for other children like him, the monsters who did this and those who do it today…you will go to a place even worse than what you made it for these children. I'll anxiously await the DNA finding. I don't have anything more to say. Thank you." She turned and walked away, Jesse's arm on her shoulder. He shook his head each time a reporter asked another question. They walked toward her car, the sound of digging behind them, and the mockingbird lifting its head up and singing from an oak tree in front of them.

EIGHTY

Maybe it was a case of half century's worth of bottled up guilt. Maybe it was because he was old, frail and thought he was on the verge of meeting his maker. Whatever it was, Zeke Wiley showed investigators where the "black boys were buried." He said he'd read and followed the case of Elijah Franklin. When Jeremiah Franklin was killed, Wiley told detectives he was horrified by a dream he had the next night—a dream where he said he saw little Eli Franklin still breathing when they tossed him in a shallow grave fifty years ago, the dark earth writhing, a small black hand clawing through the loose dirt.

He remembered Hack Johnson laughing, walking up to the grave and standing in his big boots at the head of the grave, the spot where Elijah's head was under the topsoil. In less than half a minute, the squirming beneath his boots stopped. They tossed another shovel full of dirt over the boy's hands, got off work, and went into town to hit their favorite bar.

Forensics investigators unearthed a shallow grave that Wiley distinctly remembered as that of Elijah because of the wicked death the boy had suffered. Some of the skeletal remains were rushed to the same lab that was testing for Andy Cope's DNA. Detectives paid a visit to Mrs. Franklin, telling her what had happened and took her DNA sample with them.

And now we waited. With the intense national and international interest in the case, the state of Florida accelerated the DNA testing faster than I'd ever seen. I stayed in Marianna for a few days, like much of the news media, waiting for the results.

The Florida Attorney General's office was working with Lana Halley and a strong-willed grand jury to deliver numerous indictments against almost every male adult member of the Johnson family, facing charges of running one of the largest drug operations in the Florida Panhandle to racketeering, arson and murder.

Jeff Carson was indicted for withholding evidence in potential felony cases involving Johnson family members, and causing innocent people to take the fall and be sentenced to prison. In a news conference, the Attorney General said, "Mr. Carson was involved in this egregious misconduct because he knew he could probably get away with it, which he did...until he got caught. His decision to be above and beyond the law is a flagrant abuse of powers that the people in his district had entrusted in him as chief prosecutor. He will be dealt with and prosecuted to the maximum extent of the law."

Detective Larry Lee, facing charges of bribery and accepting payoffs for selective law enforcement, took an unpaid leave of absence from the sheriff's office pending the outcome of the charges. The judge slapped him with an ankle bracelet and a stern warning not to leave the county.

Cory Wilson had tried in vain to secure an interview with the CEO of Horizon and Vista Properties, James Winston, after the corporation rescinded the offer to buy the reform school property. His Gulfstream jet left in the middle of the night, the pilot somehow failing to file a flight plan.

I was filling my tank with gas when Lana called. "Sean, it's a match. The mitochondrial DNA testing came back. The body in the first grave is Andy Cope. And the child in the second grave is Elijah Franklin. I'm calling Caroline and Mrs. Franklin with the news. Hack Johnson is facing first-degree murder charges. In the meantime, the university forensic anthropologists are conducting ground penetrating radar testing. At first pass they say they've found at least a dozen unknown graves. Could be more. Looks like that property won't be on the auction block for a long time, if ever."

"Normally, I don't like attending funerals. But these are two that I wouldn't miss."

"If you don't mind, I'd like to join you. They're funerals, but they're also two reasons to celebrate. We can celebrate because heinous crimes, murders never even on the investigative radar, are seeing justice because you received that letter."

EIGHTY-ONE

The Shiloh Baptist Church couldn't hold the crowd. Some people gathered near the open doors to the front entrance, using hand-fans to circulate the motionless air. Although it was only 11:00 in the morning, the Florida sun was hot, the air humid. Other people stood in the shade of leafy oaks, listening to the service on a loud speaker wired to the pulpit. Attendees, black and white, packed the old church to pay their respects to the family of a murdered child.

I stood in the back of the church with Lana and listened to the Reverend Joseph Hart deliver a passionate eulogy for Elijah Franklin. Caroline and Jesse sat in a middle pew. Caroline would bury Andy's remains at 4:00 in a cemetery less than five miles away. I could only imagine what was going through her mind.

Reverend Hart talked about the injustice and shortness of little Elijah's life. How God has a special place in heaven for children, especially those abused and killed by adults. He added, "Last week we buried Elijah's brother, Jeremiah. Killed, just like Elijah, by the hands of others, the influence of Satan. Let God be the judge, and brothers and sisters he will! Amen!"

Half the congregation said, "Amen," people nodding and using hand-fans. Elijah's mother and other family members sat in the front row. Mrs. Franklin staring at the small white casket, the diminutive size reminding the crowd just how little Elijah was at the time he was killed. When Reverend

Hart invited family members to share their thoughts, Sonia Acker stepped behind the podium.

She looked out across the packed church, a baby crying in his mother's arms, the mother comforting the child. Sonia talked about the uncle she would never know, except for the pictures in her grandmother's house and the stories from aunts and uncles. She said her grandmother spoke of Elijah often, and how much she still missed his smiling face. Sonia told the audience that she did know Elijah's brother Jeremiah and how he had been a special uncle. Kind and considerate. But all his life, he carried the scars from the months he'd spent in the Florida School for Boys, the same place where Elijah had died.

When the eulogies were done, the congregation, and those waiting outside, walked behind the old church for the burial. Members of the Franklin family carried the small casket down the church steps and to the gravesite. Carefully. Step-by-step. Tears flowing. Reverend Hart said a short prayer, nodded and the cemetery workers slowly lowered the coffin into the hole. It was very close to a fresh grave, sandy soil still piled in a small mound. Jeremiah Franklin's name on the headstone.

Five members of the Franklin family tossed yellow roses into the open grave, Mrs. Franklin sobbing softly. She just buried two sons in one week. When the service concluded, people embraced the family again, offering condolences and prayers. Wet faces. Tears. Jesse and Caroline spoke with Mrs. Franklin, both giving her long hugs. I watched Jesse walk over to Jeremiah's grave. He bowed his head. Hands in his pockets. Shoulders quivering as he wept.

Lana and I stepped up to offer Mrs. Franklin our sympathies. "My name is Lana Halley. This is my friend, Sean O'Brien. I want you to know how deeply sorry we are for you and your family."

The old woman looked up, variegated sunlight popping through the magnolia trees. It was her eyes that struck me. Compassionate eyes. Wise eyes. Eyes reflecting a deep longing—a sadness cutting to the bone. She studied Lana a moment and said, "Thank you. That's kind of you."

"Mrs. Franklin, I'm one of the prosecutors in the district. I will do everything in my power to find justice for Elijah. I just want you to know that, ma'am. We have a man in custody who we believe killed Andy Cope, and he probably was responsible for Elijah's death."

She nodded. "Thank you. Like the preacher said, our Lord will deliver the real justice. Here on earth, wit' the wickedness and the hate, I don't know if I have ever experienced real justice. Lots of judgment, but not a whole lot of justice."

I said, "Mrs. Franklin, the man who took Jeremiah's life is dead. I suspect that real justice you mentioned has already happened."

She nodded, looked up at me, looked at the cuts and stitches on my face. She touched my hand. "Mr. O'Brien, I recognize your name from the stories on the TV news. I cain't read the papers much on 'count of my vision, but I can hear the TV, 'specially on Sundays when I cain't get out to Reverend Hart's church." She smiled. "I don't get on the road much no more either. The only road I travel is cemetery road, and that's a real lonely place to be." She patted the top of my hand, smiled and used her cane to walk toward family members.

— —

Even after my military service in the war-torn Middle East, after working homicide in the dark vice sewers of Miami, I couldn't remember attending two funerals the same day. But here in Jackson County, in view of the unearthing of two graves, graves of children who died close together in time and place, it seemed fitting to have two funerals a few hours apart. Many of the people would attend both services. They began arriving at the funeral for Andy not long after Elijah was laid to rest. I estimated that at least 150 people had come. Black. White. People all here to say goodbye to a little boy who'd suffered horribly so many years ago.

A large white tent was erected over the gravesite. Dozens of flower arrangements near the casket, maybe fifty chairs supplied by the funeral home. The vast majority of people would stand near the grave in a cemetery filled with live oaks, pines and maple trees. A place filled with sorrow. Caroline and Jesse sat in the front row. There were other people there, too. A woman in her forties, and a man about her age. They had two teenage children, a boy and a girl. I assumed the woman was Caroline's daughter, the man her daughter's husband, and the kids their children.

The minister was a tall man who resembled Abe Lincoln without facial hair. He spoke eloquently about life, death, and the absolute power of faith at all times, especially dark periods and times of doubt. He talked about the unconscionable and senseless death of a child—Andy Cope, a child taken by violence. The comfort, if it could be found, was in knowing that Andy Cope went to a much better place than what he inherited. The minister invited family and friends to speak a few words about Andy.

Caroline stood slowly. She stepped to the casket, placing her hand on it. She bowed her head in silence and then turned to address the people. She looked exhausted, her face aged in the last few days. She wiped a tear from her cheek and said, "It's been many years since my brother was sent to the Florida School for Boys. His crime? Truancy from school. He was just a kid. When he was never released, when he never returned home, we were told he'd run away. And now, all these years later, the forensic investigators found buckshot in Andy's remains. They say he was shot in the back." She couldn't hold back the flow of tears. Her hands trembled. Lips quivering.

"My brother was a good boy, a good son, and he would have become a good man, had he been given the chance. I'm so grateful to those people who helped me find and bring Andy home. I wish my mother had lived to know what happened to her son. But that was not to be. As Reverend Lawton said, Andy's in a better place...I just so wish he could have had more time in this place."

Jesse stood, nodded at Caroline and stepped beside her. He held a white rose in his hand. Jesse cleared his throat. "I grew up with Andy...at least I grew up with him until he never came back from the school. He was a good guy, always grinning. Andy wouldn't even play boyish pranks 'cause he didn't want to hurt anybody's feelings. He was that way. Sort of wise beyond his years. Even though he was just a kid when they killed him, he had a wiser soul than any of us boys. So maybe Andy was already halfway to heaven because of who he was and what he did for others. What he stood for, even as a boy, I wish as a man I could have combined more of those qualities that Andy showed me. If he's lookin' down here today..."

Jesse glanced up, his voice breaking, eyes watering "If you're looking down at us today, Andy, I want you to know you had a positive influence on me. And I swear to God, for what ever time I'm allowed to remain on this on earth…my intentions will be for good—for others." Jesse wiped tears from his face, handing the rose to Caroline. She touched him gently on the shoulder. They turned and together set the rose on the casket.

I could hear gentle sobbing coming from family and friends. Crying that was long overdue. The release of buried emotion. A painful wail. A sniffle. A soft cry. A cardinal warbling from a mimosa tree, the scent of magnolia blossoms in the warm breeze. I stood with Lana near the back row of chairs. She dabbed her eyes with a tissue. I lifted the small black and white picture out of my pocket again, looking at it and then looking as they lowered Andy Cope into his final grave.

EIGHTY-TWO

It was late afternoon the next day when I arrived back at Ponce Marina, the breeze over the mangroves laced with the scent of salt water and baitfish. I felt like I'd been gone for years, everything in the marina seemed refreshed, or maybe I was just more aware of what I missed—the sounds of gulls overhead, the dinging of halyards jingling in the breeze against sailboat masts, fishing captains laughing and swapping stories at the Tiki Bar.

I walked down L dock, longing to see little Max and her unbridled passion for all things living. My face was still bruised and stitched from the beatings I'd undergone, first with Deputy Parker on the trail, and then with Solomon Johnson in his barn. I hoped Max would recognize me. I walked past a forty-foot Bertram, rigged for fishing, just easing away from the dock, two guys in golf visor hats going out the inlet and into the Atlantic. A Leopard catamaran entered the marina, its sails down, one man at the helm, a tanned woman in a white bikini sipping a drink next to him.

It felt good to be back. And it would feel better doing some sailing.

I didn't know if Max would be on Dave's trawler or on Nick's boat. It usually depended on who was cooking. When I got a whiff of grilling fish, spotting the white smoke swirling from Nick's grill on his cockpit, I knew. A few more steps and a furry reddish-brown head popped up from a deck chair, ears perked, and then she looked down the dock my way.

If a dog can smile, Max grinned. She jumped from one of the canvas chairs, spun in a circle, barking three times, her tail moving like a humming-bird's wing. I approached. "Hey kiddo, you really recognize me?"

Another bark. A tilt of her head and another full circle turn. I stepped from the dock onto the *St. Michael* and scooped up Max, holding her against my chest. She flattered me with kisses. Considering my face, it was the true example of unconditional love. "I missed you, Max. Have you been helping Nick and Dave? Picking up food that Nick drops, not getting into Ol' Joe's whiskered and scarred cat face? Maybe I'll start looking like that darned cat." I rubbed Max behind her ears as Nick came through the open cockpit doors, dressed in a faded blue swimsuit, a tank shirt, a towel in one hand, a Corona in the other.

"Hey, Sean!" he grinned, lifting his beer in a toast. "Did you check yourself for ticks before you walked on my boat? Sounds like you've been so far out in the country even the Internet won't go there. Maybe that's where the World Wide Web stops."

"I'm clean." I smiled.

He raised both bushy eyebrows. "Dave said you had to face some tough dudes. Looks like they did a helluva drumroll on your face. Tell me the other guy's in worse shape."

"He's dead."

"I'd say that's beyond worse shape."

"Where's Dave?"

"Should be back on *Gibraltar*. He went to restock his bar."

"Is that because he knew I was coming back?"

"Could be. Or maybe because he's generous, and I don't have to stock mine as much. I have the beer, Dave has the craft beers. He has the premium booze, which means I'm less likely to get a hangover hangin' with Dave. We have a lot more in common than you might think."

"Oh, yeah." I smiled. "What would that be?"

"Basra. He's damn good. He's the only non-Greek that can beat me with the cards."

Dave stepped from *Gibraltar's* bow onto the dock. He wore a red and blue tropical print shirt, shorts and sandals. "The prodigal friend returns from the west." He looked at my face in the setting sun, shook his head. "Well, you've undergone a physical transformation of sorts. Let's have a drink and hear about the psychological ramifications. Nick, do you have any more bounty from the seas?"

"Got fifty pounds of snapper. Some grouper left too."

"Since I restocked the bar for this occasion, let's cook 'em on *Gibraltar* and have a cocktail before hand."

Nick nodded. "I'll wrap my piece in foil, bring over some nice fillets, and we'll experience the thrill of the grill."

— —

We sipped cold chardonnay, ate fresh grilled fish and Greek salads in *Gibraltar's* cockpit, piano jazz coming from speakers in the salon, the setting sun igniting the western sky in hues of deep reds, pinks and clouds with lavender bellies. I told Dave and Nick about the two funerals, the arrests and charges leveled at the Johnson clan, Jeff Carson's quick departure from office and the charges he is facing.

I mentioned the buckshot taken out of Andy's remains matching the shot I dug out from the tree. "Police believed the murder weapon was a 12-gauge shotgun Hack Johnson handed down to his kids. They often kept the gun in a rack in one of the trucks. I'll be going back to testify. Lana Halley will ask for life in prison if Hack Johnson is convicted, and there's no doubt that he will be. With all the evidence and the fact that Zeke Wiley agreed to testify against Johnson, life in prison for a man Johnson's age is the death penalty—a slow death."

Dave said, "It's big news all over the nation, Sean. The state attorney general is overseeing the prosecutions herself. The governor is trying to fold this into his campaign for the utmost political correctness mileage, saying, and I'm quoting here, 'Our office will work with the attorney general to make sure no stone is left unturned, ensuring a thorough and complete investigation into allegations of criminal activity on the former reform school property.' End quote. Blah-blah-blah. Nothing would have moved if you hadn't moved."

Nick wiped olive oil from the tips of his fingers, sipped his beer and said, "It's like you stepped back into a page from the book, *Gone With the Wind*, up there. It's amazing how those guys got away with that much shit through the years."

Dave nodded. "When the state attorney is in cahoots, the law of the land becomes the law of one man. You knocked the hornet's nest down, Sean."

I smiled. "But if you hadn't tracked me so well, alerting—no, managing to find the guys in white hats, I would have been stung to death."

Dave sipped his drink, pushed back from the table, his eyes following a jet trail above the horizon in the darkening sky. He looked at me. "All in a day's work. I live vicariously through your journeys. You're a video game in the flesh, the bruised flesh." He grinned and sipped his wine.

I said nothing for a few moments, the gentle wake from a passing Hatteras rocking *Gibraltar*. Dave said, "I've seen that look. You're trying to make sense out of the futile."

"I'm trying to see what I missed in Deputy Ivan Parker. I've been fooled before, but never quite like that."

"We all live our lives in shades of gray. So there was nothing black or white that would have popped out in your dealing with what appeared to be a very honest cop."

"He was a sociopath, and I had no clue. But, in retrospect, subtle signs were there. Either I chose to overlook them, or in comparing Deputy Parker to Detective Lee, and in needing an ally in law enforcement, I made a hasty choice that backfired. I wound up with a few broken pieces. The irony is that I told Caroline that sometimes we're made better by having had a few pieces broken and welded back together again. At some point, you have to ask yourself…when do you learn your lesson?"

Nick raised his shoulders, palms up. "Maybe if there's no pain, there's no gain."

Dave chuckled. "Spoken like a Greek philosopher, Nick. The obstacles, the confusion and even the fear…it's all there to remind you there's something better, something more just, and it's worth fighting for. The broken pieces mend, and the scars are the visual reminders it was worth it. Often it's the loss that teaches us about the worth of what's right. " Dave lifted his glass. "To wounds, welts and life's blemishes because we can't hit the rewind button on our lives, leaving out the crap without losing the very thing that made it meaningful."

We sipped our drinks, Max dozing on my lap. After another hour, I bid my friends goodnight and opened *Jupiter's* doors and windows to air her out. I fixed Max a bowl of dog food, probably a food she didn't have while I was away. She walked over to her bowl, sniffed and then jumped up onto the couch in the salon. I laughed. "Suit yourself. In picking you up, I did notice that it seems like you put on some weight." Max closed her eyes, ignoring me.

I removed my keys from my pockets and felt the photo in my shirt pocket. I lifted out the picture of Andy, walked over to my refrigerator and used a small magnet to stick the photo on the refrigerator door. The phone in my pocket buzzed. I looked at the ID. Lana Halley. I answered and she said, "This little town's not the same when you're not here."

I smiled. "Bet it's a lot quieter."

"That it is, but sometimes too much quiet can be deafening in a weird way. Where are you?"

"Back at Ponce Marina. I just opened up *Jupiter*. Max and I have opened all the windows, and we're airing out the boat. The old boat's been locked a little too long."

Lana was quiet a few seconds. "I can relate. Sean, I have a little time before things get intense around here. The state attorney general's office is handling some of the heavy lifting in the cases, Jeff Carson's included. I have a week or so to just get the hell out of here. God knows I could use it. I was online looking for places with white sand beaches, tropical flowers and the best rum punches in the whole Caribbean."

"The Caribbean? What'd you find?"

"Two tickets to St. Vincent and the oh-so-lovely Grenadine islands. You told me how much you enjoy sailing a catamaran. They have a great special. It's an eight-day rental. We'd leave from St. Vincent, sailing for Bequia and onward. I don't want to sound presumptuous and I haven't ever initiated this sort of thing...but after what we've seen...life's just too damn short not to enjoy it more."

I said nothing for a few seconds.

She said, "Are you there?"

"You said two tickets…can we make it three? One's not really a ticket because she can fit under the seat in front of us on the plane."

"She?"

"Max. She's sleeping on my couch. And when she heard me mention the Caribbean, she opened one eye. Max is my ten-pound dachshund. She loves to sail. Takes up hardly any room. Understands the meaning of privacy."

"I love her already."

EIGHTY-THREE

We rented a thirty-six foot catamaran out of the Blue Lagoon Marina on the south side of St. Vincent. The itinerary would have us stopping at an island about every thirty miles. We cast off and sailed toward Bequia and Admiralty Bay, stopping in a secluded cove, dropping anchor and snorkeling the reefs and an underwater wreck. Max kept vigil about the catamaran. She sat in the shade of the cockpit and watched a pod of dolphins fifty yards off our stern.

Lana slipped into a black bikini. We stepped from the dive platform into gin-clear water with a visibility of more than one hundred feet. She loved snorkeling and was good at it. She had breath control, able to stay down for a least a minute. We snorkeled for about an hour, surfacing, laughing and talking about what we'd just seen underwater. I held her hand diving to depths of fifteen feet. She tapped me on the shoulder, her eyes wide behind the facemask, pointing to a half dozen black seahorses swimming in and around pink and orange coral and sea fans. She gripped my hand when a five-foot barracuda came up to within a few feet of us, pausing and then darting away, its silver body catching the sunlight through the water.

We swam back to the boat, Lana removing her fins at the swim ladder, tossing them on the deck and then climbing aboard. I followed. We towel dried and she said, "This is so beautiful." She used a brush to comb her thick hair, her eyes following dolphins as they came closer. She smiled. "Maybe we should jump back in and join them."

"They can hold their breath longer. They'd get bored with mere humans."

Lana laughed, petted Max, and sat in one of the deck chairs. "Sean, let's just say 'screw it' and sail around the world. I've always wanted to do that. This boat seems big enough."

"Don't tempt me."

"It wouldn't take much, would it?"

"No, it wouldn't."

"Unfortunately, I have some unfinished business in Jackson County. But after that's done, let's rethink this crazy but oh-so-delightful dream. Hungry?"

"As matter of fact, I am."

"I'll make a scrumptious salad, lobster included."

She entered the galley, Max following, Lana chatting with Max like a girlfriend. Twenty minutes later, we were eating at the deck table under the shade of the canopy, Lana had an Adele song streaming from satellite radio. We ate a delicious salad, kale and mixed greens with chunks of fresh lobster in a special dressing that Lana had made. We sipped rum punches and absorbed the beauty. The water was an emerald green within a mile of the shore, tapering off to a deep blue further out.

We set sail again. Lana was a quick study, grasping the sails, moves, and the simple physics of sailing a cat. The Leopard cat was nimble, drawing about two feet of water, scooting over the surface at about fifteen knots. Lana sat with me at the helm, the wind in her hair. She looked behind us, laughed and said, "The dolphins are following us."

I turned and looked. More than a dozen dolphins easily caught up with the cat. They jumped and played to our starboard side, and then they cut under the boat, resurfacing on the port side. That got Max's attention. She stood on a deck chair and barked twice, her long ears flapping in the wind. After a few more minutes, the dolphins left us—left us to cobalt blue seas, and gentle trade winds from the south and a perfect day. Max retreated back to a chair and napped.

Lana sat next to me. She sipped rum from a tall glass and then set it in a cup holder. She took off her sunglasses and looked at me. Her eyes were as beautiful as the Caribbean waters, just as blue and just as full of life. She leaned in and we kissed, softly. Her lips warm and sensuous. I touched her cheek with one hand, her eyes almost hypnotic in their beauty. She smiled and said, "Do you know how long I wanted to do that?"

"No, how long?" I smiled.

"Too long." We kissed again. Then she rested her head on my shoulder, watching the islands in the distance, singing softly to a song on the radio. "Sean, this is so relaxing. Thank you for joining me here."

"Thank you for inviting me."

"I'm already beginning to feel like putty. After a week of this, I'm not sure if I could ever go back."

I said nothing, leaning down to kiss her shoulder. She smiled and said, "When I became a prosecutor, it was because I thought I could change a little corner of the world. Sweep evil back under the door when it came across the threshold. Now, I'm not so sure. There's just too much of it. I feel overwhelmed, and maybe I entered the wrong profession."

"You've gone through a lot these last few weeks. The wringer. It squeezes your heart."

"It's wrung out my soul...causing sleepless nights. Causing me to rethink my purpose in life."

I said nothing. Listening.

She exhaled and said, "After these upcoming cases, I'm thinking about going into defense work. And I'm only thinking about it because I saw how easily Jeff Carson could cheat the system. Maybe a good defense lawyer could have kept some of Carson's victims out of jail."

"Follow your heart, Lana. That's the best road." I massaged her shoulder, a soft moan coming from her lips. I kissed her again. When we broke, she said, "Does this boat have an automatic pilot?" She smiled wide, the wind in her hair, sun on her face.

"We can drop anchor. We're only in thirty feet of water. You can see the bottom. We're in no hurry. Time, in terms of having to be somewhere, is overboard. Buried at sea. You're here to relax, to put Jackson County in the rearview mirror. Captain's orders." I smiled.

"Does that mean I'm your first mate?"

I answered her with a kiss. I lowered the anchor, the cat drifting onto a semi-stationary position, and then I took Lana's hand leading her into the master cabin. Max stayed outside, napping in the shade.

At the bedside, Lana and I kissed again, building in passion. I held her face in my hands. She touched my bare chest with the palm of her hand and looked into my eyes. Then she removed her bikini. Her body was amazing, curvaceous, firm and feminine. The sex was slow and sensuous. We took our time, lots of kissing, and exploring and then building to mutual climaxes.

Afterwards, we took a shower together, dressed in light clothing and went topside, Max lifting her head. We decided to continue our southward trek, staying out of Admiralty Bay. Keeping away from the lights of island civilization. Within two hours, we were greeted with a fiery sunset in the western Caribbean. Just as the sun slipped beyond the sapphire sea, there was a quick green flash. Lana pointed. "Did you see that?"

"What?"

"The green flash."

"What green flash?"

"On the horizon."

"You mean the one that pops when the sun sinks, right?"

She playfully pushed my shoulder. "You did see it!"

"I saw it. It's not rare but if you blink, you miss it."

"I wonder what causes it."

"It's the way the atmosphere is at the moment the sunlight slips over the curvature of the earth. The last rays are, in essence, trapped for a second. Their original source, the sun, now gone and the weaker light penetrating the atmosphere is green as it dissipates."

She smiled. "Was that meteorological trivia you learned in sailing school?"

"No, I was curious so I looked it up online a few years ago."

When the sun left, the stars joined us. The Milky Way seemed to be a living thing above us. Pulsating. A heartbeat surely somewhere tucked between the stars. Lana looked behind the boat and said, "Wow…I'm not sure I've ever seen anything like it." There were twin trails of blue-green light churning in the water from the boat's wake. The kinetic energy from the double hulls skimming through the warm sea was creating an explosion of phosphorescence in the water. Baitfish jumped from the surface, flitting through the water causing the same lightshow. Two dolphins joined us, and it was as if they were swimming through an ocean of blue-green fire.

Lana snapped pictures with her camera. "I hope I'm getting this. It's simply incredible."

"This kind of lightshow doesn't happen that often. The water temp has to be right. The season has to be right. The tiny microscopic life has to be in abundance. It all comes together to create a bioluminescence that glows unlike any manmade light source."

Max stared at the light explosions in our wake. I looked up, a meteor shot through the heavens. In the water, a dolphin created a blue comet just under the surface. It was as if the heavens knew no boundaries between earth and sky. We'd sailed across a planetary threshold, the universe turning fish and marine creatures into meteor showers of aquatic life, moving like fireflies in orbs and orbits of undersea starlight.

I looked to the south and caught my breath. There it was. Just above the horizon. An ornament hanging from the sky due south, beyond the dark sea. The Southern Cross. "Lana…look at that." I pointed in the direction.

"Sean, what is it? It's beautiful. Like a cross."

"It's the Southern Cross."

Lana stared at the twinkling constellation, its reflection over the sea. "Dear God…I'm getting a chill. There are goose bumps on my arms. We're looking at a heavenly designed cross…and when I think about Hack Johnson, his old tattoo and what he told children about the 'Southern Cross of Justice'…I have no words."

"And now justice for Andy and the others is his cross to bear. Dante referred to the Southern Cross as the *Crux*. He'd ascribed four human virtues to each star you're looking at; *justice, temperance, prudence* and *fortitude*. But just down in the lower right, you can barely see a darker star—a faint fifth star. Does it remind us of the omnipresence of darker forces?"

"Possibly. But right now, at this moment in time, Sean O'Brien, the brighter stars, fortitude, temperance, prudence and justice are what we see the clearest. Maybe there's a celestial metaphor in the starlight. I've never seen the Southern Cross before tonight."

I smiled and held Lana close to me. Her skin had a slight floral scent from the soap. "Before my wife Sherri's death a few years ago, we were sailing the Caribbean. She used to love to sing an old Crosby, Stills and Nash song…*Southern Cross*. Tonight, sharing this with you—you seeing the constellation for the first time, has helped me appreciate the lyrics a little better.

"What are the lyrics?"

"*When you see the Southern Cross for the first time, you understand now why you came this way. 'Cause the truth you might be runnin' from is so small…but it's as big as the promise, the promise of a new day.*"

She looked up at me, the starlight in her eyes. "Tonight Lana, you're the promise of a new day."

She smiled and we kissed, the Milky Way above and under us—the universe and sea dancing and seamless in the cosmos of light.

The End

Coming Summer 2016

A MURDER OF CROWS

A Sean O'Brien Novel

The following is preview from the novel

A MURDER OF CROWS

(Prologue - Florida wilderness – 1835)

Only a few people knew the name his mother had given him. Millions would know the name he took to his grave. He was born by a river, and throughout his short life rivers would speak to him. He stood on the banks of the Withlacoochee River deep in the heart of Central Florida. Watching. Listening. Looking for signs. The water was the shade of tea, moving slowly through the wilds, flowing at the base of giant cypress trees, limbs heavy with hanging moss. A brown limpkin screeched across the river. Cypress knees grew beneath the ancient trees, the knees protruding upright from the dark water, reaching for the hard blue sky. The current made slight eddies swirling between the cypress knees, the river whispering to him— warning him. *Something was coming.*

Osceola looked across the opposite shoreline, the sunset coming less than an hour. He would meet the elder tonight. There was no wind, the Spanish moss hanging straight down, the knotty eyes of a large alligator just above the surface. Osceola listened for the sounds of gunfire in the distance, on the edge of the Green Swamp. He watched the wildlife, eaves- dropping on nature, heeding sounds that weren't native to his environment. He observed a cardinal singing from an oak, the bright red bird watching him near the river.

Osceola stood at six feet, handsome, dark hair and eyes, his skin lighter than most Seminoles. He wore a cloth shirt, buckskin vest and pants—a chest plate made from shell, three eagle feathers protruding from a black turban on his head.

He turned from the river, looked at his camp a hundred yards away. Tribe members—men, women and children mingling in and out of the chickee homes—primitive structures with roofs made from dried palmetto fronds. There was excitement in the camp. Some of the men had killed a large manatee. Two of the men dressed the fresh meat, the women preparing the meal. The animal would feed the entire tribe for at least a week. All parts of the manatee, snout to the thick tail, cooked and devoured.

Osceola watched his people for a moment, the Panther, Bear and Otter clans descending from women in the tribe. In the previous months, some of his brothers and sisters had been captured and sent away to a faraway land west of the great river called the Mississippi. The Indians were housed like cattle in camps of no return, the destiny found at the end of the Trail of Tears. Osceola would not go. Not surrender. Not submit to the relocation demands of men dressed as Army soldiers.

He walked a half-mile through the woods, heading in the direction of the temple mound and cave. The old man would be there. He was the oldest of the elders. And his medicine bundle was so powerful that he kept it away from the camp. He told Osceola to come at sunset. To receive medicine needed to prepare his spirit for war.

The sun was on the edge of the world when Osceola entered the partial clearing, a sacred place. A primal temple mound stood in the center of the clearing. It was more than twenty-five feet high by two hundred feet in diameter, centuries old and built by the ancients. The ancients had vanished due to war with the Spanish and disease exported from Europe. Osceola looked at the temple mound and felt a kinship, a powerful pull that often brought him here to be alone

On the perimeter of the clearing to the right of the mound was a slight knoll, a natural uplifting of earth by limestone formations, some of the old boulders protruding from the earth. It was the entrance to a system of caves. And it was in here where the medicine man kept the most powerful medicine, far away from others.

Osceola looked up to the peak of the mound, the old man a silhouette in the setting sun. He used one hand, motioning Osceola to climb. Within a minute, Osceola joined the elder at the summit. They could see across the flat forest and jungles of southwest Florida. Nothing but wilderness in any direction, the western sky was now a fiery red.

The old man's face was carved by time. Skin dark, weather-beaten and creased from age and sun. He wore a vest with red, green and white beads sewn onto it. Buckskin pants. No shoes. A black scarf around his neck. His pewter gray hair hung from the sides of a dark green turban on his head, three flamingo feathers jutting from the turban.

He'd made a very small campfire in the center of the mound. He motioned for Osceola to sit. In the language of the Seminole he told Osceola to extend his arms, palms up. And then the old man used teeth from the jawbone of a garfish to cut into Osceola's forearms, to scrape, the sharp bones leaving bloody trails. Osceola said nothing. He stared at the sunset, his jawline hard, the tinge of fire in his dark eyes.

The elder man chanted in song, dropping some dried leaves on the campfire and then blowing smoke into Osceola's face. After a minute passed, the medicine man lifted a hollowed gourd and instructed Osceola to drink the black liquid inside. He did so, holding the drink in his stomach for as long as he could before turning his head to vomit.

The medicine man chanted, his eyes unblinking, staring into the ember of the fading sun, white smoke swirling around his craggy face. He opened a buckskin sack. Osceola could see powder the color of silver inside the sack. The medicine man produced a long black crow feather. He dusted the feather in the silvery powder and lifted it from the sack, placing the tip into the fire. When the feather ignited, he held it in front of Osceola and blew smoke into his face. He told Osceola to inhale through his nostrils. To, *"Breathe in the spirit of the crow."*

Tomorrow at dawn the spirit of the crow would guide Osceola when two hundred men came to kill him.

ONE

(Florida Wilderness – Present Day)

Some old timers wouldn't go there. They said there was something about the land—the place itself that was not welcoming, as if Mother Nature cast a spell on a few hundred acres tucked away in a primal spot that time overlooked and man left alone. The family, descendants of cattle ranchers, had tried for years to sell most of the land. And now, as urban sprawl crept like a disease over Florida, the environmentalist and nature conservation people were looking to buy and set aside tracts of pristine land, especially acreage that bordered rivers and lakes.

Today it was still private ranch land. Fenced along its massive perimeter. There were more than ten thousand acres, many bordering the Withlacoochee River. At one time, years ago, the ranch family ran herds of cattle over some of the property. Other sections, acreage encompassing part of the Green Swamp, were left to nature. Due to the remoteness, swampy terrain, poisonous snakes, ticks and leeches, folklore of hauntings—especially near the temple mound, there had been very little trespassing.

Today the remaining family members were anxious for an estate sale. Environmentalists had petitioned and encouraged the state of Florida to buy the most unspoiled areas and designate the property as a nature preserve or maybe even a state park. A large mound built centuries ago on an isolated piece of the property would make a perfect study in native cultures, some dating back thirteen thousand years.

Dr. Beverly Sanchez, an anthropologist for the state's Department of Cultural Affairs, and two of her colleagues, steered four-wheel ATVs, following the ranch owner through the scarcely marked trails of the primeval ground. They looped around wet cypress hammocks, tannin water more than two-feet deep.

They traversed under live oaks that had been here since the Civil War. The property was thick with bromeliads, cabbage palms and saw palmetto. The rancher stopped near an oak, shut off the ATV motor. He wore an old Stetson hat, the lower third long-since stained from sweat. He was in his mid-sixties, rangy face filled with gray whiskers. "We're almost there. Anybody need some water? Got a half dozen bottle in my saddlebags."

"I could use some hydration," said Dr. Sanchez, early thirties, dark hair pulled back in a ponytail. Even with no make-up on her face, the rancher thought that she was a striking woman.

"Here you go." He stepped from his ATV and handed her a bottle of water. "How 'bout ya'll?" he asked the two graduate students, both men.

"I'm okay," said one.

The second man shook his head. "You have any bug spray in there? I was fine until we stopped and then the mosquitoes got into a frenzy." He swatted a mosquito.

The rancher nodded. He reached in one of the compartments on his ATV and lifted out a can of insect repellent. He tossed it to the man. "Help yourself. Pass it around. Skeeters don't see people too much out here."

Dr. Sanchez nodded and smiled. "We really appreciate you taking the time to show us the property. It's like Florida of days gone by. It's so beautiful. I can see why your family originally bought the land. I think it'll make an excellent acquisition for the state."

He grinned, removed his hat, wiping his furrowed brow. "When my daddy bought it, they were almost giving land away. He needed enough to run herds of cattle. A thousand acres would have done it. But because a lot of it was underwater, the sellers were glad to get rid of it. The whole parcel is less than eleven thousand acres. And the stuff ya'll are interested in is no doubt the closest to Eden you'll find left on earth. Let's saddle up. We're almost there."

He cranked his engine. The others did the same and followed the rancher toward the northeast, to a place in Florida that hadn't changed much in thousands of years.

They rode through nearly impenetrable bush, the sable palms slapping faces and hands with fronds interlocked across the trail. The rancher used his left hand to wipe a massive spider's web from his face, while continuing to steer is ATV. After another five minutes, the sables and palmettos weren't as thick, they seceded to oaks and pines. A half a minute later they entered an open space in a forest that was unique—nature's own garden, a clearing in the midst of jungle, swamps, springs, rivers and dry woodlands.

And there it was.

A temple mound. A mountain in place of no hills.

Dr. Sanchez stopped. She shut off the ATV and started photographing the ancient mound. The others on her party followed.

The rancher circled back and said, "Wait 'till you see the view from the top. Some people have told us that mound is older than the pyramids of Egypt. And on the backside are caves that go on and on. There's a karst system of underground water, limestone…lots of springs bubbling up and flowing into the Withlacoochee. Like I said, this place as a direct descendant from the Garden of Eden. Some say it was Osceola's hideout before he was captured under a white flag of truce. The state better buy it before somebody builds a theme park here."

Dr. Sanchez looked up from her camera, her eyes following something in the sky. She watched three carrion birds ride the warm air currents, circling above them. She pointed. "Maybe there's an dead animal nearby."

The rancher nodded. "It's life…and its damn sure death. This land has a motto: eat or be eaten. It's all about survival and where's the next meal coming from. Probably a deer carcass. Something left over from a panther or bear attack."

They started their ATVs. The two graduate students following the rancher as he headed toward the right of the temple mound. On a whim, Dr. Sanchez decided to go to the left, to meet them somewhere on the other side. She drove the ATV slowly, taking in the majesty of the work that went into constructing a mound of this size.

She thought about the doctoral thesis paper she'd written on the Calusa Indians. They had been a fearless tribe. The men and women were tall. For more than two hundred years they resisted all attempts from the Spanish to convert them to the white man's religion. And in 1535, they were the tribe that killed the Spaniard famous because if his exhaustive search for the fabled Fountain of Youth. Ponce De Leon met death at the end of a Calusa arrow dipped in poison from a beach apple tree.

Had the Calusa built this mound, she wondered. *If not, who did and what happened to them.*

Her thoughts were abruptly altered when the stench of death hit her nostrils. She'd smelled the odor once before when an indigent man she knew had died in his trailer home. Dead a week before he was found. And now, here it was again, in the middle of a secluded habitat. She stopped her ATV, her mind trying to comprehend what her eyes were sending to her brain. She couldn't. The image was simply too horrible to grasp. She didn't notice the rancher and the others riding up, their voices sounding muted. The coughing. The gagging sound. Someone trying to dial 9-1-1. No signal.

She stepped closer, trying to process the horror of what was on the ground. The body looked posed—propped up for display. She stopped, clutching her throat. The man's body was at base of the tree, positioned in a kneeling posture. His hands had been tied behind his back. He was stripped of his clothes. A stick was wedged under his chin, holding his head up. He'd been scalped, dried blood coagulated in his open eyes, eyes that stared up at the top of the mound. Greenish blowflies circled his head. Some were crawling in his ears and nostrils. The others were feeding on dried blood that had oozed from his skull into what remained of his hairline.

Dr. Sanchez braced herself against a cabbage palm tree. Her knees were weak. The wind shifted, blowing the stench of death right toward her. She leaned over and vomited, the screech of carrion birds circling above her.

TWO

J oe Billie drove slowly approaching his old airstream trailer. He almost always would drive his twenty-year-old pickup truck with the windows down. Sometimes he listened to the news and human-interest stories on NPR. Mostly he listened to the sounds of nature, going deep into the Florida woodlands to harvest palmetto fronds. He spent much of his time in the fish camp drying palm fronds to use in building rustic outdoor shelters, waterfront bars at marina resorts usually. When not working, he read nonfiction books and carved wood.

He eased his truck off the hard packed dirt and oyster shell road that twisted through Highland Park Fish Camp, stopping in front of the last the vintage trailer in a remote part of the secluded camp. The once shiny aluminum exterior was stained in dried pine tree sap and age spots of oxidation from spending almost thirty summers in the harsh Florida environment.

Billie parked, glanced in his rearview mirror at the palmetto fronds that filled the truck-bed. He listened to his engine tick, cooling in the shade of large pines. He looked up at the blue sky between the limbs, the hoot of a barn owl coming from near the St. Johns River. It was a rare sound for that time of day and the time of year. Billie, a descendent from the Seminole Owl clan, thought the call of the owl was the warning of a sentinel long associated with his family. He lifted the machete from the truck seat. It was still sharp even after using it to cut dozens of palm fronds.

Billie got out of his truck. He carried a book he'd borrowed from the Volusia County Library in his left hand, the machete in his right hand.

He was just over six feet tall, mid-forties, broad shoulders, brown skin, large and powerful hands. He wore his salt and pepper colored hair in a ponytail.

He stepped up to his trailer door, checked the hidden traps he always set when he was gone for more than a couple of hours. The small sliver of toothpick he'd wedged between the door and the jamb was gone. Billie lowered his eyes to the base of the metal door. The splinter of wood was at the threshold. He turned the handle. It was still locked, but it appeared that someone had jimmied the door.

Billie stepped back. Slowly turning. Listening. There was the second hoot from the owl. And then Billie heard the cars coming. *At least three… maybe more.* As they rounded the bend in the dirt road, he could see they were sheriff's cars. Lights flashing. No sirens. They stopped quickly, dust and pine straw caught in the drafts. A large deputy got out of the first car, his right hand resting on the butt of his pistol.

"Are you Joe Billie?"

"What do you want?"

The deputy kept the opened door between him and Billie. "I want you to set that weapon down and step to one side."

"What's this about?" Billie's hand tightened around the handle.

"Drop your weapon!"

Another deputy emerged, pistol drawn and pointed directly at Billie. He dropped the machete and stepped backwards, closer to his trailer. The first deputy approached Billie, staying within ten feet of him. "You Joe Billie?"

"Yes."

The deputy looked at the palm fronds in the truck. "Where'd you get those?"

"In the woods."

"What woods? Where?"

"What's this about?"

"It's about murder. It's about scalping a man…and it's about you."

"Are you arresting me?"

"You got that right. You have the right to remain silent. Anything you say can be used against you in a court of law. And you have the right to an attorney." He paused, stepped a little closer, studying Billie. "You want an attorney or can we go on down to the station and straighten this out?"

"I want to speak with Sean O'Brien."

— —

He ran hard. Stopped, waited for little Max to catch up, and then jogged. Sean O'Brien was finishing an afternoon run along the beach near Ponce Inlet when his phone buzzed the first time. Max, his ten-pound female dachshund followed him, short legs a blur, stopping to sniff an occasional starfish or crab carried to shore by the pounding Atlantic. O'Brien slowed to a walk and then sat on a sand dune, cooling off, feeling his heart rate return to normal.

He was more than six-two, athletic build, wide shoulders, dark hair, chiseled face, hazel eyes that could penetrate the lies he'd faced conducting homicide interrogations years ago. His former partner in the Miami-Dade PD used to say O'Brien had a bloodhound's nose for sniffing out BS during questioning, often getting a confession with the first hour. O'Brien simply chalked it up to closely watching people and listening to what they said or didn't say. How they moved in the chair or didn't move. The physical hints to the psychological façades.

His phone buzzed a second time.

Max sat at his feet, her pink tongue showing, eyes bright watching seagulls hop between the breakers. O'Brien looked the caller ID. It was from the Volusia County Jail. He knew no one in the jail. He knew no one that worked in the jail. He did know plenty of people in the Florida State Prison—people he'd help send there when he was a homicide detective. There was no one in or out of the county jail that he knew. But he couldn't ignore the call. He answered, and for the first time ever, hearing a trace of desperation in his old friend's speech. O'Brien felt his heart rate kick up again.

"I hate to ask you this, Sean...but I could use your help."

"Why are you calling from the jail? What's going on, Joe?"

"I've been arrested for murder. I get one call, and it's to you. When you get here I'll tell you what happened."

Printed in the USA
CPSIA information can be obtained
at www.ICGtesting.com
LVHW012243200923
758872LV00010B/311

9 781518 718281